STAY ON THE WING

a novel
by Michael Atamanov

*Wishing you safe travels on
your fantasy journey,*

Michael Atamanov

Dark herbalist
Book Two

Magic Dome Books

Stay on the Wing
Dark Herbalist, Book 2
Copyright © Michael Atamanov 2017
Cover Art © Vladimir Manyukhin 2017
English Translation Copyright ©
Andrew Schmitt 2017
Published by Magic Dome Books, 2017
All Rights Reserved
ISBN: 978-80-88231-25-7

Also by Michael Atamanov:

Table of Contents:

The Tail-End of a Long Story

"AMRA, ADMIT IT. At the end of the day, all our searching has turned up nothing. There's no trace of them!" said the morbidly thin wood nymph in a light frock sitting on a fallen tree and yawning wide, demonstrating a set of sharp predatory teeth.

My sister hadn't gotten any sleep all night and was clearly beside herself. And the only reason she was up at this ungodly hour was me, not the light and not the dawn. Valeria had expressed her disapproval in sharp terms and refused to enter the game for some time. But the risk that some of the many killers after me might show up near the Cursed House was absolutely real, so in the end, Val apologized and agreed to come play with the rest of our group.

Max Sochnier, who I'd called on his cell phone, had promised to come in to work as soon as possible and catch up to us near Stonetown. And even Leon, after a moment of thought, asked me not to leave without him. I understood perfectly how difficult this choice was for the former construction worker, too. On the one hand, he had the half-destroyed goblin village of Tysh, where his character, an Ogre Fortifier, had work lined up for a month, providing him a steady stream of missions, experience and leveling. On the other hand, he was being asked to cast in his lot with our group, fleeing from hired assassins in peril and anonymity. Leon chose the option of staying with his friends, and I deeply appreciated that. By now, he would have already arrived by taxi to the *Boundless Realm* building, and should have been entering the game at any minute. After that, we could all run for our lives to Stonetown.

Taisha walked up to me, wrapped tight in my coat and accompanied by the clearly limping Akella. The beautiful green-skinned goblin lowered her eyes in response to my inquisitive gaze and shook her head.

"I've got nothing. I walked around the Stonetown stockade and checked the gates a few times, but the lady wasn't there. I looked over the tracks left by the farm workers again, too. There are a lot of footprints, but none from a lady. The runaway must have left a few days ago. I sent Tamina Fierce's children with Lobo and White Fang back to check the road from Stonetown to Tysh in the opposite direction. Although, as you must understand, the chances are low. We've already looked there a couple times..."

I swatted at a level-4 Fly buzzing peskily around my ear (our Naiad Trader hadn't been exaggerating — near the river, there were flies the size of a fist) and plopped down wearily next to my sister on a fallen log. Taisha carefully found herself a place next to me.

Day was dawning. The sky in the east was growing noticeably pink. But today, I wasn't afraid of the sunrise, because I could already see plenty of thick rainclouds dashing about the sky like dark tattered rags. It would probably start raining any second, then our search for the missing dark-haired girl would become utterly useless — the rain would wash all remaining evidence away. The wolves of the Gray Pack would no longer be able to smell her trail, either. The rare *Gray Pack's Past* quest threatened to remain unfinished. But I had big plans that were entirely reliant on finishing that mission — it would give me the ability to include ferocious and swift-footed wargs in the Gray Pack, which was very, very tempting!

I took a heavy sigh and removed the brightly colored headband I'd found in the warg's lair from my inventory and spun it in my hands. To look at it, it was just a headband as average as they come, the kind village girls wear to keep their hair back but, when I found it, the next mission in the Gray Pack chain initiated. We couldn't just let that pass us by and let the runaway escape. I sincerely hoped we still had a chance. If not, we might have bungled the whole Gray Pack mission chain, which would be terrible. In vexation, I slapped my palm against an impudent fly landing on my forehead, crushing it.

Damage dealt: 18 (Slap)
Experience received: 4 Exp.

Object received: Dead Fly (bait)
Your character is missing the requisite skill to use this object
Skill required: Fishing (P A) level-3

I flicked the fly away. It was useless to me anyway. Then, I shouted in a fit of anger, not clear who I was addressing:

"There's no way a pregnant lady could just go up in smoke, much less with her young niece and nephew! After all, there must have been some reason for her suddenly fleeing after such a long stay. Just imagine how hard it must have been for her to walk! Damn, all these flies really have me worked up!"

As a matter of fact, a whole swarm of the buzzing insects had come in place of the one I'd killed, and were now cutting circles above our heads with a vile whirring sound. Valerianna Quickfoot shook her right fist, and all of her hornet pets moved out to help us, taking down the insolent blood-suckers in a matter of seconds. Taisha, on seeing the dangerous overgrown wasps, crouched down and tried to cover her head with her jacket. I, meanwhile, whistled respectfully, having counted at least ten wasps, which were either black and brownish-yellow or orange-red. I even saw that some of them had already reached level sixteen.

A bit more leveling and they'd reach twenty, then the Beastmaster could choose useful perks for them. Knowing my sister, I had no doubt that Valerianna Quickfoot had already thought through a development plan for her pets down to the smallest detail, considering both the strong and weak points. Clearly, the wood nymph hadn't selected her swarm at random, given the several distinct types of wasp within it. My sister, obviously flattered at the attention paid to her variously-shaded pretties, sent her flying pets away and answered me:

"Why she ran is, of course, clear. In the last few days, eleven of her friends have been killed.

She likely knew they were wargs. She might not be, but she began justly fearing for her own life all the same. Although, Tim, we might be wrong. Maybe the dark-haired girl had absolutely nothing to do with it, and her leaving the farm is just a coincidence. In any case, we should come to an agreement on the runaway as quickly as possible — we can't just stick around near Stonetown. When the sun comes up, there might be assassins about. My opinion — we should stop searching and leave right away."

My sister then went silent abruptly and got on edge, seeing a bare-footed gray-haired old man dressed in a dark chlamys walking in our direction from the houses of the village. But based on how Valerianna immediately breathed a sigh of relief, I realized that this old man was familiar to her and presented no threat. I quickly read his info:

Umar Bonesetter
Level-45 Human Witch Doctor

This must have been the Stonetown doctor the wood nymph had met on our second day in game. She'd told me about him on a number of occasions. With a short nod to my sister, as if greeting an old friend, the gray-haired bearded man stopped next to me, looked me over and gave a kind-hearted laugh:

"You must be the big-eared goblin herbalist

who moved into the Cursed House! I've been expecting plant deliveries from you for quite some time! You're late!"

If the old man thought he could shame me with those words, he was wrong. I was seeing him for the first time. I had no obligation to sell him plants, so I didn't feel at all guilty. What was more, I didn't even have enough plants to practice Alchemy with, so the witch-doctor was absolutely wrong to be counting on me. But the man wasn't even expecting me to answer and had already turned his attention to Taisha. Under his harsh gaze, my companion grew embarrassed, shrunk and wrapped herself tighter in the jacket, covering over her thin thief's outfit, still burned through in many places.

"In my time, girls would have been embarrassed to walk around looking like that," said the old man, shaking his head judgmentally. "You may enter the village. The guards at the gates know you. They'll let you through. My home is the second on the right from the gates. You'll find a needle and thread on the shelf in the entryway. Sew that wretched outfit up."

Taisha turned to me and, after getting permission, jumped up off the log and scurried off to mend her clothes. The witch-doctor immediately took her place, croaked out like an old man and sat down next to me on the fallen tree. He gave Pirate a scratch behind the ear, truly unafraid of the level-17 Forest Wolf, dozing away under Valerianna Quickfoot's legs. Being honest, I was taken aback by the old man's lack of caution. I mean, my sister's pet Pirate was a wild predator, after all, and this old man couldn't possibly know how the wolf would react to an attempt to stroke it like that. But the wolf just twitched his ear lazily, as if chasing off a gadfly, and continued dozing.

A private message came in from Shrekson:

"Me and Leon just entered the game and are hurrying on our way to you. We're going as fast as possible, but we still need an hour to get to Stonetown. Wait for us."

So, I had one more hour to pick up the runaway girl's trail. In that time, the sun would be coming up. And after that, we would have to run as far as possible from Stonetown. The chance of us meeting a high-level enemy was increasing with every minute. Also, the residents of the human village would be waking up soon. They would be sure to take an interest in our search, making it impossible for the wolves of the Gray Pack to work effectively.

As if reading my thoughts, the old witch-doctor spoke with an old-man's growl:

"Come to think of it, this is some strange business. A whole group of goblins with a pack of wolves and a dangerous mavka came to our human village and, now, they're all crawling about stubbornly trying to sniff something, or somebody out. One might start to think you have ill intentions for our village. Perhaps I should send a runner to the garrison for more guards..."

I turned in fear to the old man and discovered that he was smiling and could barely hold back his laughter.

"I'm just joking, dumbo," the witch-doctor hurried to reassure me. "The mavka told me who you're looking for yesterday. It's just that you aren't talking, Amra. I'm only trying to start a conversation."

"We is looking after runaway farmhand from long-away plantation. Many farmhand is run, master no understand where and why workers is leaving," I said, purposely distorting my words.

But the old man answered, beaming all the brighter and shaking his head in reproach:

"Oh, goblin, you're a bad liar... Never in a million years would I believe that the greedy Kariz would go search for missing workers, especially near the end of the season when pay time is coming. For him, the farm-hands disappearing is a good thing — it means he has to part with less of his coin."

I looked thoughtfully at the man, who appeared wizened by a long life... and decided to tell him the whole truth as it was, hiding nothing. And I even spoke in normal human language without my tongue-tied "goblin accent." Umar Bonesetter listened to my story about killing the wargs and discovering their lair very carefully, without a single interruption. And when I reached the part where I discovered the headband, leading to my suspicions on the runaway dark-haired woman, the witch-doctor said thoughtfully:

"The runaway was named Belle. I knew from her first day in town that she wasn't just a simple villager. She's a short girl with short hair. She showed up in the village five months ago. The farm owner, Kariz, hired that group of farm-hands in the spring for sowing and asked me to give the lady a checkup. She looked far too thin, beat-up and unhealthy. It was as if she were ill. And also, her short hair aroused suspicion. What kind of girl would just cut off her braids like that? It spoiled her womanly beauty! The only reason I could think of would be typhus or some disease."

The old man stayed silent for a bit as if trying to remember then continued, noticeably quieter:

"At that time, Belle's belly wasn't noticeable at all. No one had any idea she was with child. But when I was looking her over, she just told me all about it. She said she'd fled back-breaking labor, squabbles, and humiliation. Even worse, she told me of her master's daily unwelcome advances. She couldn't even walk around the farm without being harangued. She told me that her former master's wife had cropped her hair like that to stop her stealing her husband away. I took pity on her, so I didn't tell Kariz anything about her pregnancy. Otherwise, he wouldn't have taken her on."

"So, what made you realize she was unusual?" the wood nymph inquired. "From my perspective, she sounds like a typical browbeaten village girl with a difficult lot in life."

For some reason, the old man looked ashamed and started coughing, then continued his story, now barely audible:

"Every woman asks the witch-doctor for help giving birth — healing elixirs, herbs, painkillers. That sort of thing. The prescription for birthing has been known since the beginning of time. It's always one and the same. First, a decoction of meadow heather, so the seed takes and turns head-down in the womb when the time comes. Then, a drink of wild honey, white chamomile and Saint John's wort, which gives her the strength needed for the birth itself. Women need many things to cope with childbearing, and I can prepare them all. But Belle asked me for something else entirely: wolfsbane, red mandrake, and enough strong sleeping potion to knock a mountain titan off its feet. Where did a poor browbeaten village woman get the money for such expensive elixirs? It didn't fit with her story. And though I'm not certain why she needed a sleeping potion, wolfsbane is known not just for its stupefying effect, but also for the fact that it stops shapeshifters from changing form. And that was when I realized something was amiss and started keeping an eye on the young woman. But still, I didn't give Belle up to the villagers, because she was behaving herself. Also, wolfsbane must have meant the girl didn't want to become a beast even at the very height of the full moon. But the birth of her child was approaching inevitably. She'd never hide the truth from the midwives, so Belle fled together with her nephews."

Having said his fill, the old man fell silent, staring with chalk-white teary eyes at the nearby forest emerging from the fog. I asked the witch-doctor when he'd last seen the runaway.

Check for Umar Bonesetter's reaction failed

"Listen here, nimble one," the village witch-doctor cringed, upset. "If you don't wish to help me gathering plants, you can't expect me to help you. For a young buck such as yourself, it should be easy — you can gather everything you need in the blink of an eye. But for me, with my injured legs, having to wade through the swamp gathering blackberries and currants..."

Mission received: Plants for the Witch-Doctor 1/3
Mission class: Class-based, training
Description: Gather five bunches of Swamp Currant, Swamp Blackberry and

~ Stay on the Wing ~

Swamp Horsetail for Umar Bonesetter
Reward: 160 Exp., Herbalism skill +1

So, that was how I was supposed to level Herbalism! Instead of wandering through the dangerous forest at night, shivering at every rustling in the bushes and constantly fearing an encounter with a blood-thirsty monster, I could have just walked up to the witch-doctor and leveled Herbalism in training quests. On the other hand, how could my goblin have gone to the human village earlier, knowing that he would have been instantly sent to respawn due to his low Charisma and -20 penalty to human reaction? Also, I wouldn't have managed to come during the day and, at night, people tend to sleep, so the gates of Stonetown would have been closed!

I looked in my inventory. I had the plants I needed and in sufficient quantity, so I was free to just complete the first witch-doctor mission right away. However, I only needed to gather a few more plants to reach Herbalism level seven, so it would be stupid to waste the free level-up. There was still time before the ogre and naiad would arrive, so I found out from the old man where to go to reach the nearest swamp and headed off to gather plants. It wasn't far, and also the mission was very simple — the plants he asked for grew densely nearby so, twenty minutes later, I returned with my Herbalism skill already at level seven.

Umar Bonesetter was still sitting on the log, speaking peacefully with the wood nymph. I walked up and handed the old man the plants he requested in silence.

Mission completed: Plants for the witch-doctor 1/3
Experience received: 160 Exp.
Herbalism skill increased to level 8!

"Good! What took you so long?" the old man exclaimed joyfully, stashing the bundles of herbs in his rumpled and dirty sack. "Alright then, I'll answer your question, as promised. I last saw Belle on the same day the undying came, packing our village to the brim. It was some time in the middle of the day. I'd be more exact, but I don't remember. She was standing by the dock and gathering water from the river in birch-bark buckets."

I felt like a light-bulb switched on over my head. That was it! River. Boats. How hadn't we guessed that right away?! Based on the way the wood nymph turned toward me with her eyes burning in enthusiasm, my sister was thinking the same. But then, she froze, grew sad and wrote me out a private message.

"Somehow, the timing isn't coming together. This means Belle must have run from Stonetown BEFORE we killed the first wargs. The death of the

shapeshifters couldn't have been what spooked her. She was already gone."

I answered my sister, also in a private message:

"It seems she didn't know about the death of the eleven wargs, but fled anyway. Her due date must have been growing near, and she was afraid to be revealed. Or maybe she left later and the old man simply didn't see her for those few days. But taking a path down the river really does suggest itself — I mean, we didn't find any footprints on land, and a boat would be the simplest way for a pregnant lady to get far away from the village."

"Have any boats disappeared from Stonetown recently?" I asked Umar Bonesetter directly, to which I got another indignant facial expression from the old man, and a second quest about engaging my main skill for the witch-doctor:

> **Mission received: Plants for the witch-doctor 2/3**
> **Mission class: Class-based, training**
> **Description: Gather ten bunches of Mountain Lily, Common Holly, Saint John's Wort of the Field, and Fire Poppy**
> **Reward: 320 Exp., Herbalism skill +1**

I read the description and froze briefly. I hadn't seen any of these plants in my last few days of gaming. In fact, other than Fire Poppy — I had never seen any of these flowers at all. Naturally, I asked the old witch-doctor where they grew. The old man's answer was not at all to my liking:

"As a goblin, you should know better than me. Far as I know, whole fields of these poppies grow next to the village of Tysh, somewhere beyond the graveyard of burning skeletons."

That was absolutely unacceptable. Even riding the Gray Pack, getting to Tysh and back would take much more time than we could afford. Well, here goes nothing! I decided to offer the old witch-doctor another option:

"Listen, Umar Bonesetter. Even though the plants you want don't grow right under our feet, they are still very commonplace. There's plenty of them in the neighboring forests, and you can easily find them yourself or send someone else out after them. Instead, I'd like to offer you the true wealth of an Herbalist — I've got hundreds of the rarest plants drying on the second floor of the Cursed House — White Lily, Shaggy Currant, Goblin Berries, Wolfsbane, and Colorful Mandrake. And near the stairs, there's a way down into a cave with a stream. Down there, you'll find Red Stinker mushrooms, Cave Morels, Black Moss and lots of other stuff you'd never find on the surface. Let's make a deal — you can have all these riches for yourself, and I don't have to stomp the wet road to Tysh in the rain."

By the way the old man's fingers were

shaking, I could immediately tell that my offer was extremely interesting to the witch-doctor. Yet he was still hesitating:

"So, you want me to go to the Cursed House? Come on... You're undying, Amra, so you will be fine no matter what. But what if some monster living there eats me alive?!"

"Don't you worry about that, old man. Last night, I killed the creature that was murdering its inhabitants. It was called a Midnight Wraith. Now, it's all safe."

Successful check for Umar Bonesetter's reaction

Experience received: 40 Exp.

Trading Skill increased to level 12!

"You better not be lying, big-ears..." the old man grumbled, upset, trying to hide his joy and impatience with all his might. "Alright, I agree to the trade."

Mission completed: Plants for the witch-doctor 2/3

Experience received: 320 Exp.

Herbalism skill increased to level 9!

Mission completed: Plants for the witch-doctor 3/3

Experience received: 480 Exp.

Herbalism skill increased to level 10!

The witch-doctor considered the goods I offered valuable enough to immediately complete two steps of his quest?! Say what you will but that was unexpected. I smiled ear to ear in satisfaction, but my joy wasn't long-lived:

"No, no boats have disappeared from Stonetown. All three of them are still at the dock. Go check for yourself."

It seemed to me that the old man was really glad that he'd managed to put me in a bind with his answer and trade such banal information for a whole load of valuable plants. And indeed, Umar Bonesetter was quite pleased with himself. He even explained the reason:

"Understand, goblin, the run-away lady was very kind to me, so I don't want anyone finding her, much less pestering or threatening her. So, as long as you don't have any more questions for me, I'll be on my way — I'll need to get a cart for your plants."

The witch-doctor stood with a creak and slowly walked toward his home, leaning on his cane. He was just seven steps away when my sister shouted out to him:

"Umar, can you tell me anything about Belle's nephews? Or are you going to make me complete some task to get the truth?"

The healer turned unhurriedly and frowned. Just when I'd decided we wouldn't be getting an answer, the old man surprised me:

"Sure, I'll tell you about those two. What's to hide? They're Belle's niece and nephew. The boy's name is Dar, and the girl is called Dara. They're around twelve or thirteen. A pair of thieves, villains, and hooligans — not much more to be said about those two young whippersnappers. If something went missing in our village, or a child was hurt, there could be no doubt it was their doing. A couple of born criminals, whose misdeeds can only be recouped by hard labor, or even the chopping block. They have no education, no discipline, and no respect for their elders. And also, the girl is no better than her brother. Completely hopeless. The villagers punished them many times: caning, locking them out in the cold, and even bringing a whipping post into the center of Stonetown... Nothing helped. When their aunt wasn't so big-bellied, Belle reined them in at least somewhat. She'd give them a good thrashing with either the rod or the whip. It was so intense that I could hear their hollering all the way at the other end of the village. Those two madcaps were afraid of her. They obeyed her. But when she got heavy, there was no longer any control. I'll be honest: I was quite glad to hear that those hooligans were finally out of our village. You can be sure no one was too upset about that."

After these words, the old man spit on the ground in annoyance and walked into Stonetown.

And at that very moment, the skies opened up, and a real downpour began. The witch-doctor, displaying a surprising agility for such a hoar-headed old man, stuck his cane under his armpit and hopped like a hare into the village. My sister and I, on the other hand, had to quickly run under the nearest wide-branched tree in order not to get soaked. There, I voiced a thought:

"I'll be direct. It sounds like these kids were pretty rough around the edges. Perhaps, we'll be able to try and find the three of them by asking in the neighboring villages about two hell-raising youths. If not, we clearly won't get anywhere — this rain will wash away all their footprints."

My sister was looking at me strangely — with condemnation or even pity.

"Tim, you're really off your game today. 'Your girly' isn't even around to distract you with her curves, but still there's a big lag in your thinking. Even though he didn't want to, the old man gave a clear hint with his answers. You really didn't pick up on it?"

I considered it, but was forced to admit that I had absolutely no idea what my sister was talking about. The wood nymph had to chew over the facts before it reached me:

"Belle was seen at the dock on the same day all the players came *en masse* to Stonetown to kill the unique flying snake Kayervina. All three of the local boats are still at the dock, so the runaway couldn't have used them. But there was one more boat, remember! On that very same day, a Naiad Trader you know well by the name of Max Sochnier came to Stonetown in his own boat, full of fresh and dried fish! But the naiad was forced to leave the boat full of goods and dive underwater, because PK-ers attacked him right next to Stonetown! Well, that fourth boat must have ended up somewhere!"

"Val, you're a genius! I owe you an ice cream," I smiled, admitting the soundness of my little sister's idea. "They're not likely to have tried taking the boat against the current — it's hard for a pregnant lady to constantly paddle like that, even with two teenagers. That means we should search down-river. But we won't catch the runaways on foot — the banks are swampy, overgrown and stony, plus they're teeming with aggressive beasts of all kinds. We need a boat. A few boats, in fact. Our whole group won't fit in just one."

"You're being obtuse again, big-ears," said the mavka, shaking her head helplessly. "No normal flat-bottomed boat would be capable of holding our gigantic ogre. And also, you're forgetting that we are gonna have to hide as well. So, there's no reason to leave our pursuers such an obvious hint as stealing boats from Stonetown."

Valeria was right again, just like always. I opened my map. The naiad trader had previously sent me his discovered map, so I could see the whole path to the ocean. A few kilometers down from the village, the nameless river made a sharp bend, curving around a thickly forested narrow headland. I zoomed in as much as possible on that part, and noticed pine tree symbols. I figured that was exactly where I should be going. I wrote out private messages to the ogre and naiad, sending them the coordinates of the place we should meet. At the same time, I asked the ogre fortifier how long it would take him to build a sturdy raft capable of holding our whole group along with the wolves. An answer came back almost instantly:

"I have the tools with me. If there really is a good pine forest there with tall, straight trunks then, with my current skills, it should take an hour and a half to build a raft, two at most. Could be less, especially if I have help."

"We'll be sure to help you. After all, it's in our shared interest," I promised.

* * *

I'd never before had the chance to see the ogre fortifier at work. Without any exaggeration, I can say it was a fantastic and captivating spectacle. Fifty-year pines fell to his ax with incredible ease. Bark and twigs flew like from a fountain. The giant carried the thick logs as if they were reeds. An hour later, Shrekson Bastard was pushing the finished raft made of heavy, tightly lashed logs into the shallows, helping the others, then finally getting on it himself.

Although the rain had grown noticeably quieter, it was still not letting up for even a second. The sopping-wet wolves of the Gray Pack were shivering, pressed up one to the next, stumbling on the slippery logs as our craft bobbed in the water. The canines were staring longingly at the nearby shore, but still, none of them had the gall to disobey my orders. Taisha and Valerianna, hidden from the rain and cold wind under a black warg pelt, were clattering their teeth in syncopation. Tamina Fierce's children, the wolf riders Irek and Yunna, despite their unseasonably light clothing, were surprisingly vivacious and happy. The goblins were laughing and joking, not even trying to hide their joy and excitement.

The weather meant nothing to the ogre, and I also was bearing the icy rain with aplomb, just yawning occasionally, tired after a sleepless night. But Max Sochnier felt best of all. The fish-man was finally in his element, sitting on the bow of our raft, excitedly stabbing river fish with a harpoon and occasionally commanding the giant to steer in one direction or the other.

For the first few minutes of our trip, I was slightly worried for the sturdiness and steering of the raft, but a half an hour on, I was now fully reassured. We were traveling at an even pace, going around obstacles and sandbanks with no effort, easily snaking around all the river's curves. According to the naiad, the path to the ocean should take about six hours, so I was hoping to get some restful sleep, taking shelter from the rain under the warg pelts. But before I managed to find a comfortable spot on the back of the raft, Max Sochnier cried out hectically:

"To the right! Over there, in the reeds!"

I grew alarmed, throwing off the warg pelt and looking. In the reeds near the shore, I saw a half-sunken boat sticking out of the water.

"That's my boat! I recognize it!" the naiad continued, his bright red back fins extending in agitation.

The fish-man jumped off the float, quickly scooping with his webbed hands and tail, trying to dig out the sunken oar-boat.

"We should pull up on that shore and do a quick search!" I ordered, and the ogre fortifier turned the rudder sharply.

We made it through the thick patch of riverside reeds with some effort. I even had to cut a passage in them as the ogre jumped overboard and pushed our raft on shore.

Finally, we came upon dry land. I was planning to assign the wolves a mission to search for signs of the people, but before I even had time, Irek had already shot up the bank and was calling the group to come see what he'd found.

~ Stay on the Wing ~

It was a small hut, which looked to have been made relatively recently, a few days ago at most. The leaves on the branches it was made of were still green.

Next to that, we found the remains of a fire pit and a ton of picked-clean bones from what looked to be a huge ruminant of some kind. The wolves came up to where we were standing, sniffed, then their fur bristled up and their tails went between their legs in fear. They scampered away from the remains of the feast. I though, took a closer look.

Successful Perception check
Experience received: 80 Exp.

On most of the bones, you could see the traces of sharp teeth and raw meat fibers. I picked up a few bones to make sure of my suspicions. Yes, the predators, whoever they were, had torn their prey to bits and devoured it. But there was something else — some of the bones had clearly been boiled in a pot. When I told my companions this, their reaction was somewhat surprising:

"Hey, we could stand to eat something, too," the ogre mumbled. "Since morning, I've had a yellow fork and knife icon flashing in the corner of my screen, and just now, it went red..."

For some reason, everyone turned toward me, as if I was supposed to be carrying food for the group. Where did they think I was hiding it?! My big-eared troglodyte was hungry himself, which I told them immediately.

"I could catch fish. I've got tackle," the naiad offered. "That would take some time, though, and I'd need bait."

"There's a crap-ton of bait by the river!" I answered, slapping yet another a red fly on my face and offering up its little corpse for the common cause. "One fisherman is not enough to feed our whole big team, though. We should go on the hunt and catch something bigger all together. I'll call my wyvern right now. She can look for prey nearby from above."

I hadn't brought VIXEN to Stonetown for obvious reasons — a horde of wolf-riding goblins was sure to attract unhealthy attention from the locals as it was. But then, if our cohort had been traveling with a three-meter flying snake, we surely would have been the object of heated discussion for many days to come, a fact that would certainly not have gone unnoticed by the undying on my trail. At any rate, it took the level-16 Royal Forest Wyvern just one minute to fly in to my call. The snout of the flying snake was smeared with fresh blood.

"What a smart cookie you are! You caught something and ate it all on your own!" I said, stroking the dangerous beast affectionately on the shoulders, at the same time noticing that my pet had leveled up and increased in size.

~ Stay on the Wing ~

My forehead pressed to the head of my winged mount, I tried to communicate the mission to her as clearly as possible in vibrant images — find large creatures from the air in the forest nearby. Enough to feed our whole big team. I do not know how well she understood but, after some time, VIXEN flew off, flapping her wings and disappearing into the low rainclouds.

"Amra, what mission did you choose for your mount in the settings: scouting, patrolling territory or hunting?" my sister inquired. I answered honestly that I did not know myself, and told her about my experimental approach to communicating with the wyvern.

The wood nymph shook her head doubtfully.

"I don't think that will work. There's a normal game interface, with popup menu describing all possible options for missions one can give pets and mounts. The option 'search for large game' is not among them, though. You could have tried using a combination of existing commands, but I'm not sure that would work either..."

Valerianna then went silent, though, because VIXEN was already back. Flapping her wide wings, wet from the rain, the green wyvern set down on the grass and crawled in my direction, not so much walking with her legs as slithering like a snake. The emerald green winged beast bowed her head and carefully touched it to mine.

Before my eyes, there came a kaleidoscope of pictures, reminiscent of screenshots taken from flight.

Breaks in the clouds. Riverbank visible. Thick brush. In it, a big animal is standing and chewing young shoots contemplatively. It's a huge Bull Moose. Wide hooves and branching antlers. Powerful back and hump. Thick black beard. Column legs. And a red skull symbol, meaning that the animal surpassed the wyvern in level by more than twenty.

I tried to figure out where these pictures might have been taken. The river was behind me. Higher up the river, it gradually turned to the left. Yep, this was about what it should have looked like from the sky. And as a matter of fact, higher up the river, I could see a hill overgrown with brush in the distance. It seemed that was precisely where we'd find our prey. I loudly announced as much to my friends:

"A half kilometer that way, there's a big moose grazing in the bushes. It's approximately level forty or fifty. I say we go hunt it."

In reply, I got a long silence, then Max Sochnier inquired cautiously:

"Fifty? And what if it decides to come hunt us? I mean, we're non-combat characters. We can't fight like that!"

"Amra, we won't even be able to seriously wound it with such a high difference in levels!" the ogre fortifier exclaimed, supporting his friend's doubts.

I exchanged surprised glances with my sister. The wood nymph didn't understand their unplaced hesitation, either.

"I'm sure we can take down a level-fifty animal as a group without any losses. But no one will force you to run at the hardened creature with your trident and sledge-hammer," I reassured the construction worker and trader. "It's just an NPC animal, even if high level. We can take it down with tricks!"

"That's right!" my sister chimed in, bolstering my point. "We can dig out a pit like the one near the Cursed House. We can stick sharpened stakes in the bottom, put branches over top and draw the moose toward us! It will all be very simple! The main thing is us going far enough away so the animal won't see us or suspect a trap."

"Uncy Amra, I can make a little horn out of bark that will bellow like a moose in spring," Yunna offered. "Shaman Kaiak Badgerleg taught me. It isn't spring now, but a mature moose will race to the call to catch a glimpse of whatever freak dared invade its territory."

And that's what we decided to do. The ogre fortifier was working at the speed of an excavator with a normal shovel, and had already been breaking fresh ground for several minutes. The space was surely big enough for a large moose, now. As he dug, the others had been gathering logs and branches, which we'd use both as stakes and cover for the trap. Taisha and I placed the branches over the pit — we were the two in the group with the highest Agility, which meant we had the lowest chance of falling into the hole.

All that was left was to solve the last problem — how to lure the animal toward the trap and force it to stand on top? Here, my sister came to our aid:

"Give me a few minutes, and I'll make an illusion of an insolent young male moose. But first, I'll need a picture of a moose..."

Valerianna Quickfoot froze motionless, and I figured my sister must have taken off the virtual reality helmet, minimized *Boundless Realm* and was looking at pictures of moose on her monitor, trying to find the most suitable representation. A minute later, my sister came back to life:

"Found one! Alright, go hide in the woods! And tell Shrekson to blow the horn — he'll be able to make the loudest sound!"

We laid down in a streambed, sending the wolves and wyvern away, so they wouldn't upset our scheme. The deafening bellow that rang out was more reminiscent of a locomotive whistle than an animal's call, but Yunna and Irek assured me it was working exactly as intended. Shrekson ran up to us and also dove into the ditch. Nevertheless, nothing happened.

"Didn't work?" I supposed, but the wood nymph stuck a finger to her lips, calling for silence.

"Quiet! He's coming," Valerianna whispered, barely audible. "I see him on the mini-map. You'll see him soon as well, big-ears."

Not even a minute later, I saw a red skull marker on the map. The moose was slowly approaching, taking long breaks to look or sniff at something. Something here was setting off the animal's sixth sense.

Successful Perception check
Experience received: 16 Exp.

Wind! That's must have been it! The wind was blowing over the trap. The moose could smell the wolves, goblins, and other creatures. All those smells were bound to be obvious, yet there was no scent from its rival — a self-assured young moose! I wrote my theory in a private message to my sister.

"Well, what can I do with that? I can't create illusory smells."

So, I answered the wood nymph:

"Change the bait. Make it a female moose."

"Tim, this isn't the season. And still, there wouldn't be any smell."

"I've got an idea! What about a young and stupid wolf, who not only won't run away, but also

has the gall to bare his teeth at the proud and strong moose! There is a wolf smell, so it might work. The moose will want to teach the impudent wolf a lesson and chase it off his territory."

Valerianna wriggled her lips, conjuring something or just repeating the new mission to herself out loud. It worked! The Bull Moose saw the newly-created illusion and started trumpeting out to the whole forest so loud that the sound Leon made earlier now seemed like nothing but a pitiful parody. This bellow was not only deafening, and literally at that, it hit all of us with a whole array of unpleasant effects:

Damage taken: 34 (level-31 Fear spell)
3 second Panic effect
15 second Deaf effect

Successful Perception check
Experience received: 80 Exp.

Successful Constitution check
Experience received: 160 Exp.

Health level: 179/216

I can't really say what two negative effects Amra managed to avoid, but those he'd been unable to stop were bad enough as it was. I got control back over my character but, by that time, the terrified goblin had already started racing off through the forest, not at all caring about finding a path. I collapsed in the grass, hoping sincerely that the bull moose wouldn't pay any mind to a little goblin hopping away in the distance, and would instead be distracted by its intended target. Irek dashed past me, his mouth open, screaming out wordlessly — he had also clearly fallen to panic. Finally, my hearing returned. Behind me, I heard the elated clamoring of my friends. I could make out distinct shouts of joy. Had it worked? The NPC marker on the mini-map changed from yellow to aggressive red, but it wasn't moving and was approximately in the spot where we'd dug the trap pit. Now more confident, I started off toward the trap first at a fast clip, then at a run. Still, though, my friends reached the trap first.

Level-48 Bull Moose

The powerful beast had fallen exactly the way we'd planned but, by some unimaginable luck, it had managed to avoid being seriously wounded by the stakes at the bottom of the pit. A few of the sharpened wooden spears had torn through the animal's hide or scraped along the ribs, leaving abundant bloody lesions. But the moose's life bar hadn't really gone down much and was still in the green. What was more, regeneration was restoring the moose's health faster than the bleeding was bringing it down. A minute later, the life bar of the cornered animal was already back up to maximum.

The moose stood looking at us in silence, though he probably could have given his terrifying bellow another try. It might just get rid of us. The moose slowly turned his head and looked over the weak creatures who'd captured him one after the next. When my turn finally came, I saw the proud beast staring at me. Looking into his teary eyes, intelligent in a seemingly human way, I started feeling unwell. Yes, I understood perfectly that the being before me was nothing but a piece of programming code made to be slaughtered in a virtual game. There was no true moral imperative stopping us from roasting its meat over a fire and simply gorging ourselves but, for some reason, I felt unwell. I didn't know how to explain to my comrades that I'd changed my mind and no longer wanted to kill the handsome moose, but suddenly the ogre fortifier burst out:

"Friends, I'm taking a pass. I can't watch him in torment like this. Split him up, but leave me out of it. I won't touch the moose meat. I'd rather go hungry or make do with mindless plants and fish."

I wasn't expecting such sentimentality from our giant. Although, I was reminded that seeing the torched goblin village of Tysh had also made a very strong impression on Shrekson, giving him a nervous condition and insomnia. Despite his thick-skinned appearance, the former construction worker was quite impressionable and kind-hearted.

The ogre turned away and, with a decisive step, started tramping off in the opposite direction of the trap pit.

"This moose would make a great mount. It could support the weight of the ogre..." the wood nymph said thoughtfully.

All at once, everyone suddenly turned toward Shrekson. The ogre stopped sharply, as if he'd hit a stone wall, turned around and... A miracle happened — the red dot of the moose in the trap instantly changed to blue, meaning ally. Over the antlered head of the animal, there appeared a name: "Lil_Timbo."

"Just a name, no worse than VIXEN or Pirate," our giant hurried to assure everyone, though no one had really looked surprised or laughed at the strange, fairly inappropriate name for the huge beast.

I didn't go help the moose out of the pit — there were plenty of helpers as it was, and the ogre would also have managed easily on his own. But, taking advantage of the commotion, I took a vial of the forest giant's blood:

Moose Blood (alchemy ingredient)

I walked a bit farther from the others back toward the shelter we'd found, crawled into it under the cover of the twigs and drank the vial down.

Achievement unlocked: Taste tester (14/1000)

My Sating the Thirst bar was practically filled, showing 18/20, so my goblin vampire could go another eighteen hours without the blood of any victims. And also, my desire to sleep was growing ever stronger. I was yawning practically nonstop. A little bit longer, and I would simply collapse from exhaustion.

I crawled out of my hiding spot and froze, drawn to some bizarre sounds. Not far from me, there was a muted combination of growling and whimpering. I entered Stealth Mode and walked toward it. I carefully moved back the bush branches and discovered the whole Gray Pack gathered in a little glade, digging into the earth with abandon. Intrigued, I walked up closer.

The wolves were throwing back the damp loose earth with determination, digging out a shallow pit. It was clear that the dirt was fresh and gave easily. There was something strange buried there. I pushed aside the forest predators, leaned over and pulled out a dirty canvas bag. I stepped back and emptied the contents onto the grass — I saw some rumpled rags, and a pair of battered woman's sandals. I stood up and started sorting through my findings.

Clothing. Village-woman's clothing. On top was a dirty, very patchy old dress. It was unclear what color it had been originally. Along with it, I found a ripped sleeveless blouse and a pair of short canvas pants, or more likely, boy's shorts. Under that, there was a relatively clean, though also very wrinkled pinafore, a set of dirty work clothes, some cheap glass beads, a pair of well-worn woman's sandals, and a four-colored headband like the ones village girls put in their hair — identical to the one I had in my inventory.

Was that all? I looked carefully at the clothes laid out on the grass.

Successful Perception check
Experience received: 40 Exp.

On the dirty gray dress, I noticed and removed a long black hair stuck to the fabric. It was sixty centimeters long and too coarse to be from a human. I wrapped the strange hair around my fingers, trying to figure out what it belonged to.

Successful Perception check
Experience received: 80 Exp.

Warg tail hair (waste)

The runaways we were searching for had scuttled their boat, hunted and eaten their fill, after which they'd buried their old clothes in the depths of the forest and changed their human appearance for an animal one. It must have been a few days earlier. Now, the warg pack could be anywhere, and the ceaseless rain had made searching for their tracks cursed to failure from the get go...

Cards on the Table

NOW, WE HAD to think about what to do given that the lady we were searching for had managed to get away. My friends suggested we set up a temporary camp and look for tracks in the nearby forests. I didn't see a particular reason for that, but I didn't argue with the collective opinion, either. Not wanting to nod off from exhaustion and be an example of idleness while my friends were hard at work, I exited *Boundless Realm.* My sister promised that our group wouldn't go far in the next day, so I wasn't especially worried. I knew I could catch up to them when I got back.

Already out of my virtual reality capsule, I spent a few minutes sitting on the stool in my work cabin, coming to my senses. It was quite the tiring and nerve-wracking game session. But my tribulations weren't in vain — my big-eared Amra managed to revive all his dead NPC companions and leveled up a good amount. I opened my stat window:

Name: Amra
Race: Goblin Vampire
Class:Herbalist
Experience, 139777 of 150000
Character level, 27
Hit points, 196/216
Endurance points, 185/185

Statistics:

Strength (S) 28 (28)
Agility (A) 30 (82.6)
Intelligence (I) 5 (15.5)
Constitution (C) 29 (35.5)
Perception (P) 3 (25.7)
Charisma (Ch) 54 (66)
Unused points 0

Primary skills (6 of 6 chosen):

Herbalism (P A) 10
Trading (Ch I) 12
Alchemy (I A) 15
Dodging (A P) 9

Stealth (A C) 13
Exotic Weapons (A P)   6

Secondary skills (5 of 6 chosen):

Veil   5
Acrobatics   8
Athletics   8
Foreman   5
Riding   4

I had yet to choose my last secondary skill, still a bit bewildered at the abundance of options. My sister was strongly in favor of me choosing Animal Control (I Ch), improving the stats of my pets. And there was a certain sense in that — I already had the Royal Forest Wyvern and four Seasoned Wolves, with the prospect of including another two beasts to the Gray Pack as soon as the opportunity presented itself. And yet, I was still hesitating — Diplomacy, Eloquence, or Animal Empathy would also be very useful for my character, letting my goblin freely access human villages or increasing the chance of survival when meeting monsters.

And then, finally, the time came to edit and upload another clip to the video hosting site about the escapades of my green troglodyte. I had plenty of respectable material in the back-log, but my crowning achievement was, of course, VIXEN.

There was no longer any sense in hiding the fact that I had a flying mount — the assassin whose pride I'd wounded had probably already blabbed about my flying snake to any and all listeners, so I made the Royal Forest Wyvern the main subject of my clip. I made the secret method of hatching the flying snake egg a separate paid video, which could be downloaded by those who so desired for just ten game coins. I devoted all the remaining time to the process of the half-meter overgrown worm growing up gradually into a beautiful winged serpent.

Perros Ruthless got some attention as well, though. His unhealthy interest in my big-eared goblin had seriously impeded my gaming for the last few days, so I felt he deserved it. I used particularly chiding expressions describing the intellectual capacity of the assassin, who'd somehow managed to die eleven (!!!) times in the last two not-even-full days. And what was more, from what I was able to piece together, his last three deaths had been due to the defensive systems of the *Goons'* castle, where Perros had demanded he respawn. From what I'd seen, Mariam Standing_Right_Behind_You [GOONS] had fulfilled her promise despite that, and accepted the star-crossed assassin back into her clan, so I didn't spare her any acrid expressions, either. One might say I was playing with fire by goading such a powerful enemy and perhaps that was true, though I didn't see what difference 'it could make — the *Goons* had already declared a two-week-long hunt for me, so I just wanted to get payback by whatever means I had available. And satirizing her like this would lower the reputation of her clan, which seemed a fitting retribution.

I kept silent about the Midnight Wraith for now, as I remained about my nighttime visit to the Cursed House in general. Naturally, the clip didn't have a single word about building the raft, or our travels down the river — it was for the best to let my opponents think, that Amra was milling about somewhere near the Cursed House, just as before. So then, my business taken care of, I headed home to sleep it all off, making a stop on my way to buy groceries. I was yawning in exhaustion and it took me real effort to think. Because of that, completely on "autopilot," I got on the electrobus to my old rented apartment in the criminal outskirts of the metropolis, and nearly let it leave. Just imagine how those gangsters would have lit up when they saw me!

I noticed just in the nick of time though, jumping out of the electrobus and getting onto the proper line. A half hour later, I was already at my destination. When I came inside, Val wasn't playing *Boundless* and met me in the entryway on her wheelchair. Pointing in surprise at the bag of groceries, she exclaimed:

"A box of macaroni, frozen cutlets, a bag of

potatoes... Tim, it looks like you forgot we don't have a kitchen at our new place. We don't even have a decent microwave here, which is to say nothing of a stove. Last night, I found a café-bar eight floors down, but I felt uncomfortable in there alone — it was all a bunch of guys drinking alcohol and making a racket. Everything is obviously overpriced. The bar and tables are too tall. It was uncomfortable for me in my chair, and I couldn't see a thing..."

"So, are you hungry?!" I guessed.

"Well, I did buy some chips and mineral water from a vending machine. I finished the hazelnuts I found in my backpack... But basically, yes. I could stand to eat a square meal," my sister admitted.

I clapped my palm against my forehead. What a mutton-head I was! While I was out yesterday having a grand old time, my disabled sister was all alone in an unfamiliar apartment with almost no money and no food. And I had the gall to call myself her brother! I immediately transferred Valeria thirty-five credits — half of everything I had left.

"I also can't figure out where I'm supposed to wash and iron my clothes," Valeria complained. "Plus, I need to buy detergent. And I need some curtains for my room. The sun here reflects off the mirror windows of the skyscraper out the window. It's blinding! I can hardly sleep. And another thing..." Valeria started sobbing for some reason. Little tears were welling up in her eyes. "Tell me, Tim: why is it so easy to live in computer games? In the so called 'real world,' life is just hard, boring and sucky..."

I didn't answer her strictly philosophical question, just walked up and embraced my little sister warmly, trying to reassure her:

"Don't you go worrying like that. I'll go buy detergent myself. I'll look for an iron too. I mean, in *Boundless Realm*, I've got five thousand in bank notes, and another fifteen hundred in coins. I'll turn it into cash as soon as possible. We can buy a microwave and curtains," I promised my sister. "Don't cry, we'll get this place up to snuff, little by little. We'll make it comfy. And for now, let's go down to that cafe and get something to eat."

Just then, my cellphone started ringing. It showed an unknown number but, when I accepted the call, the peeved voice on the other end was unmistakable. It was Kira:

"Timothy, were you thinking with your head when you published that last clip?"

"What's not to like? The wyvern?" I suggested.

"Of course, the wyvern! What else? The pissed-off chatter on the *Boundless Realm* forum is already at such a pitch that the moderators can't delete the repeat threads fast enough. And that's to say nothing of banning players who lose their temper. Around a hundred new topics are being made every second on your wyvern. It's absolutely impossible to read all of them. And that's just the beginning. By the end of the day, it'll only get worse. Such a stir, in my memory, has only come about once before — when the *Boundless Realm* developers fundamentally changed the experience-gain algorithm and took stationary NPC dungeons from the game. That was where the top alliances used to quickly level their newbies, so they were understandably upset."

I explained to Kira that my hand had been forced, and I had to show the wyvern, because an enemy had seen it. I tried to justify my position — better for me to describe the situation with the flying pet from my point of view than to let someone else do it for me. This way, I could hide a few touchy moments and emphasize others. And also, once again, the clip on raising a wyvern from an egg was for money, which could not possibly hurt in my situation.

"You know best, Timothy. Though, in your place, I wouldn't enter *Boundless Realm* right now. Just live without the game for a week or so until the hubbub quiets down. And in the future, try to do everything you can to distance yourself from your character as much as possible — no one can be allowed to associate you with the green goblin. Not your old childhood friends, not your work colleagues and not your neighbors — no one. And that's for your wellbeing and peace of mind."

It was sensible advice. But I couldn't possibly spend that long out of game — it was my job, and I could quite easily be fired if I missed that much work in a row. Also, Taisha might go any number of places while I was gone. Then, finding my NPC companion in the huge *Boundless Realm* would be an extremely challenging task. In the end, I thanked the beautiful red-head for her advice, but was not planning to actually follow it in any way. Kira then, convinced that I grasped the gravity of the situation, changed the topic:

"Timothy, do you still have that card I gave you? Good. I've had it reprogrammed. Now, it will let you take the elevator up to floor three hundred thirty-three and open the door to the apartment we were partying in last night. It's already all picked up. Feel free to show up and spend the night whenever you like. In fact, if you're feeling like it, you could even move in. It would be much easier for you to get to work and — who knows? — maybe I'll drop by for a visit every once and a while. Before we ever met, I'd already paid that whole floor off for a few years in advance, so there's no need for you to waste the money. And another thing: I took your painting to my house — it really was a fitting and unique gift."

Kira said goodbye, leaving me in a pensive state with a telephone in hand. I really didn't like depending on anyone, or feeling obligated but, in this case, Kira was offering to help me for nothing, just selflessly. What reason did I have to not take advantage of her offer? It was a big apartment, fully furnished with all kinds of appliances, plus it'd be twice as close to work. And also, my sister and I could always come back here if something in the new place wasn't to our liking, or if my relationship with Kira soured.

"Tim, you asleep or what?" Val asked, tugging at my sleeve. "Let's go eat! You promised!"

I lowered my gaze to my sister, she looked tired. I could make out dried tears on her face. She was clearly not doing well here. This cheap hotel was no good for the physically disabled, much less teenagers. The people who lived here were unmarried specialists from the neighboring large office buildings, modestly-living freelancers and young couples without children — at least, that was the contingent of neighbors I'd noticed. That must have been why there were so many bars, pubs and restaurants in the building, but no decent establishments aimed at families with children.

Choosing my words carefully, I told Valeria:

"A girl, you don't know her, said we could move into an empty apartment she owns. The conditions there are much better than here — it has a real kitchen, a bedroom, a bathroom with a jacuzzi, a big living room and the view from the windows can be changed like the channel on an old-fashioned TV. What do you say, Val?"

"In terms of the girl, I can't say anything without seeing her," my little sister said, not missing the chance to quip. "But as for the apartment, it all depends on how much she's asking per month in rent."

"She's actually offering it for free, which is what has me so apprehensive," I admitted.

"Yeah, that does sound a bit weird," my sister agreed, serious beyond her years, tossing me a long careful gaze. "Maybe she just has a crush on you, Tim? It was for her, after all, that you bought a new suit and that super expensive present, right?"

Well, she guessed it. I didn't deny it, and nodded in confirmation. Valeria smiled:

"Then let's consider these expenses a kind of rent payment for the apartment. My opinion — we should agree and go live at your friend's. All the more so given that I absolutely hate it in this abominable hotel. And this way, the cutlets and potatoes you bought won't go to waste!"

I was awoken by the tantalizing aroma of frying potatoes and cutlets. I had to rush and peel my eyes open so I wouldn't choke on my drool.

"Time to get up lazy-bones! Food's ready, and it'll be time for you to go to work soon," my sister said as she pointed me to a small table near my bed. On it, she was placing my freshly made dinner.

"We could eat in the kitchen or the living room. Why'd you bring it into the bedroom?" I asked in surprise. In response, Valeria laughed happily:

"I couldn't help myself. I already ate in the kitchen. Plus, I don't know a single better way to wake you up than the smell of tasty food on the stove!"

I thanked Val, but didn't eat in bed, first heading to wash up and get myself in order. When I came out of the bathroom, Valeria was extending me a telephone:

"Someone named Jane called for you. She didn't want to talk to me, but said someone was waiting for you, and that you would know where. After that, she hung up. I hope you at least understand what she wanted to communicate."

Yes, I understood perfectly. Jane was the pretty assistant of Mark Tobius, director of special projects for the *Boundless Realm* Corporation and my direct boss. That meant my boss wanted to see me, which probably had something to do with all the chatter on the game forum after my clip showing the winged mount. My chest was seizing up a bit — being called to meet with the director, as a rule, meant unpleasant things. On the other hand, if my boss really was upset, Jane would have said as much in no uncertain terms.

"That wouldn't happen to be the same girl whose apartment we're moving into, would it?" my sister clarified.

I laughed and answered that Jane was a totally different person who had nothing at all to do with our new place.

"Good. Because, based on her voice, she really didn't like me. I was even worried she'd had a change of heart on the apartment."

While I was stuffing my face, my sister told me about the results of the day in-game. As I figured, the search for warg prints had ended fruitlessly, although my friends had checked the surrounding forest very thoroughly and even looked over the opposite bank of the river. They did find something of interest though: a respawn stone in a secluded glade. Valerianna Quickfoot had suggested the ogre and naiad change their respawn points to it, so they wouldn't end up dozens of kilometers through forest and swamp away from the group, back near the Cursed House.

After that is when it all started...

"In the next half hour, I was literally flooded with letters and private messages," my sister complained. "And they weren't even all free, meaning the sender was within a ten-kilometer radius. Some were actually quite expensive. All the messages and letters had one common theme slipping through: they wanted to know where to find a Goblin Herbalist by the name of Amra. Some simply asked politely, some offered money. Some even tried threatening me. Max Sochnier and Shrekson Bastard also complained that they got a huge amount of spam. Then, I closed the game and went on the *Boundless Realm* forum to figure out the situation. It took me just a couple minutes to grasp the scale of the problem. Tim, there are a huge number of people searching for you, and most of them have the very unkindest intentions. Because you were offline at the time, they tried searching through other players — all the ones you mentioned in your video clips. I advised our friends not to answer such letters under any circumstances and leave the game for a day. I sent our goblin companions away to an inn we discovered, gave Taisha plenty of money and told her and Tamina Fierce's children to stay inside until we came back. Lastly, I told the Gray Pack to hunt deep in the forest, then logged off immediately, because I saw a big boat full of players coming down the river from Stonetown. Fortunately, I saw them before they saw me..."

"What was that about an inn?" I asked, hoping to clarify part of my sister's story.

Val told me passionately about her find:

"Today, in the process of searching for the wargs, I hit upon a road. It was approximately five kilometers to the west of our camp. By the looks of things, the path was fairly well trod. I rode Pirate four kilometers to the south on it and, at a fork, I found a huge sturdy building, or maybe more like a small fort. A group of kobolds run the place. There must be around fifty of them. They have a copper mine not far from there and, near the inn, they have a copper storehouse with wood coal and ore, as well as a little trade depot. Merchants and travelers can stop at the fort. Staying the night there isn't expensive at all, and the food is more than tolerable. I thought this was the best possible place to hide 'your girly.' I mean, your green-skinned girlfriend is too conspicuous — the players instantly notice her attractive face and alluring curves. So, I decided to just let Taisha sit for day or two among NPCs, not poking her head out."

I praised my sister for the very proper and reasonable actions in the complicated situation and started getting ready for work. The municipal electrobus took about fifteen minutes to bring me to the *Boundless Realm* corporation skyscraper. It was seven thirty in the evening, so I was counting on catching the director at work. However, Mark Tobius wasn't in his office, just his assistant Jane, looking bored as she polished her already well-kept nails.

"So, as promised," I said, handing the director's secretary the chocolate I still owed her. "Where's the big man?"

"Mark didn't come in today. He called in this

morning and said he twisted his ankle. So, the big man is at home resting his leg," Jane answered in a none-too-affable tone, without even looking at me and not stopping her nail-care routine for even one second. "Tim, who was the young girl that answered the phone for you?"

What? I smiled back happily, because what I was hearing was very unexpected, but completely distinct notes of jealousy came through in Jane's voice. Strange. What was all that about? I didn't think I'd ever shown any interest in my boss's secretary, not even subtly or vaguely. Also, she was accustomed to expensive gifts, luxurious attire and apartments in the very center of the metropolis, so she was not likely to be looking on me as a perspective beau. I told her about how I lived with my sister. Janey finally tore her gaze from her nails and put the file in her cosmetic bag.

"Oh, with hazelnuts, just like I asked!" she exclaimed, giving a very positive evaluation to the chocolate bar lying before her. Then, suddenly wanting to return the favor, she offered to make me some coffee.

"Timothy, I actually called you just for myself. I thought you might appreciate what I have to tell you. Today, I put Mark through to all the head corporate honchos — marketing guys, economists, creative types. At one point, they were all together on one big conference call, and I involuntarily overheard. It was mostly about you..."

The girl went silent next to the coffee machine and turned, clearly expecting some kind of confirmation that I was interested in the topic. I then inadvertently noticed how dressed up Jane was. My boss's assistant always looked glamorous but, today, she was dressed in a bright red ultra-short party dress (a few centimeters shorter and it would've been inappropriate) with a very deep neckline. She was also wearing a red-coral-bead necklace, a pair of earrings, and gold rings on almost every finger. Finally, the girl's intricate hairstyle had clearly been done especially for this day. Was Jane celebrating something? Maybe it was her birthday? That said, I didn't see any flowers or presents on my colleague's desk.

"You look nice!" I admitted, and the girl smiled sorrowfully.

"Thank you for the compliment, Timothy. I had some plans tonight, but they didn't come together. Here's your coffee."

Jane extended me a glass of burning-hot liquid and, as I took little sips, she continued telling me about what she'd overheard from the leadership:

"Your video clip caused quite the fuss! A lot of players were very unhappy with the fact that such a valuable mount went to, forgive me for the harsh words, a totally green noob, who barely even knows how to play the game. And that included veterans and even top players, who've devoted years of their lives to *Boundless Realm* and earned their popularity and authority among the players. There were even a few petitions signed by famous gamers threatening to leave *Boundless Realm* if the situation isn't rectified."

"It's gone that far...? I didn't think a player's mount could raise such a commotion," I said thoughtfully. Jane exclaimed emotionally in response:

"Timothy, I've actually been understating things! You should have heard what the directors were really saying! The public relations director used nearly only curse words, shouting in annoyance at Mark that this incident could eradicate the trust of our player-base, which is fragile enough as it is. There's been a stream of hateful messages coming in from players to the developers in all day and it won't let up. In fact, it's only picking up strength!"

These were the same general terms I'd already heard from my sister, but I was interested in finding out the opinion of the corporation's employees on what had developed. And that, as it turned out, wasn't the greatest either. Jane continued sharing her discoveries:

"Initially, the forum admins harshly banned the most unrestrained, but then they got an order from the upper directors to soften their position and not to touch high-level players or any members of top clans. The corporation has always positioned itself as sensitive and open to player opinion. That is why the highest directors are now meeting to come to a decision that will allow them to take advantage of the current frenzy of activity for their benefit. They're talking about letting the players blow off some steam and voice their frustrations. After that, they plan to 'act in line with user opinion,' add some new rules to the game and redirect the negative attitude of the crowd at something other than the developers..."

Jane went silent, offering to let me think over the rest.

"Am I understanding right that they want to direct the rage of the masses against me?" I hazarded in fear. Unfortunately, I was correct.

"Yes! The details are still being discussed but, overall, they have come to an agreement. It will be a big hunt that will be announced to all of *Boundless Realm* tomorrow, and you will be its target. They will imbue an object in your inventory with the ability to control your flying mount — a token or an amulet, and there will be a certain chance for it to drop every time you get killed. If that amulet does drop, the player that kills you will become the owner of the unique flying mount! The directors did a survey of some top clans, and the results are in — they all found the idea intriguing. Seeing that, the hullabaloo must have been unprecedented."

"I have no doubt..." I said gloomily, my view on the situation growing dimmer with each passing moment.

My mood sunk below the floorboards. The leadership wanted to deprive me of my VIXEN — the pretty little wyvern, which I had earned fair and square, and raised from an egg. Was that really just?! Where in the game rules was it written that a successful player has to part with his property in order to calm a faceless herd of less-successful losers? I asked that last question out loud.

"Such a thing is, of course, not in the rules," the director's assistant agreed. "Appropriate bylaws will be written in, though, and along with them, your voluntary agreement to play the victim in the hunt will be obtained."

Seeing my slain state, Jane smiled and tried to perk me up a bit:

"It's not all that bad, Timothy. As far as I know, the hunt will only be for a limited time. And the biggest thing is that, at the end of the hunt, if you do manage to keep your pet, you can officially sell it at a *Boundless Realm* auction and legally convert the game currency to cash. I heard them mention a figure in the millions!"

I looked at Jane incredulously, but she reaffirmed her statement. For faithfully executing the role of victim of the great hunt, if I could manage to keep the trophies to the end, the

Boundless Realm corporation would give me an official, public job offer. That was exactly how the directors were planning, not only to once again hype working for their company, but also to explain the legal method of withdrawing game currency. However, I would be strictly forbidden from revealing the fact that I was working for the *Boundless Realm* corporation until the end of the hunt — otherwise, I would just be fanning the flames of a false narrative that the corporation greased the wheels for "their people," and preferentially awarded unique quests and objects to corporate employees.

There really was something to think on here, as well. Mark Tobius had said before that there were buyers ready to invest ten million coins of in-game currency just for an unhatched wyvern egg. Now that she was at level 16, my Forest Wyvern had to be worth a bit more, especially if sold at open auction, where she could be bought by any player with enough cash. But a million credits in real life was a ton of money. That could provide a comfortable and safe dwelling for my sister and me. That could be our future provided for. That could be a pair of new biotic legs for Val. That possibility was the very reason I had gone to work for the *Boundless Realm* corporation in the first place. But getting that million would be damned hard work. Otherwise, the corporation wouldn't have set up this whole mass-hunt spectacle in the first place...

"I see, Timothy, that the gravity of the moment has already reached you," said Jane, standing up from her desk and walking over to the doors leading into the hallway, then locking them from the inside with a key. "And now, I want to have an even more serious conversation. Just accept this as a fact — without outside help, you'll never manage to keep your pet. Already, your character is under thick cover from a few large clans and tomorrow, after the hunt is officially announced, your goblin herbalist won't even be able to enter the game without being killed immediately. After that, the players will wait for you at the respawn point, killing you off again and again. Sooner or later, the item will drop, and you'll lose your wyvern. And you won't be able to do anything with that. All your attempts to hide or change the respawn point will have no effect, because you have no concept of the methods being used to track you."

"I'm starting to suspect you have an ulterior motive for telling me this. Do you have a concrete offer for me?" I asked carefully. The girl laughed:

"That's exactly right, Timothy. You're a good guesser. I wanted to offer you a mutually beneficial transaction. You see, my position as director's assistant allows me to stay in the loop on a great many processes underway in the corporation. Finding out about upcoming events, items and new rules in the game world, as well as various cunning tactics used by players. The directors and other highly placed employees don't take me seriously, thinking me just a classic dumb blonde — a living piece of furniture or a wordless coffee-fetcher. Just so you know, I have a very good education, high ambitions and my own plans for life. Also, my current hair color is not natural. All that said, director's assistants don't get paid very well. Without alternative revenue streams, I'd never manage to survive, if you understand what I'm talking about..."

I nodded curtly, confirming that I understood all the advantages and subtleties of Jane's work, and also the girl's high demands. She sighed sorrowfully:

"On nothing but a secretary's salary, a young lady would never manage to rent an apartment in the center of the metropolis and provide herself with good cosmetics and decent clothing. My last boss understood that. He valued me and sent me bonuses at every opportunity, or even just gave me valuable gifts. But when Alexandro Lavrius left, the situation changed. Mark pretends not to understand my transparent remarks. Maybe he really doesn't. But I, meanwhile, am having trouble making rent — I mean, my salary is lower than the monthly on my one-room downtown! My offer — I'll tell you how to not get caught, and you help me with rent money.

I need seven hundred credits."

What a request! I had thirty in my account right now all told so, despite the attractiveness of Jane's offer, it was beyond my means. The thought of in-game money flickered by — the fifteen hundred coins my big-eared goblin had could have been withdrawn from the game in the form of one hundred fifty credits. But that wouldn't be enough, either. The rest of the funds in my character's possession were in the form of promissory notes from the Most Reliable Bank of Gremlins and the Subterranean Bank of Thorin the Ninth. Getting to a branch of theirs would be absolutely impossible under present conditions. Amra would just die repeatedly, if I tried. I'd never even leave the respawn point. Although...

"Here are the keys for a two-room suite in a hotel," I said, extending Jane a clinking key-ring. "It's a long-term hotel for young specialists in a calm residential neighborhood. The room's paid up two months in advance. It wasn't good enough for my sister and I, because it isn't adapted for non-walking disabled people, but there was no way to get our money back. If that sounds good, here's the address."

If I were in *Boundless Realm* at that time, I'd surely have seen a series of lines on raising my Trading skill run past. Jane grabbed the keys from my hand and wrote the hotel's address in her phone.

~ Stay on the Wing ~

"Thanks! You really bailed me out, Timothy! Now, listen carefully. Probably, before you enter the game, you'll see a bunch of messages from unknown players. And that's no coincidence — your pursuers are not so naive as to expect an answer. They just need to know you received the message — if you did, you must be within ten kilometers. After that, they can place a circle with a ten-kilometer radius on the map — the receiver must be inside. From that point, they can narrow down their search. They go five or ten kilometers away and try sending another free message to the offline player. If it works, they draw another ten-kilometer radius and look at where it intersects with the previous one. Then, a few hours later, they've got a fairly small area to search for their victim in. By the time the victim decides to return to the game, the location of the character has already, as a rule, been established to within a few meters. Then, they set up an ambush there and wait for the victim to enter the game. Usually, these murderers work in a group — in that case, figuring out the location of the offline character can be done in less than an hour. Avoiding this method of pursuit is not hard, though. All you have to do is change your private-message receipt settings for free messages from unknown players."

What could I say? It was really valuable information. On its own, though, it was hardly worth seven hundred credits.

"That's all well and good, but what should I do if the killers are already sitting there when I enter the game?"

Jane laughed. Now, the expression on her face was very similar to the look of sympathy my sister wore when I was acting blatantly stupid, misunderstanding elementary things. I had already figured it out on my own, though, coming up with methods to get rid of them off the top of my head. So, I asked Jane not to get distracted and tell me about the other methods of detection — after all, *Boundless Realm* was huge and, in the majority of cases, players could not count on finding a given character within ten kilometers of their location.

"It's impossible to turn off paid messages in the settings — the *Boundless Realm* corporation gets a steady income from them and it's pretty considerable. There are very many forms of paid message, one of which involves the players using magical messengers. The pursuer sends out such a magical being and simply notes the direction it was traveling with a compass, drawing a straight line along that trajectory. After that, they ask a partner to send the victim a message from another city, or use a teleportation scroll to another city and do it all on their own. On the map, they see where the lines intersect, and that's where the runaway must be. It's a fairly inexact method and, in the majority of cases, it gives an area dozens of square kilometers in size so, from then, they use free or cheaper private messages to determine the exact coordinates. Sometimes, an entire clan will engage in a search using these methods."

What could I say? The information I got from Jane was very valuable. As it turned out, there was nowhere, even in the farthest reaches of *Boundless Realm*, for my big-eared goblin to feel truly safe. But all the same, I saw some weak points in the detection methods — after all, finding out approximately where a person is located doesn't amount to much. They need to be able to get there, as well. But if that place is in a distant wilderness, hundreds of kilometers from the nearest city and there are no teleportation scrolls easily at hand, they'd have to walk for days through mountains, forests and swamps. After that, they'd have to just comb the wilderness in search of the runaway, at which point they'd discover that the victim hadn't been there for some time, and was now a thousand kilometers in the other direction. After all, no one had outlawed teleportation scrolls. Amra just needed to get his hands on a few.

An incoming message beeped out. Jane walked over to her desk and read the text on the screen.

"Tomorrow morning, Mark Tobius is preparing to come in to the office, despite his injured leg. He just gave me the assignment to get in touch with you and call you back here in the first half of the day. He'll almost certainly be telling you about the final decision of the board and the rules of the 'great hunt.' I hope, Tim, that you understand that our conversation must remain a secret. So, try to act surprised tomorrow and get at least a bit outraged, just for appearances."

I promised the girl I'd put on a real spectacle for the director tomorrow, so he wouldn't have any doubts that I was in the dark, and felt truly incensed.

"But, look, just don't overdo it. Mark has a pretty short fuse and can easily get out of control. I mean, he recently fired an employee just for having the gall to argue with him. I hope you have enough tact and acumen to drop your guard when the time comes to accept his offer."

"Don't you worry about that. After all your warnings, I'm morally prepared for a conversation with the big man."

Jane smiled in satisfaction and, pumping her thighs alluringly, walked up to the door and opened it, showing me that we were done talking. I bid the girl a polite farewell and headed for the exit. But when I walked past her in the doorway, she unexpectedly grabbed me by the hand and turned me toward her, placing her hand on my shoulder.

"I really hope, Timothy, that we can work together for a long time to come. I really do have something to offer a successful corporate tester.

And, if you play your cards right and follow my advice, you'll have plenty of money to afford my services."

Jane stood up on her tip-toes and kissed me right on the lips. To be honest, I was completely caught off guard. Also, now, her offer of other services sounded like it had a good deal of double meaning. But she was satisfied with the effect she'd produced, smiled and pushed me out into the hallway, wishing me happy gaming.

Already in the elevator, thinking over my conversation with Jane, I concluded that the fancy clothes she was wearing, her saying her plans for the evening hadn't come together, and Mark Tobius not showing up to work due to a suddenly sprained ankle, were possibly connected. At some point today, Jane had realized I could serve as a backup, probably when she overheard upper directors talking about the grand hunt and its main prize.

On my floor, it was very crowded and noisy — the work day was just coming to an end. The corporate testers were all leaving the game together to go home. I took advantage of the crowd and hurriedly slipped through to my work cabin — there was absolutely no time for me to get acquainted with and talk to my new colleagues. I did notice that

Kira was already at work, though — over the door of her cabin, there was a glowing red light. My sensor suit already donned, I was still in no rush to enter the game. I just loaded up my character's "work space," changed the message receipt settings and opened my mailbox.

Yes, there truly had been a great deal of messages... I didn't waste my valuable time reading them, just took down the names of those who'd managed to send me free messages — they must have been relatively nearby and so would be the most dangerous. There were twenty-six such players. I placed all of them on my black list, so I could always know whether they were in *Boundless Realm* or not. Three of them put me particularly on guard. They had sent a few messages each at intervals of thirty to sixty minutes. It looked very much like they had determined the location of my goblin by the method Jane had described.

None of the perfidious trio was playing now, but that didn't really mean anything. Valeria and I had quite often used the "login-trap" in other games when a person we'd marked for death noticed the threat and managed to leave the game. We would just log right off after them and watch from another account to see when our victim logged back in, at which point we would also enter and kill them.

But in *Boundless Realm*, a player could only

have one account, and I could hardly imagine someone convincing a partner to help them with an endeavor like this — there was little joy in sitting watch for hours at a stretch to see when the victim entered the game, especially at night. Also, the main prize for killing me now — the ability to join the *Goons* — was only for one person, and had already been claimed. Nevertheless, I was in no rush to start playing. It was only around ten, and night had already fallen in *Boundless Realm*, but two players from my black list were still in the game for some reason. That put me on guard.

I called Valeria and asked her to check if she'd also received messages from these characters, and what they wanted. But while my sister was finding that information, the green circle opposite one of the names changed to gray — the player left *Boundless Realm*. Of my pursuers, the only one left in the game was a woman, a level-80 Elemental Mage. Based on her high level, the night monsters of this area were of no threat to her whatsoever, so I had no hopes the magess would be leaving the game any time soon.

"Answer her message," I suggested to my sister, "and better to talk in a private channel. If they ask about me, say I definitely won't be playing until morning. You can think up a good enough reason on your own."

Three minutes later, the last of my pursuers had also left the game, after which I almost instantly got a call from Val:

"Yeah, she really was asking about you. But I feigned ignorance. I just told her gladly and willingly, that you were studying for a test and wouldn't be coming back today. After that, I asked her to accompany me to Stonetown. I pretended like I didn't manage to get into the protected village before dark and was now afraid to go alone through the scary dense forest. But the magess said she had stuff to do in real life, apologized and left."

"Good, Val. Then log in and check the area! If everything near the camp is clear, give me a call," I replied, then crawled into the virtual reality capsule, ready to log in at a moment's notice.

However, it took no less than six minutes for my sister to confirm that it was safe near the camp. I closed the virtual reality capsule and, thirty seconds later, found myself standing near our shelter, getting accustomed to the darkness of the night.

"What took you so long?" I asked, jumping on Valerianna Quickfoot with reproach. But I abruptly went silent, as there was a bright crimson criminal marker shining out like a beacon above the wood nymph's head. My sister's life bar was also in the orange, and there was an arrow with red fletching sticking out of her right shoulder.

"There were two players by the river keeping watch for us," my sister explained, wincing in pain.

"A berserker and a bow-woman. They didn't notice me at first. They were too busy doing... something else. This will serve as a good lesson for them — this place is a dangerous world with full PVP, and not a bedroom in a whorehouse, after all... Basically, I got lucky."

I helped the wood nymph remove the deeply embedded arrow and gave her some Healing Potion.

"Oh, now that's a lot better!" the mavka said, instantly starting to smile, her health now almost fully restored. "Amra, there are many pieces of equipment on the shore over there, sitting in the grass. Go look through them, maybe something will be of use to our wolf riders."

On the bank, there was a complete mess including a whole set of berserker armor and, right next to that, there was a carefully folded dress, chain-mail, a helmet, and pair of boots. It wasn't all from a surprisingly generous drop, it was just that the owners had removed their own clothing, caught up in an unexpected surge of passion. Why they hadn't placed their clothing in their inventories, I did not know. Clearly, they didn't think it sufficiently romantic. I didn't see the star-crossed lovers in the flesh, though. Their bodies had been carried away by the flow of the river.

After gathering the equipment, I called the Gray Pack. The wolves were close at hand. No more than five minutes away.

"Amra, take this. It's a more complete local map!" the wood nymph said, sending me a transaction offer for zero coins. "Look! Just half a kilometer from here, there's a respawn stone. You should make sure to visit it and add it to your list of stones. But before that, I have a pleasant surprise for you!"

Valerianna headed for the thick bushes on the riverbank, waded up to her knees in the water, fiddled about for a bit, then pulled out a stringer of live fish.

"The naiad has been fishing since morning. I asked him to leave a portion of his catch for you. One of each species. All fresh, alive and full of blood — just the way you like them! If you're too ashamed, I could turn away."

"No matter, go ahead and look..." I said, taking the stringer in my hand and looking at the silvery flopping fish:

Level-4 River Catfish
Level-2 Common Roach
Level-13 Mature Bream
Level-8 Muddy Tench
Level-1 Common Redeye

Five new species all at once! The perfect gift for a vampire! Let the feast begin! As they say, I won't stuff my face, but I might take a nibble!

~ Stay on the Wing ~

Damage dealt: 30 (Vampire bite)

Experience received: 20 Exp.
*Object received: Catfish meat (food) * 2*
Racial ability improved: Taste for Blood (Gives +1% to all damage dealt for each unique creature killed with Vampire Bite. Current bonus: 8%)

Achievement unlocked: Taste tester (15/1000)

Damage dealt: 89 (Vampire bite)

Experience received: 96 Exp.
*Object received: Tench meat (food) * 4*

Racial ability improved: Taste for Blood (Gives +1% to all damage dealt for each unique creature killed with Vampire Bite. Current bonus: 9%)

Achievement unlocked: Taste tester (16/1000)

...

Racial ability improved: Taste for Blood (Gives +1% to all damage dealt for each unique creature killed with Vampire Bite. Current bonus:

12%)

Achievement unlocked: Taste tester (20/1000)

Regeneration improved to 3 HP/Minute

My big-eared troglodyte burped in satisfaction and patted his puffed-out belly. Great! I managed not only to sate my hunger, but also to fill my Thirst for Blood bar to maximum. This had to have been the fastest and safest method of leveling my vampiric abilities in the game. I'd have to visit the fish market of the underwater village of Ookaa — I suspected that, there, I would find a true abundance of different fish and a happy hunting ground for bloodsuckers like me.

"Stuffed, big-ears?" Valerianna inquired compassionately. "Then let's not stick around here. The Gray Pack has already come to your call. Let's hurry. We need to mount the wolves and get on our way!"

Despite the late hour, we managed to reach the respawn stone without meeting any of the dreaded forest creatures. After that, I told the Gray Pack to head for the kobold inn — I'd have to get Taisha, Irek and Yunna out of there. We passed the eight-kilometer ride on wolfback in just half an hour. On the way, I raised my Riding skill to level 6, and Athletics to 9. Akella was limping badly and lagging behind the rest of the pack, but we were trying not to let them out of sight, though they would wait for us if need be — a wounded level-28 lone wolf would be easy pickings for the kind of creatures that roamed these woods.

With two hundred meters between me and my target, I jumped off the wolf, hoping not to frighten the inn workers with the predatory canine. The wood nymph and I made the rest of the way on foot.

"Stop, who goes there?!" a sentry called out. Hearing that, I raised my head and saw a small figure wrapped in a dark cloak lurking up a tree with a crossbow in hand.

Level-62 Kobold Guard

Perception check failed

I suspect that the guard was not, in fact, alone, and had friends hiding in the thick crowns of the neighboring trees. But I didn't manage to detect any other archers.

"My going in tavern eat-eat! There many goblin. That my friend."

"But why is mavka? Mavka — tricky and sharp-tooths."

"Mavka already be here today in daytime. Eat tavern, coin pay for kobold. Now she go with me."

Although kobold language was similar to goblin, it did have its differences, so we spoke in clipped, awkward phrases. But still, we understood one another.

Valerianna, though, was patiently awaiting the results of our negotiations.

Successful check for Kobold Guard reaction
Experience received: 80 Exp.

The gate opened with a creak, letting us inside the walls. Despite the late hour, the inn was bubbling with life. There were lit oil lamps hanging from posts lighting the way for a chain of gray- and blue-skinned kobold workers loading heavy bales onto a great many carts that belonged to a traveling merchant. All of this was, of course, performed under the watchful gaze of the merchant's guard team. No one paid my sister and I any mind. We walked over to a two-story building separate from the walls. In its windows, there burned a bright light, and I heard the sound of dishes clinking.

"No vacancy for sleep in night! All room to guest occupied! Only you can is going in munch-hall," a big fat kobold standing at the dining hall entrance cried in dissatisfaction.

But I reassured him that we weren't looking for rooms, we were just going to eat dinner with our friends — I pointed at Taisha, Irek and Yunna, sitting modestly at a corner table. On hearing my voice, our friends turned and ran to meet me with joyful whooping. And although Irek and Yunna just ran up and stopped, Taisha jumped right up onto my shoulders, saying:

"Where have you been all day, Amra?! You can't just leave me in a strange place like this!"

I nearly collapsed under her weight — my character was still not distinguished by particular Strength, but I embraced my NPC bride tightly and even managed to twirl her around.

Athletics Skill increased to level 10!

Whoa there! Even the game system considered my actions strenuous and exhausting. Nevertheless, I joyfully assured Taisha that I had come after her at the first opportunity. The people eating at the neighboring tables (clearly more of the merchant's guards) watched us two goblins kissing with a fair degree of hostility, but they didn't say anything or try and stop us. Nevertheless, my sister touched my shoulder and said:

"Big-ears, that's enough PDA. You and your green beauty are attracting attention. Tomorrow, the players searching for us will ask the local NPCs and quickly figure out that you were here. We need to leave and get as far away as possible."

"You know, you're right," I agreed. Then, I turned to Taisha: "The wolves of the Gray Pack are waiting for us beyond the gates. We need to leave."

Taisha let go of me, looked at the empty table in sorrow and asked:

"Can we please wait for the dinner we ordered first? It's just that Tamina's children and I are hungry, and we've already paid," the green-skinned beauty begged. "We've been sitting here for an hour already, but they still haven't brought our food."

The wood nymph and I had to go figure out what was taking so long. I wasn't allowed into the kitchen, but the kobold chef came out on his own and, wiping a shaggy blue arm on his sweaty brow, started speaking:

"It is devil's delight this of evening. Important merchant men is coming. Twenty-five guard with hungry gullet. They need eat. Many pan I use, all fire is took. And too, is birthing human, aristocrat lady. She want food also, with two grown children. And now is for her almost finish the food. Your goblin be next."

The chef pointed at a wooden tray stacked with dishes and plates meant for the human woman, who had either already given birth or was preparing to do so in the near future. My sister and I exchanged glances without a word. A woman giving birth, and two grown children with her? Interesting. Very interesting...

"Am can bringing tray for lady human. Like this, you no losing time and can cooking dinner for hungry goblin," I suggested to the chef.

~ Stay on the Wing ~

Successful check for Kobold Chef's reaction
Experience received: 80 Exp.

"Good. Goblin take and bring — help," the chef mercifully allowed and handed me the plate-laden tray. "Going stairs up and door is of left."

Successful Agility check
Experience received: 16 Exp.

I nearly spilled. Due to the large size of the tray, I couldn't see in front of myself and tripped on the first stair. The wood nymph helped me, setting the plates and glasses back in their places on the tray, and speaking with a trembling in her voice:

"I seem to have caught a bit of the jitters. It is now night, and those people are like, supposed to change into their alter ego. I mean, what if it isn't just some harmless big-bellied countrywoman and her nephews behind that door, but a pack of hungry killer wargs of an unknown level?! Or what if they're people now, but go alter-ego when they find out we've discovered their secret?"

I stopped sharply. What was there to say? It really was a very possible way this situation could develop.

"Hold the tray!" I said, passing it to my sister. "I need to take some precautions first. I have a tiny bit of wolfsbane in my Inventory. Just one lone leaf, but it should be enough to powder up and add to one of the big food dishes. If they don't attack us right away, and start eating, we'll neutralize the biggest of them right off the bat. And if we're wrong, and those people aren't our wargs, the garnish won't do them a bit of harm."

Valerianna returned me the tray of goodies, pushed her green hair out of her eyes, and took the wand in her hands.

"You go in, leave the tray on the table and start the conversation. They're expecting someone to bring in food, so they won't be surprised. In the meantime, I'll wait and see how this plays out behind the door. I'll butt right in if something goes wrong. Try not to die too quickly. If it starts going bad, lead them out into the hall. There's a bunch of human guards there, and they'll be able to help us against the predatory wargs. And also, our goblin allies can come help..." said Valerianna, thinking things over. I could read alarm and indecision in her face.

"Let's go up there, Val. At the very least, we won't know who's in the room until I've opened the door. So, here goes nothing! Let's hope they're just humans."

Holding the tray in one hand, I politely knocked and entered the room. And... I stopped dead in my tracks.

When my sister and I were considering the

two options — humans or wargs — we hadn't even considered this possibility. It all turned out much worse...

Until the hunt Begins

ALL THE WORDS I had prepared in advance for the NPC runaway got caught in my throat. I mean, they weren't going to be tricking the character before me now. I found myself being stared down by a living player — a woman with dark, short hair of thirty years in a long bright-red dressing gown. Even her loose clothing couldn't hide her huge stomach and impending birth.

Belle Sweetypie
Human
Level-78 Druid

Not really believing my eyes, I opened the information on the character, and my last doubts were finally unraveled. The person before me really was a player, I could even read her primary skills:

Animal Empathy (P Ch) level 56
Transformation (C S) level 44
Thick skin (C S) level 39
Animal Control (P Ch) level 29
Hand-to-Hand Combat (S A) level 50
Tracking (P A) level 89
Stealth (A C) level 67

Well, well! I had no words. My little goblin Amra had no chance against her, even considering the woman's present extra weight and difficulty in maneuvering. On a carpet next to the pregnant woman, there were two NPC children sitting and playing quietly with stuffed dolls: a boy and a girl.

Darius Violent
Level-19 Human Townsperson
Darina Violent
Level-18 Human Townsperson

The room was immersed in gloom. The oil lamps on the walls were not lit, but there was a candelabra on the table with three candles, giving off just enough glow for me to make out everything. I took a quick look around. It was a spacious room, with expensive furniture. The floor was carpeted with thick rugs. On the wall, there was a painting of a battle scene. All three of the windows were adorned with thick blackout curtains. By the standards of the modest kobolds, this wasn't just a room, but a true palace.

In the prolonged silence, I made a few steps forward and placed the dish on the table. The woman looked at the dinner, then at me and said quietly, not hiding her surprise:

"What is this all about then?"

I decided to return to my initial plan, and answered the high-level player innocently:

"Down here is NPC chef, very busying. Merchant to come with guard division. All is hungry. I saying to help kobold man. Me bring plates. We was hungry already, and chef is making food slow for goblin. No me expect see undying here."

"I see..." the woman replied, unable to hold back a smile as she listened to my incomprehensible gabbing. "Alright then, boy. You've done your job. You brought me and my companions dinner. Now leave us so we can eat in peace."

I was being forced out the door. Fairly politely, but still adamantly. Should I just leave? Or was it better to find some pretext to chat, so I could find out a bit more about this mysterious Belle? I pointed at her big stomach and asked:

"Is really a woman play *Boundless Realm* with so big tummy allowed? Is dangerous in virtual world. Stress, worry, heavy lifting. Game can to harm baby health. Is especially bad in last of pregnant time."

Belle laughed heartily, tears welling up in her eyes:

"Boy, you must understand perfectly that we don't always look the same in the game as in real life. I mean, do you really walk around with green skin and massive ears outside *Boundless Realm*?"

I shook my head so hard my ears started flapping.

"So, you see! I just play a big-bellied lady, but in reality, I'm not even considering having a baby. It's just a quest. Very rare. I have to bear it and pretend to be pregnant."

Just then, the girl sitting on the floor, who was wearing a well-kept light-colored dress and playing with toys made an unexpected incursion into our adult conversation:

"Aunty Belle, what are you talking about? Does this mean you've been tricking me and Dar, pretending to be pregnant? Aren't you going to give birth to Fenrir's heir?"

Fenrir's heir?! I strained to pick up my fallen jaw.

Mission renewed: The Gray Pack's Past
Mission class: Rare, Group
Description: Find the owner of the headband in the room and return it to them
Reward: 2000 Exp., the ability to include

Wargs in the Gray Pack

What was there to figure out? The pregnant Belle had a stylish short hairdo. For her, the headband would be nothing but an extraneous nuisance. Darius was a boy. And although he did have long braids below the shoulders, young boys wouldn't wear such girlish attire. The only person in the room who could possibly have a need for the headband was Darina.

While I read the message and thought over the simple choice, the aristocrat chewed out the girl for crawling into the conversation uninvited. Belle's pretty face transformed into an evil grin as she spoke:

"Darina, how many times have I told you not to interrupt! No matter what, you don't understand even a third of what Amra and I are talking about, and only prove your ignorance! You will be punished very severely!"

"Yes, aunty," said the frightened girl, lowering her head and starting to play nervously with her waist-length hair.

"Amra, the quest updated for me!" Valerianna Quickfoot messaged, confirming my own observations. *"It looks like you're on the right track!"*

"Yeah, I know. But don't come into the room. There's a player in here over level 70, and you've still got the criminal marker for all to see. I'm gonna

give the girl the headband now and go out into the hallway. We can think about what to do next together."

"Fenrir's heir?" I asked, latching onto the girl's incautious words. I then said with feigned surprise: "This is huge evil wolf tall as house with two story? You are must confused, Darina. Your aunt... how is little kid saying... she normal person, not lady of wolf. No is head-sick zoophile, making unnatural such couple. And also, hard to imagine how to start process with such size in difference."

The girl didn't answer, just smiled barely perceptibly with the very corners of her lips. But then, her brother couldn't hold back and burst out laughing, which garnered him a stiff wallop from his aunt.

"Is that all, Amra?" Belle asked, no longer trying to hide her annoyance.

"Almost. Last topic and goblin is leave. Amra is also having quest long time. It may is boring and not so unusual as with Belle pretending pregnant. Goblin to be in Stonetown. Man in there is asking goblin to look for owner of headband to return lost-and-found item. Saying only vague: 'niece and nephew of pregnant human woman, were live in Stonetown, but is leave, not known where.' Honest admitting, I was thinking that mission is useless and 'jammed' — real bad hard finding such people in huge *Boundless Realm*. But before eyes, I seeing pregnant human aunt lady. See nephew. See niece. So Amra is ask kids: you in Stonetown no is losing this headband so pretty with all colorful?"

The girl turned in hesitation to her severe aunt, awaiting her reaction, but then lowered her eyes. The boy then unexpectedly stood from the floor and extended an arm demandingly:

"That's mine! Dara gave it to me so I could keep my long hair out of my eyes!"

"You're mistaken, Darius," the lady said with tension in her voice. "We were never in Stonetown. It's just a similar headband."

The child somehow shrank and collapsed. Nevertheless, I managed to slip him the band:

"Here! Goblin is give for you! This long hair go in back, not in front of seeing!"

Mission completed: The Gray Pack's Past
Experience received: 2000 Exp.
Ability gained: you may now include
Wargs in the Gray Pack

On the mini-map, the yellow NPC child marker changed to green — the character was now friendly to me. Taking advantage of the spontaneous break, I got a second headband out and handed it to the girl:

"Here! Goblin is see that you is want, but of shame to ask. Gift for you!"

~ Stay on the Wing ~

Passive use of artifact: Ring of Fenrir

Successful Charisma check
Experience received: 16 Exp.

Despite the druid's angry shout and the obvious threat of punishment, Darina decisively grabbed the headband from me and placed it in her dress pocket.

> **Hidden mission completed: Gray Pack's Past (additional, wolves)**
> **Experience received: 4000 Exp.**
> **Charisma increased by +2**
> **Default relationship improved by +5 with all NPC creatures of the following types: Dogs, Wolves, Wargs, Volkodlaks, Rougarous, Canine Chimeroids, Hellhounds**

"Get out of my room!" Belle Sweetypie demanded, her voice raising to a shriek and her eyes growing dark with rage.

I understood that, if I didn't get out of the druid's room immediately, the high-level player would attack me and, naturally, kill me quickly. So, I hurried to apologize and leave, closing the door behind me. My heart was beating frantically in anxiety. From behind the door, I heard Belle screaming, reproaching her "niece and nephew," but I smiled to the wood nymph, who was standing a few steps from me:

"It worked! Alright, there's nothing else keeping us here. Let's go down to the dining hall, get the goblins fed, give Irek and Yunna the new duds we took off the star-crossed lovers and get the hell out of here."

When we reached the stairs, my sister started bombarding me with questions:

"So, did you see Dar and Dara? Were they really wargs? Can they be included in the Gray Pack?"

"They're the pets of a level-78 druid, and the player is not prepared to give up her acolytes. But I gave them the headband and completed the quest so, if we do come across any wargs now, we could try and take control of them and add them to the Gray Pack."

They'd just brought in the goblins' dinner. The fat chef was setting plates on the table. Time was of the essence, so I asked Taisha and Tamina Fierce's children to wolf down the food then, together with Valerianna Quickfoot, went to visit the trade depot. Kobolds being night creatures, there was little surprising in the fact that the trader was awake to greet us in a room piled high with boxes and bales.

Would you like to choose Poisoner (A I) as a secondary skill?

~ Stay on the Wing ~

I needed a few seconds to figure out why I'd gotten that message: Belle Sweetypie had begun eating her specially seasoned dinner. No, I didn't take the "Poisoner" skill, but my mood was dramatically increased — the high-level druid would not be able to take her combat form for some time, so we didn't have to worry about dangerous aggressive animals. And that was perfectly fine by me.

"For some reason, he's only got trash," the wood nymph said, frowning in dissatisfaction as she looked over the kobold merchant's truly modest assortment. "Big ears, it looks like we've already outgrown all the equipment and weapons they suppose might be of use to the newbies who come upon this place. Hold up; someone's calling my cellphone."

The wood nymph froze motionless — my sister went afk. Meanwhile, my gaze caught on a pair of short spears with wide flat tips — they seemed well suited to a pair of goblin wolf-riders. They could be used from wolfback, or standing. The merchant didn't accept bank notes, so I had to pay in coins — ten pieces of silver for each spear. After counting the money I gave him two times, the shop owner strung the seven-sided silver coins with holes in the middle onto a leather strap and hung it from his neck.

I realized a bit belatedly that I had slightly too much in the way of bank notes from the Most

Reliable Bank of Gremlins and the Subterranean Bank of Thorin the Ninth. I opened my finance window once again and couldn't believe the reality of what was happening — I now had promissory notes from *Boundless Realm* banks to the tune of over eighty-six thousand coins! Could it really be that over eight thousand players had bought my paid video clip on how to hatch and raise a wyvern? It seemed they had! And at that, the sum was gradually increasing before my very eyes — the sales were ongoing. I'd have to make my way to some big city to cash in these notes soon. I already had up to eight thousand credits worth. That could provide Val and I with a decent car! And if I could get another two thousand credits, I'd be able to afford biotic prostheses for my sister.

The mavka started moving again — my sister was back in the game.

"It was Max Sochnier. He's also been reading the *Boundless Realm* game forum and, to put it lightly, he's in shock. The mess on the forums just won't die down. There's a bunch of new petitions demanding they confiscate your flying mount. As an argument, they're writing that you had an unfair advantage, exclusively available to goblins — the method of hatching the egg was known only to the NPC shaman Kaiak Badgerleg, and he would only share it with other goblins. A player of any other race wouldn't have such hints on how to grow a wyvern from an egg, and the fetus would have surely died. The admins are doing their best to call for patience, assuring the players that they'll announce a decision on the wyvern tomorrow. Max is asking if we need his help. He says he could get the ogre fortifier, too. Apparently, they're both well rested and are ready to enter the game. Max can pick Leon up in his car, and they could both be in *Boundless Realm* in forty minutes."

"Yeah, have them both come!" I replied, joyful at the unexpected help of my friends. "Tell them we'll meet up in forty minutes at the forest encampment, then we can keep going from there together. By the way, ask the naiad when the merchant ship comes to the Ookaa docks. Max Sochnier once told me about a sailboat that comes once a week with human NPC merchants to buy up the fish caught by the undersea residents."

My sister "froze up" for another few seconds, then said elatedly:

"Tim, you're a genius! The merchants should be coming tomorrow at the crack of dawn. They'll only be there for an hour, then they go on to some far-off islands. If we can get on that ship, it would be a very unexpected tack for our pursuers!"

* * *

Unfortunately, we were not simply allowed to leave the inn in peace. Just a hundred steps past the gates, I saw Belle Sweetypie five meters ahead of me in the dark forest, accompanied by her niece and nephew. Over the big-bellied lady's head, there was a black skull symbol hovering ominously — the player surpassed me by over fifty levels. And though the druid didn't have any apparent weaponry in hand, she didn't really need to. The druid's strength was her ability to morph into a predatory beast at any moment. Considering the fact she was level seventy-eight and had very well-leveled combat skills, Belle Sweetypie could take us all down in a matter of seconds.

"First, let's just talk," the woman said with a predatory smile, noticing the criminal marker over the wood nymph's head with satisfaction. "'Just talk' means I talk and you answer honestly and in detail. If your answers are to my liking, I might let you go. Except the mavka — I'll be sending her to respawn no matter what, because it is not in my habit to let lawbreakers off scot free."

"Why so lopsided? I'd also like to ask a few questions to such an interesting character as yourself," I said, understanding that I was being quite impudent, but not prepared to audition for the role of helpless victim. "First, answer me honestly: are you really carrying Fenrir's child?"

The druid winced in discontent. I suspect that Belle thought we would be shaking in fear when we saw her, terrified to make a peep and risk upsetting such a strong player. But our calm demeanor astonished her. And also, my big-eared goblin's ability to speak normally, I suppose, came as an unpleasant surprise as well. I thought the woman might not answer my question, but she did anyway:

"Alright, I'll answer that one question. Yes, I was one of the many wolves in the Gray Pack. One day, I caught the Pack Leader's attention. It was in the last days of Fenrir, when the Gray Pack didn't even have a tenth of its former numbers. We had just lost three battles in a row, and all our strongest and most battle-hardened predators were dead. They had once formed the military backbone of the Gray Pack, so we were done for. Players hunted us down day and night, chasing us into the impassable swamps east of the city of Lars. Fenrir was wise and understood perfectly that the end was near. But while the Leader was alive, the pack continued to fight. That moonless night, the Great Leader lay with me, then ordered me to go and take all the pups over an unsteady dike his wargs were building by placing branches over the bog. Initially, there were around ten pups, but only these two managed to make it through the swamp," the druid said, pointing at Darius and Darina. "A few days later, I found out that Fenrir had fallen heroically in an uneven battle with undying, and his Pack was disintegrated. At that time, a chain of unique quests started for me about rebuilding the Gray Pack. I am carrying

Fenrir's heir, and my child may one day rally the beasts of this forest and lead the Pack back to its former greatness!"

Mission received: Leader of the Gray Pack
Mission class: Rare, group
Description: The Gray Pack can only have one Leader. Eliminate your competition!!!

Attention! If you die, the chance of losing the object Ring of Fenrir (cursed item) in this battle has been increased to 100%
Reward: 8000 Exp., +1 to maximum Gray Pack member limit (up to seven)

The druid went on for a bit longer, giving a passionate retelling of how she confused the tracks and found a new place to live, all the while avoiding encounters with other players. Then, she described how she went into the wild unknown parts of *Boundless Realm* and taught the two surviving warg pups how to behave properly in human society and how to approach humans. But suddenly, the woman clammed up and looked at me in surprise as if she was seeing me for the first time.

"Well, well! How interesting. It's been a long time since any mission about the Gray Pack updated for me. Probably two months at this point. So then, Amra, you must understand perfectly that I can no longer let you go alive. Attack!"

At the very beginning of the druid's long speech, I already understood that our encounter would not be ending peacefully. For that reason, I'd already given my sister a curt warning and prepared my throwing net, taking it into my hands and starting to wind up. I had no desire to attack first and get the criminal marker for myself but, if there was aggression against me or any of my allies, I was prepared to strike back at a moment's notice.

Despite the gravity of the moment, I was forced to laugh as I watched the enemy camp start a maneuver that looked like a high-speed striptease competition. Both Belle's niece and nephew managed to undress in a matter of seconds and get down on all fours, quickly changing their appearance to that of fur-covered long-legged toothy predators. The druid also removed all her clothing but one piece, probably placing them in her inventory, then fell down onto all fours. But, unlike her pets, the druid didn't change appearance, remaining a big-bellied vulnerable human woman.

I cast my net at the druid, hoping to immobilize our strongest enemy.

Exotic Weapons skill increased to level 7!

But then, my sister completely surprised me — the figure of the wood nymph instantly split into two, then both copies did the same. Now, there were four identical mavkas running in different directions and starting to cast freezing spells on the still-kneeling pregnant lady. The wargs took bounding leaps at the nearest figure but when they tried to bite the delicate green-haired girl, they found themselves jumping through a phantom.

Belle gave a few twitches, trying to find the path of least resistance, then saw the wolves running across the field and the wyvern darting downward and... exited the game!

She was attempting an emergency logoff in the hope that we wouldn't manage to kill her character within thirty seconds, at which point she should disappear. Considering the huge number of hitpoints she had (many of her primary skills leveled Constitution), her incredibly high resistances and her well-leveled damage-absorption skill Thick Skin, the tactic just might have worked. But Belle Sweetypie, whether out of inexperience or ignorance of game mechanics, missed one very important factor — although she had yet to attack anyone, her warg pets had already managed to come at my sister, thus giving their master a thirty-minute delay before she could leave *Boundless Realm*. If she had ordered them to attack me or any of the goblins accompanying me, Belle Sweetypie would have become a criminal, and the leaving penalty would have been eight whole hours, but a half hour was plenty for us, given no resistance.

After losing their connection to their master, and not receiving new commands, both wargs simply laid down on the ground and looked on indifferently as dozens of malicious hornets stung the woman's body, goblins poked her with spears and daggers, and enraged wolves tried to damage the high-level druid. The wyvern, meanwhile, was spitting down acid from above. My sister was trying out various spells from her magical arsenal, blanketing the kneeling woman with a sheet of ice, or shooting her with icicles. Belle Sweetypie's life bar was going down very quickly, and had already reached the red zone. I also shot a few thorns from my blowgun, but both times did no damage and just placed the weapon back in my inventory, as it was no longer needed. Finished! All told, it took us a little under a minute.

Experience received: 780 Exp.
Achievement unlocked: Player killer (5)

I got "Player Killer?" That meant one of my NPC pets must have made the final blow. The experience gain was quite paltry, though that wasn't too surprising — we had to share the prize with a fairly large crowd.

I stopped Irek and Taisha from throwing themselves at the defenseless wargs, and also ordered the Gray Pack to lie down and get some rest. My attention was drawn by a frantically pulsating game icon, the one used for controlling mounts and pets.

Oh, that was new! New lines had appeared in the Gray Pack settings, but only the first two were available to choose:

Young female warg, level 18
Young male warg, level 19
Garm, level 0 (inactive)

Garm?! I tried selecting the last line a few times, but it never worked. What was more, the line quickly went pale and I watched as the words slowly faded into nothingness. "Garm, the greatest of dogs..." The huge four-eyed monster from Scandinavian mythology must have not been born yet. It was a great pity to miss out on the unique creature, but I was forced to make do with what I had. I put a tick next to the two wargs, confirming their inclusion in the Gray Pack. A moment later, the NPC triangles changed color from red to blue — allies.

But the quest wasn't considered complete – something must have remained unfinished. I walked up to the body of the druid lady and opened the loot window. Coins, nearly two hundred. Raw meat. Two vials of human blood. A pair of woman's boots with unknown properties. There it was! A dark metal chain with a pendant stylized in the form of a predatory claw.

Fenrir's Claw amulet (unique item)
Gives +250 Constitution, +250 Strength, +50% resistance to physical damage, +50 to reaction of the following creatures: Dogs, Wolves, Wargs, Volkodlaks

Attention! Your character's level is too low to use this object
Requisite level: 125

Based on that, the level-78 Belle Sweetypie had also been unable to use this object and was just carrying it around "to grow into." As soon as I took the amulet in my hands, the quest finally completed:

Mission completed: Leader of the Gray Pack
Experience received: 8000 Exp.
+1 to maximum Gray Pack member limit (up to seven)

Level twenty-eight!
Racial ability improved: 60% resistance to cold

A light was glowing over my head — my

Royal Forest Wyvern had reached level 17 and was now on top of the world, contorting herself into one highly complex shape after the next.

"Oof, we barely managed!" said Irek, walking up in disbelief to the body of the dead druid and poking it with the tip of his spear.

"Not at all, goblin. It was all very predictable," Valerianna Quickfoot disagreed. "Sure, Belle Sweetypie in the form of a she-wolf, or whatever else she was preparing to turn into, could have killed any of us with one swing of her clawed paw. Probably, the pregnant druid in human form also could have 'one-shotted' us with a slap. But who among us would have allowed the encumbered lady to get within striking range? Amra and I were shooting her from afar, and you two have slings. Of course, the battle would have taken longer, and she might have spent some time healing up, but the result was obvious from the very beginning. The druid just made our job easier by logging off."

Technically, I agreed with my sister — a vicious horde such as ours really could have brought down a level-78 player with strong debuffs to movement speed such as the pregnant Belle. But Valerianna stayed tactically silent on the fact that someone would have also had to distract the wargs from biting down the wood nymph, who was our main damager. Also, the slightest miscalculation or slip-up could have led to losses in our ranks.

"Am I to understand that these two man-eaters will be traveling with us from now on?" Taisha asked squeamishly, clearly meaning Dar and Dara.

I wanted to object to my green companion, saying something like, "what makes you think that, just because they're wargs, they eat people?" But instead, I turned to the new members of the Gray Pack and... stayed silent. Hrmph. The spectacle of the nephew and niece devouring their "aunt" was, to put it lightly, unpleasant.

"Woah! What are you doing? Have you gone totally mad?! Darius, spit out that filth! Darina, what are you doing?! Get away from there!" I tried to drive the predators from the corpse, but was met with two pairs of utterly wild animalistic eyes. I couldn't detect even the slightest signs of intelligence in their gaze.

I had to immediately open the Gray Pack control menu and command the two predators to go elsewhere. The wargs obeyed, but they still continued greedily inhaling the scent of fresh prey and licking their blood-caked snouts.

"In this form, they're just wild animals and cannot understand human speech," my sister said sorrowfully, also in shock. "Now, they'll remain that way until sunup, and you'll have to constantly watch them. On the other hand, that does have some pluses — they'll run like beasts, so we won't get slowed down. I'll grab the clothes and give them back in the morning."

* * *

The way back stuck in my mind because we came across a pack of Ancient Wolves who were around level fifty. They followed us for some time, but their intention seemed to be either just curiosity or trying to drive competitors from their territory, as the markers for the NPC's on the mini-map remained yellow. Our wolves, "modded" for speed, were easily able to evade the chase. And also, Akella's lameness came to an end just in time. He no longer lagged behind his high-level wolf brothers in speed. What was more, I had just raised my Riding skill to level 8, increasing the speed of my mount by 1% for each level. My sister had found some developer comments on the *Boundless Realm* forum saying that the skill also worked passively on creatures belonging to the player or in the same group as him, even if not being ridden.

Shrekson Bastard and Max Sochnier were waiting for us at the forest camp. The huge moose Lil_Timbo initially had a slightly apprehensive reaction to the wolves and wargs, but he soon calmed down and then simply paid the predators no mind. Before going anywhere, we took a short ten-minute break — my sister went to bolster her strength with sandwiches. I, though, climbed out of the virtual reality capsule and met with my friends at the employee break area near a coffee machine.

I already knew Leon quite well, but this was the first time I was seeing Max Sochnier in real life. He really was a Frenchman, too. He was a young man of average height and intelligent appearance with dark curly hair. Max used to work as a piano and recorder teacher in a music school, but had been downsized a few years ago when, everywhere on earth, most living teachers were replaced with computer programs and robots.

I heard about it all on the news. At that time, there were protests in most major cities from the newly out-of-work teachers. From what I'd heard, these episodes of civil disobedience were very harshly cut down by the police, who arrested all activists and even shot some. Max Sochnier, in his own words, was not an activist in the protest movement, but also fell in the field of view of the criminal justice system, even spending a few months under house arrest with an ankle monitor.

Branded in his personal record as an anti-government radical, it was hard for him to find work. In fact, Max couldn't find any normal employment for the next year and a half. One day, by complete coincidence, he saw the game plotline tester vacancy with the famous *Boundless Realm* corporation and applied without particular hope he would succeed. He didn't spend too long trying to perfect his game alias, and just went with his real name. The former music teacher considered successfully completing his trial period a sign that fate had given him the chance to return to a normal, stable life.

"But why did you get assigned the Trader class, instead of something musical, like Bard? I mean, the system was supposed to choose a character close to your interests."

The man just shrugged his shoulders in response:

"My father worked as a salesman for many long years, so I have some familiarity with sales and negotiation. Maybe that's why. Music just brings up sad and unpleasant memories for me now anyway, so Bard would definitely not be the right class."

I asked him to listen to me with great attention, and told him about the upcoming Great Hunt, which was to remain a big secret, as well as methods players might be using to track us. Max Sochnier, thoughtfully stroking the bridge of his nose, answered:

"Hrmm... You're really in a jam, Timothy. But I'm with you. You can count on me all the way! Participating in such a massive event on the side of the fleeing victim is, after all, a unique opportunity to strut my stuff, raising my fame and value in the eyes of the corporation. I'm sure our boss will look positively on us, if we can just wriggle away for some time and not let them catch us right off the bat. Even if it is just for a few days, we need to hold out!"

Leon said approximately the same thing, but in simpler language. Both my friends refused to believe I'd manage to hold out until the end of the hunt, but still they offered their unconditional help to draw out the unusual event as long as possible.

"Good. Let's finish our coffee and get back to the game, then. I saw that our raft is still on the riverbank. Let's use it. We need to get to the ocean before sunup, then destroy the raft and meet the NPC fish-merchant at the Ookaa docks. Max, our shared mission will be using our Trading skill and other abilities as much as possible to convince the people to let us come with them. My sister Valeria already figured out that the *Boundless Realm* player-made knowledge-base doesn't have any information on the route of the trading ship and, actually, there's nothing about its existence at all. So, this move will be unexpected for our pursuers, and we'll gain a few hours' head-start."

The hunt Begins!

"DID YOU CALL?" I asked, walking into the office of the director of special projects with a bubbly bearing.

Mark Tobius pointed me to the guest chair and immediately asked his assistant to make us both some coffee. The "big man" himself was sitting far back in his huge director's armchair, his injured right leg propped up on another chair placed in front of him. I noticed a pair of crutches leaning on the wall and saw a thick layer of bandages under his pant leg. I didn't ask Mark how he was feeling, as such questions would surely sound utterly false. But he brought it up all on his own, speaking in an upset tone:

"Well, I had to come into to work because of

you, even though my leg is injured."

"Because of me? Are you talking about the seething on the forum after that video clip I put up?"

The director frowned and nodded. Mark Tobius's mood was nothing but gloomy today. I realized that immediately, so I had to make sure to choose my words extremely carefully.

"So, what do you think about that? How are you planning to fix what you've done?"

The question being posed that way surprised me, and was an unambiguous sign of bad things to come. My boss, for some reason, considered me at fault all the problems and was expecting justifications and apologies. I didn't think that was the case at all, but pretending everything was going awesomely would have been the wrong move on my part as well. I didn't know all the details of what was going on in the corporation. Perhaps, the higher directors must have seriously chewed Mark Tobius out yesterday and even threatened him with wage deductions and other hardships for the ruckus in the player base. And maybe that was why my untimely joy and elation caused such a negative reaction. So, I started answering the director's question, attentively following his reaction and carefully choosing my words:

"On the one hand, I did a very good job with the main mission — showing the hidden advantages of playing the unpopular goblin race. Only players of that race would have been able to easily figure out the secret of hatching the flying snake. Any other person would have had to closely study the whole wyvern island, looking over the nests and considering why there were so many animal bones everywhere. It isn't true that players of other races would never have figured it out, or that the priceless egg would have inevitably died..."

"But then, why didn't you say a word about it in your video clips!" my boss flared up unexpectedly, interrupting me. "If you were able, as it is now clear, to tell your viewers in a normal way about this secret bonus of the goblin race, you should have drawn their attention to that fact! Instead, you decided to earn some money by selling the recipe, and the corporation ended up with a situation where the players are openly expressing their unhappiness. And as the players are upset, the corporate directors are also upset. Yesterday, my phone got red hot after taking so many calls from upper management, and they were all demanding I take immediate action."

I accepted a mug of hot coffee from Jane's hand, took a little gulp and cautiously inquired:

"Is it really all that serious?"

"More than you know. The petition to ban your character for fraud has now got over four-hundred thousand signatures. The number of signatures on another petition demanding your flying mount be taken away has surpassed one million signatories. This is a very rare case indeed. A great many suggestions were considered, including some radical ones: from 'give all players a flying mount,' to 'take them out of the game altogether.' Those two, of course, are nonsense, but on the whole, the corporation would be wrong to ignore the opinions of its user base — that's the surest course to losing all our players."

I fell silent in contemplation, showing my boss with all my appearance that I appreciated the seriousness of the situation. Then, I asked:

"Mr. Tobius, I could easily say whatever you like in my next video clip, but I suspect that wouldn't be enough. After all, the corporation has certain plans already, isn't that right?"

The director half-stood with a heavy groan, extended a hand and took a tablet from the table. He turned it on and handed it to me.

"You don't need to sign anything, because your agreement is off the record. Just familiarize yourself here."

Just after reading the first lines of text, I set the tablet aside in incomprehension.

"What does this mean: 'In the interest of legitimizing illegal virtual property?!' Can you tell me at which point my actions were illegal? Was it when I got the wyvern egg and raised my flying beauty?"

"I didn't write this," replied Mark Tobius, trying to wave off my concern as if it was insignificant. "The text was simply written in dry, perfunctory language, as it was composed by the legal department."

"I mean, god damn!" I replied, turning off the tablet and setting it back on his desk. "In the first paragraph, the corporate lawyers are already suggesting I confess to being a criminal, a thief, and a fraudster, who used illegal methods to obtain virtual property from the company."

My boss barked back with a heavy rattle, clearly this conversation and my stubbornness were seriously annoying him. Behind Mark Tobius's back, Jane was gesticulating wildly, trying to communicate something to me. Her pantomime looked to mean that I should be more careful with my wording and not test Mark's famously long patience. My director's face was growing red as he bored into me with a severe dissatisfied gaze, but he still didn't take any hasty decisions. Instead, he tried to convince me:

"Timothy, tell me in your own words what you think it should say, ignoring all the legal mumbo-jumbo. We cannot simply ignore the fact that so many of our customers are upset. I mean, the company stands to lose more than just reputation. This threatens all our financial, marketing and production plans. This could mean a reduction in stock prices, or not paying out dividends to the company's beneficiaries. In the eyes of the upper management, that is all a serious problem. And at that, it isn't just an abstract problem for the *Boundless Realm* corporation but also a personal problem concretely for me and you. After all, the owners of the firm aren't going to care whether some random tester broke the rules of the game or not. They'll just fire whoever they determine to be at fault for their lost profits. And at the same time, that person's direct boss will be fired for not having followed and intercepted the problem before it got started. I trust you understand that?"

I stayed silent and lowered my gaze to the floor. Arguing with a superior is always more trouble than its worth. All the more so given that Mark Tobius had a true Sword of Damocles hanging over his head, if I understood his words properly. So, I just nodded, confirming my understanding.

"That is excellent, Timothy. Don't worry about that dreary legalese. I'll just tell you the main points. Successful people live their lives by one simple rule — if you see a huge wave taking out everything in its path, it would be dumb to try and stop it. Instead, you should try to ride it. For that precise reason, the *Boundless Realm* directors decided not to try to extinguish all the righteous indignation on the forums, but to direct into a specially made event, which will attract attention and work for the benefit of the corporation. It was decided that your wyvern, the cause of so much envy and negativity, should be made the main prize in a global contest. Any player, who manages to find Amra and kill him in the next two weeks, will have a thirty-percent chance of receiving a medallion that controls your flying mount in the drop. As is only fair, that player would then become the new target of a free-for-all hunt for the next two weeks, and so on until the flying mount finds a worthy master, capable of holding the valuable prize for a whole two weeks."

"So then, in other words, somewhere over two million players will be chasing down my big-eared goblin in order to kill him and take VIXEN, which is my legal property. I can see why the players would like that. Such a hunt will surely be fun for them. But what reason do I have to even log in to *Boundless Realm* for the next two weeks?"

"Whoever manages to keep the flying mount for two weeks will become its fully-fledged master and can do with it as they wish from then on. And that includes selling it at auction, which would bring in very significant money. The *Boundless Realm* Corporation will officially offer to hire said player, so withdrawing the game currency after that would be legal. There are only two main rules for the wyvern master. First: they must spend over eight hours per day online to give the pursuers a chance to find them. Second: you must post video clips about your adventures, the length of which must be no less than thirty minutes, and the delay for uploading must be no more than twenty-four hours. That's all, we have no more restrictions. You can use any methods available to throw them off the trail. What do you say, Timothy? How must that be? After all, you might become a millionaire in two weeks!"

The director laughed, clearly having thought his joke funny. He personally had no faith I could emerge victorious. That was clear. I shook my head reproachfully:

"Yeah, but this whole thing still seems rather spontaneous and poorly thought-out. What is the point of running and hiding if the players after me can just use service commands to determine my precise coordinates? I'm sure, after all, that such commands exist, and that top players know them. And if they do not, what percent of the sale do you think it would take to bribe a corporate employee to follow me and tell a friend my coordinates in real time?"

Mark Tobius laughed again, but this time sincerely and with approval:

"Timothy, you're impressing me with your savvy! We noticed that risk last night when discussing the event. Let me reassure you: any attempt to use service commands to determine the coordinates of your character will return a corrupted value from the server, and the person who sent the command will be instantly removed. If it's a player, they will be banned at least until the end of the event. If it is a dirty corporate employee, the harshest possible methods will be applied. For every rat you expose in the corporate ranks, you'll get a special bonus of one hundred credits. Any other commentary?"

"Yes, sir. First, I could also be found through my companions — both the NPC's and living players. It seems fair to me that they shouldn't be able to be detected through unfair means, either. Second, any player with a flying mount, and there are already seventeen in *Boundless Realm*, could just fly straight to me."

"How would they do that?" the fat man asked in surprise.

"Very simple! It isn't very hard to tell from my video clips that my goblin is somewhere in the Lars province. So, the hunter buys or prepares a teleportation scroll to either the city of Lars or Weiden, or even perhaps jumps directly to Stonetown, which is much closer. Then, as soon as I'm in the game, the pursuer could periodically send magical messengers to me and follow after them from the sky. These messengers do, after all, give a fairly clear indication of what direction the intended recipient is in. Sure, it isn't the cheapest method, but such a valuable prize justifies such minor financial expenses, and it wouldn't be very far to fly, either. Just five minutes after I enter the game, five snow-white pegasuses could be landing next to my big-eared goblin, the ones already in possession of the *Legion of Steel*. It certainly wouldn't take me any longer than that, if I were them, and they're quite a bit more experienced than I am. I'm sure they know not only this long-known method, but also a great many others."

The director didn't answer in any way, but started thinking hard, and even asked for another coffee. Jane, behind her boss's back, showed me a raised thumb, approving of my tactic. Mark Tobius was already reaching for the telephone to call a colleague of his, quickly explaining the essence of the new problem — the grand hunt that the corporation was preparing to make a global event risked ending too soon. They only spoke for five minutes, and I realized from the clipped replies I could hear that the number of people on the line was constantly increasing. Finally, my director hung up and turned to me.

"You don't have to worry. There won't be any raids on you from above. Everyone who owns a flying mount has been disqualified from the event. A few more organizational decisions were made as well, but you don't have to know about them. Just understand this: the corporation is not planning to aid you in any way, but it also wants the hunt to last a decent amount of time. We would consider the result acceptable, if you manage to hide for at least three days. For every day on top of that, you'll get a special bonus from the board of directors. Also, you can earn a bonus for activity exceeding eight daily hours. The hunt will begin today at precisely noon. Each *Boundless Realm* player will receive a special notification. After that, your goblin will be invisible to other players until six PM. No seeking spells or other methods of detection will work, either. That whole time, you'll have complete immunity to any type of damage, and even sunlight won't do any harm to your vampire. Take advantage of this time, spend it wisely! That is all. Best of luck to you, Timothy!"

* * *

I was standing on the upper deck of the oared trading galley *Tipsy Gannet* under the scorching midday sun. I had unusual sensations — for the first time in *Boundless Realm,* I didn't have to hide from the rays of the sun. In fact, placing my body in the outpouring of golden warmth was quite pleasant. I wasn't afraid to overheat — my huge ears flapping in the breeze served as a natural temperature regulator. The steady wind allowed our galley to move quite quickly using just the foresail, so the oarsmen were resting and sleeping on their benches.

The oarsmen on *The Tipsy Gannet,* I immediately realized, were all slaves — mostly human, but there were plenty of other races represented as well: orcs, dwarves, and even a minotaur. I also met members of my own race among them — there was a huge veiny goblin sleeping on the dirty floor, having ceded the bench to his orc partner. The whole green back of the oarsman was covered in a mesh of old and fresh lashes from the overseer's whip. On his frail body, through the skin, I could clearly make out his ribs and spine. I didn't wake the goblin up, though, and continued on.

There were around sixty oarsmen in total. Each of them had a wide metal shackle around their ankle, which was chained to a loop cut into the deck. As for clothes, they only had loincloths. The whole living space of these slaves was the two-meter radius they were chained into. The oarsmen were sleeping, working, eating and defecating all in the same confined area. The ill, weak, or rebellious oarsmen were simply thrown overboard to be eaten by the many marine predators of *Boundless Realm*. To be honest, I was shocked by what I was seeing — I'd personally prefer death to such a pitiful existence. But, my curiosity satisfied, I hurried away from the oar deck, as the stench there was simply unbearable.

On the aft of the galley, not far from me, were the four NPC teenagers — Irek, Yunna, Dar, and Dara — they were flailing away with determination on the ogre, who was stripped to the belt. Shrekson Bastard maintained his composure, as if none of it even had anything to do with him. From time to time, our giant's life bar would go down into the red, and I would give the ogre fortifier yet another healing potion, totally curing him.

"Thick Skin skill level fifteen!" said the giant, boasting of his success. "Maybe that's enough for today? I mean, my whole body is in pain. I'm about to give out!"

"No, let's stick with the plan and continue leveling you. You need to get Thick Skin up to level twenty today so you can choose your first specialization," said my sister, ever the taskmaster. She never took any excuses. "No matter, just bear it for a few more levels, then I'll release the wasps on you, and the leveling will go much faster."

Our Ogre Fortifier made a blatant shiver at the unpleasant perspective, but continued standing stoically and serving as a punching bag nevertheless. The naiad, overhearing the conversation, his fishing pole dangling over the edge of the galley, laughed:

"No matter, you can bear it. They spent all morning punching me, and nothing came of it. I'm alive, and I've even almost come back to my senses! Ugh, what torture! But the reward for the suffering is pretty sweet: a perk to reduce physical damage by a quarter. It's like a dream!"

My sister was the one who had

recommended that both of our close-combat fighters rapidly level Thick Skin — our group needed "tanks," who could take blows on the front lines and hold back the enemy. And though the naiad trader had this skill as a secondary, the mavka had been insistent in recommending the ogre fortifier make it a primary, due to its leveling Constitution and Strength. The giant took Heavy Armor as a secondary skill on my sister's advice, as well. We hadn't actually found any armor for the ogre yet, but it was at the very top of our purchase list.

"My Hand-to-Hand is up to seventeen!" Dar boasted, and almost immediately, his sister echoed out the same.

Amazing! That was the main combat skill for our warg shapeshifters. It impacted their damage ability and increased their Strength (which also governed the wounds caused by their claws).

Foreman Skill increased to level 10!
Stealth Skill increased to level 15!

I wasn't suffering from lack of things to do on *Tipsy Gannet* either, and was improving my skills as quickly as possible — my NPC goblins and the wargs in human form were working actively, leveling the Foreman skill of their master at the same time. In the galley's hold, the Gray Pack was hunting down the ship's rats with determination, increasing my Animal Control skill. Also, even in human form, the wargs leveled this skill as well. In the end, I'd agreed with my sister and filled my last free secondary slot with that skill. I had even raised Animal Control to level six already.

What was more, until six this evening, I would only be visible to NPCs. Living players couldn't even see me at point blank, and I used this fact shamelessly to level my Stealth. Although there was also a downside to being invisible and invincible — all of Valerianna Quickfoot's plans to level her Beastmaster and Water Magic skills by using me as an indestructible target for spells and pets came to naught. My sister couldn't see me, so she couldn't choose me as a target for attack. My own companions, the wyvern, the goblins, and the Gray Pack, had a programmed-in rule against attacking their master, so I couldn't use them to level Dodge or Acrobatics either.

All that said, I was leveling the Veil skill very quickly, making a couple punches on the ogre every so often, then changing the game logs to hide that fact. In just a few hours, I managed to raise Veil to level twelve, but this method did eat up my endurance, so my big-eared troglodyte was barely able to stay standing. My sister had set me the mission of raising Veil to level twenty in a few days — then, I could choose my first specialization, and among the various skill improvement options, there existed the ability to hide my character's real name for some time. That could come in very handy, if my goblin had to pass a checkpoint at the port or when entering a city, or if I needed to walk past a group of living players.

Alright, my endurance had come back up a bit. I came up to the Ogre Fortifier and struck the titan in the chest with my fist. I did no damage to him, just hurt my own hand. Hand-to-hand combat was certainly not a strong point for my big-eared goblin, but I didn't need to do any damage now. I clicked on the Veil icon, lowering my endurance points to 1 of 195 and corrected the logs to show that Irek had struck him instead of me.

Veil Skill increased to level 13!

My weary legs were giving out, so I had to sit down on the boards of the deck again. It was quite hard work levelling a character... Taisha appeared from the stairs leading to the hold. Today, she was looking especially green — the goblin beauty was feeling nauseated. Seasickness was very rare for NPC's, yet Taisha was the only one on the whole galley that couldn't bear the boat journey. And now, barely glancing at the white-capped waves, the salty splashes and the deck rocking underfoot, the thief threw herself toward the edge of the ship and vomited overboard.

It was precisely her temporary infirmity that had caused Taisha not to take part in the active skill leveling organized by my sister for the whole group. The goblin girl just sat in the hold on bales of dried fish and passively leveled her Stealth skill — I looked, and she had already brought it up to level eighteen. Not bad, but too little for truly comprehensive character progress. Valerianna Quickfoot was planning for Taisha to increase her main thief skills in our days of marine travel — Dodge, Dagger, Lock-Picking — and it was very unfortunate that these plans were not to come to fruition. I was distracted from the bad thoughts by my sister's voice:

"Amra, the *Boundless Realm* corporation just released a series of advertising clips on the event." Valerianna Quickfoot couldn't see me, but she deduced based on the reactions of the nearby NPC's approximately where I was, and was looking there. "I have to admit, I really liked the videos. Say what you will, but the corporation has great marketing and advertising specialists. The clips of the winged green snake were really cool. They showed it growing up from a worm to a thirty-meter giant python. By the way, in these videos, it says that the wyvern should be able to carry one average-sized player at level twenty-five. So, our shared mission is to quickly level VIXEN to 25, then no one will be able to catch you!"

"But it isn't all puppies and rainbows," I replied. My sister still couldn't see me, but immediately turned her head toward my voice, though her eyes were looking through me, rummaging through the emptiness. "Yes, with equal levels and conditions, my VIXEN will outpace any creature in *Boundless Realm*, other than the uncatchable Phoenix. But VIXEN is still very small, and mounts get a speed and endurance boost at every level. Also, the Riding skill adds one percent speed to the mount for every level. So, players with high-level skills and high-level riding creatures, not only would not get left behind by my wyvern, they would be constantly catching up to me, if on the ground."

I had actually made the calculations this morning, taking as my initial data the speed of the most common mounts in *Boundless Realm*. Being honest, in the end I even deflated the results a bit. But what I got was that a well-leveled player on a lively steed of level one hundred (giving the mount three perks) wouldn't go any slower than my wyvern, due to the multiplying speed coefficients. And well leveled riding cheetahs, rhinoceroses, hellhounds, ostriches and some other animals would be able to move much faster than VIXEN, even if on the ground. Of course, in the distant future, the picture would be completely different, and the Royal Forest Wyvern would be able to teach a thing or two to these cheetahs and ostriches, but who would give me that much time to level? My winged child needed to grow and grow just so she could hold the weight of one rider without getting tired too fast.

"Oh, what a beaut!" said the naiad, pulling a meter-long silvery fish from the water.

Level-8 Minor Mullet

"Great! You haven't caught one of those yet. Give the trophy to Amra!" the mavka ordered.

The naiad trader meekly placed the mullet on the boards and returned to fishing. I stashed the fish in my inventory so I could eat it later in a secluded corner. My biggest disappointment of the day was the fact that we didn't manage to get to the Ookaa fish market. I had plans to visit the live seafood market there and quickly level my vampire skills, but the underwater merchants weren't going to show up at the stalls on shore until eight in the morning, and the *Tipsy Gannet* left the docks at seven. We couldn't afford to wait a whole week for another ship, so I had to make do with what the naiad caught underway. I told my companions that I needed samples of various kinds of blood to level my Alchemy skill. The explanation was to everyone's satisfaction, and no questions followed.

The naiad slipped another piece of bait on his hook and cast his line. For bait, he was using the meat of the mollusks that gathered in huge numbers on the shore in the morning. Valerianna asked Max Sochnier how much more time he needed to level his Fishing skill to twenty. The fish-man answered almost instantly:

"I'm at level sixteen in it now, and every trophy increases the bar by four percent. It's currently up to seventy-two. So it will be level seventeen in about fifteen minutes, and we can see from there. On the one hand, they'll start biting a bit more often, but on the other, I'll need to catch more to reach the next level."

Valerianna started calculating in her head, perhaps even opening skill tables in the built-in guide, and told him it would be about three hours. Max Sochnier sighed heavily:

"I cannot keep staring at that damned bobber... I never thought I'd get sick from fishing... By the way, friends, shouldn't we be going west?"

"Yes," I replied in surprise, opening the map.

The amount of discovered area on it had grown considerably, though it was mostly sea and coastal areas. Far to the east was the underwater village of Ookaa, where the *Tipsy Gannet* had departed from early this morning. Now, our marker was in the area of a group of nameless islands. But the Naiad Trader was right: for some reason the galley had deviated from the path and was now going north. My sister confirmed this observation:

"Based on the map I bought this morning from the captain, we should be on a direct westward path all day. That's how we get to the

Island of the Wanton Widow, where the captain promised we'd be spending the night. But now, we're heading for these tiny islands for some reason. Something must have happened."

"I'll go and figure it out," I said, standing with difficulty. My green goblin was slightly swaying in fatigue.

On the galley, meanwhile, clear changes had taken place: the sleepy atmosphere of the last few hours when the sailors, beaten down by the hot sun, were just barely moving around the deck or even just sacking out in the shade was no more. There was now a storm of activity. The overseers had already awoken the slaves and were now giving all the oarsmen water and bread with corned beef. The middle-aged bearded skipper, despite the burning sun, pulled on a mail shirt and donned a helmet. His first mate opened the normally locked arsenal and gave the sailors their weapons.

"What is going on?" I inquired, scanning the sea, but not finding anything out of the ordinary or dangerous.

"The lookout on the crow's nest saw a sail on the horizon," the captain said, pointing a finger at the top of the mast, where there was a light-haired boy looking out from a little platform. "What do you see up there, Johnny?"

"I don't see anything now. It's behind the island," he shouted from the crow's nest.

~ Stay on the Wing ~

The captain was stroking his disheveled beard with abandon, as if there were some biting insects pestering the man. And perhaps that was the case — *Tipsy Gannet* did have quite an abhorrent hygiene situation, after all.

"Maybe it will just pass by," the skipper stated hopefully, as if he didn't truly believe in the auspicious outcome. "A sail in these waters either means a patrolling military ship of the Kingdom of Lars, or pirates. And I don't want to meet with either of them. Ugh, we should have gone further south, but I didn't want to squander the favorable wind. Pirates sometimes stop here on the unpopulated Skeleton Islands for careening."

My big-eared goblin made a surprised face, not understanding the unfamiliar term. The captain noticed my incomprehension and smiled awkwardly:

"Eh, that landlubber ignorance. You don't know something so basic... In these warm waters, any ship will quickly get bogged down with barnacles and seaweed, which makes it go much slower. That is why, at high tide, we bring the ship into shallow sandy bays and tie it down, so that at low tide, we can get all the shells off and, if necessary, resin up the bottom..."

The captain's explanation was interrupted by a shout from Johnny the lookout:

"I see the sail again! It's off to the north-west, past the very farthest island."

"Well, scurvy!" the captain cursed, clearly having seen something over there, though I still saw nothing. "It's pirates. An orcish drekar of the *Brotherhood of the Coast.* They're coming against the sun. They might not have seen us yet. Hey, helmsman, head for that narrow channel between the two nearest islands. We'll try to hide behind the palm trees. If it doesn't work, we can try to negotiate. My cargo won't be of much interest to the orcs — what do they need dried fish for? It's all over the place! If they ask for protection money, I'll pay..."

"Captain, they're turning. They're making a course for us! We've been spotted! They're raising a flag — its black with a white shark!"

"Anything but that..." based on how the captain went pale, I could immediately guess that the black flag with white shark was well known to him. "It's the Merciless Aarsch, a hardened orc pirate from the *Brotherhood of the Coast.* He has a seething hatred for all humans and is known to kill them without exception. Sometimes, he lets sailors and slaves of other races go depending on his mood, but never people. He says it's his revenge for the time humans burned down his home village — he swore to kill all people he came across from then on. Oars in the water! Double-time! Don't spare the lash for these lay-abouts!"

~ Stay on the Wing ~

* * *

I returned to my companions and told them the reason for the alarm on *Tipsy Gannet.* Soon the wood nymph, and then all the others also saw the ship after us. The long dark bireme had a predatory monster on the bow baring its teeth and was going much faster than our merchant galley. Two rows of oars were methodically lowering into the water, pulling through, and rising up. A big slanting sail drove the pirate ship over the waves, its black flag flapping in the wind.

"They're definitely gonna catch us," the wood nymph said, stating the obvious. "There will be a boarding battle, and we'll be dragged into it one way or another."

"Well, maybe it's for the best?" Max Sochnier suggested, not overly confident. "Amra is invincible, so we should take advantage of that. Set him in front, and the pirates will shoot him from afar. It's a good opportunity for us to make a scene about a pirate attacks, as testers I mean."

"I'll try. It's currently one thirty, I've got just four and a half hours of invincibility left, so it would be dumb to miss the chance."

All the same, Valerianna wasn't in such an optimistic mood:

"There must be over a hundred pirates on a bireme big as that. There aren't even thirty defenders on this ship, including our group. Of course, we still have to see what levels they are but, it seems to me that NPC's tend to all be around the same level in the same region. So, they should be around thirty, plus or minus a few levels. That means they'll take us with sheer force. Sure, Amra is invincible, but that won't stop the pirates from wrecking everyone else. What's more, our enemies might free the oarsmen slaves of nonhuman races, thus increasing their numbers."

"Can you stop them with magic? Like, maybe reverse the direction the sea is flowing, or tear through their sail with a big icicle."

My sister shook her head "no," and I understood why perfectly: using spells would take too much mana, and the effect wouldn't very last long. What was more, we were out of magic range. My other suggestion — sending out VIXEN to rip a hole in their sail — was blasted by all the others. There were too many enemies for them to allow a flying wyvern to just calmly tear apart and break their rigging. A heavy pause followed, which made it all the more surprising when the Naiad Trader spoke up:

"I'll stop them! I can poke holes in the bottom of their bireme with my trident, then they'll have bigger problems to deal with."

The tall giant looked the naiad and his weapon from top to bottom, after which he shook his head skeptically:

"You think you can do that with your big

fork? It won't work. You simply lack the Strength to get through those thick boards. Although... Your idea isn't bad, you just need a different weapon, and some help. Let's go together. We'll need a tree trunk. Any of those palms on the islands will do. We'll also need a bundle of rope and a couple of the metal bars from the hold we're using for ballast. Just a couple minutes to get ready, and we'll be on our way. Make sure you don't leave me and the naiad behind afterward, though. I really don't want to become a new Robinson Crusoe on these tropical isles!"

Under the Black Flag

THE CAPTAIN took the news of our planned attempt to stop the pirate bireme with surprising ease, and said ambivalently:

"Sure, give it a go. Then, I'll send my galley over to that narrow channel between the islands. Based on the waves, it can't be too deep there, so you'll be able to work the stakes into the sandy bottom, making the strike on the bireme even more grave. Though it's a pity to lose cargo, a new ship would also cost money. For some reason, I was feeling generous and paid the crew wages and expenses for this voyage in advance..."

I was somewhat taken aback by the man's value system — for the captain, the potential loss of money was the only thing that mattered. The lives of his crew had no meaning to him, much less those of his oar slaves. The captain himself, from what I could understand of his words, was not afraid to die in the battle with the pirates at all, because he had long-ago purchased a teleportation scroll to a safe port and kept it on his person at all times.

"Without the ability to slip away unharmed, I'd never set foot on a seagoing vessel," the captain said in self-satisfaction, but at that patting the inner pocket of his doublet. "Sometimes, you end up in a nasty typhoon, or the ship gets caught on reefs, or sea snakes attack, or like now, you get set upon by pirates. In all those situations, I can be standing on dry land in a blink of the eye next to a branch of the Most Reliable Bank of Gremlins. Insurance covers part of the losses, and a week later I've got a new ship and crew. It's a pity about the lookout, though — he's a clever lad. He could have gone far, if not for these pirates..."

To my view, this was all somehow incorrect — I was accustomed to a captain going down with his ship, or at least being the last to leave it, not just abandoning his crew and saving his dear self. Although it was possible that, from the captain's point of view, the behavior of the undying also seemed incorrect and even cowardly — we, after all, did not have to fear a final death and, even in the most extreme situations, were guaranteed to survive, even if that meant being reborn.

A sharp command sounded out from the overseer on the oar deck, and oars lowered from both sides of the galley. A drum started booming, and the ship lurched forward from the synchronized movement of two dozen oars.

From behind me, I heard two splashes — the first was barely audible, while the second was a deafening boom, as if someone had chucked a stone the size of an automobile into the water. It was the naiad and ogre jumping overboard, at which Shrekson sounded to have belly flopped. Not long after, a message came in from Valerianna Quickfoot:

"We totally forgot that Shrekson doesn't know how to swim. It's a miracle he didn't drown. His height helped, as well as the fact that the water here is relatively shallow. I helped our friend reach the shore by making a current. But you should go down into the hold to eat the live fish while everyone's busy."

It was a reasonable suggestion, so I went right down the stairs into the hold. Once down there, I saw Taisha lying doubled over on the bags of dried fish. The girl was still troubled but now, my companion was expressing at least some interest in what was happening, and asked why the drum had suddenly started up, and if they could possibly stop, because the loud rhythmic sound was making her head spin. I told her about the pirates after us. The goblin beauty went silent for a bit, then said:

"I don't want to end up in the mitts of orc

buccaneers, they always have very harsh methods of treating their prisoners. And with female captives, well... What do you think Amra, should I commit suicide? You did say, after all, that I am now impossible to kill, so it won't be too bad — I'll just pop up somewhere else, alive and well. By the way, where will I be reborn if I die?"

"Taisha, I can't say for certain. You don't seem to be able to use respawn stones like normal undying. So, most likely, you'll respawn where you died — either on a galley teeming with bloodthristy pirates, or in the middle of the open ocean, where you'd then have to come ashore somehow. And how would I find you after that in the huge *Boundless Realm*? So, you should give up the idea of suicide, and try to survive unless it gets extremely bad. But in general, you're right, we'll have to take care of this problem somehow in the future. For example, make you a teleportation scroll like the captain of the merchant vessel has, so you can always run away to a safe place in case of danger."

Letting my ailing NPC companion rest, I went away from the stairs and used my Vampire Bite in a hidden spot on the fish, my eighth new creature in half a day.

Damage dealt: 109 (Vampire bite)
Experience received: 56 Exp.

*Object received: Mullet meat (food) * 2*

Racial ability improved: Taste for Blood (Gives +1% to all damage dealt for each unique creature killed with Vampire Bite. Current bonus: 20%)

Achievement unlocked: Taste tester (28/1000)

My endurance went down to zero, wasted on the bite. My big-eared goblin fell face down, smacking his forehead on one of the cast-iron bars, which served as ballast against the high buoyancy of the galley. Damn! If it weren't for my invincibility, I'd surely have a bump from that. Despite the pain, I stretched out my lips into a happy smile from ear to ear — I was successfully leveling my vampire skills, and had already begun to feel the effect of its coefficient increasing my damage. And that was, after all, only the beginning! What would happen when the damage done by my Amra increased not by a pitiful 20%, but let's say, 300%? All the same, I didn't have time to think it over for long. I got a private message from my sister:

"Amra, I need your help. Our friends already made the sharpened stake from a log, and dragged it ashore. But the ogre can't swim, and Max Sochnier can't drag the log into position on his own.

I also jumped overboard and am now underwater. I'll help the naiad as much as I can but, as you know, my Strength is very low."

"And how can I help here? I don't have gills, or underwater breathing spells!"

"Amra, don't be silly! For another few hours, you're invincible, so water cannot kill you!"

She was right. Had I really turned into such a complete pinhead? Clearly, this was evidence of the sleepless night and sixteen hours of playing with just two small breaks: one to talk with the director and the other to prepare the video clip I was planning to upload this evening. Struggling to stand, I dug around in my inventory and got out the last of the Strength Restoration Elixirs I was keeping for emergencies. This seemed like a sufficiently dire occasion, so I popped the cork and poured the bitter orange liquid down my throat. My Endurance Points instantly went up by a third.

"Don't poke your head out, wait for me here!" I ordered Taisha as I ran up the stairs.

While I was in the hold, the pirate bireme had made significant headway on our merchant galley. There was now less than a kilometer between us. Irek and Dar pointed me to a sharpened log bobbing in the ocean. On the shore nearby, the ogre was frantically waving his paws, no longer capable of helping his companions. Not wasting time, I climbed overboard and went headfirst into the water. I was expecting to bob back up, hoping to get a sense of my character's buoyancy via the Archimedean force, but the laws of the game world were much simpler: Amra could not swim, so I sank like a stone to the very bottom.

Anyhow, the descent was not very long. The depth was just four meters, maybe five. I felt hard earth underfoot and opened my eyes. First of all, I noticed a bar with bubbles pop up. That must have been the countdown until I drowned. I watched it in alarm for some time, but it didn't go anywhere, remaining at maximum the whole time, so I stopped paying it any mind.

The rays of the bright midday sun easily penetrated the water and lit up the underwater world vibrantly. I could see just fifteen meters, but that was plenty for me to look around. The sea floor in the channel between the islands was quite clear — there was light sand mixed with small stones and shells. In some places, there grew bundles of shaggy seaweed. I didn't notice any dangerous undersea beasts, so, after getting my bearings on the mini-map, I walked toward my two nearby allies without fear. The waves were the biggest detriment — here in the shallows, the passing rollers pulled, spun and tossed my goblin every which way, knocking me off my feet. I got a few messages about successful Agility checks, then a double skill raise:

Acrobatics skill increased to level 9!

~ Stay on the Wing ~

Dodge Skill increased to level 10!

I either felt the level-ups immediately, or I was simply getting the knack, but it got easier to walk after that, and I soon saw my friends not far away. The wood nymph was inside a big air bubble helping the naiad hold onto the log, which was quite buoyant. The bright red fins on Max Sochnier's back were extended. Our friend was not wearing shoes, so his long flexible webbed toes were now visible. I came closer and asked how I could help. My sister shuddered in surprise and pointed me to a pair of metal bars lying not far away on the sea floor.

"Those ones weren't attached well, and fell off. You need to hammer them back into the log. While you're up there, try to wedge in some stones so they'll hold better this time."

Mission received: Bottom from below
Mission class: Normal, group
Description: Damage the ship as it goes by using an obstacle set in its path

Reward: 800 Exp.

Would you look at that! We were already going to do this without any quests, but with the reward, it was even more pleasant. I walked up to the nearest bar and tried lifting it.

Successful Strength check
Experience received: 8 Exp.

All in all, bearable, though I was straining. I brought it nearer my friends and went back for the other. At that point, the main problem became clear — I'd never manage to hammer the slippery metal spike deep enough into the gnarled log.

"Faster! The pirate ship is already on the mini-map!" Valerianna spurred me on, but it still wouldn't work.

I couldn't see the ship yet, but I could hear the sound of the beating drum through the water from afar, as well as the splashing oars. At the last moment, I thought to get out my throwing net and use it as a rope bag, placing the two metal bars in it and hammering the net into the log. Now, not only the mavka, but also the naiad and I could see the ship on the mini map. Based on that, the bireme was on course to pass about fifteen steps to our left, so we hurried to reorient. Soon, I managed to see the pirate ship up close — the big black mass was racing directly for us. Either the orc captain was taking a risk, or he knew the area well, but he was blazing through the shallow water. There couldn't have been more than two meters below the ship's keel. With our combined forces, we hammered the log at an angle into the sea floor and managed to get away just a few seconds before it struck.

Bang!!! The sharpened stake went right into the bottom of the bireme on the right side and, breaking boards, carved out a five-meter-long hole. The ship spun in place and started tilting severely. A few of the bireme's oars reached the sea floor, and one nearly chopped my goblin in half. It was a miracle I dodged it. The water around grew cloudy from sand being raised from the bottom, and the many air bubbles coming from the hole. I could no longer see anything in the murk, though I did clearly hear the scraping of the long heavy oars breaking on the bottom, and the frightened screams of the oarsmen.

Mission completed: Bottom from below
Experience received: 800 Exp.

Experience received: 460 Exp.
Experience received: 512 Exp.
Experience received: 390 Exp.

...

Exotic Weapons skill increased to level 8!

Exotic Weapons skill increased to level 9!

Dodge Skill increased to level 11!

Stealth Skill increased to level 15!

Level twenty-nine!
Racial ability improved: 65% resistance to poison

Woah! I was again thrown off by the mass of changes to my character, though they weren't so extreme as when I got a few levels in a row earlier. I slightly caught my breath and quickly skimmed the messages before my eyes, trying to figure out what was going on. Either the stake dug into the sea floor had been interpreted by the game system as an Exotic Weapon (and in fact, it was quite an exotic mode of dealing damage), or it was interpreting my use of the net in the construction of our trap.

In the crash, over forty pirates died, and we got experience for all of them. Even divided between four players, it was enough for me to level up. As it was, it should be noted, enough for the others — Valerianna Quickfoot hit thirty, and Max Sochnier reached twenty-six. I couldn't see Shrekson from underwater, but I suspected he was also at a higher level now.

"Done deal. Now let's go ashore to the ogre, wait for the dinghy from *Tipsy Gannet* and go back to the boat," the mavka suggested, leading by example. We all got our bearings in the murky sea and set off for the beach.

~ Stay on the Wing ~

* * *

Seeing the huge, bulging titan trying to hide himself on the white sand beach with nothing but palm branches was a spectacle that was nothing short of hilarious.

"I don't see anything funny here," said Shrekson, offended. "I had to watch the pirates somehow. Over on the next island, they took their bireme out into the shallow water, lashed it up, and they're dragging it onto the sandy beach now. The island is tiny, just bushes and sand. There aren't even palms or any other trees. So, unless the orcs have boards and resin with them to repair the ship, they'll be stranded there for quite some time."

Max Sochnier shook his head skeptically:

"We shouldn't underestimate them. The passage to our island there is very narrow, and a division of one hundred fifty pirates is almost sure to have some members who know how to swim. So, they'll be able to swim over here for materials, cut down trees and ride the logs back."

The wood nymph stood in contemplation for some time, then announced:

"Based on the map, their bireme has at least three large dinghies, so the pirates don't even need to know how to swim, they can row here. We shouldn't stay here on this tiny island if we don't want to come up against a gang of enraged sea robbers. But for some reason, I don't see our galley anywhere around here..."

What? Overcome by anxiety, I scrambled through the plants to the opposite side of the little island. Far in the distance, I saw a white slanted sail on the sea. Below it, the oars were flying up and down at a rapid pace, showing that the captain was not planning on slowing down, much less turning back.

"Damn! What thankless scoundrels! They abandoned us!" panted the naiad trader as he jumped on shore next to me.

"Bastards! I'll kill them! I'll tear them up with my bare hands!!! Their taking my Lil_Timbo!" cried the ogre fortifier, his paws serving as a megaphone. He then shouted out a few unprintable sentences as the ship sped away.

Was it just me, or did I hear a barely audible bellow of anger from the moose a few seconds later? No, I was not wrong — the wood nymph confirmed that the huge moose had broken free of its restraint, jumped overboard and was swimming to us. And at that, with the moose, there was another blue marker for another of our NPC allies. I didn't see anything, but didn't doubt my sister's words either — the Cartographer specialization not only increased the mavka's viewing distance, but also allowed her to detect and track markers on the mini-map from much farther away.

My goblin was not capable of yelling as loud as the titan, but that wasn't necessary. Instead, I opened the Gray Pack control menu and gave the wolves and wargs an order: "Return to master immediately!!!" I supposed that all the wolves knew how to swim, and probably quite well at that. Also, I figured Darius and Darina would be able to turn into predators and jump off the galley. And there, look, the goblins Irek, Yunna and Taisha are also figuring out how to jump overboard and swim away, clutching the animals' backs. One of them managed (I hoped greatly that it was Taisha), and the others tried following their example.

Nevertheless, my hopes were not to be — Valerianna Quickfoot declared that she could already see and identify the swimmer: the goblin girl Yunna had grabbed onto the moose Lil_Timbo, and beyond these two NPCs, none of our other companions managed to make it off the galley. I cried out in despair and rage, filling the surroundings with my voice. And the words that followed contained at least as many curses as what the ogre had shouted at the retreating ship a few minutes earlier.

Wet as a drowned rat, Yunna crawled up on shore, jumping off the moose when they were in the shallows. She spent some time on shore trying to cough up all the water in her lungs and catch her breath. She had drunk a lot of sea water and was scared to death. Finally, the girl squeezed out some foamy words:

"They... attacked us! They attacked and tied up... Irek and... all the others! As soon as all the undying... left the ship, the captain ordered the drummer to pick up the pace, saying not to stop no matter what. And when the lookout... shouted that the *Brotherhood of the Coast* ship had run aground, the skipper ordered 'all non-crew on deck' bound and thrown in the hold. Irek stood to my defense, but he was quickly caught and stunned. I escaped their grubby mitts, dodged and jumped overboard! I would have died, but the moose plopped into the water next to me, and I grabbed onto him. Then... when I was in the water, I heard the captain order the hold locked, because 'the wolves went rabid for some reason.'"

It all became abundantly clear — we had made a huge error in allowing the treacherous skipper to get the upper hand and sail away. In fact, what were we even thinking when we all left the galley at the same time so rashly?! Were we relying on the good nature of that rapscallion? In the morning, the skipper had agreed to take us on board with all our beasts at a very fair price. It now all seemed far too easy. He'd asked for just two hundred twenty coins each for three days underway! And also, the shameless eyes of the experienced trader had been undressing my beautiful Taisha, looking at the two matching daggers on her belt with particular greed. Now, after everything that happened, I thought the skipper must have been up to no good, even then. If it weren't for our haste during the pirate attack, the captain would have simply taken advantage of another opportunity at one of the many stops or any other convenient chance to get rid of the undying and take possession of my companion's bejeweled weaponry.

I was shaken from my thinking by the decisive voice of my sister:

"Have you all rested up and restored your Endurance? Let's go over to the pirates, then!"

"What for?!" tore itself simultaneously from several mouths, not excluding my own.

"Because they have the only ship for three hundred kilometers around here, even if it is a bit damaged. And when they fix it and sail away, we risk being left here on uninhabitable islands for an indefinite length of time. Well, to be more accurate, the players searching for Amra will find us fairly quickly, but I doubt that will be a pleasurable encounter."

* * *

Our arrival was noticed at a good distance — it was hard not to notice the huge moose swimming through the channel with a titan and pair of goblins saddling it, the naiad with a trident swimming next to them, and the wood nymph walking on water like dry land (my sister was using a spell to walk on water from her water-magic arsenal). The pirates abandoned their work and huddled around their broken ship, exchanging hesitant glances.

I had plenty of time to see them in detail. I have to admit, it was quite the diverse bunch. Almost all the pirates were orcs — classically wild, tusked and fearsome. Although I also noticed a few goblins, one mountain troll and one member of a race very rare in *Boundless Realm,* the dog-headed rougarou — a human-dog hybrid covered in black fur that walked upright.

Above all else, I was interested in the levels of our potential enemies. I looked for deadly black skulls, meaning the player surpassed me by fifty levels, but there were none. There were some red skulls, but I could count them all on one hand. Chief among them was the captain, the Merciless Aarsch — a huge level-56 Orc with giant tusks and coarse red fur. He was sitting right in the scorching sun wearing a leather vest and worn pair of pants, showing a shaman-healer his broken left arm, which was hanging motionless. Then, there was the healer. He was a level-fifty Orc Shaman, unexpectedly young and muscular. I was anticipating a hunch-backed gray haired old man in his profession. The first mate was also showing as a red skull for me — a level-50 Orc Bodyguard bound in a heavy armor suit, he was holding a huge two-handed poleax. As a matter of fact, only he was wearing armor.

The other pirates were barefoot, and most of them were wearing no clothing other than a loincloth. I didn't even see weapons on all of them, and those who were armed mostly had just clubs or primitive spears. Many of the pirates were also wounded — their life bars were not full, and some of them were even hovering down in the red.

It was obvious that the Merciless Aarsch kept his crew "in the doghouse." Either that, or luck had been passing the dreaded captain by for some time, as the equipment of his pirates didn't merely leave something to be desired, it was more suited to the very poor, the kind one sees digging through garbage bins for bones. That changed my plans sharply. Earlier, I was preparing to prove my worth and ask to join their crew or, in the worst-case scenario, offer the captain money to bring us to the continent but, now, I had another idea. Just after coming ashore, I cast my gaze on the pitiful troops and started laughing with purposeful mockery:

"To this very day, I have only known one captain of the *Brotherhood of the Coast* to be this unlucky — the Merciless Aarsch. It is said that he is so bad at being a pirate that he cannot even provide his crew with grub, booze or even decent garb! I figured it would be simply impossible for someone to do worse than the worthless Aarsch, a complete loser, who brings shame on the *Brotherhood of the Coast*! But now I see there is an even worse captain, and he's blind to boot. This loser couldn't see the breakers in the channel between islands, so he didn't realize that it was shallow!"

I was speaking in a normal language this time, not warping my words. I was afraid that, otherwise, my sarcasm would go over the pirates' heads, and have no effect. Even still they heard me, but didn't understand. Based on their hanging jaws, the impudence of the little big-eared goblin came as a shock to the pirates. In the silence that came over, the hoarse voice of one of the pirates standing nearby emerged:

"Hey, this ship belongs to the Merciless Aarsch. You can see his flag on the mast: a white shark on a black flag!"

I put my hands on my hips and laughed once again:

"Well of course! How could I have been such a fool?! Only Aarsch could be this freakishly stupid! You'll never find a more worthless pirate than that idiot! Well, where is our 'hero,' then? Ah! There he is, sitting behind a bush. He broke his little bitty paw, the poor cripple..."

A private message came in from Valerianna Quickfoot:

"Amra, what are you doing?! Why are you

provoking the captain? He's not gonna take us with him now!"

"Don't get in the way, I know what I'm doing."

Seeing my approach, the huge orc pulled off the bandage being placed on his arm by the healer and stood up, sticking out his yellow tusks:

"Before I kill you for your insolence, I want to know: who are you?"

"My name is right above my head. But if you can't read, wretched soul... Alright, I'll tell you. It says that I am your future master. I'll even allow you to clean the latrines, if you behave yourself."

The orc growled in rage and grabbed the handle of his wide curved blade with his good hand. But the captain was stopped by the shaman, who placed a hand on his shoulder and stepped out in front.

"Tell me, for what reason do you seek death, little goblin? Our captain does not appreciate jokes at his expense, and is renowned for his short temper."

"Look around, shaman, your crew is half naked and poor. Many of the sailors are also hungry. That's why I came over to your pitiful crew — to challenge your loser captain to a duel, take his place and give you all what a bunch of fearless strong pirates deserves: glory, good weapons and nice clothes, so you won't be ashamed to show yourselves in port pubs! And money, lots of money for you to spend on drink and women."

Successful check for Orc Pirate's opinion
Experience received: 120 Exp.

Successful check for Troll Enforcer's opinion
Experience received: 120 Exp.

Trading Skill increased to level 13!

Just in time! I sensed that my words were hitting their mark in the hearts of the pirate crew, and the Charisma boost was very timely, allowing me to speak even more convincingly.

"You must be hopelessly stupid, if you've never heard of the famous corsair Amra!" I was planning to keep speaking for some time, but an orc interrupted me with a menacing roar:

"I know you! You aren't worthy of an honest fight!" The Merciless Aarsch let out a roar, brandishing his weapon. "You're no captain, you aren't even a pirate. I'm going to kill you and feed you to the sharks!"

"Not so fast, Aarsch. You can always kill him later," the shaman stopped the captain again. "As strange as it may sound, I do know the name Amra, and it really is the name of a pirate captain."

Mission received: The Right to a Duel
Mission class: Unusual, personal
Description: Successfully confirm your

***identity as a pirate captain by answering
the question on the life of a corsair by the
name of Amra (external library activated)***
      ***Reward: 8000 Exp., +5 to relationship
with members of* Brotherhood of the Coast**

Quite an unexpected turn of events. I even froze in surprise for a bit with my mouth open and my lashes batting. I mean, it wasn't like the computer system really knew the names of every player, and found where they were from, right? This case was fairly complex and tracking down the info would have been hard! I had chosen the name "Amra" back when trying to play *Boundless Realm* for the first time as a human barbarian. I took the name from a book by Robert Howard, where it had been used by the very famous literary character Conan the Barbarian when he was a pirate. Was the game system seriously asking about that episode?

That all said, the orc shaman didn't waste any time, asking me his first question:

"Tell us, what was the name of your ship, Amra?"

"Val, I need your help! Open a second search window. I need information about Conan the Barbarian as a pirate!"

"I already figured that out, I'll take a look. Give me a few seconds. Answer: the galley Tigress*, the captain was a woman by the name of Bêlit, then*

after her death, Amra became captain."

"That's correct!" The orc shaman's marker on the mini-map changed to a neutral yellow color. What was more, I could now see the previously hidden name of the NPC character:

Ghuu-Ghel All-Knowing
Level-50 Orc Shaman

A few more questions followed, and I was able to answer them with Val's help. Then the shaman issued his verdict:

"Aarsch, this really is Amra, the famous corsair captain! According to the laws of the *Brotherhood of the Coast*, he has the full right to challenge you to a duel and fight for the role of leader."

Mission completed: The Right to a Duel
Experience received: 8000 Exp.
+5 to relationship with members of Brotherhood of the Coast

A number of NPC pirate markers instantly changed color from red to yellow. I even saw a few green ones.

"All the worse for him!" the ghoulish orc crowed out. But in his cry, I caught notes of uncertainty. "I have only one good hand, but even like this, I'll tear this tiny goblin to shreds!"

~ Stay on the Wing ~

"Captain, as the party accepting the duel, you have the right to choose the battle conditions. You can allow the participants to choose a helper for the battle, or even put another duelist in their place," suggested shaman Ghuu.

"I won't allow anyone to deprive me of the joy of killing this little whelp! But I will take a helper..."

The orc leader turned to his crew, choosing a partner. I was certain he would take the armor-bound first mate, or the huge muscular troll, but Aarsch pointed his good hand at the rougarou:

"You're with me, dog-face! You're the fastest and most agile in my crew, so you'll easily be able to catch that goblin if he tries to dodge my cutlass!"

"Tim, the pirate captain isn't the brainless idiot you imagined. He understands that pure force won't help here, and it's important to not let you get a speed advantage."

"I don't know, Val. To my eye, Aarsch made a very bad choice. The rougarou is likely to obey the ring of Fenrir and join my side."

"Maybe you're right, we'll see. In any case, take me as a partner, I have a few interesting ideas for the battle. Also, I've been wanting to try out the racial abilities I got at level 30."

For appearances, I walked up, looking over my troops and chose a partner. The ogre looked very, very menacing with a huge poleax. The naiad was playing with the trident, demonstrating a willingness to fight. But I pointed at the wood nymph — the skinny green-haired girl in a thin short dress was looking down at her sharp claws with a detached expression. My choice was not to the pirate captain's liking — he screwed up his face and began whispering something to his helper.

He chose a sandy beach as the duel site. Shaman Ghuu walked around it cantankerously, threw out a few sticks, and was left satisfied. But at the very last moment, when he was just about to declare the beginning of combat, the shaman suddenly stopped.

"I warn you in advance: this will be an honest battle, so there cannot be any more helpers. I know you, undying — you never fight for yourselves, you just sic others on your enemies, like animals, undead and demons. And no magic!"

"A rougarou is a magical creature. He's a shapeshifter, capable of transforming and even using magic," I instantly objected. "So, I think we should also be allowed to use magic, to even the playing field. The mavka can't fight any other way. All her attacks are magical."

Trading Skill increased to level 14!

Successful check for Orc Shaman reaction
Experience received: 80 Exp.

"Alright, I agree. But as for additional

helpers, the proscription remains. Just two fighters per side, and no other participants!"

This extra condition forwarded by the shaman was clearly to the disadvantage of the wood nymph and me. I even saw my sister's swarm of angry wasps hidden in the nearby bushes, and my wyvern circling in the sky. But Valerianna Quickfoot unexpectedly suggested that I not balk, and agree to the conditions.

"Amra, we can win without pets. They're both close range. They can't strike from distance. We can just fall back on old methods we developed back in *Kingdoms of Sword and Magic.* You be the tank and fight them close range. You've still got your invincibility, after all. I'll be the 'glass cannon,' I'll 'kite,' keeping my distance and shooting the pirates from afar. My damage abilities are already quite leveled, and I've got more than two thousand mana, so I've got more than enough to bring down both pirates."

Strangely, there was no extra quest for winning this battle. On the other hand, the game system had already given me a lot of experience and reputation for earning the right to duel, so I wasn't too upset. My sister and I were standing at the very brim of the sea on the sand. The waves were rolling up to our feet and washing our boots with foam. Valerianna Quickfoot grabbed onto her magic wand and stood with her eyes closed, concentrating or reciting a spell to herself. I was only armed with a dagger — in close combat, my blowgun would be worthless, and I'd lost my throwing net when the pirate bireme crashed.

Our enemies were ten steps from us. The muscular orc was baring his tusks and making figure eights in the air with his wide cutlass, warming up his right wrist. On his left, broken hand, Aarsch clipped a round wooden shield. The rougarou stripped nude, not having any obvious weapons, but he grew out huge claws on his front paws and thick black fur over his whole body, protecting him at least as well as a set of armor.

"Begin!" shouted shaman Ghuu and, at that very moment, the rougarou dashed forward. A few seconds later, he reached Valerianna, flailing his paws and cleaving the air with his terrifying claws. The momentary burst forward was a move not even his partner was expecting!

However, the wood nymph was no longer there — in a barely visible indistinct shadow, the mavka raced down the shore, immediately reaching a safe distance. It must have been some racial ability, allowing nymphs to instantly dash away from attack. So that's what my sister meant when she talked about new abilities! I ran fifty meters away. Valerianna Quickfoot then did a trick I'd seen before — her body split into two, then each double split another time. The four identical-looking girls ran in different directions. Mirror images, illusion magic!

- Stay on the Wing -

Watching my sister's actions, I nearly missed the attack — the orc leader was approaching me and trying to split my goblin in half from top to bottom. Ha! How naive! I just had to think about dodging for my body to instantly step aside and turn away from the terrifying strike. And then the cutlass passed me by, having gone just one centimeter over my head.

Dodge Skill increased to level 12!

So, that was how my invincibility worked — as long as I didn't want to get hit, my body would go into action automatically! I needed to make use of the unique chance and level up as much as possible while I still had the opportunity! I even sheathed my dagger, as the weapon was now of no use to me, and easily ducked away from a few of the orc's strikes. Then I heard a short, frightened cry and the sound of breaking glass — it must have been the rougarou, having somehow managed to catch up to and destroy one of the mirror images of the mavka, in the very limited duel space. The three other magesses were ceaselessly shooting the dog-faced creature with lightning and icicles. His life bar had already gone down by three fourths. Just a bit more and... Suddenly the rougarou lit up red and his health fully restored! What was more, I saw the dog-head suddenly make a twenty-meter burst and slash another mirror image of the mavka with his claws. I heard a cry and the sound of breaking glass. Bad news! The duel space was too small for the magess to get away from such a blistering fast enemy.

"Quick, into the water!" I cried, and Valerianna heard me and understood.

The two remaining green-haired girls cast spells in concert and were brought onto the sea, walking over the waves with ease, putting some distance between herself and the beach. The shapeshifter, having thrown himself at one of them, stopped when up to his chest in the brackish water and started howling in frustration.

Dodge Skill increased to level 13!

Acrobatics skill increased to level 10!

I watched my sister in alarm, and almost didn't see the splash of spit from the impotent rage of the Merciless Aarsch, who was still trying to catch me with his broad heavy blade. The orc was clearly tired, but was still cutting the air deliriously, trying to do away with the impudent goblin. Finally, when the orc was totally out of breath and finished the attack, I turned to my enemy and suggested he surrender, promising to let him keep his life.

"Now you dare mock me, whippersnapper!" the pirate captain shouted, barely breathing he was so tired. "Dog-head, help me!"

That was a huge error on the part of the pirate captain — as soon as the rougarou turned his attention from the wood nymph onto me, the shapeshifter stopped sharply and froze, his eyes glassed over.

Passive use of artifact: Ring of Fenrir

Successful Charisma check
Experience received: 80 Exp.

The canine beast roared furiously, made one uncertain step forward, then another and... threw himself at Aarsch the Merciless, striving to bite through the orc's throat! The terrifying jaws of the shapeshifter plunged into the orc's throat, causing blood to gush out in thick streams. The orc stepped back, tore the enemy off, and ran the rougarou through with his cutlass, trying to deflect the attacks of his clawed paws with his shield. The two enemy markers shown on the mini-map were fighting one another! At that, the wood nymph's two copies were shooting both pirates from the water, not particularly caring which of them got hit by her sharp magical icicles as they burst into shards.

The life bars of both pirates were going down fast — both the rougarou and the orc were bleeding profusely. They were under the fire of

Valerianna Quickfoot's spells and, at that, were still trying to slash and pummel one another. If I were a bit quicker on my feet, I'd have helped the rougarou out — in theory, I could include him in the Gray Pack and make him a companion. But I was a bit distracted and didn't manage. The shapeshifter froze, stopped by some freezing spell of the mavka's, and Aarsch didn't lose the chance, driving his cutlass directly into the rougarou's chest.

Experience received: 400 Exp.

"That's what's up, pup," exclaimed the orc leader, gurgling out blood from his torn throat. A few seconds later, though, he fell dead on the corpse of his opponent.

Experience received: 680 Exp.

"Whoo-ee! Amra, you have to make sure to put this battle in your next video clip. It was an awesome fight! I leveled up Water Magic, Illusion Magic, and Thaumaturgy, increasing my total mana!" said both girls at the same time, creating a slight echo effect.

After that, both copies of Valerianna Quickfoot returned to shore, exchanged glances and ran to meet one another, opening their arms for an embrace. I heard the sound of breaking glass once again, and my sister was back to one.

"Val, how high is your Intelligence, if you were able to kill enemies twenty levels higher than you with such ease?"

"One hundred fifteen is the raw number in my character description but my effective Intelligence, considering primary skills and worn objects is two hundred fifty-six."

"How much?!" I froze, not believing my ears, and my sister repeated.

The wood nymph's intelligence had already reached 256! That's what I'm talking about!!! I had a pretty amazing sister! My own highest effective stat was Agility at 97, then Charisma at 74. But two hundred fifty-six, was beyond belief... It was no surprise, then, that her magical attacks were so crushing. No wonder she was taking down "red skulls."

"Amra, quick loot the corpses and take blood, especially from the rougarou — you might never get that chance again. They're very rare."

I followed my sister's advice and looked at the trophies.

Orc Blood (alchemy ingredient)
Rougarou Blood (alchemy ingredient)
Captain's Cabin Key
Thirty-five coins
Bronze medallion of a Brotherhood of the Coast *captain*
    Chipped pirate cutlass (Damage 2-

4*Strength, +2% chance of critical hit, 6% chance of causing 5 seconds of bleeding damage)

Under the steadfast gazes of dozens of pirates, I took the heavy cast-iron octopus medallion and placed it around my neck then turned back to the silent crew:

"If any of you have anything against me or want to challenge me to a duel for captainship, this is the time to say so. Because, after this, any mutineers will find themselves hung from the boom!"

The crew got on guard and kept silent. No one was opposed. I waited a few seconds for order, after which I shouted at full throat:

"Then from this moment on, I am your new captain! And I ask, why are you lazy sacks just sitting around?! I'll show you the meaning of idleness, shark bait! Ten sailors in each dinghy, make haste over to that island to cut logs! First mate, your mission is to help these slow-moving mollusks with heavy kicks to get those boats in the water! Shrekson, you give these degenerates tools and help them split the logs into boards. The tide will come in soon, and the *White Shark* must be fixed by that time! Shaman, don't be stingy with the magic. Heal the wounded! Max Sochnier, Yunna and Val, I need you to find provisions on the bireme and cook up something for the crew to eat! I'll need them strong and healthy soon — every hour you delay, *Tipsy Gannet* gets farther away, and I plan to catch up to that impudent trader before nightfall!"

At a Crossroads

THE BIREME FLEW over the waves as if soaring through the sky. The wind was at our backs, and the big sail was confidently pulling us forward, but I didn't let the oarsmen rest, because time was too precious. *Tipsy Gannet* had a nearly three-hour head start on us, and I wanted to catch them before they stopped for the night in a protected port, where the local garrison might come out to help the trader.

The huge Ogre Fortifier, panting heavily, came up onto the upper deck and stopped a few steps from me. The giant was glistening with sweat, having worked for more than an hour as the lone oarsman with a huge five-meter oar. He couldn't see me, but supposed I was somewhere above him.

~ Stay on the Wing ~

"You really ran me ragged today... Tell me, Amra, how do you generate missions?"

"What are you talking about? What missions?" I didn't understand.

The titan turned to my voice, searching the empty space with his gaze — I was invisible to all living players for another forty minutes.

Stealth Skill increased to level 18!

"What do you mean 'what missions?' You gave me three quests in the last few hours: 'Saw boards,' 'Fix the bireme,' and 'Take the ship out of the shallows.' I completed all your quests successfully and got significant experience, even enough to reach level twenty-seven."

"And you gave me and the wood nymph the quest 'Feed the crew,' but we're still working on it," the Naiad Trader cut into our conversation, pointing to the dozen orc pirates sleeping on the deck. "Valerianna and the goblin girl caught fish, cleaned them and cooked them in the galley. They're almost done with their mission already, just twenty sailors remain unfed. How did the pirates even have the strength to row to us? In the hold, there wasn't even a morsel of food! The mavka and I scavenged the whole ship, but there was no flour, biscuits, corned beef, or even clean water. Thankfully, we gathered a few baskets of fruit and bags of coconuts on those islands, otherwise the provision situation would be really dire."

That was right. I really was still in shock at the abhorrent conditions previously endured by the pirate crew of the *White Shark*. Hungry, dirty, ragged, practically untrained, with no armor or weapons... the Merciless Aarsch thought losing half of his crew when storming a ship was just business as usual. Having no pity for his subordinates, he simply replaced his losses with utterly untrained wild orcs from seaside villages, who had no understanding of sailing, much less particularly astute minds.

The only thing that moved the blood-thirsty orc leader was a quest for revenge, and inconveniences like losses among his own crew meant nothing to the harsh captain. Aarsch punished the disaffected with his own hand, cutting off their heads and throwing their corpses into the water, so the crew was ghastly afraid of their leader and suffered his tricks. What was more, many orcs were accustomed to their chieftain being such a person since childhood — it was always the strongest, cleverest and most bloodthirsty among them. They had simply never known any other way.

My appearance on the bireme was still being taken with caution. The crew was blatantly afraid of my goblin, as the big-eared Amra, despite his short height and low level, had managed to take down the strongest pirate of them all. But I had no doubt that nearly all the crew members would be glad to stick a knife in my back if I gave them the chance. I was hoping that the crew would notice the improvement in their condition with time, would stop being so afraid, and start respecting and appreciating their captain, but I couldn't say as much yet.

And I had absolutely no confidence that my friends and I would be remaining on this pirate ship for long. On the one hand, the chance to be on the open ocean and not get randomly spotted by other players was great in my current circumstances; however, I had no doubt that my pursuers would soon take responsive measures, and the *White Shark* would be truly mobbed by a great many combat ships. I needed to prepare for that in advance and, at least, arm my ship with long-ranged weaponry.

"Shrekson, how possible would it be to make a catapult with the logs and boards that we have left over?" I asked the ogre fortifier. The titan shuddered:

"Woah, Amra, I just got a new quest from you: 'Strike from Afar.' How are you doing that?!"

I didn't know, which I told Leon honestly. He shook his head in uncertainty, but promised he would think over a ballista or catapult for the pirate ship. The captain's first mate came up to us. I could now see his name:

Ziabash Hardy
Level-50 Orc Berserker

"Captain Amra, a group of five orcs has come to me. They suggested all six of us cut you down without warning. I ordered the other sailors to tie up the mutineers and throw them in the hold. What are your orders for them? Hang them off the boom as a warning to the rest? Or cut off their legs and throw them overboard for the sharks?"

Well, well. I was starting to like this first mate more and more. Of the whole crew, he was the most judicious, which was quite unusual for a berserker, a class that typically goes into battle after eating toxic mushrooms so they won't feel fear, pain or exhaustion. Also, Ziabash Hardy had a lot of sailing experience. He'd been on both human and orc galleys nearly since he was a baby. And he was also capable and lucky, given he'd managed to survive dozens of bloody boarding operations.

"No, we'll do something else with them, as a lesson to the other sailors. Give each of them a rag and order them to clean the dirt and shit off the oar deck. If they try to refuse, threaten to make eunuchs of them and sell them to slavers for perverse entertainment."

The orc stretched out his lips, revealing a set of uneven yellow tusks, which must have been intended to be a smile. It seemed this type of punishment was unusual to him, but the experienced sailor immediately appreciated its plus sides.

"So the other sailors don't come under any illusions about how easy it is to cut me down, call up everyone who isn't busy rowing to come on deck. We'll hold a training session. By the way, you can have the previous captain's saber. It's not a good weapon for me," I said, extending the wide cutlass to Ziabash. "And I also invite you to participate."

I glanced at the time shown at the bottom of the screen. I had another thirty-eight minutes of invincibility, so it'd have been stupid not to take advantage of the unique opportunity to level my Dodging and Acrobatics skills, while building my reputation as utterly impossible to kill. Hopefully, that would stave off attempts on my life in the future.

"Done! Moderation in all things!" I said, stopping the pirates five minutes before six in the evening.

Twenty weary soldiers took their weapons and, following the example of the first mate, bowed in respect to their captain. The many onlookers started applauding and expressed their enthusiasm with shouts. I myself was not tired at all, despite the fact that my little goblin had been strenuously hopping about, bending, squatting, falling to the ground, rolling on the deck and somersaulting for a whole half hour without rest. My endurance bar stayed at maximum the whole time, and none of the pirates managed to hit me for thirty minutes. It was a very, very beneficial training session, and it was a pity to see it come to an end — in that half hour, I'd raised my Dodging skill to level eighteen, Acrobatics to Fourteen, and also grown my Athletics and Foreman skill.

And I finally saw unhidden admiration in the eyes of the pirates, which was also quite important. They had begun to take pride in their captain! I took another look at the clock and hurried down the stairs into my cabin — it would be stupid to let myself burn up in the rays of the sun while my whole crew looked on! The captain's cabin was furnished in a very spartan fashion. There were no rugs, mirrors, paintings, expensive furniture, or anything else the orc had considered a luxury. Only a big clunky bed with a straw mattress, a round dining table fastened to the floor, a wobbly stool and a locking chest with fairly dirty orcish clothing. Against the cabin wall, there was a large sturdy box approximately one meter by one meter at the base and one and a half meters high.

On my first visit to the cabin, the box hadn't been of much interest to me — it must have contained some pirate booty, which Aarsch had taken for himself. The wooden container was locked with a stiff latch, and I didn't spend much time messing with it, as I had some more important business. But now, I could no longer ignore it — something inside the locked box was scratching and howling. Also, the narrow crack I had earlier written off as simply unevenly hewn boards, could have been for the creature locked inside to breathe. I returned to the stairs and caught the first mate, asking him about the container. Ziabash just shrugged his shoulders:

"I do not know, Captain Amra. Our last captain dragged it from a seaside village we attacked a few days ago. What is inside, no one can say — the captain never showed us. He immediately took it into his cabin."

"Whatever it is, it's alive, though. It's moving around, howling and scratching the boards," I said, admitting my confusion.

"So just open it and look," Ziabash suggested.

I smiled a crooked smile and went back into my cabin. Easy enough to say: "Just open it and look." I didn't even have the key to the locked box, which closed with a normal latch. But the latch was very tight! The pirate crew would burst their bellies in laughter if they found out their captain simply lacked the Strength to open the box, although it required just fifty points! Any of my pirates could open it with their left hand, without even trying. But not me — my Goblin Herbalist's effective Strength, considering all my skills and worn objects was just thirty-six. I could have temporarily raised my Strength with Alchemy, but as bad luck would have it, I didn't have the ingredients to make a Strength Restoration Elixir.

I hung a piece of old fabric over the porthole and prepared, walking away from the window just in case. There was just one minute left until six, so my time of invincibility and invisibility to players was coming to an end. While the last seconds ticked by, I decided to drink the orc and rougarou blood in my inventory.

Achievement unlocked: Taste tester (29/1000)

Achievement unlocked: Taste tester (30/1000)

ATTENTION!!! Resistance to light improved
Your character will no longer die instantly in sunlight
Sunlight will now cause damage at a rate of 1000 HP/second

I looked at my Goblin Vampire's maximum hitpoint stat: it was just 255. I couldn't really tell a particular difference between dying instantly, or dying in a quarter second. Nevertheless, the news was very positive — in the end, leveling Taste Tester would reduce the damage I took from light and increase my character's ability to survive.

The clock was showing exactly six in the evening, so I was now vulnerable and visible to players once again. The mail signal beeped, telling me I'd gotten new messages. To its rhythm, the box in the cabin again began to shake. I heard a muted howling sound from inside. But I had no patience for mail or the mysterious chest now — I noticed that the fabric I'd placed over the porthole was fairly ragged, and lots of little needles of light were poking through into the room. I walked cautiously back into a corner of the cabin, called up the menu and exited *Boundless Realm* — it was still impossible to walk around the lower decks of the bireme without serious risk to my life, and I was not planning to take that risk that for no reason.

What was more, I was exhausted and famished after so many hours spent in the game, and it was time to upload the video clip on the first day of the hunt. I'd already prepared the material in the morning, but I was in no rush to upload it — why give my pursuers hints before I had to?

But I didn't have time to do anything at all. As soon as I got out of the virtual reality capsule and put my clothes on, someone started knocking frantically at the door of my work cabin. In the doorway was Veronica — a familiar *Boundless Realm* corporation employee who played a dryad dancer and was considered the most successful in our group.

"Geeze, finally! I couldn't get ahold of Leon, Max or you no matter what I did — for some reason, the private messages wouldn't send, and I didn't have money for paid ones."

"That must mean the distance is too great," I said, not giving the girl's words any meaning. "So, Veronica, what do you want?"

"The distance, as a matter of fact, is minimal, but you still can't hear me. I can't shout any louder because I have a gag in my mouth, and other ways of contact are unavailable. What do I want? I want you to finally let me out of that damned box!"

Woah... I shuddered in surprise. Over the next few seconds, a million thoughts stampeded through my mind. So, it was the dryad scratching and howling away in that big box? What was she doing in there? Had she seen me drinking the raw blood? There was an air hole in the box, so she certainly could have. Although, I should have still been invisible to all players. So, had she seen or not? The answer to that question was very important to me. Also, what should I do with the unwanted passenger now? Maybe I should just toss the box into the sea and put an end to it. As it was, the dryad might be spying on my crew and informing on my coordinates! In that case, all my ploys to get away from pursuers would be useless. Although... I wonder if a player can actually see on the big map where they are located while in a locked box? Probably not. Although, who knows? I'd never checked.

"Whatever made you decide that Leon and I were anywhere near you?"

"Timothy, don't take me for some subhuman idiot!" the girl exclaimed, offended and puffing out her lips. "I could hear you talking perfectly, I saw you write stuff in the local chat a few times. I read the messages, but couldn't answer. Then, I saw your Goblin Herbalist next to me in the cabin. I even tried to get your attention, but you walked into the room and immediately exited the game. I need to get out of that damned box right now, though! My dryad's hunger and thirst bars are already in the red! My health is falling fast!"

What the...? So, what should I do here? I could just not react and let the dryad starve. That way, she'd respawn somewhere far, far away from the pirate ship and not mess with our plans. Perhaps that would be simplest. That thought must have shown itself on my face, because the girl then said angrily:

"Just don't think of killing me! I'll hold a grudge against all of you forever! After all, I've gone through so much after those NPC savages captured me that there's nothing on earth that would make me want to respawn in that accursed village! I was nothing but happy when the savages paid off the orc pirates with me, even though the Merciless Aarsch was a headache and perverted bastard! But I'd already thought up a plan to flee. The ropes cannot hold my dryad. At any moment, she can remove her manacles. But I didn't want to do that too soon and was waiting for the pirates to dock somewhere, because it would be stupid to try to flee a ship at open sea teeming with bandits. But then you showed up and the situation changed completely. Now, let me go or tell Leon, and he'll do it. With him, the pirates won't push me around!"

I imagined the sight of a naked dryad walking around the deck of the pirate bireme while dozens of orcs gaped, drooling lecherously. That was the opposite of what I wanted. A woman on a ship is always considered a harbinger of fights, stabbing sprees and lots of problems in general. But this dryad dancer, renowned for her easy ways... There was quite a bit to be afraid of here. The orc pirates had even started glancing at little Yunna, even though the goblin girl was clearly immature and I immediately took her under protection, by declaring her my relative. The wood nymph also sensed the attentive leering gazes of pirates, but found her own way out, having remembered an instructive story as if incidentally, and telling it to them, saying any male of another race who lusted after a mavka was forever deprived of masculine force. The wise shaman Ghuu confirmed the truth of the story for all to hear, and now the pirates would recoil and jump away every time they saw Valerianna Quickfoot.

In such conditions, releasing the naked dryad to the pirate crew would have meant a situation guaranteed to spin out of control, possibly even leading to blatant disobedience and subordination. Veronica had strongly underestimated the gravity of the problem and overestimated the role the Ogre Fortifier could play as her protector. The giant would be able to watch her every step, but he wouldn't manage to stand up to a team of wild orcs. Even the Merciless Aarsch understood that and hid her from his crew. Nevertheless, I wouldn't have managed to hold her prisoner in the box any longer — Veronica was very friendly with Leon, and the former construction worker would come to her aid. What could I do? The girl, standing in the doorway, was awaiting an answer.

"Alright, go back in the game. I'll tell my friends, and you'll be let out soon."

"Excellent! But, could you maybe open the box? It's just that my dryad... how can I put this... is a bit too exposed. Aarsch entertained himself in his orcish manner, binding the dryad in various perverse positions, drawing designs on her body and then admiring the result. I'd prefer not to have

Leon or Max Sochnier see me looking like that. I need to get myself back together first."

"Alright, until your dryad is back in order, I won't tell my friends," I promised my colleague. "Go into your work cabin and log in."

As soon as Veronica closed the door, I took out my cell phone, called my sister and described the situation. Val immediately appreciated the seriousness of the problem, but told me not to clutter up my mind with that now, promising she'd handle it herself. Finally, I got around to my daily video clip. The Cursed House, the Midnight Wraith, then looking for traces of the wargs in Stonetown and the forest camp. Catching the lovers unawares (my sister provided that material, though some scenes had to be blurred out a bit) and the battle with the pregnant druid Belle Sweetypie. I watched the material one more time and was left very satisfied. The viewers would be sure to get the impression that my goblin herbalist was somewhere near the Cursed House, just as before. And if the pursuers tried to predict the movement of my group based on the coordinates and times shown in the video, the trajectory would lead them in the opposite direction of the submarine village of Ookaa, which was more than fine with me.

Now it was time for the hardest part — I wanted to say something about the hunt myself. This morning, I went onto the *Boundless Realm* forum and was unpleasantly surprised — topics on the flying wyvern and her big-eared master were still in the top positions. The interest of the players was nowhere near dying down. And at that, in the consciousness of millions of players, a steadfast image had formed of an enemy that had cut them all to the quick, a fraudster that absolutely had to be punished by the most severe methods available, given that the corporation didn't want to do that on its own.

This treatment of the events was not at all to my liking, and I wanted to try to change all their minds. There could be no doubt in the fact that my video would be watched by a great many players, at which a large number of them had an initial prejudice against me and were in a very aggressive mood. Well, what could I say here? They practically all wanted to kill me! So, I wanted to show them all that I was a player just like them, and describe the events from my point of view. Of course, it would have been naive on my part to suppose that one video would be capable of changing the focused negativity of the masses, but I was still hoping that my point of view would at least be heard.

So then, my initial bearing: no despondency, and especially no despair. Nothing of the sort. In fact, I should be telling them all how lucky I felt! Representatives of the globally famous *Boundless Realm* corporation had contacted me and offered me the chance to take part in the largest-scale event of the year! The corporation appreciated my ability to play *Boundless Realm* well in an unconventional fashion and said I was of great interest to them! My modest big-eared Goblin Herbalist was even held up an example to be imitated, because I had tried from my very first day in *Boundless Realm* to stay away from the traditional well-trodden path, constantly experimenting and trying out new things. And that proved the soundness of my approach — after all, I was able to find interesting locations, rare missions and unique objects, and that was precisely the kind of gameplay the *Boundless Realm* corporation wanted to see from its players. But the players, for the most part, were concentrated in large cities and were too lazy to leave the gates into the huge unknown world, instead trying to discover new things in locations checked thousands and thousands of times each day by other players.

I wrote out the speech, turned on the microphone and considered it. I was lacking a sense of finality, and satisfaction at a job well done. What was the purpose of telling my pursuers what a great guy I was if that didn't change the situation whatsoever? They'd still be hunting down and killing my goblin, and no words on the soundness of my method of obtaining the wyvern egg would change the end result of the great hunt

— sooner or later, Amra would be caught and the trophy would be taken. But what if...

A thought came to mind that was utterly barbaric. Nevertheless, I didn't throw it out, and started thinking over the consequences. After all, the corporation hadn't truly stated any concise rules for the hunt yet, having considered such restrictions unnecessary and excessive. In the official announcement, the only thing communicated was the name of the victim, the requirements for the wyvern owner and the time for the whole mass-scale event. There was a serious slant to advertising support in this event. In that regard, the corporation had done gloriously, releasing stylish video clips, describing the value of the trophy and agitating the already-active player-base. In the opinion of the board of directors, the main thing was quickly occupying the minds of the indignant gamers and trying to draw them into an event they concocted on the fly, thinking they could handle all the questions and collisions that came up during the process.

But what if I said the upper management of the *Boundless Realm* corporation had gotten in touch with me to tell everyone the rules of the hunt, thus slightly correcting and adding to them to my advantage? After all, I would have millions of interested players watching me, and they would blindly believe anything I said, so any rules I stated would be perceived as official. And if I didn't especially dig myself a hole, but in fact described totally believable and beneficial additional conditions, the corporation would have a choice: quietly agree to them retroactively, or once again come up against millions of unhappy users.

Going out for a coffee, I thought over the speech for the next hour. The sentence, said as if in passing among the other information, should have been to the interest of the players, and would be taken positively by them, but at that I didn't want to worsen my runaway character's position, or cause financial issues for the corporation. Finally, I made up my mind, and put on the microphone helmet.

After telling them about the simple rules of the hunt and the valuable trophy, I mentioned that the flying wyvern would only drop for players who confirmed their participation in the event by registering in a special section of the official *Boundless Realm* website. All registered participants of the great hunt would get a special souvenir token in the form of an emerald green winged snake in flight, which could be obtained right there on the official site of the corporation for just ten game coins (how could it be any lower? that was just one credit in real life!).

The special property of the token, in my words, was to make a character's death cause half the experience loss it usually did — thus the corporation could count on stimulating the players to leave the stale, boring and safe cities and go off and explore *Boundless Realm*. By the end of the event, the token would lose this property and become just a nice memory, that could then be seen in their profiles.

Then, the total from the sale of the tokens would contribute to a prize fund for the whole great hunt, which was supposed to go to the wyvern owner, if they managed to escape (perhaps, this person would change periodically). It would be paid daily in proportion to the number of days that person managed to hold onto the wyvern. I gave particular emphasis to this point and asked the viewers if any of them seriously believed that such a responsible and legally scrupulous organization as the *Boundless Realm* Corporation would really just confiscate a valuable trophy from its owner given that it was obtained honestly, without giving anything in return.

I took another look over the speech, and was fully satisfied with the result. Sure, I didn't have any right to promise the players these new rules, but I did have a perfect understanding of the effect. Before the day was out, the corporation would be flooded with demands from the players wanting to officially register for the great hunt and get the attractive and useful token. What was more, it was already the very end of the work day. The leadership had already gone home and the forum admins were simply not able to stay on top of the situation. And that would lead to a repeated scenario: refuse millions of users and seriously upset them, or agree and take money from those who were desperate to part with it. It was no more than five minutes' work: create a section on the site to arrange for collection of clients' money.

Of course, I was taking a risk and might take a walloping on the head for taking things into my own hands. I could even have found myself flying out of work with a whistle for this. But for some reason, I was overcome with a foolhardy joy. The sea itself seemed knee deep to me now. The video clip uploaded, I got undressed and climbed right into the virtual reality capsule without entering the game.

* * *

I was awoken by a call on my cell phone. It was my sister. The clock on my phone showed that it was ten thirty at night.

"Timothy, where'd you disappear off to?! I've been calling you for an hour, but you won't answer!"

"Sorry, Val, I just fell asleep and didn't hear. What happened?"

"Oh, sure. The *White Shark* has reached the Island of the Wanton Widow, and is in raid position at the bay's exit. We didn't manage to catch up to the merchant before dark, but that might be for the best — they don't seem to have noticed us. It's a small, rocky island with very jagged cliffs on the shore. According to First Mate Ziabash Hardy, the bottom is very bad with submerged rocks and reefs all around. You need to know the channel to get into the bay. *Tipsy Gannet* is in safe harbor as expected. I ordered all lights on the *White Shark* extinguished so they wouldn't see us from shore. The weather is getting worse. The sky is cloudy. And now is the very time to decide what to do from here."

I answered my sister that I'd come in. Already preparing to turn off the phone, I discovered a balance increase message from my bank. I got four hundred credits, and it came with a note: "For exterminating corporate rats." I gave an involuntary chuckle — the first four unclean employees had been caught trying to slip players the coordinates of my big-eared goblin.

Before logging into the game, I went to the *Boundless Realm* forum. The biggest topic of discussion was, as I supposed, the delayed registration for the goblin hunt. The players were actively demanding it, and the admins were giving vague answers, not really knowing what to do. The most sensible message I read from a corporate employee said that the patch with new rules was currently in testing, and there were a few bugs left to be fixed. So, the players were asked to remain patient and assured that the work was under way. Most importantly — none of the corporation's employees were denying my words, though there were no confirmations either. I suspected that the corporation was actively working to find the department or director responsible for promising all these new rules to the players.

I now had over two hundred unread messages in my mailbox, but I still couldn't find any time for them. It was nothing. Once I fired up the game, I'd take a look through as much of it as possible.

My goblin appeared in the captain's cabin, where I'd exited the game. In the room, there was a single tallow candle burning, and the weary wood nymph was sitting on a stool.

"So, where's the dryad?" I asked, pointing to the open box.

The mavka shuddered and nearly fell off the stool. It seemed my sister had been dozing off, and I had awoken her. I had to repeat my question.

"Angelica Wayward? At eight fifty-five the dryad said that she only played when it was light out, and that her work day was over. The ogre fortifier exited the game with her. From what I could understand of their conversation, Leon was planning to go visit Veronica's stylish new penthouse."

"And Max Sochnier also left?"

"Yeah. He said he needed to rest. But he

promised he'd stay in his work cabin, and asked to be woken up if his help was needed."

Now that's better. If we planned a night-time excursion to the shore to rescue our NPC companions, we could fully count on the help of the naiad. It was too bad, though, that the titan would be unavailable — his strength and height might well prove necessary. But I fully understood Leon and had no complaints — the ogre fortifier had already been a big help last night and all day today with just a small break for a short nap. I couldn't possibly ask for more from the man — he was, after all, a living person and was allowed to have interests and plans outside our shared virtual world.

"And how'd you like the dryad? Both as a person, and a character."

Val shrugged her shoulders indecisively, seemingly not particularly wanting to discuss the topic, but still decided to answer in more detail under my gaze:

"The dryad dancer has unique high bonuses to reaction of NPC characters she meets and a whole spectrum of useful buffs that she can give to a group by dancing for them. Today, I thought up some progress plans for such a character, and I was very impressed. Potentially one of the best buffers in the game, and in some areas simply the very best. Nearly an ideal 'bonus-giver' for PvP groups: restores health, speeds up any action, refills endurance, increases damage done and critical hit chance... You could even just put a tambourine in her hands and have her beat time for the oarsmen. The *White Shark* would go thirty-six percent faster, and the orcs could work for sixty-two percent longer."

"Is that right?" I couldn't hold back the surprised exclamation. "So, she'd be very useful to our group!"

"Exactly. And she also has a racial ability to evade detection in forests or swamps. She'd be an invisible buffer that could give sweet bonuses to our group, all while remaining beyond detection. I'll admit, I was tearing out my hair and telling myself off for not having discovered such an 'imba' earlier — if I had, I would have played that combination of race and profession myself. But Veronica doesn't want any of that. She basically isn't thinking of leveling her character as a group buffer, instead making an emphasis on individual play with her high Charisma and racial bonus to attracting members of the opposite sex. And at that, the girl's personality is, being direct, pretty rough. She wants to be the leader all the time, the center of attention. She thinks the world revolves around her. Like that, she's of no use, only harm. Timothy, I really don't see a place in our squad for a character like that."

I completely trusted my sister's opinion, so I not only didn't argue, but adopted it as my own point of view. But how should I tell Leon that I didn't want the self-involved nude dryad in our group?

The Island of the Wanton Widow

MY GOBLIN opened the door of the captain's cabin, went up to the upper deck and stopped, growing accustomed to the darkness and cold rain. My sister hadn't been remotely exaggerating when she'd said "the weather is getting worse." The weather now was nothing short of horrible — the sharp cold wind was driving loose leaden-black clouds across the night sky. Waves were rocking the anchored bireme and lapping against the seaside cliffs in the distance. Even with night vision turned on, I could barely make out the features of the island. The first mate came up to me.

"Captain Amra, the wind is growing stronger. By morning, there will be a very strong storm. We need to bring the *White Shark* into safe harbor or go out into open ocean. The anchor is barely holding. If the chain gives out, we'll crash against the cliffs."

"in order to get into the bay of the Island of the Wanton Widow, we need to know the local channels, which are quite complicated. Do you know them?"

Ziabash Hardy grew embarrassed, lowered his head and answered that he, of course, did not.

"Then order two dinghies lowered into the water and choose the fourteen most agile and experienced sailors. You stay here on *White Shark* and take over in my absence. Me and the crew of daredevils will try and find someone who can lead our bireme into port."

Perhaps, for such a dangerous and substantial operation, I should have taken more soldiers. But my level-14 Foreman skill limited me to that precise number, and I wasn't going to risk bringing more pirates than that. A few minutes later, I walked around the lined-up rows of the ghastliest-looking cutthroats around. Wild orcs, a couple goblins, a troll... They were all standing in silence and listening carefully to their captain.

"This is the first time I'm going on a serious mission with you, so I'll be watching each of you to get a sense of what you can do. If you really are the best as Ziabash Hardy says then, after tonight, you'll become something of a captain's personal guard. You'll get armor and weapons better than the rest of the crew, and your share of the loot will also be higher. But that is only if you are deserving of the honor. We should hide and get near the trade galley in the harbor, climb aboard, quietly take out the lookouts and tie up the crew. Any sound could raise the alarm, and we'll be met with steel. What's more, the local guard team might come off the island to the aid of our enemy. I mean, we'll win no matter what in that case, but there will be more blood. So, I will personally feed to the sharks whichever clumsy simpleton causes the alarm to be raised. If any of you are afraid to boat at night in the stormy sea, or unsure of your Strength or Agility, better to say so now, and I can just swap you out for a more capable sailor."

> **Mission received: Silent assault**
> **Mission class: Normal, group**
> **Description: Capture the merchant vessel and free your companions**
> **Reward: 3200 Exp., +5 to relationship with members of Brotherhood of the Coast**
> **Optional condition: None of the soldiers or overseers raise the alarm**
> **Reward: +5 to relationship with members of Brotherhood of the Coast, +1 to Stealth skill**

My crew stood in silence as I read the

mission conditions. None of them refused. The orcs were baring their tusks fiercely, demonstrating a readiness for combat. The troll was clenching and unclenching his huge fists, easily capable of crushing the skull of a person.

Foreman Skill increased to level 15!

"Great! But from now on, we will work in silence. You should all stick a piece of fabric in your mouth and not even grind your jaws until the mission is over. If any of you open your mouth out of turn, or even remove the rag, you will get no reward!"

The wood nymph handed each of the pirates a strip of fabric, which they humbly squeezed between their teeth, then started down to the dinghies, sitting on the benches and grabbing the oars. I'd ordered the oar hooks greased with fat from the kitchen so the oars would be practically silent as well. I was at the head of the first dinghy, and Valerianna Quickfoot was at the bow of the second. I decided not to wake Max Sochnier without good reason — our Naiad Trader was tired after the endless day, and I figured I could do this without him.

The sea was stormy, our craft was tossed and turned. It was all strongly reminiscent of riding a roller coaster at an amusement park. I thanked the heavens a number of times that my belly was empty, otherwise the contents may have evacuated.

"I see blue markers on the Tipsy Gannet *in the bay. Our NPC companions are still on board. The Gray Pack and my Pirate are locked in the hold. Taisha is there as well. But Irek, Darius and Darina are not on the galley."*

The absence of the wargs and goblin was very curious, but I was hoping for an answer soon. The two dinghies entered the bay cautiously and went directly over to the anchored galley. Here in the harbor, the sea was much calmer, now lacking the powerful foamy breakers that threatened to overturn our boat on the way to the island. But at that, the rain had grown stronger, and was now a real downpour. In such nasty weather, I didn't have to worry that we might be seen from the shore, and Valerianna saw only one lookout on the anchored galley.

With a gesture, I ordered the oarsmen to row back, as our dinghy had accelerated a bit more than I wanted. I pointed my finger at the three nearest orc sailors, then at the oars lowered into the water and a hole high in the side of the galley.

"To the upper deck! Take out the lookout!" I mouthed, giving an order. And they all understood.

Soundless shadows, three figures crawled up the oars, reached the oar-deck, then pulled themselves up and hid from view. A few seconds later, I heard a muted cry, a strike and a splash of water. One enemy sailor down.

Experience received: 54 Exp.

"Tim, let's try to avoid unnecessary killing. Half of the crew is on shore right now blowing off steam in a tavern. The rest are mostly sleeping. And they're probably unarmed — after all, the captain locks up the armor and weapons in the arsenal, remember?"

Hey, that was right! As my sister had correctly noted, most of the sailors on *Tipsy Gannet* didn't carry weapons, they were handed them only before a battle. I turned to the pirates awaiting my order and gave the command to tie our boat to an oar and for everyone to climb onto the upper deck, and not to lower down yet into the inner spaces of the galley. I then also climbed up.

Successful Agility check
Experience received: 20 Exp.

I reached the hole in the side of the oar deck and carefully careened my neck to look inside. Despite the storm and rain outside, the oarsmen shackled to their oars were sleeping soundly. Probably, the gray-haired skipper had worked them half to death today, trying to race away from the pirates following them, then trying to leave as fast as possible from the island where they'd left the undying they'd betrayed. I already wanted to jump into the ship and crawl across the dirty oar deck, but I was stopped by a sudden message:

Stealth Skill increased to level 19!

One of the slaves or crew members wasn't sleeping, after all, and might have seen me! Not wanting to take a risk, I followed my orcs onto the upper deck. I took a look around, made sure there were no enemies and, at the same time, took a tally of my soldiers. All fourteen were still there, and one group had thrown a rope ladder down to help the wood nymph climb up. The stairs, leading directly into the hold, were crisscrossed with nailed-in boards.

"Troll, over here! Remove the boards, but be quiet, no sound!"

The huge, three-meter-high shaggy troll had elongated arms that practically reached the floor. He ran up nimbly to the obstacle and quickly removed the boards blocking the passage.

"Four stay here on guard, four to the other stairs, but no one go down! Another three to the port side as lookouts. If you see a boat coming in from the village, tell me, but be quiet! Troll and a couple of the strongest orcs, here's the locked door to the arsenal. Open it, but don't make too much noise. There are weapons and armor there. Take some for yourself and give the rest out based on preference and size. I repeat, no one go down, everyone await my signal!"

"Val, order Pirate to lie calmly and sit in silence! I really do not want him to start whining or howling in joy. I commanded the same to the Gray Pack. And find me the captain. Where is he?"

My sister began thinking for a few seconds, then shook her head:

"He's not here. He's probably on shore."

Resetting my Night Vision skill in any case, I threw open the hatch, immediately noting how deeply scratched up it was from the inside. After that, I started down into the dark hold.

The level-29 Akella was lying at the bottom of the stairs and wagging his tail in joy just like a dog, greeting my arrival. The forest predator's life bar was in the orange for some reason. Then again, so were the life bars of all the other members of the Gray Pack I could see. The aftermath of a squabble? Hunger? As it turned out, no. The wolves were suffering badly of thirst. Out of all the food available to them in the hold, they found only a great number of bags of salted fish, and had downed a few of them.

Soon, I saw Taisha. The goblin beauty was sleeping in a secluded corner of the hold, having fashioned herself a bedroll out of the bags that used to contain fish, and squeezing one dagger in each hand, her form-fitting clothing emphasizing alluring curves. Also, the thin fabric of her thief's costume was ripped in a few places, allowing me to see details normally hidden by her clothing. But it wasn't the most appropriate moment for gawking — at any second, any of the crew members could come on deck and see the orcs and raise the alarm. So, I carefully tapped Taisha on the shoulder and immediately jumped aside as the shuddering girl, half awake, tried to jab my Amra with a dagger. And she actually hit, nearly sending my goblin to respawn in one strike!

Dodge check failed

Successful Agility check
Experience received: 40 Exp.

Damage taken: 234 (270 Dagger strike — 36 armor)
3 second Bleeding effect

What about the programmed-in rule against harming one's master?! I grew alarmed for a second due to the unexpected turn of events, and that delay nearly cost me my life, as the bleeding was reducing my health by six points every second. Fortunately, I had plenty of level-15 Elixirs of Healing. In fact, I'd even put them into my quick-actions icons at the bottom of the screen. I had to drink two at once to be sure I wouldn't kick the bucket.

Three steps from me was Taisha, spinning in place, and flailing her weapon about, blindly looking around and shouting in fear: "Stay away!" Realizing too late that the goblin beauty did not have night vision, I hissed at my panicking friend so her shriek wouldn't wake up the whole crew of the *Tipsy Gannet*.

"Amra!" she exclaimed, the daggers instantly falling from her hands. The girl ran to my voice and nearly knocked me off my feet, hanging from my shoulders. "I just kept remembering your directive to not go anywhere from the hold and wait for you! And I believed you'd come, even though the captain tried to convince me otherwise! He tried to get me to leave and give him the daggers all day, promising to leave me on the shore if I did. But before that, he tried taking them by force, and the Gray Pack intervened. You wouldn't believe the fight we had in the hold! Teeth, claws, fists and daggers, everything was flying! The captain and his gang just barely made it back to the stairs. And by the way, during the day, I pulled this out of the skipper's pocket when he came into the hold."

Taisha extended me a rolled piece of parchment tied with a thin ribbon.

Insufficient Intelligence to identify object
Intelligence needed: 80

But even without that, I could guess what I had in my hands — a teleportation scroll to a safe port, the one the skipper had been bragging to me about, and about which I'd later told Taisha.

"I put the bales of fish against the far door leading into the crew's living quarters so the captain and his bandits couldn't make it in from the back. And the skipper ordered the exit from the stairwell boarded up so I wouldn't run away. Since then, I've been sitting here under siege. No water, no light, no way out. But over all these worries, my sea-sickness retreated unnoticed. I'm not nauseated anymore!"

I carefully placed the girl on the floor and ordered her to go upstairs, but first get her clothes in order — the beautiful NPC didn't want to provoke the orcs with her frivolous outfit. Taisha, in the diffuse light penetrating unevenly from the stairwell, looked herself over and gasped in fear, immediately covering her perforated clothing with her hands. The goblin beauty did have a needle and thread (the old Umar Bonesetter in Stonetown had let Taisha keep them), so the girl immediately got to work. I, then, went deeper into the hold and started pulling down the bag barricade Taisha had made.

The door, once freed of the heap, was not locked. I walked in and found myself in a semi-dark room, carpeted with a layer of fresh-smelling hay. The sailors slept right on the floor. I counted twelve bodies. Another was lying separately on a wide bench. It was a big half-orc — the main overseer of the oar-slaves.

Well then, let's get started! I walked past the snoring and sniffling bodies, rewarding each sailor with a Vampire Bite. I didn't kill them, instead choosing the option "Deep Six-Hour Sleep." But when it came to the overseer, I couldn't resist — I was expecting good experience from the level-47 NPC, and I didn't have a half-orc in my "vampiric collection" yet, so the temptation was too great. I mean, I could level not only Taste Tester but also Taste for Blood.

Experience received: 3760 Exp.

Racial ability improved: Taste for Blood (Gives +1% to all damage dealt for each unique creature killed with Vampire Bite. Current bonus: 21%)

Achievement unlocked: Taste tester (31/1000)

For trophies, I was left with the Overseer's Whip, which had the unusual bonus of restoring 3% of maximum health and 5% endurance with every strike. It was a ghastly, terrible thing — the overseer himself would always remain healthy and full of strength, leeching life force from the slaves under his care.

The quest to capture the ship was not yet considered finished — clearly, to complete it, I would have to render the rest of the crew harmless. I opened the door and called the pirates, ordering them to tie up all the stunned sailors tight. The muscular orcs, who'd already managed to open the arsenal and equip themselves with decent weapons and armor, on seeing the dozen bodies lying passed out, stroked their heads thoughtfully and looked at my puny goblin with noticeably increased respect. At that moment, I was called out to by Valerianna Quickfoot:

"Amra, a ship started off in our direction from the village. There are eleven people in it, including the captain of *Tipsy Gannet.* They're taking a somewhat strange path here, though. It's as if their dinghy is going in circles. Clearly, they've been carousing on shore."

I asked if our other NPC companions, who we'd yet to locate, were on the ship: Irek, Darius and Darina, but my sister shook her head.

"Then we'll have to interrogate the skipper, but first take him alive. What do you think: will he turn his boat back to shore when he sees the bogeymen greeting him on *Tipsy Gannet?*"

"I understand, big-ears. I'll make a quality illusion of human sailors, but only the three to meet them — I don't yet have the abilities for more. The other orcs should hide and jump out once they're on deck."

My sister did a great job, turning the troll and two of the strongest orcs, who I selected to meet the boat, into two of the bound sailors. All the same, our preparations were in vain — both the skipper and the sailors who'd come with him were drunk as hogs, and couldn't stay on their feet. In that condition, they could barely tell an orc pirate from an elven princess. I ordered the sailors tied up and thrown in the hold. But the captain, despite his clouded mind, I was planning to have a very serious talk with. I ordered him given a few slaps to bring him to his senses, and commanded:

"Tie him up and keelhaul him!"

The pirate crew shrieked in delight all together, sensing the foretaste of a rare moment of excitement. Keelhauling often ended in death for the victim, who would inhale lots and lots of sea water. But even those who survived were generally quite mutilated by the sharp barnacles stuck all over the bottom of the ship.

The skipper seemingly came to — he was now looking around with purpose and shivering when meeting my gaze. In that time the mavka, rope in hand, jumped overboard and soon appeared on the other side of the galley. Everything was ready to start the punishment.

"Please!" the bound captive prayed. "I beg mercy! Give me the chance to buy my way out of this!"

"This pitiful worm wants to deprive us of entertainment!" I turned to the crew and got a predictable reaction of rambunctious whistling and howling.

I raised my hand, calling the crew to silence. After that, I turned to the skipper.

"This damned trader thinks money can buy him anything. But no, our crew wants blood. Although... I suppose I will give you the chance to defer your punishment, or even totally avoid it. But first of all, answer me: where are the children I left with you?"

"They're with the island elder. They were my gift to him, a sign of gratitude for a trade concession we signed with the Island of the Wanton Widow."

> ***Mission change: Silent assault***
> ***Mission class: Normal, group***
> ***Description: Buy your companions back from the island elder***
> ***Reward: 3200 Exp., +10 to relationship with members of* Brotherhood of the Coast, *+1 to Trading skill***

Would you look at that! The noiseless capture of the ship was already completed but now, in the updated conditions for the mission, the reward was higher. Beyond that was the fact that I'd gotten a bonus Trading skill increase — clearly, the negotiations with the local elder were expected to be quite problematic.

"Give me the papers, on the double!" I

demanded, but the captive captain just smiled guiltily, as his hands were tied.

I stuck my hand into his pocket and felt a greasy scroll, a ring of keys, and a heavy coin purse, all of which I placed in my inventory. After removing the ribbon sealing the parchment, I acquainted myself with its contents. It conferred the exclusive right to sell goods and purchase marine fish from the Island of the Wanton Widow on the owner of the *Tipsy Gannet*. An intriguing little thing — just write the proper name in the document, and get a stable source of purchases of cheap goods. That said, it was a small island. The population was just three or four hundred people, but for the start of a big project creating a fish-trading network on the Southern Continent of *Boundless Realm*, it would do quite nicely. Max Sochnier was sure to like it — it was his name I was planning to write in the documents.

"Where are the documents for ownership of *Tipsy Gannet*? Although, you don't have to answer, they're probably in your cabin. Well old man, this is what you get for the treachery and horridness you committed against my friends. I should be leaving you for crab food or tying you to an oar on my bireme, the *White Shark*. But I'll give you a second chance. I'll let you keep your life and set you on the shore alive and unharmed if you can lead the *White Shark* through the difficult channel into this safe bay."

The crew of orcs started hooting in dismay, but I sharply cut them off:

"Cram it, you buffoons! If the deal comes off, you'll all get a handful of coins and be set free on the shore where you can relax and spend the money on drink, women and fine clothing. But I have one condition for you. Just one, and it's very important: anyone who harms the locals will be hung from the nearest tree! Other than that — make merry to your hearts' content!"

The crew screamed out in joy, having immediately rethought punishing the gray-haired skipper.

I heard elated cries and shouts, proclaiming the glory of Captain Amra.

Trading Skill increased to level 15!

Foreman Skill increased to level 16!
* * *

For some reason, it seemed wrong to go into the negotiations without the Naiad Trader, so my sister called and awoke our French buddy. The fish-man initially tried to object, saying that the galley assault could get on without him. But he abruptly mellowed out when he found out what a great reward awaited him — his very own trading ship! And it would start following a regular route, buying fish and seafood from the island of the

Wanton Widow and Ookaa, then selling its wares in the large port of Vaant in the Lars Province, or in any other city the ship owner ordered the hired captain to visit.

Max was clearly taken aback and first spent a long time refusing the generous gift. But nevertheless, he eventually agreed to write his name in the ownership papers for the *Tipsy Gannet.*

"I free all the oarsmen! Free people work better than slaves!" said the naiad, working through his plans on the way to the home of the island elder.

In that regard, I was in full agreement with my friend, although I also asked him to allow the oarsmen slaves a choice. After all, my *White Shark* also needed to top up its crew. If any of the former slaves wanted to become pirates on my bireme, I asked Max not to stand in the way. Taisha had her own point of view — she thought the Naiad Trader should not free the most mutinous and wild slave oarsmen, otherwise he risked mutiny. The girl also suggested the slave ranks be filled out on the galley with the tied-up sailors. But my companion was unable to give any explanation for this other than the fact that the sailors had tried to capture her and given her a nasty fright.

The mavka didn't join our conversation, and just walked next to us, yawning as she did — it was already midnight and my younger sister was supposed to be sleeping. I even reminded Val of that, pointing to the clock, but my sister asked that she not be made to — here at least she wasn't alone, but being all by herself in the empty, strange apartment was scary.

Distracted by the conversation, we didn't even notice that we had finished walking the path all the way up to the elder's home on the mountainside — it was a two-story stone building with a good-sized garden containing bushes of flowers that were largely exotic to me. Unfortunately, the relentless rain didn't allow me to take in their aroma — all the buds were closed. I also didn't have the opportunity to level Herbalism — Valerianna and Max dragged me onward to the entrance of the house, not allowing me to tear up the man's garden.

"Look at the map!" Valerianna exclaimed, first to notice a nearby marker made of interlocking gray rings.

On the summit of the nearest hill, there was a respawn stone, but getting up there at night in the rain was something none of us wanted to try, so we stayed on our path. I saw no guards at the entrance to the manor, nor did I see any servants. First, I was impressed by the carelessness of the owner, who seemed to have no fear of robbers or break-ins, but then I saw the elder, and my questions all evaporated:

~ Stay on the Wing ~

Arlen Proud
Level-211 Human Demonologist

The elder was a tall bald man of middling years in a long burgundy silk robe and funny slippers with the toes pointed upward. Over the wizard's left shoulder, fluttering a pair of short leathery wings, there was a little violet devil giving off steam. The demonologist's servant was around cat-sized and was holding a full glass of wine in its front claws.

All my plans to start the conversation from a position of strength by frightening the naive and timid island-dweller with a pirate attack and demanding he return my companions, were instantly dashed — if he so desired, this magic-specialized conjurer could easily sink both of the ships in the bay at a moment's notice. Despite the late hour, the elder was not asleep. His hands crossed behind his back, he was standing at the window and watching the ships in the bay through the sheet of rain.

"What business do three undying have in my home?" he asked, not even turning to the sound of the doorbell, or the opened door.

I didn't hear any fear in the wizard's voice. As a matter of fact, no night-time guest could really pose a threat to him. The elder paid Taisha no mind, or considered the goblin girl unworthy of individual attention.

"Arlen Proud, we came for justice," I answered. Max Sochnier and Valerianna Quickfoot were keeping silent for some reason.

"And just who was it, little goblin, that committed an injustice against you?" Was it just me, or was there poorly hidden mockery slipping through in the man's words?

"No one here, yet. I can handle those who have on my own. The captain of *Tipsy Gannet* betrayed me and my friends by basely abandoning us to be torn to shreds by bloodthirsty pirates under the orc the Merciless Aarsch. First, I defeated the pirate captain and captured his bireme. Then, I came here to *Tipsy Gannet* in the bay and also captured it, taking the oath-breaking fraudster captain prisoner. But while I was gone, he captured my companions by force — two human children and one young goblin — and, not having any rights to those children, he gave them to you as a gift."

"Won't the orc pirates cause problems in the village?" the demonologist asked, completely out of turn, either asking us that question, or talking to himself.

I rushed to reassure the wizard that I had only let three sailors come ashore, and told him they got enough money for drink and entertainment. And at that, the tavern owner assured me that the doors of his establishment would remain open all night, and that his guests would be shown the most equitable reception. Also, I threatened my orcs, saying that if any of them started fights with the locals, I would hang them like dogs. They respected and feared their new captain, so it wouldn't be a problem.

Successful Charisma check
Experience received: 480 Exp.

"Alright then, why not?" the wizard asked thoughtfully. "Other than a few local fishing schooners, few other ships visit my island. *Tipsy Gannet* is the only trade ship. Once a week, they come to buy our fish and bring us news and goods from the continent. The captain also transported goods and messages for me, when I needed to get or send something."

Max Sochnier, as the new owner of the merchant galley, hurried to assure the wizard that it would all remain the same in the future, but that the captain of the *Tipsy Gannet*, having proven himself a scoundrel, would be replaced by a more respectable seaman.

"That's good. He always was quite dodgy. Pangs of conscience never stopped the captain from accepting illegal money. But he was a talented conversationalist. It was always interesting to sit with him over a bottle of wine or two and be regaled with his stories of an adventure-filled life at sea. Also, he always came bearing gifts of respect — sometimes unusual trifles, other times, bunches of rare flowers for my collection. Last week, he brought a whole barrel of dwarven homebrew infused with subterranean mushrooms. But he made a poor drinking partner — he'd get drunk very fast. So then..."

The wizard cast his long, studious gaze over us all and said:

"I cannot simply give you back the three young ones just like that. After all, they were a gift and part of my compensation for the trade concession. Well, to be perfectly honest, I have no qualms giving up the goblin boy. I have no need for him whatsoever — he's too clumsy and poorly mannered to make a decent servant. Also, I've heard goblins are prone to thieving..."

Arlen Proud didn't change the tone of his voice, didn't point with his finger and gave basically no hints he was talking about a specific person. But Taisha suddenly blushed, pulled something out of her sleeve and placed it back on the table: a porcelain statuette of a dancing girl.

"So, I can give the goblin back," the wizard offered, as if nothing had happened. "But the wargs are of interest to me. I'd like to study the mechanics of their shapeshifting and see if it can be used on or by demons of the lower worlds. And also, fortunately — I've been given a young male and female, so they can procreate."

"But they're brother and sister!" the wood

nymph objected. The demonologist retorted that, when in predator form, they were entirely deprived of human reason and were in no way different from wild animals.

The wizard snapped his fingers, and one of the room's walls dissolved into thin air, as if it had never been there at all. We all saw a big metal cage. Inside of it, the wargs were on a rampage, roaring in rage, foaming at the mouth and gnashing at the metal bars, testing them for sturdiness.

"They're good specimens — young, ferocious and with excellent regeneration. Good subjects for studying shapeshifting. But, if my offer is of interest to my guests, I am willing to bet the wargs in a game."

With a barely noticeable gesture, the wizard conjured two horned demons, carrying a heavy table laden with victuals. The little demons that ran in after them placed four carved chairs around the table. The bald island elder took one of the chairs and gestured for the rest of us to take our seats. We lingered a bit, as there were only three chairs, and four of us. But Taisha said that, in her father's house, she had never been invited to sit at the common table, so she was more accustomed to standing.

"Smart girl. I'd welcome you into my home. There's something worth studying in you," the demonologist laughed. "As you've volunteered, pour everyone a glass of this barberry infusion from the Land of Gloom. As I said, the previous captain of *Tipsy Gannet* was a worthless drinking partner. What need did I have for hundreds of the rarest wines and infusions if I had no one to sample them with?! I couldn't share them with the uneducated rabble, much less those stinking fishermen from the village. Imagine how they'd react to elven meads or dryad flower infusions! But now, I've been given the very rare chance of treating a group of undying. And what's more, you're from three different intelligent races. We have plenty of time — the whole night's ahead of us, and there will be a nasty storm for the next two days. Your ships will never manage to go anywhere. So, here is my condition: if you manage to keep up interesting conversation long enough, I'll give you my wargs."

> **Mission received: The Respect of the Demonologist**
> **Mission class: Unusual, group**
> **Description: Keep up the interest of the master of the Island of the Wanton Widow in conversation**
> **Reward: 4000 Exp., Darius and Darina will be returned to the Gray Pack**
> **Optional condition: Outdrink the master of the island**
> **Reward: +5 to relationship with members of Brotherhood of the Coast,**

~ Stay on the Wing ~

random variable reward

"And what if we cannot manage? I don't see anything in the quest for that eventuality," my cautious sister asked me in a private message.

"In that case, we won't get the wargs and, at the same time, we will be bungling the still unfinished quest on capturing Tipsy Gannet. *But you don't need to worry much about the main quest — we have plenty interesting stuff to tell the NPC wizard. I'm not quite so sure about the optional part, although Max Sochnier and I will do our best. And you, sis, don't drink too much. You're still too young."*

Valerianna Quickfoot snorted contemptuously and asked Taisha to hand her a glass of the ruby red beverage.

"Alright, then. Let's drink to new acquaintances!" said the thin green-haired girl, who was then first to drain her glass. Everyone followed her example.

Poison Resistance check failed
Drunk effect received for 12 minutes

hungover Morning

I WAS AWOKEN by the beeping of an alarm clock, although its sound was somehow too short and immediately cut out. I cracked open an eye... and froze in incomprehension. The porthole was covered with a curtain. The bed was hard, uncomfortable and too big for my body. Next to me was sleeping Taisha, having swept her bright red hair over the pillow, which was adorned with a sewn floral pattern. Her leg was bent at the knee over my stomach.

Cool. My first time falling asleep right in the virtual reality capsule. What time was it, and how had I gotten to the ship? Finding an answer to the first question was no problem at all. With a simple glance at the clock in the bottom of the screen, I read: eight twenty-three in the morning. But as for an answer to the second question, I couldn't say.

~ Stay on the Wing ~

The last thing I remembered clearly was us drinking wine in the home of the high-level demonologist. After that, I had a few fragmented memories that I just couldn't put together into a complete picture.

I seemed to remember the wizard and I hand-feeding meat to VIXEN, and the wyvern nearly biting off the man's right hand. At another point, I saw my goblin all soaked through with rain on the top of a mountain giving a toast of some kind and waving a bottle. After that, I must have stolen the flowers from the demonologist's garden, while the owner was at home standing watch to make sure none of his servants saw us. From there, I remembered a ship, but it wasn't my *White Shark*, it was *Tipsy Gannet*. Taisha, on a bet, had picked the locks on the shackles of the oarsmen slaves one after the next. I was reminded that the thief girl had won the bet and was very glad at that fact, but who the bet was with and what for, I couldn't recall. Then we drank some more, or so it would seem. There were these strange scenes of my big-eared Goblin Herbalist walking underwater along the bottom of the sea in a bubble of air, gathering seaweeds practically by touch alone in the darkness. All in all, some disconnected nonsense, probably a dream.

I was very careful trying not to awaken the goblin beauty. I tried to move her leg over so I would be able to stand up. By the way, why was

Taisha sleeping in my bed all of a sudden? Although my NPC companion was Amra's official wife, she was always embarrassed to even sit on my bed, to say nothing of sleeping together. There hadn't even been discussion of taking the liberty of embracing or kissing the girl yet, and here I suddenly found Taisha in my bed! Although, on the other hand, there were no other beds here in the captain's chambers, so the girl had no choice — after all, she wasn't going to sleep in the common bunkroom on the straw with the sailors!

I carefully moved her leg off me, sat up and tried to stand. No such luck! As it turned out, I was significantly over-encumbered! After glancing at my inventory, I spent some time looking over the contents in astonishment, not believing my eyes. The whole bag was filled with long wet strands of shaggy green seaweed, as well as the clipped buds of exotic flowers. In my inventory, there was also a new barrel of beer, a silver wine goblet, a Demon Gardener skull fragment (based on the length of the teeth, the size of the gardener's mouth must have been around that of the prehistoric megalodon), a two-meter dinghy oar and the very same porcelain statuette of the dancing girl that Taisha had earlier attempted to steal.

Also, Amra, it seemed, had taken a serious debuff called "Hangover," which reduced Intelligence, Agility and the speed of any action by two times. Based on the timer, my troglodyte would be spending another nine hours and change hungover. By the way, I remembered, how had the drinking contest with the elder ended? I opened my menu and brought up my quest history. Well, well. Looks like I'd burned the candle at both ends!

Mission completed: The respect of the Demonologist
Experience received: 4000 Exp.
Darius and Darina will be returned to the Gray Pack
Optional condition fulfilled

+10 to relationship with members of Brotherhood of the Coast, *+1 barrel of the dark dwarven beer* King of the Depths

Mission completed: Silent assault
Experience received: 3200 Exp.
+10 to relationship with members of Brotherhood of the Coast, *+1 to Trading skill*

Mission completed: Bloodthirsty Demon Gardener
Experience received: 4000 Exp.
Stealth +1
Mission completed: Seaweed is also a plant
Experience received: 320 Exp.
+5 to relationship with members of

Brotherhood of the Coast, *Herbalism +1*

I was especially intrigued by the strange mission on the demon gardener. I opened the description of that finished quest. I needed to clip ten buds from one of the wizard's bushes, evading an encounter with the bloodthirsty garden caretaker as I did. I looked in my bag once again. Based on the inventory slots filled with hundreds of bright petals, I hadn't limited myself to just ten buds. And based on the gardener's jawbone, the owner of the garden and I had kicked the ghastly bloodthirsty demon caretaker to death so he wouldn't get in our way and stop us ripping out flowers.

I even found some lines in the logs about getting over ten thousand experience for killing the Demon Gardener and Amra reaching level thirty. Based on the logs, I had shot the demon from my blowgun for more than twenty minutes (increasing my exotic weapons skill by two in the process), not doing him particular harm, then the enemy had abruptly died for some reason. Either Valerianna Quickfoot or Max Sochnier had come to my aid, or the elder had simply grown bored with the lengthy game and undone his demon servant. My goblin vampire had sampled the blood of the demon immediately, and I was very much hoping that the big-eared troglodyte had at least done so out of view of others.

~ Stay on the Wing ~

A short beep rang out again, similar to my normal alarm clock, but this time, I immediately recognized the sound as that of an incoming paid message. Yesterday, I'd managed to acquaint myself with some of the messages that came in and was entirely disappointed to find nothing useful in any of them. Half of them were offers to meet up in some pre-determined place in *Boundless Realm* to allow myself to be killed for a reward. The rest could be split into approximately three equal categories: invitations for Amra to join some entirely unknown clan, offers to meet in real life and "discuss mutually beneficial cooperation," or simply cursing with threats.

Joining a third-tier clan would do me nothing in terms of protection, it would just reveal the location of my Goblin Herbalist. Letting myself be killed or meeting with some unknown people in real life didn't sound too good either. So now I, also without particular interest, pressed down on the mail box icon, but gave an abrupt shudder when I saw something interesting: next to the mail symbol, there was a little flower shield, meaning the sender was from one of the top one hundred clans. I looked closer at the letter. The sender was a rock dwarf, a level two-hundred-fifty warrior named Headshots_For_All. The name seemed familiar to me, and I rummaged through my memory, recalling that my sister had once told me he was the main tank of the *Keepers* clan, who didn't even take a piss without ten support players.

"Amra,

you may not know me personally, but you probably have heard of our clan, the Keepers. We are one of the strongest clans on the Southern Continent and the largest in number. No, we are not offering to let you join our ranks, as you may have thought. We have very strict requirements in level and combat skills for our candidates, and your character has a long ways to go yet before meeting our selection criteria. That said, we can offer you something else that is sure to be of interest. You see, we have common enemies — Mariam Standing_Right_Behind_You [GOONS], along with the whole rest of her clan. In your clips, you've already done significant damage to that detestable lady's ego. In fact, you've done such a good job at it that, on an order from their leader, a large part of the Goons are planning to take part in the hunt against you. So, here's my offer to you: keep trying in each of your releases to bruise Mariam's ego with your acrid comments. Ideally, this will lead to her removing the rest of her soldiers from her territory. The Keepers, then, will try to make sure the Goons simply have nothing to return to.

P.S. As leader of the Keepers clan I am authorized to promise you ten percent of all future loot taken from the castle on the Goons' territory."

Not bad, not bad. Such high-level clans

didn't make idle promises, as it would have too detrimental an effect on their reputation. It was too bad, of course, that I was offered just a percentage of the value of the "loot," without considering the castle itself — in *Boundless Realm*, the value of even the smallest castle was one million game coins. Ooh-wee, how I'd like to get ten percent of that! But here, I shook myself for being overly ambitious. I was already going to keep teasing the *Goons* for free, so ten percent of the loot on top of that was just amazing!

In a great mood, I opened my mailbox to look at the message that had awoken me, as well as all the other unread ones. Would you look at that! The last letter was also marked with a shield for a top-100 clan. And what a clan it was! *Legion of Steel*! The clan with the most combat power on the whole Southern Continent!!!

"I don't think there's any need to introduce our clan, so I'll sidestep that and get straight to business. As you may know, the admins have already forbidden the Legion of Steel *from participating in the mass hunt. And although it's not an official rule, it was entirely unambiguous. Of course, it is unfortunate, but our clan abides by the law, and we will not be breaking the rules set by the* Boundless Realm *administration. But no one forbid us from observing the developing events and sharing our observations with players that have caught our eye.*

So then, Goblin Herbalist, don't think you've made a clean getaway on that merchant galley. Sure, it was unexpected to the majority of your pursuers, but we'd already tracked your group from Stonetown to the sea coast. In the village of Ookaa, we found a group of fishermen players, who told us about a trade ship that regularly visited the village, Tipsy Gannet, and even remembered the main points the trader stopped at: the Island of the Wanton Widow, the Coast of the Striped WIldmen, and the port city of Vaant.

The Legion of Steel*'s analysts believe that, at present, you and your friends are located on the Island of the Wanton Widow. You can be sure that, if our clan managed find that out, then at least ten other strong clans have that information already as well. By midday at the very latest, fast-moving drekars and triremes will be paying the Island of the Wanton Widow a visit. And on the Coast of the Striped Wildmen, there will also be people waiting for the* Tipsy Gannet. *I hope you take this information into account.*

P.S. If, in the future, you become interested in protection or reliable cover, in your next video clip, just say the key word 'Steel' or mention the Legion of Steel *in any context.*

Alexander the Great3st. Human. Level-230 Priest of the Sun [LEGION]"

I felt as if a tub of cold water had been poured over me. Not a trace now remained of my once relaxed, and tranquil demeanor. After throwing everything I didn't need out of my inventory to get unencumbered, I went into the hallway and found myself nearly face to face with the first mate. He was standing stick straight and reported in a loud voice:

"Captain Amra, we bought everything you asked for on shore. Ten barrels of corned beef, groats, salt, flour, fish, vegetables and fruit. The whole crew got cutlasses, and another twenty bow and arrow sets with plenty of arrows. Also, a spyglass, and a tricorn hat with a feather for the captain, plenty of resin, screws, tools, five bags of saltpeter and wax. The tavern on the island had just one barrel of rum. We bought it and rolled it into the hold. There wasn't enough coins for everything, but the trader agreed to accept notes from the Underground Bank of Thorin the Ninth at half their value."

What? In horror, I checked my character's wallet and discovered that there really were no more coins. Not even one. And at that, in the logs, I found a record saying that at four seventeen AM, I gave Ziabash Hardy nearly two thousand silver coins. Plus, I added another ten thousand in underground bank notes. A while after that, five minutes later, I gave max Sochnier notes for... here I nearly had a stroke... one hundred thousand!!!

My eyes glazed over. My big-eared character stumbled and could barely stay on his feet. The first mate had a slightly inaccurate assessment of the reason for my stumbling and shouted to someone down the hallway:

"Bring the captain some brine!"

"Don't scream like that..." my head really was splitting. The debuff worked in a very realistic manner. "Cutlasses I understand. And the food too. But remind me, why did we need so much wax?"

Ziabash Hardy shrugged his broad shoulders ambiguously:

"It's not for me to know, captain! But I remember you saying something about Alchemy and flaming projectiles for our new catapults."

Greek fire? An incendiary mixture of tar, saltpeter and wax, used back in Ancient Greece to destroy enemy ships, and which could not be extinguished with water? Had I really decided to do such a thing last night in a drunken fit? Well I'll be... This might actually work!

"Did you buy clay pots to hold the fire in?" I asked, starting to worry.

"Yes sir! Three hundred of them, just as you ordered, captain! We bought all the local potter's supplies!"

At that moment, a human boy ran up and extended me a bucket of brine. I thanked him, drank half of it, then asked in a more kindhearted mood:

"You're that kid... what's your name, dang

it... Johnny. Yeah, that's right! Johnny the lookout from *Tipsy Gannet*! What are you doing on my pirate bireme?"

The first mate answered for the boy:

"Captain, last night, when you offered the liberated oarsmen from the trade galley the chance to become pirates, the lookout boy asked to join us. None of the other members of the galley crew wanted to. Of the oarsmen slaves, twenty came over to *White Shark*. A dozen orcs, six humans, a couple goblins and one dwarf."

"A dwarf sailor?! A thousand dead squid! I have to see that!" I burst out, then started laughing. "That's like a troll ballerina or a mermaid merchant riding a camel!"

"That's exactly what you said last night, captain," Ziabash Hardy informed me, smiling with his tusked mouth. "You also, to be honest, said something about a man-eating warg embroidering a cross. But the dwarf answered that he's a good mechanic and knows how to repair anything you might come across. Also, he has fairly good skill working with military machinery like ballistae and catapults, so you agreed to accept the dwarf into our crew, captain."

Good then. A mechanic-repair-man really would make a valuable crew member. In that regard, I was in complete agreement with my past self. Although, all that — new soldiers, provisions and ammunition — was of secondary importance now. What mattered most was the fact that our enemies now knew where we were docked. The chance that my crew could withstand the expected assault by high-level players was zero, with or without cutlasses. That was why we absolutely had to leave the bay of the Island of the Wanton Widow no matter the cost!

The pickle brine took effect — although the Hangover debuff time was not removed, the negative effects to Intelligence, Agility and movement speed were reduced by half. Now walking entirely confidently on the lurching floor, accompanied by the first mate, I went up onto the upper deck. The weather was as bad as it comes — it was downpouring with a very strong wind, making the *White Shark* lean to the port side. The anchor chains were creaking in strain. And this was all happening here, in a safe harbor beyond the breakwater! Calling what was happening at sea anything other than "complete and utter shit," would be hard. Huge breakers slammed into the seaside cliffs with a deafening roar. The water was foaming and misting, as if we were in a gigantic hellish cauldron.

"What do you think, Ziabash, will we be able to overcome this madness and get out to open waters?" I asked the first mate.

He spent a long time gazing into the ghastly howling of the tempest at the exit from the bay, after which he asked tentatively:

~ Stay on the Wing ~

"Captain, are you seriously asking me that? The chance of the boat overturning, or being broken on the cliffs is nine out of ten! Finding the safe passage is hard enough as it is, but in weather like this, the only way to make it out is with the help of the gods!"

I looked the huge orc from top to bottom several times, then stated quietly:

"Drekars of undying are coming here to the Island of the Wanton Widow. They'll be here by midday and destroy all pirates they can find, whether in the bay or on the shore."

The orc took another look at the fervent water and stroked his bald head in contemplation:

"We will have to completely remove the sail, of course. We'll have to go fast, using all our oar-power until we get to that cliff... then we'll have to turn hard to the right... then go backward and catch a wave... then make it through the breakers in the gauntlet... Captain, if we can do this, it will be a sure sign the gods are on our side!"

Mission received: It's not the Gods, who Fire the Pots

Mission class: Rare, group, time-limited

Description: Take the bireme out of the bay to open sea within one hour

Reward: 8000 Exp., +10 to relationship with members of Brotherhood of the Coast, Foreman skill +1

"Ziabash, order the crew to prepare. Three strong oarsmen on each oar, three watching out on the nose, five port and five starboard. You'll be steering. Order a barrel of rum brought out of the hold and placed on the oar-deck. As soon as we raise anchor, have that barrel opened, and have the shaman stand next to it with a ladle. Then, let Ghuu personally give out the medicine to calm both the nerves and noses with his blessing."

Foreman Skill increased to level 17!

I was hoping for help from the gods of *Boundless Realm,* but I was more counting on my sister's Water Magic, which could calm the waves for some time. But, unfortunately, Valerianna Quickfoot was offline, so I had to leave the game and call Val on my cellphone. Valeria answered, but it took her some time.

"Tim, what the hell is wrong with you?! I was forced to go messing around with you all night, entertaining the master of the island and getting him drunk. I only got to sleep two hours ago! Let me rest!"

I apologized to my sister for waking her, but still painted her the worrying picture I had before me. Val snarled like an animal, then snapped through her teeth:

"Alright, I'll log into *Boundless Realm* and help you with my magic. But then I'll need something from you. A half hour ago, I got a call from an employee of the Department of Human Services. She said that I've been missing the legally mandated conferences and medical checkups for two years now, and that my personal record is missing school information."

"Wait up Val, what do they mean there's no school information? Officially, you attend distance learning. Not so very long ago, you took the grade seven exams and passed with honors. You and I also sat and studied geometry together. It even made us miss a few raids in *Kingdoms of Sword and Magic*!"

"I don't know, Tim. She said they didn't have the info. And that I would have to update my details, otherwise they might take away my disability card, and that would be a huge problem. They want to see me in their office today at three thirty. Tim, please, come with me. You know I get all agitated when I talk to strangers!"

Of course, I promised my sister that I'd go with her for moral support. Although it all looked somewhat strange — both the lack of important documents in my sister's personal record, and also the never-before-mentioned conferences and medical checkups for the disabled to confirm their status. It was hardly likely that these bureaucrats thought a disabled girl could suddenly grow a new pair of legs, right?! We had never hidden from the organs of social welfare and, if their employees had not once found the time to visit our place in the criminal outskirts of the metropolis, that was their problem!

Before entering the game, I tried to call Max Sochnier a few times. There was a fully founded risk that the Naiad Trader was not on the *White Shark*, but on his galley or on shore. But my French friend wasn't picking up for some reason, so I had to simply leave him a message asking him to call me back, and close the cover of the virtual reality capsule. I didn't try calling Leon, as I was absolutely sure that the Ogre Fortifier and his flame were on my ship and could log back in later.

So then, the screen lit up, although it wasn't very bright out. The thick black rainclouds made day seem like night. Everything was ready for our mad dash through the raging sea. The sailors began blustering, steeling their courage with exclamations. The oarsmen, based on that, had already begun taking the "medicine," and were calling out the gods of the sea with scornful words. The shaman Ghuu Ghel All-Knowing, it seemed very likely, had personally tested the quality of the rum, as he was shouting loudest of all and singing out indecent songs, which was a bit strange for the normally respectable shaman.

I went up to the bow of the bireme and called the pirate crew to attention.

"So then, he-men, let's show these water demons where to stick their raging wind and bubbling sea! They must be taught that we are above tempests, and that storms are nothing but joy to pirates like us! All sailors on the upper deck, lash yourselves together and tie the ends down! Lift anchor! To oars, crab meat!"

Just then, VIXEN came down onto the deck next to me and folded her wings up compact. The level-20 Royal Forest Wyvern was all wet from the rain, but the flying snake wasn't at all thrown off by the bad weather. She lowered her long, flexible neck, revealed her toothy maw and set before me on the wet boards, a live level-12 squid. Yet another piece for my vampiric collection! I embraced my beauty!

"Who's my little hunter? What a little smarty-pants!" Then I turned to the sailors and shouted at full volume: "A good sign! Despite the storm, success and loot await us! Oars in the water! Forward!!!"

I cautiously lowered my sister's wheelchair onto the electrobus platform and, after getting my bearings on the palmtop screen, rolled down the quiet street bathed in summer sun. There was still plenty of time until Val's appointment with the Department of Human Services, so we were in no hurry and simply enjoyed the quite rare opportunity to spend some quality time together outdoors. Once upon a time, we had taken walks in the park quite often but, after selling our old apartment and moving, the walks stopped. I realized with horror that I had no memory of the last time Valeria and I had taken a walk like this. A year and a half ago, probably. Maybe even earlier.

Both of us were in an excellent mood, in no small part thanks to the cloudless day and blue sky. Unusually, the smog that hovered over the metropolis had been purged today by a morning rain.

"This is just great!" my sister said, bending down and trying to reach the fluffy white head of a dandelion growing up through a crack in the asphalt.

I stopped on Val's request and helped her pick the flower. The girl smiled happily and said with a smile:

"Timothy, do you remember when we used to gather dandelions in the park, making wishes and blowing with all our might? And if the fluff flew away, we used to say our wish would come true."

"I remember, of course, Val. What are you gonna wish for?"

"Hey, Timothy, that's not fair! We didn't used to play like that! We would wish quietly to ourselves, then blow. And if it came true, only then would you say your wish. Otherwise, someone knows your secret wish, but it still hasn't come true. That just sucks."

I laughed happily and suggested that my little sister do just as we'd done before. Val considered it briefly, then with a very serious look, told me she was ready. We both blew together, and all that was left of the dandelion was its little white head and green stem.

"Cool! It worked! What did you wish for, Timothy?"

I answered my sister honestly that I had asked to survive to the end of the hunt and keep my VIXEN — I'd already grown far too attached to the unique winged mount to lose it or sell it to anyone. For some reason, Val got upset and puffed out her cheeks.

"You're an idiot, Tim... Even though you're twice my age, you're just such a naive dreamer. Remember how, a week ago, we didn't even have money for food or rent? We still don't have our own roof over our heads and are living in a rented apartment just out of the goodness of your girlfriend's heart. If she has a change of opinion, we'll find ourselves out on the street. And last night, you gave all your bank notes to a Naiad Trader you've barely known a week! The value of that was over ten thousand in real money! And what's more, without any signatures or contract, just taking him at his word! Now you've taken it even further and are wishing to say no to a million credits you haven't even earned yet!"

I'll admit, my little sister managed to make me feel ashamed, and I lowered my head. I already felt pretty bad about just giving practically all the bank notes I earned from the paid wyvern-hatching clip to the new owner of the *Tipsy Gannet* to grow his business. But the Naiad Trader needed funds, and quite significant ones at that, to buy goods and set up a trade route. Max Sochnier was preparing to personally captain the *Tipsy Gannet* through all the points of the route, and establish firm relationships with traders in those places before entrusting such a weighty mission to a hired NPC captain. So, the naiad would be leaving our group for some time. And though I fully trusted Max, neither I nor my sister had one-hundred-percent certainty we'd get the money back.

"Val, you're right, as usual," I agreed in conciliation. "What did you wish for?"

Valeria chuckled sadly with the very corners of her lips, but still admitted:

"Not so long ago, in a burst of enthusiasm, you promised to buy me a real virtual reality capsule. I'll admit, I have very little faith in that, given how you hand out bank notes like candy, and refuse future money in advance. But you have no idea, Tim, how unbearably I want to try *Boundless Realm* with the full spectrum of sensations! Even if it's not in my own virtual reality capsule, there are probably some kind of gaming clubs where you can pay to rent one and play with full immersion!"

"There probably are," I agreed, promising to find such options for my sister.

"But..." the girl giggled, "I'm afraid to even try. For example, our escape from the bay this morning. I was nearly pissing myself in fear when *White Shark* was tossing and turning between the stones. I was especially impressed by those two jagged cliffs at the exit. A real Scylla and Charybdis! After our bireme got past them, I took off my virtual reality helmet and realized that all the hair on my head was soaked with sweat! I do not understand how your heart didn't just stop in panic, in the virtual reality capsule, seeing all that with the full spectrum of sensations!"

That was true... The feeling of being on the bireme in the storm was one of the most vibrant, and at the same time, ghastly things I'd experienced in all my time in *Boundless Realm*. The realism of it all was off the charts. Cold waves rolled over the deck, knocking me off my feet and washing away everything in their path. We almost immediately lost one badly lashed-down dinghy. Another ripped off not long after, but not all the way — the boat was still tied with a rope on its fore, causing it to flail about on the upper deck for some time, crippling sailors, before it broke in two with a strike against the mast. I then hurriedly told the sailors to get down below deck, other than two observers and the helmsman, as being on the upper deck had become a deadly endeavor.

The gusty wind was causing our ship to lurch horribly. At times, it seemed that the top of the mast was about to touch the surface of the sea. If it weren't for the well-tied-down freight and significant ballast in the hold, we certainly would have tipped over. Nevertheless, the water was coursing fairly quickly through the drainage holes overboard. The situation on the oar-deck was especially dire. We lost three of the orc sailors, who inhaled far too much sea water sitting at their oars. Nevertheless, we managed to pass the storm, after which the *White Shark* raised sail and dashed like an arrow across the sea, driven on by the squall.

When the quest "It's not the Gods That Fire the Pots," was considered complete, a wave of bright illumination rolled over the ship — nearly all the sailors aboard leveled up. I got enough experience to reach level thirty-one, and Valerianna Quickfoot reached thirty-two. After distributing my character's stat points as usual — into Charisma and Agility, I handed control to the first mate, then exited *Boundless Realm* together with the wood nymph, having promised the crew I'd return by evening.

The video of the howling tempest and *White Shark* being hurled by huge breakers, contained lots of very high quality material, which simply had to be shown to my viewers. But I only planned to upload the footage tomorrow — I had no reason to show my pursuers that I'd changed ships. If the cleverest wyvern hunters already knew about *Tipsy Gannet*, no one at all (or so I hoped) knew about the pirate bireme.

As I pushed my sister's wheelchair down the street, Val suddenly started laughing. My sister informed me with a smile that it was her character that had defeated the island elder in the wine-drinking contest. The Goblin Herbalist and Naiad Trader had gotten drunk too fast, and started behaving rowdy and dropped out of the race. Successfully completing the optional condition of the Demonologist's Respect quest was entirely the wood nymph's doing. She told me she periodically got messages about penalties to Agility or Intelligence, but they had no effect on the wood nymph's ability to behave herself. My sister supposed that she simply didn't know what being drunk was like, so the computer system was unable to put her into such a state. In the end, the master of the island had admitted his defeat last night, and hobbled off after my big-eared goblin up to the very summit of the hill to the respawn stone.

"Ugh... I still can't get away from thoughts about the virtual reality capsule. I read that some gamers get so into the game world that their consciousness starts to get digitized and they then live in the game separately from their body... By the way, Timothy, we're here. There's the building."

Conversing actively, we really hadn't noticed the dingy imperceptible building. Over its doors, there was a washed-out banner reading: "Department of Human Services." Other banners hung next to it informed us that the building was shared by a medical clinic and a center of gerontology.

I got slightly on edge — this place was just half a kilometer from the criminal neighborhood Valeria and I had lived in not so terribly long ago. There was a certain risk we'd meet an old neighbor or acquaintance — many of the residents of the ill-fated neighborhood were on the Human Services rolls, or visited the medical clinic for various things.

There was still a whole forty minutes until Valeria's appointment, but we didn't stay on the street getting sun, just went into the building. A large freight elevator brought us up to the third floor. In the hallways, it was deserted, and we didn't see any line into the office we were headed to. We knocked and entered.

Inside the small office, there were two fairly plump ladies of "a bit over forty" sitting and drinking tea with chocolate candies. For some reason, the simplest question of all — could they see us now, given that there was no line — caused the pair of clucking hens to fall into a prolonged stupor. For some time, they exchanged glances and even tried to claim it was their lunch break. But I pointed to the sign on the door showing operating hours, which clearly stated that lunch break had ended fifty minutes ago. One of the two ladies gave an upset frown and, finishing her tea in one big gulp, tossed on a white hospital gown over her blue business suit and walked out into the hallway. The lady who remained agreed to see my sister, turned on the monitor on her table and handed a form to Valeria.

"Young man, you can wait outside," she suggested in a tone that wouldn't bear objection.

"Timothy, you go, I'll manage on my own," Val assured me.

I left the office and paced the hallway looking bored. On the stairs next to the elevator, the lady who we'd stopped from gossiping with her friend was standing and smoking. She turned away from me demonstratively and unhappily. I kept walking. Just then, I got a call on my cell phone. On the screen, the name Max Sochnier was shown.

"Greetings, Timothy. I have a great video for you. I sent it to your mailbox to download. I was up on the seaside cliffs filming two ships of players pass not far from the entrance into the island's bay. A drekar belonging to the *Night Predators* rammed through the *Power-Brokers'* galley. You'll never believe it! Grappling hooks, clouds of gunsmoke, lightning bolts, magic shields, wisps of toxic smoke... It looked amazing! The *Power-Brokers* won and even captured the attacking ship, though they did sustain quite heavy losses. After that, a bireme with one hundred *Goons* tried to take the drekar, which was barely floating, with the rest of the *Power-Brokers* still on board. But they didn't consider the strong wind, and scuttled on the reefs, sinking in half a minute together with the whole crew!"

I couldn't resist laughing, imagining the spectacle. I'd have to download the video and tell them in my daily clip today about the *Goons'* latest act of idiocy.

"Max, overall, how's the situation on the Island of the Wanton Widow?"

"The storm isn't stopping, and seems to even be getting stronger. There are five player-controlled ships next to the island but, in this weather, they can't get near the shore, nor enter the bay. What's more, the water is just lousy with marine predators. Any player or NPC who falls overboard gets devoured by them instantly. The players saw me on the shore and even tried to get in touch with me, but I haven't yet answered. I say let them think you're also somewhere nearby, and waste time near the island. When they realize their error, you'll already be far away! It'd be great if the storm stayed like this until dark, then you'll have the whole night ahead of you."

"Thank you for the help, Max!"

"Thank you. With your money, I bought so much cheap fish from the Island of the Wanton Widow that my galley is nearly sagging down to the oarsman's benches in the water. As long as the players don't sink *Tipsy Gannet* in rage over the fact that they wasted so much time searching for you in vain... You really shouldn't have given me that teleportation scroll — you need it more!"

I could barely hold back a surprised gasp — had I seriously given up such a valuable rescue scroll to the Naiad Trader?! Although, I remembered that I really hadn't seen the scroll in my inventory this morning.

"Alright, Timothy, I'm going back into the game. If something interesting happens, I'll be sure to send you the footage!"

My cell phone stashed back in my pocket, I walked slowly down the hallway, thinking over our current situation. My attention was caught by a muted woman's voice whispering animatedly from the stairwell. If the woman had been speaking in a normal tone, I may have not noticed, and just walked by, but she was clearly trying to speak quietly so no one would overhear.

"That's right. They're already here, nearly a whole hour early. Anette is trying to delay them. We'll send her to medical checkup or something, if need be. But don't you be late, otherwise they'll leave and you'll never find them! In how long? Yeah, they'll definitely be here for five minutes, so you'll make it. Alright, that's all. Bye-bye!"

From what I overheard, I had easily enough to realize that she was talking about Valeria and I. These base animals, taking advantage of their position in government, had found my sister's phone number in the human services database and contrived a reason to lure her here so they could give me and Val up to their co-conspirators. We're in a trap! And we only have five minutes to get out!

More Than Just a Game

UNTIL TODAY, I never suspected that I would be capable of striking a woman — I figured I was too well-raised to do something like that. But all my culture, education and politeness, which I considered natural qualities of my character, left me in one moment. I felt exasperated and stripped bare. If anyone wanted to bring harm to my sister or I at that moment, I would tear their throat open with my teeth. Punching the fat lady in the ear was a pointed and savory feeling. The woman flew to the side and hit her head on the wall with a dull thud. Her cell phone fell out of her unclenched fingers, and was crushed under her high heel with a crunch. Next to the fragments of phone on the floor, there was a large key ring that fell out of her hospital gown pocket, including an electric key fob to a car. I saw it with the corner of my mind, but I didn't take her property, just hurried to my sister.

"Young man, I told you to wait in the hallway!" the social worker met my entrance reproachfully.

But I wasn't listening to her now, and entered decisively, closing the door behind me. Valeria was pensively and unhurriedly filling out the fifteen-twenty page-long form, and the social worker was entering some information into the computer database. It was all typical and natural. There was nothing to speak to the fact that something criminal was afoot. A belated thought flashed in my head that I might have misunderstood the overheard conversation on the stairs. But my gaze caught on a little placard on the woman's suit: *"Anette Crisby, social worker."* A phrase I'd just heard instantly flashed by in my memory: "Anette is trying to delay them." Unfortunately, I was not wrong!

Anette didn't even manage to realize what was going on, much less grow afraid before I stepped forward and twisted her arm behind her back, pushing her face into the table.

"Val, give me that roll of scotch tape!" I said, pointing to a dispenser nearby.

Valeria's composure in extreme situations had always impressed me. I even admired her for it. And now as well, my sister didn't ask any questions and, as if she did this every day, helped me in a business-like manner to tie the fat lady to the chair.

"Who did you and your co-conspirator give us up to?" I asked, looming threateningly over the lady.

"No one..." she first tried to just lie, but after getting a hard slap and seeing the decisiveness on my face, immediately lost her nerve and admitted to it. "It wasn't my idea, I swear! I was threatened by gangsters from the Grave Worms! They said you borrowed a bunch of coin from them and had run off with the money. But they figured the disabled girl was probably on the human services rolls, so they demanded your new address from me. I didn't know it, but promised to figure it out and called the phone number shown in the girl's personal record to make an appointment."

God damn it! My rage subsided just as quickly as it had rolled in, ceding its place to disgust. This animal, using her government job, was prepared to give us up to a bunch of gangsters. The idiotic story had nothing to do with my flying mount and was just more of the same racketeering scheme that had made my sister and I leave our old neighborhood in the first place.

"And what sort of relationship does that other lady have with the bandits?"

The plump bound lady winced unhappily. She must have preferred not to address that topic. However, she did answer my question honestly:

"Irene works a floor above me in the medical center as a nurse with the ambulance team. In her free time, she sometimes comes down to gossip. Her younger brother is a lookout for the Grave Worms. He first tried getting information on you through his sister, but there was nothing in the medical center database. Then, Irene pointed her brother to me. According to their gang rules, if a person helps them track down someone in their debt, they get a portion of the loot. Irene was counting on this — she said it was a very large amount of money, and she'd give me a good bonus for it."

Everything became extremely clear to me. I had to leave immediately — the gang had a very nasty way of dealing with those in their debt. A former neighbor of ours had both his legs broken a year ago, because he hid some of the income from selling his pictures. They left him with his hands intact, though, so he could keep working and pay up faster. And another neighbor, who owned a second-hand clothing store, refused to pay protection money and was burned alive in her shop.

"Val, let's get out of here! Make sure to bring the survey with you, though!"

Leaving the woman tied up, we hurried to the door. I took a belated look around for security cameras, but didn't see them in the office, on the stairs, or in the hallway. Good — that meant my attack on the woman must have gone unnoticed by security, and we still had a chance to leave in peace. My sister screamed out in fear when she saw the plump lady lying unconscious on the stairway landing. Yeah, it was pretty rough, but I had to do it. I had no regrets.

It took a long time, and was very uncomfortable to get down the stairs in the wheelchair, so Val called the elevator. At the same time, I looked out the hallway window. And it was good that I guessed to do that — down the street, there was a jeep racing our way covered with skulls and graffiti and lacking windows or doors. There as a grand total of ten people in the vehicle, riding on the seats, standing on the running boards, and even clinging to the roof. With a horrible screech of the brakes, the car came to a stop, and the bandits poured out holding chains, brass knuckles and knives. The gang immediately ran into the building.

The elevator reached our floor and its doors opened, but getting into it now would be suicide. We had to stick to the stairs, and we'd have to go up, given that our pursuers would be coming from below! Damn, Vals' wheelchair weighed around forty kilograms all on its own, and I had to carry my sister in it, as well! Lifting the load with massive effort, I took a heavy step up.

"Leave the wheelchair, Timothy! Leave it, or we'll never get out of here!"

With a nod to my sister, I took Val in my arms, kicking the chair down the stairs — let them think we went down to the third floor. Here, my gaze caught on the unconscious lady's keyring. The car! It was probably parked somewhere nearby the building or was in the building's underground lot. That was our path to freedom. Obviously, running away down the street with my sister in my arms would have been impossible. I bent down, grabbed the keys from the floor and hurried up the stairs. When I got there, I saw that the elevator had already started moving — the criminals had pressed the button on the first floor.

On the fifth floor, there was a medical clinic. The on-duty doctor was a decrepit old geezer. He had a tablet on his knees and was talking to a friend of his over a social network app. He only tore his eyes from the screen for a few seconds, leading his surprised gaze over me, but didn't stop. Perhaps, he figured I was dropping off an emergency patient, or something like that. I hurried to the end of the hallway — as far as I remembered from when I was waiting for my sister, there was a service elevator there.

There really was an elevator there, but the buttons didn't work. Damn! The last thing I needed! But the light over the elevator door lit up. Somehow, it had worked anyway. I looked at the keys I'd taken from the nurse. One of them, as it turned out, was to unlock the elevator. The doors parted ways at a positively comatose pace. After familiarizing myself with the various buttons on the panel, I chose the underground garage. The elevator doors also closed very, very slowly.

"Where'd they run off to?!" I heard far-off cries at the other end of the hallway but, just then, the door closed and the elevator started unhurriedly downward.

There were twenty or so cars in the underground lot. I pressed the button on the fob, hoping it would activate one of them. And it did — the headlights flashed on the front of the ambulance. Oof, now I'd be arrested for stealing a medical vehicle! But those distant problems could not stop me now, as I had more substantive ones close at hand. I set Val on the front seat next to the driver, threw a white hospital gown over her shoulders and fastened the seatbelt.

The ambulance raced to the garage exit. I even purposely turned on the siren so the guard would rush to raise the gate and wouldn't look at us too long. It worked! To the howling of the siren, the ambulance flew out of the garage and started a course for the center of the metropolis.

* * *

What should we do now? Call the police? Sure, and be instantly arrested for attacking a human services worker, adding to that violence and the ambulance theft? How could I ever prove that my actions were forced, if all their evidence came from one very frightened woman tied to a chair? She'd tell the police a totally different story, and when her friend came to, she'd confirm that some badly-behaved man had attacked and beaten them, stolen their property and taken the ambulance.

No, calling the police was not the way out of my situation. But what should I do, then? Probably, for a start, I should try to get rid of the flashy mode of transportation as quickly as possible. Let's say I did that, what could I do from there with my legless sister? Hold her in my arms? We'd be too obvious, and where could we even go? The taxi option also fell through — both the police and gangsters would be searching for us, and the first thing they would do would be to ask transport companies about clients originating in this area, and would soon figure out where the taxi driver had brought the man and his legless sister.

We needed a reliable person with a car who could take Val and I home. I ran through a list of old friends and college buddies in my head, as well as former clan members from *Kingdoms of Sword and Magic*, and even ex-girlfriends. Either I was a bad friend, or there was some other reason, but I couldn't think of anyone who'd help Valeria and I out, then be guaranteed not to talk. Maybe I should try my new friends Leon and Max Sochnier? But Leon didn't have his own car, and I absolutely did not want to have him find some third party to bring Val and I home. We were left with Max Sochnier.

According to an ancient Eastern wisdom, friends can be divided into three categories: one can be trusted with money, the other with your wife (or sister in my case), and a third to hide a dead body. And only the friend who fell under all three categories could be considered truly reliable and trustworthy for this matter. I knew only one such person. I thought about it and chuckled: I'd already entrusted Max Sochnier with money. Val would clearly not be harassed by my French friend, and all that remained was finding out about "hiding bodies" (or in my case, helping me get away from the racketeers and police at the same time). But... Max Sochnier didn't answer any of my calls — he must have been in *Boundless Realm.* What a shame...

There was only one more person in my list, a woman, though this option I had left for the most extreme circumstance. I was, naturally, thinking of Kira. The red-headed beauty tried to avoid notoriety in her life. She was a mystery even to her closest friends. Kira had quite a bit to lose, and she had absolutely no need for trouble with the police so, I really had no idea how the girl would react to my request for help. Kira might easily have agreed to help. But she could also not only refuse, but also demand that my sister and I immediately leave the apartment so no one would associate her with law-breakers. But there was nothing to be done. I had to take the risk and dial the beautiful red-head's number.

Kira answered the call almost immediately and with reproach in her voice. She was asking why I'd forgotten about her and not called for two days. But when I told her about my problem, the girl's reaction was unexpected.

"How much is the social aid that you and your sister get each month? I mean, that is what made you go down there, right?"

I answered honestly that it was eighteen credits a month. Kira took a heavy sigh.

"Timothy, is your head alright? You know perfectly well that a ton of people are searching for you, and with quite unkind intentions at that. I already told you to disappear and just sit quieter than water and lower than grass, especially for the first two weeks. There's a million-credit prize riding on this horse. And now you're telling me that you revealed information about yourself, and risked your health as well as that of your sister all over eighteen credits a month?! If you have such a severe need for money, you could have just told me! I would have sent you however much you needed on the spot. And if you're so scrupulous that you wouldn't have accepted it as a gift, I could have loaned you the money!"

From just a purely financial point of view,

my sister and my actions really did look extremely weird and hard to explain. I tried to argue that the reason for our visit to the social center wasn't only to do with maintaining her stipend, but also to update my sister's documents after we moved so everything would stay above board.

"And, did you update the documents? Has your situation improved, legally speaking?" Kira quipped, but immediately changed her tone to business-like. "Alright, don't answer. I already understand everything. I cannot come now — I'm currently at the opening of a new designer clothing collection. In fact, I'm on the opposite side of the globe from you. I hope you understand. It isn't that I really care that much about all these dress orders and the fashion lovers around me. It's just that it would take me at least four hours to get to you. But I'll send the head of my security and his guys. I'll give them your number now. They'll get in touch with you and explain what to do. That's all. Good luck!"

Kira hung up. Not even a minute later, I got a call from an unknown number. A raspy man's voice said:

"We've determined your coordinates via your phone. Everything is okay. We're not far away. At the next intersection, turn right toward the square. There, turn off the siren and find somewhere to pull over. Do not leave the vehicle. Lock the doors and sit inside. Don't open up for anyone. Not even cops. We'll be there in twelve minutes."

* * *

It was already dark, but I was in no rush to get to work today — I'd finished my required eight daily hours in *Boundless Realm* this morning and, now, I was recommended not to go outside until the situation was cleared up. So, Val and I were sitting in the apartment on the 333rd floor, eating delivery pizza and playing around with all the functions of her sophisticated new wheelchair. My sister had chosen the model she wanted herself in an online store and ordered it for immediate delivery. I, then, paid all the expenses. A call to my cell phone tore us away from testing the autopilot mode. I picked up my phone. On the screen was the number of Kira's head of security. Finally, some news!

"Timothy, I wanted to tell you that everything turned out just fine. We returned the ambulance. No one even missed it. We left the keys in the vehicle. All the prints were scrubbed. We carefully checked with our connections — no calls came into the police about the medical center. All's quiet. The police are definitely not searching for you. All the same, I hope greatly that this story with the bandits will teach you to be more careful in the future."

~ Stay on the Wing ~

I felt like a heavy stone had been lifted from my shoulders. I wanted to scream in elation at the top of my lungs, which is exactly what I did, surprising and even slightly frightening Val. The man on the line laughed, sharing my joy. I thanked him for the help, promised to be more careful in the future and hung up. My mood was just amazing. I couldn't see anything else standing between me and playing *Boundless Realm,* so I started off to work.

Fifteen minutes later, I was already flying up the marble staircase in front of the corporation's building. I made it past security and hurried to the elevators. I walked up near my game cabin, 4-16A, and, as I was taking out the electronic key, a call from an unknown number caught me off guard.

"Finally, you're in the building, Timothy! This is Andrei Soloviev, head of in-game security. You might remember me — we once talked in the office of the director of special projects. To be honest, I'm pretty sick of waiting for you at this point — it's almost ten in the evening, and you just wouldn't show up..."

Of course I remembered the light-haired strong-man. He had cold attentive eyes and a sharp analytic mind. Honestly, being in his company made me feel very uncomfortable, even though I had no sins to be worried about at that time. It was just that he had a prim and proper army bearing, so he just reeked of danger and even death. I had no doubt whatsoever that Andrei Soloviev had killed people before. What did he want from me? I immediately grew restless inside.

"Timothy, a very important person would like to have a talk with you. Go to elevator eleven. I'm unblocking it now. Go up to the seventy-seventh floor. I'll meet you there and accompany you."

Intriguing beginning to a work shift! I returned to the elevators and looked for the usually inactive elevator eleven which, unlike the other fragmented elevators, shot straight through the entire *Boundless Realm* skyscraper. Now, the elevator was working, and its doors instantly split as soon as I pressed the button. The high-speed elevator shot up like a bullet. My ears even popped. Literally ten seconds later, I was already there.

Andrei Soloviev was awaiting me at the exit from elevator, but instead of a greeting, he asked me to put my arms out to the sides, and took a multi-functional scanner or detector from a holster on his belt and led it along my body.

"Just standard procedure," the security man said in a irrefutable tone. "The security guards normally check guests, but the lady let them go early today so, I have to do it myself, even though it's not in my job description. Everything is fine. Follow after me. Don't keep her waiting."

Her? That said, I'd already seen enough to

realize that. The whole seventy-seventh floor was one huge stylish office, and its occupant was now up on a little ladder feeding the bright tropical fish in a huge aquarium. She was a lady of average height, her age somewhere "over fifty." She had on a dark blue business suit, black stilettos, and a number of gold rings with huge gems. The lady's ashen-gray hair was pulled up in a tight bun on the back of her head. If she dyed it, no one would guess she was over forty. But she preferred not to hide her age.

"Walk into the small room, Timothy. You can sit in any of the chairs. I'm finishing up now, then I'll come in."

Andrei Soloviev pointed me into the next room, enclosed with thick transparent walls. In it, there were two dozen chairs spread out around a huge touch-screen table. I took the first chair I came across and, trying not to show my confusion, started searching this room and the next one over in an attempt to discover a placard showing the name or title of this gray-haired lady. I didn't find a thing, though.

Seven minutes later, she entered the room, wiping her hands with a wetnap as she walked. Then, with an accurate flick, she sent the rumpled napkin right into a trashcan halfway across the room.

"I hope you didn't have to wait too long," the woman said, sitting opposite me and starting to stare at me unabashedly. "So then, you're the corporate tester that's stirred up so much trouble! Somehow, I imagined you quite different — small, nimble, crafty. Like a goblin!"

I smiled at the joke, but I could barely believe that this lady had not taken the pains to open my personal file before the conversation. I mean, it did have a picture in it.

"Alright, let's get right to business," said the woman, her voice instantly changed from warm-hearted to cold as sharp steel. "All day, I've been trying to figure out where this whole confusing story started. It seems someone promised the players a wyvern-shaped token. All the departments are pointing the finger at one another, and no one wants to take responsibility. Be frank with me, Timothy, which of our employees told you about this? Your boss Mark Tobius? Or was it someone else?"

The gray-haired woman looked me severely right in the eye, demanding a fast and honest answer. Well, it took them a while, but they got me... I now felt like a rabbit just about to be eaten by a boa constrictor. But still, I found the force in myself not to avert my gaze. I answered in a voice no less calm than before:

"No one told me about the token. I thought of it myself."

"What do you mean? Why?!" exclaimed both people in the room nearly at the same time.

"Because this whole story with the hunt for the wyvern looked poorly thought-out, like a quick and dirty hasty, botched event. Like, if my Amra had been found yesterday or today, and the medallion had dropped, that would have been it — all the fanfare about drawing players out of the boring cities into the mysterious and unknown world would have fizzled out just like that! The wyvern hunt would go down in the collective memory as nothing more than a reminder that a successful player could be deprived of a valuable trophy at any minute just because of envious losers raising a ruckus on the forum. So then I decided, as long as the company itself wouldn't, I should try to remedy the situation with my video. I tried to find a way for the *Boundless Realm* Corporation to save face, both raising player interest in the event and redirecting their activity in a positive direction. And I also gave the players an extra stimulus to finally leave the cities — for the whole length of the event, experience loss is reduced. It's the perfect time to explore!"

When I finished my long emotional speech, Andrei Soloviev and the unknown lady spent some time in silence. Finally, the woman said with a nervous smirk:

"I really don't even know what to say... I have to admit, I wasn't expecting such a simple answer to the riddle of the wyvern token!"

Either the security head said something

quietly to the lady, or showed her with a gesture I missed, but she began speaking hurriedly:

"No, no! There's nothing to punish Timothy for — he was just doing his job, warming the interest of the players in the hunt for the flying mount. And Timothy has some very sound ideas. I like it."

Andrei Soloviev relaxed noticeably — the lady clearly changed her rage to sweetness. The security head instantly got his bearings and hurried to change the topic:

"Yes, the ideas are correct. Now is the time to think about why these simple, obvious truths are being spoken by a simple tester, while the corporate employees of higher rank hadn't noticed them earlier or taken measures."

The gray-haired lady looked at her assistant and laughed magnanimously.

"Andrei, let's cool it with the repressions. Enough heads have rolled over this great hunt as it is. The director of player outreach was fired. The marketing director was fined and received an official notice that he did not fully meet the qualifications of his profession. The director of special projects admitted that he didn't have the situation under control and was not aware of events in his own department, and asked to be transferred back to his post as test-group leader. I'm inclined to approve that resolution for a transfer, as well. Mark Tobius is a valuable employee. We should keep him for our corporation. But he just doesn't seem to have grown to director level yet..."

As I was listening, my head was sinking lower and lower. Just imagine of all the thunder and lightning today! I mean, directors were sacked! And it was all because of my arrogance and a few careless phrases said into a microphone... I was afraid that, after today, I had earned myself some enemies in the corporation. And also, I couldn't understand what the lady had decided about me. How was this story all going to end?

As if reading my thoughts, she continued:

"After weighing all the plusses and minuses, I give my approval to your additions. Exactly as you described them. Also, the decision was made that players who have bought the token will be marked gold on the map to attract attention and encourage other players to get the tokens as well. There was one real change, though. After meeting with accounting, it was decided that the price of a token should be increased to five credits and that it should only be allowed to be paid with real money. Over the first day, sales of the 'token of the wyvern hunter' have provided our corporation with twenty-eight million credits, and that's just the beginning. Of course, on a wider corporate scale, that's just a drop in the bucket, but as unplanned income, it is quite respectable. I suppose I'll give an order that ten percent should be set aside as a daily prize to go to the wyvern owner. That's good money, and you've earned it honestly, Timothy. Congratulations!"

The head of in-game security shook my hand and also congratulated me. But my head was spinning in agitation and worry. Meanwhile, the woman continued:

"Timothy, in that a new director of special projects hasn't yet been appointed, for some time, you will have no immediate boss. For a day or two, you'll have to act on your own without oversight, and without getting every little action approved in advance. Whether that's good or bad, we'll see. What's important now is that the event continues as actively and fervently as it began. The clans are active, top players are in motion. The inevitable skirmishes are underway. Lots of items and money is sure to change hands. Your mission, Timothy, is to continue to serve as a bothersome lure, hopping before their very noses, tempting the players to want to catch you. If you manage, you'll be promoted to senior tester and will receive a monthly salary of two thousand credits on top of the payouts you already get. If, though, you have any other questions, or actions that need someone's permission, send them through the director's assistant... What's her name? She's quite young and wears lots of makeup..."

"Jane?" I suggested.

~ Stay on the Wing ~

"That's her! For now, solve all the complicated issues through her. And another thing..." Here, the gray-haired lady suddenly started smiling somewhat ashamedly, "this is a personal request. You see, Timothy, I've lived quite a long life. I even remember news stands on the street and stores selling paperback books..."

Paperbacks?! Those hadn't been published for thirty years, if not forty! A long time ago, everything changed to electronic and audio-books. So, she must have been a real dinosaur! My estimation of the lady's birth year quickly moved back into the previous century. She might not have been from prehistoric times, but she was quite old. And meanwhile, the lady continued with a note of nostalgia for her bygone era:

"Yes, young man. It was once normal to read paperback books, and keep the most interesting of them in a special cabinet at home. In my childhood, I had whole shelves of nothing but books. And also, as a teenage girl, I was most drawn not to tear-jerking melodramas, but to adventures on the high seas and pirate romances. Rafael Sabatini's Captain Blood. Arthur Conan-Doyle's Captain Sharkey. Flint, Silver, Blackbeard, Francis Drake... Right before this conversation, I was watching your game sessions from the last few days, and I was flooded with memories from distant childhood. The smell of the salty sea, tar and powder. The creaking of rigging, the flapping of sails in the wind..."

The woman started smiling and even closed her eyes for a few seconds, under the spell of the pleasant memories.

"So then, Timothy. I would really like you to show this side of the game in the best light in your future video clips. In *Boundless Realm*, we have a lot of seas and oceans, thousands of unknown lands and islands with treasures awaiting the brave, but the players are quite lazy and haven't yet done much exploring of the seas. It's expensive and dangerous. You've already gotten a good idea how pricy it can be to outfit a ship and buy everything necessary for a crew. But in *Boundless Realm,* there are rich clans and players capable of emptying their wallets to equip marine expeditions. I'd like that to become more popular! I'd like there to be virtual equivalents to Magellan and Columbus, giving their lives to the spirit of adventure, exploring new lands and returning with hitherto unseen trophies! Can you do that for me, Timothy?"

Of course, I promised to do it. The woman thanked me and told Andrei Soloviev that she had no questions left and our meeting was over. I stood, bowed to the woman and headed for the exit. Once near the elevator, I took a risk and asked the security head who I was talking with back there. Andrei found my complete ignorance hilarious.

~ Stay on the Wing ~

"Timothy, you've just had the chance to speak with Inessa Tyle herself. She's a legend in our corporation. Five years ago, she was the first person who, after hearing out a team of unknown developers, agreed to take a risk and invest her personal funds into buying servers and hiring employees. Now, Inessa Tyle is the vice president of the *Boundless Realm* Corporation, second in the hierarchy and one of the richest women on the planet. She owns one third of the shares of the *Boundless Realm* Corporation. She's God and King here. Her word is law for all employees. Timothy, you have no idea what kind of support you'll receive if you can fulfill the whims of this influential lady and create a magnificent pirate romance."

I nodded in silence, dumbfounded at the head of in-game security's admissions and the new perspectives revealed. It seemed very much that the leadership's opinion of me was directly dependent on how eloquently and convincingly I could depict the charms of a pirate life in my upcoming video reports. Now, I would have to go balls to the wall to provide the material she was after!

Return to the Bireme

IT DIDN'T TAKE me long to edit the video. The material, in large part, had been ready for some time — the raft voyage down the river, then the dock near the undersea village of Ookaa, loading our animals onto *Tipsy Gannet*, then the attempt to flee the pirates and the log driven into the sea floor, stopping the bireme. Sure, I had to cut down the scenes of my walking along the bottom of the sea, and my other underwater tasks, as I had no desire to show the viewers that big-eared Amra had been given invincibility. That would just be another headache. Also, I was trying very hard to get around all the moments connected with *White Shark* and immediately went to the Island of the Wanton Widow. Thankfully, there was plenty of material on our night out. Although my character didn't remember nearly everything that had happened, Valerianna Quickfoot had provided footage of the most interesting moments, and Max Sochnier had helped as well.

I paid particular attention to the *Tipsy Gannet* coming under my team's control, as well as Taisha freeing all the slave oarsmen. The half-hour video finished with some shots taken from shore of the sea blockade and the battles in the harsh storm between the various crews of undying. I mocked the *Goons* in the harshest terms, showing how they'd wrecked their ship with their own idiocy on the seaside cliffs and drowned their entire crew.

I didn't forget to say the key word "steel" either, given that aid from the *Legion of Steel* would now come in very handy. From all the logic of the clip, it followed that my big-eared goblin was still on the Island of the Wanton Widow surrounded by the many ships of his pursuers. Let the viewers think just that!

After uploading the video report, I set about going through my huge backlog of messages, which turned out to be a huge waste of time. Of the two hundred messages there, I didn't find a single one useful — just more of the same: requests to allow myself to be killed in *Boundless Realm*, or offers to meet in real life. Alright then, enough! I had already encountered a group of strangers today, and it was very much not to my liking.

Finally, I finished my business, crawled into the virtual reality capsule and closed the lid. So then, how am I looking?

Name: Amra
Race: Goblin Vampire
Class: Herbalist
Experience, 228172 of 240000
Character level, 31 (ATTENTION!!! Level-30 modifications not chosen)
Hit points, 276/276
Endurance points, 133/241

Statistics:

Strength (S) 32 (32)
Agility (A) 34 (122.4)
Intelligence (I) 5 (16.5)
Constitution (C) 35 (45.5)
Perception (P) 3 (43.3)
Charisma (Ch) 64 (80)
Unused points 0

Primary skills (6 of 6 chosen)

Herbalism (P A) 15
Trading (Ch I) 16
Alchemy (I A) 15
Dodging (A P) 20 (ATTENTION!!! Level-20 skill specialization not chosen)

Stealth (A C)21 (ATTENTION!!! Level-20 skill specialization not chosen)
Exotic Weapons (A P)   12

Secondary skills (6 of 6 chosen)

Veil   13
Acrobatics   15
Athletics   14
Foreman   17
Riding   8
Animal Control   6

Simplest of all was managing the modifications — just as at character level twenty, at level thirty, I chose Invisibility: another minus 2% to detection radius for my goblin by any NPC or living player in *Boundless Realm.*

Now, the time had come to choose my first perk to the Dodge skill. The abundance of options made my eyes go in opposite directions:

　　　☐　　+30% chance of dodging arrows and metal ammunition
　　　☐　　+30% chance of avoiding AoE spells (area of effect spells that hit a large area)
　　　☐　　+30% chance of dodging spells aimed at character
　　　☐　　+30% chance of dodging close

combat weapons

☐ +30% chance of dodging the fangs/claws/mandibles/tentacles/tails etc. of NPC monsters

It was all useful. I wanted them all! I considered it for three minutes before deciding it would be best to avoid AoE spells. I was reminded that, once upon a time, I'd been caught by a frost spell from a magical grenade, which nearly led to my death. Also, the panic effect from the moose bellowing was very unpleasant. I wasn't at all sure that the perk would help me avoid panic. I'd have to look at detailed guides on the forum. But the fact that Amra's chance of surviving all kinds of fireballs, magic shrapnel, poison clouds and other such spells with an area of effect would be certainly increasing was very, very nice.

It took me much less time to choose a Stealth skill perk. Sure, increased movement speed while hidden, or improved chance of hiding in illuminated places were alluring abilities, but I decided to continue on my chosen path and took a Stealth perk that reduced my character's discovery radius by a further 20%.

So then, loading. My big-eared goblin appeared in the captain's bunk on the *White Shark*. Taisha was sleeping on my bed. What was more, she was in the very same position I'd left her in this morning. It was as if the whole long nerve-wracking day had never happened. I pulled a thin woolen blanket more snugly over the girl, and the beautiful NPC muttered something indistinguishable in gratitude, not opening her eyes.

In the meantime, there had been clear changes in the room — the huge empty chest that had once held the dryad was now gone. In its place, there was a shelf and bedside table made from the boards that had once constituted the chest. Elegant and I'd even say ornate, also having a little railing so the contents wouldn't fall out as the boat rocked. And what was most surprising was that the shelves weren't empty. In fact, they were densely packed with bottles of woman's perfume, powders and mascaras, some other cosmetics, and a folded semi-transparent shawl. Were these all Taisha's? I turned to my NPC companion and shook my head in doubt. It didn't much look like the goblin girl used cosmetics.

Well, whose things were these, then? The dryad's? But where had she managed to get them on the bireme at open sea? Or had my pirate ship visited a port of some kind during the day? But then, all the efforts undertaken by Max Sochnier and me to keep Amra's location a secret would be going down the drain! This fundamental question had to be answered immediately, and I headed for the exit from the bunk in order to find the first mate or any other member of the crew.

"What, you won't even hug your wife?" came a reproachful voice from behind me, and I turned around instantly.

Taisha wasn't asleep and, the blanket thrown back, was staring at me. Her eyes were sparkling in joy.

"How'd I get stuck with a man like you?! Disappears to gods-know-where all day, only comes back at night and leaves as soon as he shows up. And I, meanwhile, missed you so, Amra!"

I approached the beautiful NPC, plopped down next to her on the bed and, my mind suddenly made up, stretched out to Taisha and kissed her right on the lips.

My modest and well-mannered NPC companion was taken aback by the unheard-of impudence for a few seconds, only beginning to try and wriggle free after that.

Successful Strength check
Experience received: 25 Exp.

Successful Strength check
Experience received: 40 Exp.

Successful Strength check
Experience received: 80 Exp.

With every second, Taisha was squirming all the stronger, trying to get free, but I embraced my

NPC bride tightly and didn't let go. The girl's resistance suddenly gave out and she started hugging me back, then giving me a smooch. We kissed for a long time and hugged one another, then my hand very slowly slipped under the thief-girl's clothing.

Check for Taisha's opinion of you failed
-15 to Taisha's opinion of you

"Hey now, none of that!" she said with a sudden frown, escaping my embrace with ease.

So much ease, in fact, that I didn't even have a shadow of a doubt that Taisha could have escaped my embrace at any second. She simply didn't want to and allowed herself to be kissed. The thief girl understood that I had realized it, and decided to explain her behavior:

"I won't hide it, you've become much more attractive and strong, Amra. You're no longer the clumsy unknown ragamuffin I once knew. Even the most terrifying orc cutthroats respect you and obey you unquestioningly. And I'm also prepared to go through fire and water for you as a leader. But your reputation as a terrifying pirate is not enough for me to give myself to you entirely without restraint. I must know that you deserve me beyond all shadow of a doubt. I need to know you're stronger, more capable and more agile than I am. And finally, it's important for me to know that you truly love and appreciate me. Convince me that you need me! Take me with you into the world of the undying!"

So, I'd been given the brush-off... I looked at my present +85 relationship with Taisha and realized that my companion wouldn't even allow herself to be kissed now. The thief, though, not waiting for any reply from me, stood up decisively from the bed, shook her luxurious red hair, adjusted her clothes and headed for the door.

"I'm going to sleep in the nook by the kitchen, with Irek, Yunna, Darius and Darina. It will be a lesson for you in the future about wandering hands!"

-10 to Taisha's opinion of you

With some kind of sixth sense, I realized that trying to persuade her in this situation was absolutely useless and would only make things worse. Evidently, Taisha was attracted to decisiveness, confidence and strength. My big-eared Amra would have only fallen further in the girl's eyes if he'd tried to beg her to stay. However, the quite abrupt reaction of my NPC companion was still quite uncharacteristic. I had allowed my mischievous hands to wander somewhat in the past. If Taisha didn't like it, she immediately gave me a smack with her finger, but it had never risen to this point. I suspected that the outsized reaction today had a reason, and I supposed I knew what it was. So, I didn't try to talk the thief girl out of it:

"You're free as a bird. Don't let me hold you. But before you go to the servants, I've got a few things to tell you."

The green-skinned beauty had already opened the door into the hall, but stopped in the doorway and turned involuntarily.

"I don't even recognize you today, Taisha! You were always proud and confident, considering yourself prettier and more beautiful than all others, and not without good reason. You announced your right to sleep in the captain's bunk yourself, the most prestigious place. All the orc pirates see you as the captain's companion and think of you as their master. But after meeting with the liberated and licentious dryad, you put your tail between your legs like a coward and decided to run into the tiny servant's room, even though with this act, you're immediately lowering yourself in the eyes of the pirates to that of a common servant, who doesn't deserve ceremony. Why'd you give up without a fight? Just ceding your place next to the leader to a prettier female? Taisha, you can't seriously consider yourself worse than the dryad in any way, right?"

"Angelica Wayward is a fully fledged undying, but I'm not!" Taisha blurted out in reply, nearly screaming. Angry tears started welling up in the girl's eyes immediately. "The dryad had a whole arsenal of the best and most expensive cosmetics. What's more, she dresses so flagrantly and behaves defiantly sexually. All the men always turn to look at her. I can't act like that, and don't want to!"

That must mean I had guessed, and the problem wasn't just Taisha and her bad manners. The Dryad Dancer and her provocative ways had made a very strong and onerous impression on the goblin girl. Now it was at least clear what to say in this case and how to reassure the upset beauty.

"Taisha, if you started behaving like that Dryad Dancer, I'd throw you out on the first island we came across and try to forget about you as fast as possible. I value you for entirely different qualities and would get very upset if you tried to imitate the lewd undying lady."

The green-skinned thief girl was standing in thought, then she returned into my cabin nevertheless and closed the door.

+10 to Taisha's opinion of you

"Maybe I really did give in to my emotions and act foolish. Forgive me if I did. It was just that Angelica Wayward put the devil in me today. She behaves like she's sovereign ruler on *White Shark*. When they see the naked dryad, all the sailors are dumbstruck and obediently do whatever she orders. And after the way Angelica danced for the crew on the upper deck, the orc pirates went in droves after her with wild eyes and caught every word, racing one another to fulfill her every wish."

I listened carefully to Taisha and frowned all the harder. I'm no specialist in the skills and abilities of dryads. It was better to ask my sister — she'd studied the issue. It must have been that Angelica Wayward had placed charms on my entire pirate crew. And meanwhile, the goblin beauty continued her tale:

"This evening, when the storm had slightly subsided, I saw the bay on the horizon with a bunch of fires and tons of sails. A big port. And though the first mate was categorically opposed to going there, Angelica Wayward wanted to see it. And the crew agreed! They nearly mutinied, demanding the dryad's wish be fulfilled! Ziabash Hardy and Shaman Ghuu couldn't do a thing, and were forced to agree. They just ordered the black flag lowered, and for the banner of a trade ship to be raised. The Dryad Dancer returned to the ship only a few hours later. And the Ogre Fortifier, who went ashore with her, was dragging all these vessels of perfume and boxes," Taisha pointed at the shelf of cosmetics.

"Stop, stop! The *White Shark* went into port?! Were there undying there?" I asked, immediately alarmed.

The huge ogre was quite head-turning all on his own. It was hard to miss him coming down a street. But if he was accompanied by the naked dryad, the couple were sure to have attracted attention. I'd mentioned the name Shrekson Bastard in my video clips several times, and even shown the Ogre Fortifier's face more than once. He was probably in the list of players being tracked. His appearance in the port must have been noted, and messages on his discovery were probably sent to interested clans. It wouldn't be very hard to connect the Ogre Fortifier's arrival to port with *White Shark* docking. Or, they could have just followed the titan and watched to see what ship he was returning to. This was the end of the secret of Amra's flight from the Island of the Wanton Widow... Didn't Leon himself understand that?! So, were there living players in the port or not?

Unfortunately, Taisha didn't know the answer to that question. The goblin girl herself didn't go ashore — first of all, no one had offered to take her and second, the thief girl was afraid of leaving the ship and getting lost. According to Taisha, after returning to the bireme, the dryad had thrown a fit to the titan, demanding he immediately take up his tools and make her some little cabinets to store her personal things. In doing so, the dryad had both cursed the ogre decisively, and made obvious remarks to the titan about the reward that awaited him for his labor. The goblin girl was put out the door fairly unceremoniously, and the howling of the saw and knocking of the hammer from the captain's bunk were interspersed with passionate groans for some time. Only when night fell had both undying left *Boundless Realm* and then Taisha returned to the cabin.

"The dryad called me a 'stupid bot,' and wasn't polite at all. She talked to the titan as if I wasn't even there, like I was a piece of furniture or an empty spot. You don't even know how insulting it was!"

"And what did they talk about, if it's not a secret?"

Taisha shrugged her shoulders and admitted that she didn't understand even half of what the undying had said in her presence. But the dryad's offensive words and disdainful remarks hadn't upset the thief girl so much as her behavior.

"Amra, the way Angelica acted for those orc pirates was disgusting to watch! The Dryad Dancer was constantly in a crowd of pirates, provoking them with her behavior and appearance, allowing all takers to paw at her, laughing at their filthy jokes and giving out lecherous promises. The Dryad Dancer teased the hot and bothered wild males all day, constantly walking the line, balancing on the blade of a knife. At times, it seemed to me that the lustful, drooling crowd would throw themselves on the dryad at any minute and rape her. But Angelica behaved as if that was totally normal. She simply lapped up the attention of all the men, leading the crowd and controlling it. These wild orcs were prepared to do anything just to get a tiny bit of attention from the naked dancer!"

"And how did Shrekson react to all this?" I wondered.

"The giant was very jealous of the others, but didn't dare oppose her and was always racing off to fulfill the Dryad Dancer's every wish. I'll admit, I even felt bad for him. Especially when he watched wide-eyed as his girlfriend kissed, hugged, and pawed at other men. But he didn't dare intervene and stop all the nonsense. I even..."

Taisha stopped her speech mid-word, because a bluish aura suddenly flickered up in the middle of the room. A crouching Valerianna Quickfoot slowly materialized inside it. My sister had entered the game? Strange. When I left, she was about to go to sleep.

"Hello, Taisha!" the green-haired girl greeted the NPC thief, stood to her feet, turned around and saw me. "There was no other way for me to get in touch with you, Tim. You aren't answering your phone, so I had to load up *Boundless Realm.*"

"Has something happened?" I asked, getting on guard, as I could hear panic in Val's voice.

"You could say that, Tim. Some lady I don't know came into our apartment. She opened the door with her own keys and came in without knocking. She said her name is Kira and that she owns the apartment. Quite young, and tall. She's rude and has red hair like a fox. She was asking about you, but I answered that you were at work. Then she put on a dressing gown and fluffy slippers and went into the kitchen. She said that pizza and soda was bad for my young body and that she'd make me a decent dinner. Tim, is all this ok?"

Despite all her impressive, and I'd even say exceptional abilities in virtual games, Valeria remained the very same home-body thirteen-year-old girl in real life, timid in conversation with other people and not at all accustomed to the idea that a stranger might come into her apartment.

I hurried to reassure my sister not to be afraid, and said that Kira really was the owner of the apartment.

"But she said she'd be staying the night!" Val said, notes of obvious panic slipping through in her voice.

On top of the little girl's stress, she now had to spend the night under the same roof as a total stranger, even if it was the owner of her apartment! In the virtual game, my sister wasn't afraid to fight in the dark night, at an unquiet cemetery with a whole host of ghastly undead, but in the real world, Valeria was very shy and easily embarrassed.

"Tim, she left the kitchen, and she's coming

this way!!! Bye! I need to leave *Boundless Realm* right now before Kira sees you on the ship!"

"Hold up, Val! There's no need to exit! You don't even have to turn off the monitor — I'm sure Kira isn't taking part in the hunt for the wyvern. She has no need for it. In fact, give her the microphone. I want to talk with her."

If Valeria was surprised, she didn't show it. I listened to my sister's indistinct explanation, then Valerianna Quickfoot's voice in the game changed:

"Hello, Timothy! Your videos are almost always first person. I feel like I've never seen Amra. You're such a big-eared little cutie! And who's the curvy barbie next to you? Ah, this must be that Taisha you're always droning on about. She really is a rare beauty for a goblin. Clearly not just a common model, but a character handmade by designers."

+10 to Taisha's opinion of you

It was funny to watch the green-skinned Taisha blush in embarrassment and lower her eyes to the floor. It was strange as well, of course. Normal NPC's in virtual worlds were programmed to entirely ignore things said by players not directly concerning them or the game. But the thief girl was listening carefully to the conversation of the undying about another world, and even reacting to it. I wondered how much of it all she understood.

Kira told me that she had returned by plane an hour ago from the designer clothing exhibition and immediately headed to my see my sister and me, as she was very worried for us and wanted to personally make sure that the unpleasant story with the gang trap had ended favorably. According to the beautiful redhead, she was horribly burnt out after the long day, and so just wanted to get some sleep in whatever room was available, if my sister wasn't opposed. I couldn't make out Val's reply, but it didn't seem like she'd objected.

"That's great, then! Dinner is almost ready. And it isn't that factory plastic you poison yourselves with, but natural and healthy food. So then, Valeria, go wash up and take your seat! And I don't want to hear any nonsense about you already being full."

Valerianna Quickfoot smiled laboriously at me, crouched down and exited *Boundless Realm*. As soon as the silhouette of the wood nymph had entirely faded, Taisha threw herself at me with questions. The girl was shaking with curiosity and impatience. But here then I, having long noticed the unhidden interest of my NPC companion in any information on the life of the undying, sniffed out an excellent opportunity to negotiate and, at the same time, have a heart-to-heart discussion with Taisha.

"Weren't you going to go sleep in the nook

with the servants?"

The thief girl grew obviously ashamed and, smiling uncertainly, answered:

"Amra, I've already apologized for my behavior. Yes, I was wrong, but I explained myself. If you'd like, I can tell you how stupid I was again. You can even call me a silly girl, if that will make things better. I won't get offended."

"Taisha, that's too much," I laughed. "I'd just like to avoid such misunderstandings in the future, because they cause problems in our relationship. And the best way to do that is for me to get to understand you better. I'd like at least to have complete information on your condition, skills and abilities. Ideally, I'd like to see your potential reaction to my actions in advance so I don't make such stupid errors in the future, too."

The thief girl thought for a moment, then decided to argue:

"Only skills. Everything else is too personal."

"No, Taisha. It's too little to understand you. It's important for me to see your hitpoints, endurance and hunger, opinion of me, all skills and characteristics. I mean, you demanded I become more agile than you. How am I supposed know your Agility in the first place? What if I've already surpassed you there long ago, but you won't admit it?! I have no interest in your inventory or wallet, and would never claim control over your actions. I'll even remove the demand to know your reaction in advance — that one really does seem a bit extreme to me. No girl would agree to be read like an open book, so others could shamelessly take advantage of their moments of weakness."

"That's better, but I still need to think seriously," my NPC bride warned me, and the world started lagging, becoming a slide-show of separate pictures.

Once again, the *Boundless Realm* servers lacked the power to calculate my companion's reaction... I didn't think I'd put the girl in such a difficult position this time, but for some reason, the beautiful NPC had a very serious outlook on my request to see her statistics. It was as if Taisha wasn't even there... I led my hand before the girl's eyes a few times, but no reaction followed. Still frozen.

Five minutes passed, then the surrounding world abruptly "caught back up with itself," but Taisha still looked like nothing but a lifeless wax statue. Leaving the girl in peace, I left the captain's cabin and headed out to inspect my ship. I was strongly upset by the tale of the chaos wrought here during the day, and the charms the Dryad Dancer had placed on the pirate crew. And unfortunately, I'd heard the truth — the first mate, with untold joy at my arrival, fully confirmed the words of the NPC thief girl about the crew getting out of control.

Ziabash Hardy also told me that, in the port

of Piren, where *White Shark* had docked this evening, he had seen several undying watching the Ogre Fortifier and Dryad Dancer closely, then milling about on the pier near the anchored bireme. It seemed my worst fears had come true.

"I should have just thrown that damned chest overboard while I had the chance!" I flared up angrily.

"Captain Amra, it's hard for me to talk about it, but the truth of the matter is that, in the case of a conflict between our undying, the crew would be sure to side with the Dryad Dancer. Only a few sailors remain true to their captain, I among them. But we'd just lose numbers in the case of a big fight."

I already understood that perfectly. Having beguiled my orcish crew with her witchery, Angelica Wayward was just one step away from becoming master of *White Shark.* I guess I should have listened to the sage advice of my sister and immediately gotten rid of the dangerous creature on my pirate bireme, even though it would have ruined my friendship with Leon. I was sure Shrekson would still be on the side of his flame now, would find justifications for her behavior and say that the dryad had yet to do anything bad to the captain of *White Shark.* It would have been good to speak with Leon or at least send him a message before taking any action against the ticketless passenger.

~ Stay on the Wing ~

By the way... it turned out I had two unread private messages from the Ogre Fortifier. The first had been written by Leon this morning:

"For some reason, we never are in Boundless Realm *at the same time to talk. You mostly play at night, and I can only play during the day. We're just living out of sync. I wanted to tell you that I might not be with our gaming team for a little while due to issues in real life. I've hired lawyers to start the divorce process. Yes, Timothy, I've made the difficult decision. Twenty long years I've been in the family yoke. My wife and three daughters, meanwhile, have spent the whole time taking advantage of me. They've squeezed me dry. My family only wanted my money, and they didn't give a damn about my desires, interests or dreams. After talking with Veronica, it was like my eyes were opened. I saw the light and suddenly understood that I could have achieved much more if not for my tunnel vision in the past and pointlessly wasted years."*

Well there's a twist... It was hard for me to form my own opinion on Leon taking such a consequential decision without knowing all the details of what had happened. No matter what, I wasn't planning on judging the former construction worker out of hand — maybe he and Veronica really were in love. Maybe it was a boundless love that simply washed away everything in its path. But now, at least,

Shrekson's behavior in the game was becoming more clear.

The Ogre Fortifier had written the last message three hours earlier, before he'd exited *Boundless Realm* together with his new mistress:

"Timothy, I thought I should write you some commentary so you wouldn't take Veronica's behavior in the game the wrong way, and all the more-so so you wouldn't think her a perverted nymphomaniac trying to tempt your pirate crew. She really has a very rare talent. She's a genius and beauty in real life, who set herself a high goal and is confidently pursuing it. In the virtual world, though, Veronica is a very particular and complex character to play. You know. The dryad dancer gains experience by dancing and speaking with members of the male sex. Tempting them with her evident availability, teasing, but never allowing anything. This is a very subtle gameplay style that simply must be seen to be understood. After a few mistakes at the beginning of the game, Angelica learned brilliantly how to balance on the edge, earning good experience and money. Just imagine it: she's already reached level thirty-five without ever picking up a weapon or killing anyone! And she is stopping direct streams of her gameplay now, even though that was her main source of income. She understands that, otherwise, the viewers will see the location of White Shark *and her captain."*

Just as I expected, Leon saw only the good

in his girlfriend. I then started thinking, staring into the distant night. Maybe we were demonizing the dryad too much. She never killed anyone and didn't even have weapons or weapon skills. After all, a corporate tester has to gain experience somehow. She's just playing the best she can. For her character, this is natural and normal. All the same, insuring myself against possible foul play wouldn't be a bad idea...

"Captain Amra," the first mate broke off my considerations. "There's one more aspect that's upsetting me. When we left the port of Piren, Angelica performed a strange ritual with our ship — she broke a bottle on the bow filled with fresh blood. She said: 'To good fortune.' The dryad said when doing it that the undying usually perform this ritual with a bottle of wine. But because, she said, the ship was a combat ship and named *White Shark*, she had to christen it not with wine, but blood. Shaman Ghuu was strongly opposed — he said blood would attract predators, but the sailors were elated by the dancer's idea and didn't let the shaman stop the ritual."

I had read at some point that, in ancient times, instead of breaking a bottle of wine on the bow, they would make a sacrifice to the gods, slitting the throat of a sheep or chicken on the deck and bathing the boards in blood. But that was all done with freshly built ships, not those that had already been sailing for some time. What was Angelica thinking? After all, the shaman was right: sharks and other maritime predators would be able to detect the fresh blood for dozens of kilometers. But what if that was her intent? She may have wanted to bring tragedy upon us. Or perhaps this was a method of tracking our bireme?!

"Ziabash, that ritual makes me very, very worried also. And the problem isn't only predators. Order the number of lookouts doubled. Or better yet tripled. Pay particular attention to the north-east, where we came from. I'll even give my spyglass to a sailor in the crow's nest. If the lookouts see any sail, even that of a rickety fishing boat, tell me at once! Also, order the sailors to bring the barrels of wax, saltpeter and tar to my cabin. And command them to also bring the empty pots. Pray to the gods of *Boundless Realm* that my suspicions are unfounded. But if they aren't, at least we'll have something to use against them!"

The captain's cabin immediately filled up with barrels and boxes. I even had to pick up the petrified Taisha and place her in the corner so she wouldn't get in the way of the orc haulers. But I had to be patient with the traffic — there was a nice little table made by Leon here, and no curious crew members would get under my feet while working, distracting Amra from the laborious and dangerous task.

~ Stay on the Wing ~

Alchemy Skill increased to level 16!

After making fifteen of the bombs for the ship's catapult, the chat window suddenly started flickering hysterically. Someone was desperate to talk with me, despite the late hour, the setting restricting anonymous contact and the distance of the pirate bireme from any settled areas. Of course, before reading the name of the sender, I'd already guessed that it could only be a corporate support employee. And in fact, it was: support_82. Some tech support guy.

"Greetings, Amra! Explain to me how you were able to do that?"

A somewhat strange question — nothing concrete. Not even a topic. What had I been "able to do?" Supposing this was related to the latest incident of my NPC companion freezing up, I began writing out my answer that Taisha had earlier started taking up massive amounts of processor resources and freezing up, which had caused complaints in the past.

"Yes, I know. We've already talked about that. But that's not what I'm referring to now. How did you manage to decrypt the library files from NPC number $FF0076-BB0733? Where'd you get the password to remove the external protection layer?"

I batted my eyelids, dumbfounded. He clarified that he was referring to my NPC companion by the name of Taisha Spark. Many programmers had long wanted to dig around in her files, but no one had managed to gain access, as everything was coded very intricately. But now, changes had been made to her password-protected archive — the protection had disappeared from the library and database portions, which had made many files available to see, but not edit.

I had to admit honestly that I had no idea about the files of the goblin thief girl, as I had never seen them.

"Very strange, Amra. It's just that, from what we managed to read in the now exposed libraries, you're a 'second administrator with read rights.' Actually, not you, but your character. The code is specific. You don't know? Well, alright. My apologies then, for distracting you from your work."

The man signed off. I, though, didn't stop filling pots with Greek fire, thinking hard as I did. This all meant that, after thinking for a long time, Taisha had agreed to give me access to her statistics after all. Now, I just had to wait patiently for my NPC companion to stop lagging, and she would tell me that herself.

Tracked Down

OH, THE FIRST hundred catapult rounds down! My big-eared goblin wiped the sweat from his forehead and straightened up, stretching his stiff back with effort. What hard work! Chop off a piece of the yellowish-gray stinking wax, mash it up in a big mortar, mix it with ground saltpeter and pour warmed tar over the resulting mixture, intensively mixing while risking catching fire at any moment. And I had to do it all on my own, because none of the orc pirates on board *White Shark* had the Alchemy skill. The most I could entrust to my assistants was heating the pitch in the kitchen, pouring it into pots and bringing it to me in the cabin to finish the process.

Three and a half hours of exacting, laborious work allowed me to level up several skills. I opened the logs and read the most recent events, causing me to melt into a satisfied smile:

Alchemy Skill increased to level 17!

Foreman Skill increased to level 18!

Alchemy Skill increased to level 18!

Athletics Skill increased to level 15!

Alchemy Skill increased to level 19!

Not bad at all. Another level of Alchemy and I'd be able to choose a specialization. What was more, the experience for making the incendiary rounds was also quite significant — eighty for each of the one hundred bombs. All in all, a good way of leveling my character, but it was very tiresome.

I walked up to the frozen Taisha and placed the tricorn pirate captain's hat with magnificent feathers on the living statue. Would you look at that! It looks good! Slightly adjusting the headwear, I took a few steps back and snapped a number of excellent screenshots. Then I took a few more, placing the spyglass into Taisha's hand. The pirate girl looked spectacular and even erotic in her form-fitting clothing. Ugh, when will you stop lagging and return to normal life, Taisha?

Looking at the guide on my companion, I shot up in surprise. How had I not seen this earlier? The NPC thief's stats were now available to see! Is this what the technical support guy had been talking about?

Taisha Spark
Goblin
Level-27 Thief
Hitpoints: 380 of 380
Endurance points: 302 of 302
Primary skills:
Lockpicking (A I) level 17
Trap Disarming (A I) level 7
Dagger (S A) level 10
Stealth (A C) level 18
*Dodging (A P) level 21 * Perk taken: Arrow Dodging*
Crossbow (S A) level 1
Secondary skills:
Pickpocket (A P) level 6
Athletics (C S) level 11
Culinarian (P A) level 10
Light leather armor (C P) level 6
Riding (A C) level 9
Lothario (Ch P) level 1

Next missions to trigger: Taisha's Envy (normal, personal), Taisha's Insult (normal, personal), Taisha's Silence (unusual, race-based)

There were three quests I could get from Taisha now? But under what conditions? How could I get them to trigger? I looked the settings over in various ways, flipping through. But more detailed information about the potential missions was unavailable. What a pity. I'd have to experiment in conversation with the girl to get the missions.

Now, onto my companion's skills... So, this all meant that, at level twenty-five, the thief girl had chosen Crossbow as her sixth main skill. All in all, it was logical, but Taisha hadn't yet had the chance to level it, so there was just a modest one next to it. As for a secondary skill, Taisha had chosen Lothario. Quite the strange choice... Just the right one to generate the rare quest Amra's Envy.

So then, what about the character parameters? First of all, of course, I was interested in Taisha's Agility, as the mission to overcome the thief in that parameter was still active. Woah! Taisha's effective Agility, considering all her skills, came to 151. Not bad, not bad at all. My big-eared Goblin Herbalist was currently at an agility of 128. Over the last few days, I'd noticeably reduced my lag in this statistic, but finishing the quest soon didn't seem likely.

Someone started knocking stubbornly on the door. In the doorway, there stood a thickset level-40 Dwarf Mechanic wider than he was tall by the name of Gnum Spiteful. His red beard looked singed and uneven, as if it had been nibbled at. Gnum, as I'd already figured out, was a nickname attached to the diminutive subterranean being, as the dwarf didn't reveal his true name. Spiteful was also unlikely to be the name of a subterranean clan, and was more likely a characterization of the hot-tempered and difficult nature of the mechanic.

"Captain Amra, the bow catapult tests were a rousing success! The bombs fly sixty or seventy steps, quickly catching fire in flight. When they splash down into the water, they're already a huge flaming ball, and the water where they fall stays on fire for some time. I need to keep practicing my aim, but all in all, the bombs fly fairly true. Also, we found out experimentally that its best to light the fuse after placing the bomb in the bucket of the catapult." At this, the dwarf gave an involuntary tug at his tormented beard with his thick, stubby fingers.

"Wasn't that obvious?" I asked, surprised at the strange urge to light the fuse before loading the catapult. "Did the deck suffer badly?"

Gnum Spiteful grew embarrassed, lowered his gaze to the floor and answered that a couple of the floorboards needed to be redone. It seemed the dwarf was expecting the captain to fill with rage, but a sigh of relief tore itself from me: a couple boards was nothing. I was worried there might have been a much worse outcome like a fire on deck. After allowing the dwarf to pick up another ten of the finished bombs, I closed the door after him and continued my work.

A flashing red icon suddenly appeared before my eyes: Thirst for Blood was in a critical condition! If I didn't solve the problem within an hour, my goblin would turn into a mad beast, throwing himself at anything alive. Somehow, I'd missed that. It had been far too easy for me to get blood in the last few days, and I hadn't taken measures in good time. Where could I get fresh blood in the depths of the night? My gaze involuntarily caught on the petrified Taisha, but I dismissed this apparently attractive idea out of hand — who knew about this complex next-gen NPC? Maybe the girl could have determined somehow what had happened while she was frozen?

I was forced to find another route. I left my cabin, found the first mate, and ordered him to bring the troll to me, along with the strongest of the orcs, and the dwarf mechanic. Soon after, the trio of pirates were standing at the entrance to my bunk, shifting from leg to leg in uncertainty.

"Here's the thing, young bucks. I'll be direct — I need a vial of blood from each of you! I want to try and create an antidote against poisoned arrows that I can use on each of you, if need be."

The huge troll just smiled gladly, revealing his yellow tusks. With his race's excellent regeneration, restoring the loss of two hundred milliliters of blood was just one minute's work. But then the orc, and especially the dwarf were on edge. I had to immediately add to my proposal:

"I have a barrel of good beer here," I said, plopping the barrel of *King of the Depths* onto the floor from my inventory. "So, my offer is this — a whole mug of foamy beverage in exchange for a dose of your blood for alchemical experiments."

Trading Skill increased to level 17!

"Captain, this is a different matter entirely!" said Gnum Spiteful, immediately starting to smile as he rolled back his left sleeve and took a sharp knife from his pocket. "Why not give a bit of my blood for a good cause?! Give me the vial, captain!"

The barrel half emptied, the trio of sailors left my cabin in an excellent mood. I then locked the door tight and started drinking.

Achievement unlocked: Taste tester (34/1000)
Achievement unlocked: Taste tester (35/1000)

I got nothing for the orc blood — I already had such a specimen in my vampiric collection, but all the same, the three vessels increased my Thirst for Blood scale to 10 of 24. Much better —

now I had a whole ten hours of sated peace.

-50 to Taisha's opinion of you

"Amra, what were you doing?!" came the voice of my NPC companion, having awoken at a very bad time. I could clearly hear notes of disgust and fear. "I trusted you!!!"

The law of unintended consequences. Murphy's law. The law of the fallen sandwich... If something nasty could theoretically happen, its sure to happen at the absolute worst moment. Why couldn't Taisha have unfrozen a minute earlier or later...? But no, she chose this very moment, and saw my big-eared goblin vampire drinking his fill of blood!

Now, the girl walked back from me and pressed herself to the wall in fear — she knew everything. Well that was it. The secret of my vampirism, and with it my peaceful life unhampered by vampire hunters had come to an end! That was the last thing I needed given the *Goons* and wyvern hunters already after me!

Mission received: Taisha's Silence
Mission class: Unusual, race-based
Description: Convince Taisha Spark to keep your secret, no matter what
Reward: 3200 Exp., +6 to maximum number of Thirst for Blood points
Optional condition: Taisha agrees to

~ Stay on the Wing ~

remain your companion
   Reward: +10 to Taisha's opinion of you, Stealth skill +1

Naturally, I immediately recognized that the name of the quest: Taisha's Silence. It was one of the missions listed as "next to trigger." That must have meant that the quick-thinking computer system of *Boundless Realm* had already figured out that Taisha might uncover the secret of my vampirism. Perhaps, the fact that she'd awoken at such a horribly uncomfortable moment was no coincidence at all.

But what should I do with her now? Kill her to stop her gabbing? She'd respawn in an hour anyway. Bite her and make Taisha a vampire? For that, I'd have to take the girl down somehow, or at least manage to get within Vampire Bite distance... No, not that!

After adopting an utterly calm, even careless demeanor, I said:

"I simply thought that, since you agreed to reveal your information to me, you deserved openness in return. I decided I could trust you with my biggest secret. Yes, Taisha, I am a vampire, and there's nothing that can change that. That's why I prefer to be in *Boundless Realm* at night, unlike other undying. And that is also the reason I need to periodically drink blood from little bottles or hunt for wild animals."

"Does Valerianna Quickfoot know?" the thief girl clarified with a frightened shivering voice.

"Of course," I said, demonstrating composure and calm. "I trust my sister completely. I keep no secrets from her. For my bride, this is the very moment of truth — are you prepared to accept me the way I am? I no longer desire to hide my secret essence from you. I will not hold you here if you'd like to leave, though."

Successful Charisma check
Experience received: 80 Exp.

Successful check for Taisha's opinion
Experience received: 800 Exp.
+10 to Taisha's opinion of you

The girl relaxed somewhat and moved her hand off the daggers on her belt. But the quest wasn't yet finished.

It seemed I had to continue the speech of reconciliation to fully reassure my NPC companion.

"I didn't say anything to the others. Neither Leon nor Max Sochnier are aware. I only trust the very closest to me — you and my sister. I was infected with vampirism very long ago from a bat attack. That was four years in the past. I couldn't get help right away, and now, it's too late. The bad part is that I cannot go into the sunlight and, as you've just seen, I have to drink blood sometimes. I know that it's a nasty spectacle to watch. My sister told me. And also, blood tastes fouler than foul. Especially fish blood. But, to me, blood is a necessary medicine I have to take to avoid losing my mind. The good sides — absolutely all undead from skeletons to bone dragons will ignore me and not attack. It isn't of much use, but it did save me from a ghastly Midnight Wraith once upon a time. And that's about all I can tell you about my disease."

"So, have you ever bitten me?" Taisha then started patting her neck to check for vampire tooth marks.

"I have not bitten you, nor the wood nymph, and I never would. The world around is full of potential prey, and, if need be, I can ask those near me for a bit of blood in exchange for drink or gold."

Successful Charisma check
Experience received: 80 Exp.
Successful check for Taisha's opinion
Experience received: 1600 Exp

The girl sighed noisily, then laughed and said with a happy smile:

"Now I see why you always looked so cute! They say vampires are very attractive, and you're no exception. Alright, Amra. I'm prepared to accept you as you are with all your flaws. And I won't tell anyone about your secret, I swear! But if you do decide to bite me and make me your nocturnal companion, at least warn me in advance so I can wash my neck off first."

Somewhere beyond the porthole, I saw a flash and a blast — lightning had struck the sea very near the *White Shark*. Taisha and I exchanged glances and both smiled at once. Such a thing had happened once before. And at that time, my NPC companion had said that such lightning was confirmation that the gods of *Boundless Realm* had heard our oath.

> **Mission completed: Taisha's Silence**
> **Experience received: 3200 Exp.**
> **+6 to maximum number of Thirst for Blood points (current value: 30), +10 to Taisha's opinion of you**
>
> **Stealth Skill increased to level 22!**
> **Level thirty-two!**
> **Racial ability improved: 70% resistance to poison**

And here, I didn't even have time to enjoy the new level and successful end to the crisis with Taisha before I heard someone drumming frantically on the door to the captain's bunk. I immediately recognized the alarmed voice of Johnny, the lookout boy:

~ Stay on the Wing ~

"Captain Amra! Sails on the horizon! And they're coming from the north-east, just as you warned! A big ship, following right after us!"

* * *

The horizon was glowing in the east, allowing me to see the large dark ship rowing against the wind in our direction through my spyglass. It had quite a lot of oars. Three rows to be exact. A trireme? How many people were in their crew?!

Next to me, noisily flapping her wings, VIXEN landed on deck. The level-21 Royal Forest Wyvern, her wings folded, crawled over to me and touched her forehead to mine. I was already mentally prepared so, this time, I didn't grow surprised at the visions appearing before my eyes.

A large ship of a sleek predatory design. A crimson sail. A bow figure in the shape of a water dragon. A long bronze battering ram bashes through the waves. Lots of armed people on the upper deck. Mostly bowmen. Among the one hundred fifty NPC soldiers ready for battle, twelve undying stand out. They are covered head to toe in luxurious "hand-to-hand" armor. A gracious light-haired elven bowwoman wearing a set of miniature plates that don't exactly constitute armor, but still provide more coverage than a swimsuit. Looking at it made me mentally quip, "these three tiny flaps are sure to protect me." A severe-looking earth mage. An even more severe-looking and ghoulish necromancer. And a whole gang of pets of the most outlandish appearances — from mummies enshrouded in rotting bandages and decaying zombies to flittering brightly-colored birds and a tall stone golem.

After thanking VIXEN for her help and giving the wyvern an affectionate pat on the neck, I started thinking. The markers were golden in color. I remembered the vice-president of the *Boundless Realm* Corporation had told me about that not so very long ago — this was precisely how those hunting my wyvern would be depicted. So then, this wasn't some random night-time encounter. They really had tracked me down. And that was almost certainly with the aid of the Dryad Dancer. Ugh, if Angelica Wayward crossed my path now, I'd knock her head off without considering the consequences!

But I'd deal with the guileful uninvited passenger later, if my big-eared goblin survived this night battle. For now, the most important mission was to counter this massive horde before they executed the boarding operation they were so clearly prepared for. I didn't soothe myself with pointless illusions, and understood perfectly that all my orc pirates wouldn't hold out even five minutes against twelve undying and their massive number of pets. And that wasn't considering the at least three hundred crewmembers on the trireme, who would also take action in the battle.

Help was needed immediately! I exited *Boundless Realm* and, throwing back the lid of my virtual reality capsule, reached for the phone lying next to me. As a matter of fact, in the game settings, there was a possibility to make calls to outside numbers directly from inside *Boundless Realm.* But that was a paid and fairly expensive function. Although the developers had introduced it long ago on player request, they hadn't wanted too many people to use it. Sometimes, it really was critically important to get in touch with someone. For example, a group leader just died in battle. Their groupmates would want to know how long they'd be gone and where to expect them back, but wouldn't have the time to leave the game to find that out. So, some gamers were willing to pay very serious money to make such a call. But the leadership of the *Boundless Realm* Corporation didn't want to especially promote that feature, given that making a call out of game would immediately take a person out of their state of immersion, depriving the virtual world of its reality.

I was worried that it would take a long time to wake Val up. She might not even have answered the phone at all, worn out after the long and nerve-wracking day, but my sister answered almost immediately.

"Not sleeping?" I guessed, and my sister

didn't deny it.

"Yeah, me and Kira are up in the living room. Even though it's late, for some reason, neither of us want to sleep. We're watching a teary melodrama on the big screen. The kind you normally shut off right away. We're eating crackers with real raspberry jam, drinking tea and, of course, chatting. Did you know that Kira has her own woman's clothing store? She showed me her internet catalog and even ordered a few stylish numbers for me!"

"Val, of course that is great, but I need your help right now! There's a ship with a dozen players and a bunch of aggressive bots quickly catching up to *White Shark*."

A very inappropriate phrase tore itself from Valeria's lips, with a meaning close to "boss, the jig is up!" But I didn't tell my sister off for her sharp tongue this time, just asked her to hurry up.

"Timothy, can Kira watch the screen when I play? She says that she's wanted to try out *Boundless Realm* for a long time but, for no good reason, she just never got off her butt to download and install the game on her home computer."

Generally, I didn't want random people watching my playing and seeing all the hidden details. But Kira? Was it really worth arguing over this point with the woman who owned the apartment my sister and I lived in? What bad could come of the fact that Kira saw things she had already known about for some time? And also, to be honest, I was interested in getting comments on my playing later from the highly-experienced tester. To put it briefly, I waved my hand and let her do it.

So then, I would have help from the wood nymph. Now, I had to decide if it was worth calling Leon? On the one hand, the last events connected with the Dryad Dancer did no favors to my image of the man. On the other, though... in the Ogre Fortifier's place, I would be offended if I wasn't called in for such an interesting and important battle, directly affecting the safety of my character. After all, in the case of defeat and the sinking of *White Shark*, both Leon's and Veronica's characters would go down to the sea floor with the ship, and the first things they'd see tomorrow after loading up *Boundless Realm* would be death from drowning or the teeth of a fearsome sea creature. After that would follow a character death message and something saying they'd have to wait an hour to respawn at the stone.

In the end, I took the decision to call Leon, internally worrying about the forthcoming difficult conversation on his flame and her subversive tactics on the bireme. But... "the number you've called has been disconnected," is all I heard when calling the former construction worker. I had no way of obtaining the Ogre Fortifier's help in the upcoming battle. I didn't even bother Max

Sochnier — he was on *Tipsy Gannet,* which was still in the bay on the Island of the Wanton Widow, more than four hundred kilometers away from us, so the Naiad Trader had no way of helping me.

So then, only my sister and I against twelve other players...

I lowered the lid of my virtual reality capsule and, a few seconds later, opened my eyes on the upper deck of *White Shark.* One step from me was Valerianna Quickfoot, alarmed and clearly bewildered as she stared into the distance.

"Amra, is your respawn point far?" was the first thing the wood nymph asked me, and that question was not at all to my liking — it seemed my sister didn't believe victory was possible.

I opened the game settings and saw that, in the case of death, my big-eared goblin would be reborn on the Island of the Wanton Widow. So then, it wasn't for nothing that I dragged myself up to the top of that hill in the rain at night to the respawn stone. Valerianna heard my reply and continued her thought:

"I don't have a wyvern amulet, so your valuable mount won't drop if I send you to respawn. You'll just lose some of your experience and pop up on the Island of the Wanton Widow. And from there, you can run off to the *Tipsy Gannet.* How is that not a way out?"

I cringed in dissatisfaction.

"Last night, Max Sochnier told me that the

island was under thick maritime blockade. So that's no way out. I don't consider the situation entirely hopeless, though. Our bireme is no slower than that trireme, and we have the long-distance catapult..."

"Yeah, but it's installed on the bow of the ship and cannot shoot backwards," my sister finished my sentence.

What?! I walked over to our weapon and made visually sure that the mount was well screwed into the deck. Just as Val said, the turning mechanism was capable of changing the direction of the catapult by fifteen to twenty degrees left or right, but one hundred eighty degrees was out of the question. It finally dawned on me that shooting at pursuers who were already at our stern would ultimately be impossible. And they were still gradually gaining on us, despite the fact that our orc pirates were really laying into the oars.

"How can they see us?" my sister asked in surprise. "We can only see them because of the glowing horizon at their backs. But to them, we are in the direction of the dark, cloudy skies and so would have a much farther rendering distance on their mini-maps. There aren't any lights on board. I checked right away. Nevertheless, a little while later, they accurately copied our slight turn to the left!"

I told her about the ritual the Dryad Dancer

had performed with the blood. Valerianna winced and agreed that it really was a convenient and reliable method of searching for a ship in the dark, if one of them had a pet fish swimming after the trail of blood and telling the master where to go.

"But here, it doesn't look like it's all just blood. For a long time, I've been seeing a butterfly on the edge of my mini-map flickering in and out of view behind us. So then what, I wonder, is this lone butterfly doing over the night sea? I do not know which of the rituals performed by the Dryad Dancer could explain this, but our pirate ship smells thickly of perfumes and lotions. The insect has a good sense of smell, so it could be following us that way, as if being led by a leash. I'll get rid of it now."

Next to the forest nymph, as if at the beck of her magic wand, there appeared a buzzing swarm of hornets. Valeria pointed toward the flying insect in the distance and her deadly insects dashed off into the night. Not even a minute later, a red beacon was lit over the head of Valerianna Quickfoot, meaning she was now a criminal.

"Well, I guess I was right — it wasn't just an insect, but somebody's pet," the wood nymph said, looking unhappily at the red marker over her head. "But, Tim, this didn't occur to me. Now, the pursuers have no need for pets — such a bright spotlight will be visible from afar. I've spoiled everything..."

~ Stay on the Wing ~

"Go down into the cabin for now," I suggested to my sister, and Valeria hurried to get off the deck.

Just after my sister went away, the first mate came up to me and, after nodding at the easily visible silhouette of the trireme, commented:

"A military ship of the Kingdom of Lars. I once had to spend six months as an oarsman on such a trireme. It was a frightening time. Three hundred oarsmen chained to their oars, plus another fifty slaves, who regularly come to sub in for the undernourished, ill or utterly exhausted. If you were feeling unwell, you had a week to get better or that was it. Overboard for shark bait. No need for hungry mouths if they aren't gonna work. Why I'm saying this, captain, is that they will not stop following us, and sooner or later, they will catch us."

"And what do you suggest, Ziabash?" I inquired, having a perfect understanding that my first mate wasn't merely trying to strike up conversation.

"I see two ways out, captain. For now, while our oarsmen still have life, and there's still a good distance, we could turn to that cliff shore over there," Ziabash Hardy said, pointing at a strip of darkness in the north, barely distinct from the horizon. "The shore there is, of course, horrible, and we only have one dinghy left, but if we still manage to come ashore, all the cliffs and hills there are dug through with subterranean tunnels like a moldering tree full of termites, but worse. That's the beginning of Rovaan-Dum — the mountainous abode of the dwarves, where the wee subterranean folk has lived for millennia. They say that you can get through underground from the ocean all the way to the Great Desert. It's probably all lies. But I can say for certain that we could escape into the subterranean tunnels of Rovaan-Dum and evade our pursuers. In our crew, we have a dwarf mechanic, Gnum Spiteful. He's a child of these lands and could perhaps be of some help."

My face lit up. There was a way to run, and that was good. But for me, leaving into the subterranean meant abandoning the *White Shark* and failing a mission given to me by the vice president of the *Boundless Realm* Corporation herself.

"In that case, we'd have to abandon a good ship, and also the crew — I can hardly believe the subterranean inhabitants would agree to allow two hundred cutthroats into their homes, after all. And the second option?"

"Turn *White Shark* around and try to board!" Ziabash Hardy stated decisively.

After seeing the incomprehension on my face, the experienced pirate hurried to continue:

"As a matter of fact, it isn't all so hopeless, captain. The crew on such a trireme will have one hundred warriors, one hundred thirty at most. Sure, they have well-trained royal soldiers and experienced sailors, but we have more sabers. What's more, if we can get down to the lower decks of the trireme, we'll be able to free their slaves. People shanghaied into service rarely learn to make peace with their fate, so many will join our side if we promise them liberty. As a matter of fact, I once gained my freedom from slavery the very same way — soldiers from a neighboring kingdom broke onto the oar deck, killed the overseers and declared that they would free all slaves that helped in the battle. At that time, many of the oarsmen took up the call. I was among them. To be honest, I was the only volunteer to survive that bloody skirmish. That's actually how I earned the nickname Hardy."

I didn't tell the first mate that his plan was absolutely unrealistic. And it was. The twelve undying would cut down half the crew of *White Shark* before the ships even got close enough to board. I just looked at the catapult sitting pointlessly on the bow of the bireme.

"Alright, Ziabash. We need around an hour to get ready, so don't let the oarsmen reduce speed. In that time, we need to arm the crew, and mount more wooden shields on the bow of the ship so the catapult firing unit and our boarding team don't get shot to pieces by the bowmen. I heard you bought a barrel of rum in port to replace the empty one. Now is the very time to roll it on deck. Call the shaman to my chambers — I've got a job that's just up his alley. And order this horrible trade-ship flag exchanged out for our black banner with the white shark! In one hour's time, we fight!"

Foreman Skill increased to level 19!

* * *

The hour I asked for wasn't just to mount shields on the ship. I also wanted to use the time to figure out a way of safeguarding the wyvern-controlling medallion. I had a simple idea: you cannot lose that which you do not have. If my big-eared goblin did not have the valuable medallion when dying (considering the situation, such an outcome looked entirely possible), then nothing would drop. No, I wasn't preparing to throw such a valuable object overboard — that might be seen by the corporation as an attempt to subvert the mass event. Also, VIXEN might just lose all connection with me and fly away for good.

But giving the medallion to one of my pets for a short time... Well, it was never written in the rules of the hunt that the person in control of the wyvern *had* to be carrying the object in their bag or wearing it on their person. Perhaps, there was no room in my inventory. And that really was close to the truth. I already had Irek and Yunna carrying some of my things. Who could tell me I wasn't allowed to use my companions' slots to store items? From there, the idea is easy to understand — if the NPC pet is killed a bit before its master, it will respawn at the same time as its owner in a safe place, and with all the valuable objects in its inventory.

"Irek, come over here. I've got something for you," I called the goblin boy over. "Open your bag!"

SYSTEM ERROR!
The inventory of NPC $FA1276-B00133 is overfilled
Error code #LOC/ER-009875
This message has been sent to Boundless Realm *tech support*
We apologize for the possible inconvenience

I tried to place the bronze medallion in Irek's backpack, but it fell onto the floor. Although there was room in the goblin boy's backpack, I couldn't place the quest item inside it. I couldn't put the medallion around the NPC boy's neck either. Understandable... I lifted the valuable object and left the upper deck in search of my winged mount. VIXEN was sleeping on the boards next to the catapult, rolled up into a ball like a kitten. I embraced my mount by the neck and attached the medallion to the wyvern.

LOGIC ERROR!
Infinite recursion
NPC $FF0A11-CB0223 is waiting for external commands originating from its own logic
Error code #LOC/ER-009955
This message has been sent to Boundless Realm *tech support*
We apologize for the possible inconvenience

Despite the logic error, I did manage to clasp the necklace onto VIXEN. Got it! It worked! Now, the upcoming battle with a whole dozen undying seemed more like an amusement park ride — scary and dangerous at first glance, but on a deeper level, you know nothing is going to happen. If I died, I risked only losing some experience, but not my unique winged mount.

All the same, I didn't want to merely take part in the sea battle. I wanted to win. To do that, I called Shaman Ghuu over and explained the essence of the mission:

"We're going to turn around and head toward the enemy. We'll shoot first from the bow catapult, taking advantage of its high range in comparison with normal arrows and crossbows. There won't be time to reload the catapult, though. Our ships will reach one another before we'll be able to get the arm pulled back again. We'll only have one chance to shoot, and we need to put all our rage and anger into it, doing as much damage as possible. We won't just load one bomb into the catapult bucket, but ten or maybe even twenty. However many fit. The bombs will be tied together with rope, so they will form a huge flaming mass as the net spreads out in flight, hopefully catching on the trireme's rigging — the mast, the sail, the boom — and fire will rain down from the deck."

The orc shaman, having imagined the picture, gave a nod of approval and gnashed his fangs into a smile.

"Captain Amra, normal fire won't be enough. We should also imbue our bombs with death magic. I can charm any and all objects, up to and including those bomb pots. The fire will nourish itself with the life force of the dead and suck the energy from the living, burning stronger and stronger with every dead victim!"

"These were the very words I was hoping to hear from you, shaman! We need to put as much ghastly magic into this single shot as possible, and death magic is an excellent choice! But that isn't all I wanted. The fire these bombs make is already quite hard to put out with water, but the wood nymph also said that she could place a spell from her water magic arsenal on it. That way, she said, the fire not only won't go out, if they try to extinguish it, it will only burn stronger. I want you to help Valerianna charm the bombs with this sophisticated magic! And call all the gods and demons of *Boundless Realm* to your aid. We simply cannot afford to fail!"

Night Boarding

VEN I, CAPTAIN of the bireme, was fearful when looking on the ghastly ugly brutes gathered on the deck of *White Shark*. Fierce, wild orcs in combat paint were howling, stomping their feet and waving their weapons in the air, getting themselves worked up into a state of frenzy. After eating fly agaric or some other hallucinogenic mushrooms, the berserkers were just rolling around on the deck, howling hysterically and causing themselves bloody wounds, enraging themselves further before the battle.

In the small space unoccupied by the armed horde, there stood a hurriedly constructed sacrificial altar. On top of it, wincing from the cold wind and briny spray hitting her naked body was Yunna. The girl was shivering, sneezing, and kept asking for the offering to be made fast before she got sick. But Shaman Ghuu, wearing countless skulls, coins and bones on his necklaces, was in no rush and asked the victim to bear it a bit longer, as the moon had yet to come out from behind the clouds, while the design in blood on the goblin girl's body had yet to dry. The shaman was extremely put together and serious. Periodically adjusting his heavy, feathered headdress with his shivering hands, he continued mumbling out incomprehensible phrases in orc language.

The shaman himself had announced that a live sacrifice would be necessary — in his words, there was no reason to hope for the mercy and blessing of the gods of *Boundless Realm* without such a ritual, which was to say nothing of the demons. What was more, Ghuu was instistent that the outcome of the sacrifice would be much more effective if the blood spilled on the altar came from a woman.

"I know the best candidate for such a sacrifice, but she's not in *Boundless Realm...*" I answered the shaman. Ghuu laughed in reply:

"That's right, captain! It would be the greatest satisfaction to offer up Angelica Wayward for a good cause! But she isn't here now, and we'll have to think over our options."

Yunna overheard our conversation, and volunteered all on her own, asking me a few times beforehand to make sure she would respawn an hour later alive and well. I assured her that she would, so the issue of an appropriate victim was solved beneficially. Now, though, we still had to remedy the problem of the shaman himself. The issue was that Ghuu Ghel All-Knowing had expended too much force creating the ghastly curses and was barely able to stay on his feet. Thankfully, I had a Strength Restoration Elixir on hand. It was hurriedly poured down the shaman's throat and chased with a glass of strong rum, returning the young orc to life. He finished drawing the complex pattern made up of strange symbols on Yunna's body and, now, Ghuu was waiting for the optimal time to perform the ritual, warming the crooked, serrated sacrificial knife in his freezing hands.

All in all, I had been extremely fortunate to find the shaman — the strong young orc had rich experience and, crucially, supported me in all undertakings. The shaman, in line with the first mate and another few experienced sailors, was a key NPC on the pirate bireme, and his opinion of me governed the loyalty of the whole crew.

Ghuu was also nervous, given that he'd never before undertaken such rituals. So, I gave the shaman an uplifting smack on the back and quietly assured him that it was sure to go off without a hitch. From another perspective, it probably would have looked strange — a funny-looking big-eared goblin staring at and encouraging a huge muscular orc shaman, who then smiled thankfully in reply, displaying his tusks and returning to a calm state.

Foreman Skill increased to level 20!
You may now choose your first specialization in this skill

I waited a long time for that skill to reach level twenty, and already had a perk picked out. Increasing the number of NPC's I could control by one and a half times was pretty sweet, as was the ability to slightly improve the stats of my workers. But, considering the present facts and needs, I chose a different one entirely:

Specialization chosen: Improved Worker Loyalty (+50 to all loyalty checks)

What a surprise this would be to the Dryad Dancer or any other player that tried to lure my allies onto their side in the future! What was more, I had read from the system information that this perk worked not only on hired workers (in this case the orc pirates), but also on all my pets, mounts and NPC companions as well. It was very important to VIXEN's case, given that she was not formally under my control right now, and was still with me exclusively due to her good opinion of me. And for the unpredictable Taisha, another +50 to all loyalty checks would help avoid a significant amount of eccentricity in the future.

"The time has come!" the shaman cried out loudly, seeing the moon come out from behind the clouds.

The moonlight had barely touched the body lying on the altar when Ghuu swung and plunged the crooked knife with a precise strike into the girl's heart. Yunna's body lit up a strange shade of violet, then disappeared without a trace. The victim's brother Irek, who had been standing next to me, lurched forward but I held the goblin boy back. Tamina Fierce's children had only been made undying recently, and though they had already survived one death, they were not yet used to it.

ATTENTION!!!

The blessing of the gods of **Boundless Realm** *has been received for the whole crew of* **White Shark**

For any actions requiring luck checks: chance of success increased by 10%

Resistance to all types of damage increased by 15%

All negative effects removed

The following effects are active: Night Vision, Stone Skin, Four-Leaf Clover, Keen Sight, Level-11 Regeneration

Duration of blessing of the gods effect:

300 seconds

299... 298... 297... We had less than five minutes blessing. What were we doing wasting time then?! I got up high and screamed my lungs out:

"Helmsman, sharp tack to the starboard! Everyone take hold of something!... (what followed was unprintable)... You're deaf bait for clumsy toads! I ordered you to hold on! Set a course toward the enemy! Weapons at the ready! Everyone take cover behind the big shields! Why is no one manning the catapult?! Where's that damned dwarf?!"

From the mess of fallen bodies, issuing an intricate series of curses, Gnum Spiteful emerged. I pointed him at the catapult, which was ready to fire, then motioned toward the quickly approaching trireme:

"If you hit, you can be the first to collect trophies! But if you miss, I'll order your red beard turned into a mop, and I'll force you to wash the whole ship with it!"

"Don't you worry, captain, I won't miss," the dwarf said, walking up carefully to the catapult, trying not to get too close, or touch the bucket filled with bomb pots. They smelled of a ghastly evil even to me, a character with no magical abilities whatsoever. "Give me a torch, now!"

Irek extended Gnum Spiteful a lit torch,

after which he hurried to get away from the dangerous contraption. The dwarf got down on his haunches, looked at the approaching target and turned the catapult mechanism with his free hand. After that, drooling and raising his thumb, he gave a dismayed wince and turned the mechanism another half radius. One after the other, the dwarf lit the bombs in the bowl of the catapult, quenched the torch in a basin of water, then picked up a heavy sledgehammer.

The heavy hammer hit out the stopper and the catapult cast the bunch of burning projectiles upward with a whooshing sound. Leaving behind a sparking trail of smoke, the fifteen bright stars flew up into the night sky. We all watched with a fading in our hearts as the fiery balls flew through the sky, growing brighter with every second. The bunch of flames drew out a sharp parabola, then started downward. It seemed about to miss — the helmsman of the trireme saw the danger in time and made a hard turn to the portside, maneuvering his ship out of the way. A moan of disappointment rang out from all around.

But suddenly a miracle happened — the flying pots gave a slight correction to their trajectory and slammed right into the big ship! Some of the tied-together pots got mixed up in the rigging, instantly turning the mast and sail of the trireme into a huge burning torch. Other bombs rained a deadly precipitation down on the deck. A wave of burning fire engulfed the trireme. Well, well, well! That was fucking awesome!

Once upon a time, I had been forced to sit through old videos on military conflicts from the beginning of the 21st century about heavy flamethrowing systems or thermobaric munitions. What I saw on the deck of the trireme was a faithful recreation these terrifying combat scenes — a great number of separate fires conjoined into one all-devouring flame, condemning those inside to a near certain death.

A few messages flickered up on my screen:

Experience received: 480 Exp.

Experience received: 112 Exp.

Experience received: 590 Exp.

...

Exotic Weapons skill increased to level 13!

...

Experience received: 320 Exp.
Experience received: 490 Exp.

Level thirty-three!

~ Stay on the Wing ~

Level thirty-four!
Racial ability improved: 75% resistance to cold
Racial ability improved: 80% resistance to poison

Dodge Skill increased to level 21!

The last entry was related to a meter-and-a-half long arrow that whizzed past my ear and slammed into the mast — the ship approaching us, engulfed in flames had a ballista on its bow. I spent a few seconds with my eyes peeled in horror, watching the flaring hell on the deck of the enemy ship as it approached us. For some reason, I lost all desire to board the ship and take up close combat.

"Helmsman, turn hard to starboard! Avoid the battering ram! God damn you, chop the boarding hooks off! Dim-witted crustaceans, you're dying like flies! Get behind the shields away from the arrows! Nymph, quickly make me a ghost in the crow's nest. Give them a target to shoot at!" I brayed out. The crew of the flaming trireme was trying to latch into our ship in with their grappling hooks and get onto our ship away from their flaming hell.

Such a great many different events were compressed in the following two minutes that I have to admit I got lost. I figured them all out in greater detail by the logs and recordings. First, we were rained down upon with a wave of deadly arrows from the trireme. The deck of the enemy ship was significantly higher than ours, so the enemy bowmen reaped a bloody harvest, taking down the orcs of my boarding team. My bowmen and crossbowmen were not asleep at the wheel, either though. I noticed a few dead NPC bowmen on the trireme, but we lost that round of battle cleanly. At some point, Irek died. When exactly it happened, I did not see. I only noted the death of my NPC companion by the grayed out team-member icon, that eventually faded to nothing.

After that, the ships collided with a groan. And although the experienced Ziabash Hardy standing at the helm of the *White Shark* did manage to avoid a direct strike from the trireme's bronze battering ram, the sides of our ship took a noticeable blow. The glancing impact knocked nearly everyone off their feet. There were a great many broken oars and shouts of maimed oarsmen... It all came together into a unified uncontrollable situation. But there's always a silver lining — the strike turned *White Shark* away from the heavier trireme, and the grappling hooks that did reach our boat were all cut down. The gap between the ships immediately widened to around seven meters, and was still expanding quickly. Not able to stay on their feet or simply in too great a rush to jump to *White Shark*, our opponents were plopping into the water, and among them were not only NPC's but also living players.

I led my gaze over an armor-bound level-89 human paladin as he sunk like a stone to the bottom of the sea. A few seconds later, a level-77 human barbarian went down to check up on him — this one could swim, but a blow from a heavy oar to his head turned the experienced swimmer into an amateur diver.

The next enemy, though, was a significant threat... I couldn't even hold back a frightened scream, when the flaming level-178 (!!!) human warrior made a short run and jumped at us right over the water. I didn't even have an idea of if we'd ever manage to stop such a high-level hand-to-hand fighter or not. Thankfully, Gnum Spiteful was standing near the edge and, like a tennis player accepting a serve, met the flying enemy in the air with his two-handed sledge-hammer. The ringing when the hammer hit the metal armor was deafening. The swordsman was sent flying back and headed off after the paladin to explore the bottom of the ocean. I do not know how much experience was gained for the swordsman, but the Dwarf Mechanic lit up for some time from the several level-ups he got in a row.

The few NPC soldiers that did manage to jump over to *White Shark* were given a very harsh reception — in a matter of seconds, they were torn to shreds by the enraged orcs and the Gray Pack.

A stone golem, conjured by an enemy mage right on our deck, met the same fate — he was very quickly taken down and beaten to a rocky pulp. At that moment, I noticed that one of the enemy players was shown on the mini-map with a nonstandard marker — neither a red nor a black skull, but a simple black triangle. That symbol meant the player had earlier been added to my black list, but who it was and why I didn't like them was something I didn't have time to look into. Through a loophole, I shot practically all the poisoned needles I had with my blowgun, but the enemies just wouldn't stop coming!

Then, right before my eyes, Taisha died — the second the girl stuck her head out from behind one of the big wooden shields, a crossbow bolt flew right between her eyes. I tried to figure out which of the enemies had killed my companion, but doing so nearly made me meet the same fate myself — three arrows whistled right past my head.

"Amra, behind you!" came a heart-rending cry from Valerianna Quickfoot, drawing my attention.

The dead orcs were all standing up. Irek and even Taisha stood up as well. All of their gazes were empty, not reflecting a drop of life force. Not paying any mind to the bolt sticking out from between her eyes, Taisha unsheathed her daggers. The enemies had a necromancer raising our fallen. Damn...

~ Stay on the Wing ~

"No, no, no. Not on my watch!" shouted Shaman Ghuu, pulling a little bag off his belt and throwing it at the herd of undead.

A yellow-green powder, acrid and burning the eyes, blocked my view of the deck for a few seconds and, when it settled, all the dead were again lying motionless and calm, as nature intended. Fortunately, that was the last tense moment of the battle. The *White Shark* put some distance between it and the burning trireme, and was getting further away still. Magical shrapnel flew in our direction another a few times, but it didn't do particular harm to either ship or crew.

"Report on our losses!" I demanded from the first mate just after catching my breath. In his left shoulder, there were two visually identical arrows with red fletching.

Ziabash Hardy, whose life bar was down in the orange, was in a very gloomy state and answered without hiding his annoyance:

"Captain Amra, we lost seventeen from the boarding team. Also dead are your companions Irek, Taisha and one warg. Eighty-three were wounded, seven of whom severely. I suppose the troll will regenerate, though. His arms were ripped out and his head was split in two but, in a day, there'll be no more trace. As for trophies, there were none, and our ship needs repair..."

The trophy situation had not turned out for the best... I looked dejectedly at the flaming trireme, quickly falling astern. On it, there seemed to be a battle raging for the right to ride in the only dinghy not to get destroyed. The undying won this bloody skirmish — all eight of the players who survived to that point took places in the boat and started rowing in despair to the far-off, barely visible shore on the horizon.

"Now we can take trophies!" I promised with a grin. "Turn *White Shark* around. set a course for the lifeboat! Let's see how much those undying are willing to pay to avoid meeting the sea floor!"

"Amra, don't rush it! The players aren't gonna get away from us. There's seventeen kilometers to shore. They'll be rowing for an hour at least," my sister stopped me. "Now, we'd better go to the burning ship. I can put out the flames on the trireme, but it will take some time. Such a large ship has a fairly decent value all on its own. What's more, on the lower decks, there are three hundred oar-slaves chained to their oars. And in the hold, there's probably plenty of interesting stuff as well."

"The mavka's talking sense!" shouted someone from my crew, suddenly inspired. "We should save the trophies before they burn up! And we also need to help the slaves avoid the horrible fate of being burned alive. If any of them want to become pirates, we'll take them on. The rest we can sell! They undying won't get far! We can catch them later!"

~ Stay on the Wing ~

Seeing such a rare unity of spirit among the crew, I ordered them to turn *White Shark* around.

* * *

"There's no sense in trying. I'll never let your rickety little boat reach the shore. I'll catch you first. Stop your pointless rowing and listen up. I'm giving you the chance to buy your way out of death, avoiding the loss of experience and valuable items. I offer two options.

One: you pay five hundred coins each and surrender. Then, we cast lots. Five of you remain alive and unharmed, and will be released on shore. But three will be executed — hung from the boom, made to walk the plank, keelhauled, or I'll think up something else. In any case, I am now a pirate, and the viewers of my video clips are expecting that kind of content.

Two: you pay one thousand coins each, and only one of your eight will be so unfortunate. A good outcome no matter how you look at it — seven of you will remain alive. Those seven can even watch the loser get executed if they like. I'll let you wave your hand to the camera and say 'hi' to your friends and relatives — in any case, my video clip will be watched by millions of viewers. When else will you get the chance at world-wide fame.

So then, two minutes to think, then White Shark will come sink your boat, and there will be no survivors. Goodbye, then. Think fast.

Captain Amra."

Forty seconds later, a message came into my mailbox from someone by the name of Eruta ibn-Aruta, a level-ninety earth mage:

"We discussed it and suggest a third option: we pay two thousand coins each (sixteen thousand in total), and no one dies. What do you say?"

I smiled — the eight players rushing to shore had all agreed they'd never make it. I quickly dictated a reply:

"If I let you all go alive, it will be boring both to you and my viewers. What's more, my NPC companion Taisha died in that battle, so someone has to pay for her death. My pirate crew simply will not accept any other way. And also, at the end of the day, wouldn't you like to test your luck? What else could put your nerves on end as much as Russian roulette, with your own life on the line?!"

The reply to that came in almost instantly:

"Alright. We'll transfer you the eight thousand right now. But we expect you to swear to obey the conditions of our agreement and let seven of us walk free. We then will swear not to escape and to behave peacefully."

Not long after, I had eight undying kneeling before me on the deck of the *White Shark*, their hands bound behind their backs. The level-ninety earth mage, a level-eighty-eight necromancer, a level-sixty-two elf bowwoman from the *Firstborn* clan, a level sixty-six half-elf assassin, three human warriors from the *Warlords* clan, and a level-one-hundred-two paladin from the same clan. By the way, the person in my blacklist was the elf lady.

> *Dorielle Flexible_Doe*
> *Light Elf*
> *Level sixty-two Bowwoman*

I had to search in the game logs to figure out in what way this elf lady had ever offended me to earn her place in the blacklist. The result of that search made me raise my eyebrows in surprise — this player had taken part in the night attack on Tysh, and killed Taisha's relatives. I'd promised my NPC companion to find this elf and punish her appropriately. Bad luck, knife-ears. I now already knew the outcome of my "random draw" in advance. All that remained was to wait for Taisha to respawn so she could personally be present to witness this act of revenge.

Four hard-working orcs dragged a massive chopping block normally used by our cook to chop meat onto the deck and set it before the captives. All riddled with deep chop marks and covered with dried blood, it was the closest thing we had to an execution block. The ghastly executioner, wearing a red sack over his head, nodded in approval and started sharpening his two-handed poleax. It turned out very natural and fitting to the ambiance. Based on the pale faces of the eight captives, it got to them.

At that time, I found a small empty barrel, a piece of paper and a quill. I ripped the sheet into eight pieces and wrote the name of the victim in blood. As the captives sat and watched me attentively, I provided some commentary on my actions, explaining that I was writing their names on the slips of paper, and would be letting blind fate decide who would be done in. It should be said that all eight papers had the very same name on them, as well: Dorielle Flexible_Doe. Sure, I agree. It wasn't sporting or fair to the bowwoman, but this way, I was preparing to fulfill a promise I'd once made to my companion.

By the way, as for Taisha — the goblin girl appeared next to me with a frightened shriek and spent a few seconds batting her eyelids in surprise and confusion, then led her hand over the bridge of her nose, eventually becoming convinced that she was unharmed. I walked up to Taisha, embraced her and pressed her to myself, reassuring the respawned NPC beauty. I smiled, trying to keep my unhappy thoughts to myself as not to cast a shadow on the joy of the newly returned girl. Though there was something to be upset about here — minus two levels to Taisha, she'd fallen to twenty-five. The goblin beauty was lagging further and further behind Valerianna

Quickfoot and I in level. Even the wolves of the Gray Pack were all at thirty, now.

After acquainting her with the situation, I explained to the redheaded beauty that it was she precisely that should draw the lot to decide which of our captives would live, and who was fated to die. Taisha tried to point out the elf woman with little head nods and whispering, but I asked my companion not to say anything. The thief girl stuck her hand in the barrel in silence and pulled out a piece of paper folded into a tube.

"The person being executed is Dorielle Flexible_Doe!" I loudly voiced the result, and Taisha jumped for joy, not hiding her glee.

"Let this be a reminder of the torched village of Tysh and all the goblins you killed there! May the heavens curse you for that!" the thief girl shouted, jumping around the bellowing bowwoman.

"And not only for that!" the executioner pulled the red hood off his head and everyone took a step back in horror.

The face of the person was horribly burnt and looked like nothing but one solid wound. No hair, no eyelashes, the skin in places red and in others charred. A ghastly spectacle...

"I am the boatswain from *Princess Amelia*, the only survivor from the whole crew of the trireme after it was captured by pirates. This knife-eared bitch kicked me out of the lifeboat, taking my place for herself! I spent gods-know-how-long in the water, kicking my feet and flailing my hands at the sharks, who were growing more and more impudent with every minute. I thought it was the end for me, but I got picked up by pirates. And they even gave me the chance to avenge the undying who sank my ship!"

It turned out well. It wasn't for nothing that I ordered the life of this boatswain saved, although he remained loyal to an oath given to the king and refused to join my pirates outright.

"There's nothing to accuse me of!" Dorielle squealed hysterically, turning to everyone present at once. "This burned monster doesn't even have a name over his head. He's just a stupid programmed bot, like millions of others. If one dies, another one just like him will come to take his place. Why should I have let a piece of program code take a seat in the lifeboat?!"

I walked out in front, pointing at the badly wounded executioner standing with the poleax, and objected to the elf lady:

"This burned boatswain has his own name. It's Staur Strong. It's just that you haven't earned his trust, so he didn't think it necessary to reveal any information about himself. All the sailors here," I said, pointing at my crew, "have their own names too, and a biography, but all you can see is 'orc pirates.' The goblin girls you killed in the village of Tysh also had names, but you didn't care about that, either. You just killed them no qualms. You prefer to 'farm bots' instead of delving deeper into the mysteries of *Boundless Realm*. But meanwhile, it's much more complicated than it looks at first glance. Here, look! Actually, everyone look!"

Down from the pinkening morning sky, loudly flapping her broad wings, my level-22 Royal Forest Wyvern descended onto the deck of the *White Shark*. The flexible, emerald-colored flying snake looked very beautiful — a true treasure, justifying the whole grand-scale event with her magnificence. VIXEN opened her toothy maw and carefully set a still living level-3 Narwhal Whelp before me on the deck.

"Who's my little smarty pants! What a great hunter you are. You never let your big-eared Amra go hungry!" I said, placing the prey into my inventory. I then embraced my beauty by the neck and turned to see the captives watching the valuable mount with hungry eyes. "Would you call this 'just a piece of code,' too? A mere hunting trophy? What can I say, Dorielle, you wanted to get to know my wyvern better. Here's your chance. You couldn't hope for a closer look — not only will you be able to touch VIXEN, you'll see her in the greatest possible detail, from the inside. In fact, you'll even become part of her. VIXEN, you may eat the elf woman!"

My eternally hungry winged snake didn't

need to be asked twice. VIXEN was instantly next to the crouching captive and, her mouth open wide, swallowing her prey whole like a snake, as if pulling herself over it. Dorielle screamed so loud my ears started ringing. The snake, meanwhile, quickly swallowing the victim's head, pulled herself over the elf girl's shoulders centimeter by centimeter. A toxic acidic drool started gushing from the wyvern's mouth, making the bowwoman's skin turn black. The miniature armor pieces that covered the girl's body hissed and started smoking.

To be honest, the spectacle of the wyvern devouring the elf lady whole was pretty gross. If I'd known in advance just how nasty it was gonna look, I might have chosen another method of execution. But not everyone shared my feelings, or was battling nausea. The earth mage stood up, walked closer and said with a happy snicker:

"I wonder what will go first: her health or her clothing and equipment?"

"She'll suffocate before the acid kills her," objected one of the warriors, also watching the ghastly spectacle wide-eyed. "I wonder if the bowwoman is playing with full immersion? If so, these must be quite unpleasant sensations..."

Her hitpoints ran out first. Either that or the elf simply suffocated but, in any case, the victim finally stopped twitching. At that point, the winged snake swallowed the rest of the body whole in one minute. Through the fairly thin skin of the wyvern's puffed-out belly, I could make out the shape of her body.

Achievement unlocked: Player killer (6)

Animal Control skill increased to level 8!

Level thirty-five!
Racial ability improved: 80% resistance to poison

VIXEN lit up with colorful sparks and grew visibly in size, having hit levels twenty-three and twenty-four in one go. The winged snake licked her lips with her split tongue and looked carnivorously at the seven other captives. All seven of them shuddered from her cold, emotionless gaze.

"No, no, enough out of you!" I said, poking the snout of my winged mount away from the bound undying. "We'll play fair, as we agreed. You're all free to go. Irek, unbind them! The boat's over there in the water. The shore is very near. Whoever wants to, feel free to take some screenshots with the wyvern for the memories."

"No thanks," said the necromancer. "I really don't feel like taking part in this event anymore!" with these words, the necromancer pulled the emerald amulet from his neck and threw it on deck.

The other players weren't so impressionable and took the chance to take pictures with the rare, flying snake. Though it was obvious that my ghastly man-eating acid-spitting wyvern didn't totally line up with the exaggerated fairy-tale picture in their heads after watching the advertisements.

Just after the last of the undying got into their boat, I ordered the oarsmen on the *White Shark* to take their places, and the helmsman to turn to the north-west, catching up with the trireme on the horizon, now just barely visible. I even said, purposely loud, in hopes that my words would be heard by the players, who were still quite near the bireme:

"Make for the port of New Tortuga, which belongs to the *Brotherhood of the Coast*. Both of our ships need repair."

The first mate, bandaged with relatively clean rags over his shoulder, nodded:

"That's right, Captain Amra. Repairs couldn't hurt. The mast got really torn up. Just look at it, it's totally cracking. The side has six holes in it, thankfully all above the waterline. Half the oars are broken. And that's to say nothing of the trireme..."

Ziabash Hardy bowed and picked up the wyvern amulet thrown by the disenchanted player:

"Pretty little gimmick. I saw one just like it around Angelica Wayward's neck."

~ Stay on the Wing ~

What? The Dryad Dancer was also taking part in the mass hunt?! Veronica had even purposely acquired the amulet, preparing to take possession of my mount? Very unpleasant news, indeed. What of the fact that the dryad herself didn't carry weapons or have any combat skills? Her strength was in something else — Angelica Wayward was fully capable of taking the pirate crew under her control and setting the bloodthirsty orcs against me!

The wood nymph was of the same opinion, having overheard the first mate as well. The dancer had gone too far. Taken on their own, it was possible to explain and justify the ritual with spilling blood into the sea, or buying perfume to put on the ship, or the charms on my crew, her taking the captain's quarters, our badly-timed excursion into port, the appearance of a ship following us, and her purchase of the wyvern amulet. But all together, it looked purposeful and even adversarial. But I didn't manage to answer Valerianna Quickfoot in any way, as Irek then walked up to me and asked in alarm:

"Uncy Amra, where's my sister? I respawned a long time ago, along with Taisha and Darius. But we all died after Yunna. She was first to go, up there on the altar!"

To my shame, I had to admit that only after the goblin boy's reminder did I notice that Yunna's image was still missing from among my list of pets.

It really was strange. Why hadn't the NPC girl respawned like all the others who'd died in the last battle?

A sense of shame swept over me. My intuition was telling me that something very serious had happened — the respawn algorithms hadn't kicked in, because the system considered the goblin girl a normal NPC, who would disappear forever after dying in *Boundless Realm*. Now, if I didn't take immediate and decisive action, the unique Yunna would be replaced by some utterly new NPC character created by the *Boundless Realm* algorithms, while my wolf rider would never return and be lost forever.

That said, although I understood the problem perfectly, I had no idea how to fix it. Unless...

Perfumer

"**K**EEPER!" I SHOUTED in a voice not my own, my face raised to the pinkening heavens. "Keeper, damn you!"

I shouted at full throat for no less than a minute, frightening the pirate crew and my sister with my strange behavior. I had already begun to despair when suddenly, an opaque winged shadow descended from the heavens onto the deck of the *White Shark*. All at once, as if on command, the pirate crew fell to their knees. The shimmering angelic figure looked over all the kneeling orcs with an ambivalent gaze, then created a golden magic dome dividing the two of us from all the others, and inquired in a grumbling voice:

"What are you screaming for, Amra? I can't even get up from my desk for a minute anymore. Someone needs me all the time."

At first, the Keeper's words threw me, not at all tallying with his majestic appearance. But then I felt inspired — this meant our conversation could be very direct without any lofty phrases or epithets.

"Are you the guy I talked to about that Midnight Wraith? Or are you a different employee of the Global Simulation Department?" I immediately clarified, and the Keeper chuckled:

"That wasn't with me, but I know about that conversation. The situation is that the directors of the *Boundless Realm* corporation still haven't decided if there should be just one Keeper in the game or many. For now, they're sticking with one, and we play for him in shifts. All understandings are recorded, so I know about the black arrow bargain."

Now that's better. It would have been much worse if this new employee knew absolutely nothing about the arrow confiscated from me and the invulnerability gifted to my goblin companions.

"Then tell me, Keeper, why hasn't Yunna respawned yet? She was my NPC companion, a goblin girl, level-26 wolf rider."

"Wait up, I'll take a look at the game logs," the glimmering figure lowered further down and stood motionless for some time. "Because she's done. She wasn't supposed to be reborn! That NPC sacrificed herself voluntarily, and for some pretty solid bonuses at that. The kind of divine blessing you wanted, Amra, don't just get handed out for free, you know! Just so you know, the only reason your catapult hit that trireme was this girl's self-sacrifice — the bombs were gonna just fly past, but the divine blessing bonus kicked in."

"Wait, stop! Keeper, I gave you a valuable item from a future game patch. Back then, we agreed on full immortality for these two goblins. There were no limitations, and no one said a thing about reincarnation being impossible! But now, I feel like I've been cheated! One day they respawn, but the next they won't!"

Was it just me, or did the Keeper get embarrassed and turn away?

"If only you knew, Amra, the kind of thunder and lightning that came down from the department head for taking matters into our own hands with the respawning NPC's... What's more, due to the mass event with the wyvern hunt, the patch adding shadow creatures to *Boundless Realm* has been postponed... And look who's talking about cheating, right?"

I didn't understand what the Keeper meant to accuse me of, and honestly told him that.

"I was talking about the amulet controlling your mount, which is now around your wyvern's neck. I won't deny that it looks pretty, but if such a valuable object won't drop when your character dies, the mass hunt loses all meaning. That bug is being patched out today. You must understand that there are a bunch of people following this event, and our corporation is monitoring every step. When you and the eight players in the boat swore to play fair and even invoked the gods of *Boundless Realm* as witnesses, we in the Global Simulation Department were sitting ready to immediately intervene if any of you broke that oath. Just in case, we zeroed out both of the bound mages' mana so they wouldn't mess around. By the way, you caught a bad break with the lots — if the necromancer or earth mage had been drawn, that wyvern would have hit level twenty-five, and you'd be able to ride on its back now. After all, it's much harder to catch a flying player..."

"Uh... yeah... I caught a bad break," I replied, not wanting to clarify that the draw was rigged. If the Keeper himself hadn't noticed anything unusual, I wasn't gonna rock the boat.

It was a pity that my trick with giving the amulet to VIXEN had been uncovered, though. That meant the error would be fixed, and I'd have to go back to wearing the valuable object myself. Although... I shuddered. This conversation was going in the exact wrong direction — these topics were of interest, but had absolutely nothing to do with Yunna's death. I was even getting the impression that the Keeper was simply running out the clock, hoping I'd drop it. I had to answer with his own words:

"There really are a lot of people following the

event. You're right there. I'm bending over backwards to make sure the viewers like it, and to keep the interest level in this wyvern hunt high. I understand how important this revenue is to the corporation. But now, explain: why hamper me in this complicated matter by taking my pets away? What's more, my viewers are already aware that my NPC companions Yunna and Irek have been promised invulnerability by the Keeper himself. There was even a touching scene of the children bidding their mother farewell as she blessed them on their travels. But now tell me, do you really think it will be good, if I have to tell my viewers that promise was broken in my next video clip? After all, the players of *Boundless Realm* associate you or the whole group playing the Keeper with untarnished honesty, and the ultimate truth. And you have to agree that it would look bad — the Keeper of *Boundless Realm* himself promised immortality to an NPC girl by the name of Yunna. She believed him and voluntarily laid on the altar. If Yunna is not reborn, many will be upset. The board of directors might take notice, too. The thunder and lightning in your department will fly even more ferociously, and the troubles for the front-line workers will be greater, which is to say nothing for your boss."

"My department always stays neutral and doesn't interfere directly in game events! So, there's no use in trying to spook me. There won't be any thunder and lightning!" Despite the loud words, I caught distinct notes of uncertainty in the Keeper's voice. "Here, Amra, let's not argue. Everything will be in accordance with the rules and regulations of the corporation. I'll need an official statement from your department saying that this NPC must be respawned and on what basis. The statement will be considered in due time, and as our leadership decides, so it will be."

My big-eared goblin chuckled, displaying a row of sharp little teeth:

"Now you're talking business, Keeper. I accept your conditions. But at the moment, the Special Projects Department is temporarily lacking a head. The former director, Mark Tobius, has been transferred to a different position by decision of Vice President Inessa Tyle. She then gave me temporary authority to make big decisions on my own. The head of the in-game security service, Andrei Soloviev, can confirm my words. So, consider the official statement requesting Yunna's respawn already sent!"

I managed to back the Keeper into a corner. The glowing figure flew higher and asked me to give him time "for consultation." I waited patiently for four minutes before the transparent angel started moving again and gave an answer:

"Alright, request approved. Your NPC goblin girl will be respawned in the next few minutes, but she will lose all the skills she earned and will be reset at level one. Unfortunately, that's the best I can do — divine intervention is a very rare treat. It needs to be repaid in kind. I was also asked to tell you unofficially that such an indulgence wouldn't be given a second time, and the next person you decide to sacrifice to the gods for the sake of group bonuses will die once and for all."

"Even a living player?" I asked, holding a fully real candidate in mind.

The glimmering angel shuddered, and rushed to clarify that he was talking only about NPC's, not about real *Boundless Realm* players.

"Alright then, on that note, my thanks to you, colleague! I wish you a happy shift without any more emergency calls!"

As the Keeper disappeared, the golden dome he brought with him also went, so I was no longer isolated from the rest of *Boundless Realm.*

A wave of sounds and scents suddenly rushed over me. Message lines ran before my eyes:

Trading Skill increased to level 18!

Foreman Skill increased to level 21!

+15 to relationship with members of Brotherhood of the Coast
+10 to Taisha's opinion of you

+ 20 to Ziabash Hardy's opinion of you

=25 to Ghuu Ghel All-Knowing's opinion of you

+25 to Gnum Spiteful's opinion of you

In the eyes of my crew, I saw admiration, adoration and even reverence. Just think! They'd just seen their captain speak on even footing with the Keeper himself! The fierce orcs bowed their heads in respect and made way, allowing me to walk over to Irek, who was nervously shifting from one foot to the other.

"Your sister will respawn soon," I reassured the boy, "but she will be much weaker and she'll lose many abilities and skills. In fact, Yunna will have to learn everything all over again..."

In confirmation of my words, the goblin girl appeared on the sacrificial altar, having miraculously avoided all the twists and turns of the battle. Yunna shouted out in fear, jumped to the floor and started looking all around. But then she saw her brother, pressed herself to him and started sobbing. Irek gave his sister his clothing, and the level-1 Wolf Rider immediately got dressed.

"That might not even be bad," the wood nymph commented as her, Taisha, and I walked down into the captain's bunk. "The goblin girl was leveled with a rare ambivalence — she even had Culinary kicking around in her skills, along with

Agriculture and, for some reason, Foot Race. Yunna now has the chance to be reborn and make herself into an adequate wolf rider from a blank slate. I'll give the girl tips on better skills, and also help her level fast."

"That's right. Yunna really does need help. Oh, Taisha is yawning bad... By the way, Valerianna, shouldn't you also be just about collapsing?" I asked, sharply changing the topic.

The green-haired girl shrugged her shoulders in uncertainty, then shot me a crafty smile and asked, barely audibly:

"Amra, are we gonna leave the ship now?"

"How'd you guess?!" tore itself from me.

Taisha sharply perked up her ears and jumped from the bed. There wasn't even a trace remaining of her sleepiness.

"I know you too well, Tim," the mavka laughed happily, impossibly satisfied with my surprise and the reaction of my NPC companion. "You'd never have mentioned New Tortuga in front of our pursuers unless you were trying to create a false narrative. But New Tortuga really is the nearest port of the *Brotherhood of the Coast.* Any pirate ship can come there for repair, no questions asked. The other ports are too far away, and we have practically no way of getting to them. From there, I came to the conclusion that you were planning to send the hunters to New Tortuga after the ships on their way there, while you yourself left the *White Shark.*"

Bingo! I mean, I'd long known that my sister was a genius, but her abilities in making complex conclusions still continued to delight me. Valeria had explained everything just right. All that was left for me was to fill in the details:

"All in all, you got the idea. Both of our ships need repair and will go to New Tortuga. They'll get there by this evening. Perhaps there will be ships of undying waiting for them when they get there. But even if that is so, our pursuers won't attack: trying to board a pirate bireme in a harbor with fifty *Brotherhood of the Coast* military ships is an utterly mad idea. But that isn't even the most important thing. Our pursuers will not see player markers on board the *White Shark*, so there will be no reason to attack — that will only startle their intended victim, or even worse, risk sinking the bireme with me on board. With such a valuable prize riding on it, they won't want to take risks and will wait patiently for me to enter *Boundless Realm.* But when our pursuers realize their error, we'll already be far away! An hour or so from now, we'll go ashore with our companions and Gnum Spiteful — we'll need the dwarf to lead us through the underground tunnels of Rovaan-Dum."

On hearing the name of the subterranean land of the dwarves, Val clapped her hands in elation and exclaimed:

"Excellent move! From what I've read in the

guides, they have a true multi-level labyrinth that goes down into the very heart of the mountain. There are abandoned dangerous tunnels, as well as very lively shafts. The coolest thing is their high-speed trains with rails and mine carts for fast transportation."

"That's exactly right, Valerianna. I already asked Gnum Spiteful and marked on the map a small freight dock which leads to one of the rail lines. *White Shark* will soon be passing not far from it and, there, we'll get out on shore. We can make use of dwarven transport there, buy tickets to somewhere deep inside Rovaan-Dum and, in one day, be at least a few hundred kilometers from the coast. I don't even know exactly where we'll be by evening. So, our pursuers can't possibly know a thing! *White Shark* and *Princess Amelia* will be going toward New Tortuga that whole time, attracting the attention of all interested eyes!"

Valerianna Quickfoot thought for a bit and agreed with my conclusion. Although she did mention that there were two undying on the *White Shark* other than us, and they could upset all our plans.

"Don't you worry about that," I assured my sister, smiling predatorily. "I've got an hour and a half or so before coming ashore, and I'm planning to spend that time preparing. I'd like to protect the ship and crew against the bad influence of that damned dryad. When everything is ready, before we leave, I'll give secret instructions to the first mate, and the most loyal orcs of my 'guard.' I'll tell them how to deal with the ships and the two undying, as well as what to do when they arrive in New Tortuga. It's just that a crew of three hundred loyal NPC pirates is a valuable resource, and I want to hold onto it. I'm sure it'll come in handy at some point."

"So, we still have time? Then I'm gonna get an hour's nap, without my character leaving *Boundless Realm*. If you need, give a sign of some kind, and Kira will wake me up."

"Kira isn't asleep?" I asked in surprise, somewhat embarrassed at having completely forgotten the presence of the outside observer.

"Come on, Tim, how could she be sleeping?! Kira's sitting next to me on a chair, watching the monitor with rapt attention. She's even making comments. See? She just said 'hi' to you. And she's saying she'll turn off the microphone when I'm asleep so you don't get embarrassed."

Valerianna sat Indian-style on the floor and closed her eyes. I waited for thirty seconds, but her character wasn't about to exit *Boundless Realm* — my sister had simply removed her virtual reality helmet and sensor gloves, leaving the game switched on.

"Amra, you were planning to tell me about the land of the undying, remember?" Taisha asked wearily, struggling with all her might not to doze off. "First tell me, who is Kira?"

I heard notes of jealousy in the voice of the NPC thief. I got an urge to initiate the Taisha's Envy quest, but held back. It wasn't a good time for that now, as I was already struggling desperately against sleep and might have made a real mess of things if I just answered wrong. So, I answered neutrally:

"Kira is the owner of the room my sister and I rent. She owns many rooms. Kira is quite a rich woman. She even has her own security team..."

Taisha took the information totally ambivalently, not reacting in any way. Quickly changing the topic away from my landlady, I continued telling my NPC girlfriend about the real world. Taisha was sitting on the bed alternating between dozing off and listening. Not stopping talking, I was working with alchemical reagents and thinking at the same time.

What was the strength of the Dryad Dancer? Her attractive appearance, very high Charisma and, based on that stat, her irresistible charms and submission spells. The player's easy behavior was secondary — without the Charisma and appearance, the pirate crew would not be following her like dogs, and certainly would not have obeyed the girl's orders. Accordingly, if the dryad's

Charisma went down, the strength of all her charms would significantly wane. If I could mar the beautiful girl's appearance even slightly, all her control abilities would disappear.

I came up onto the upper deck and approached VIXEN, who was wound up into a ball asleep. Fearlessly unlatching the ghastly jaws of the flying snake, I filled an alchemical vial with wyvern poison. I desperately wanted to comment on these scenes: "Do not try this at home! Dangerous!!!" as the wyvern was very upset with my manipulations and, even groggy, bit into my arm with her jaws.

Damage taken: 55 (Bite)
Damage taken: 32 (Poison)
Successful check for Poison Resistance

After recognizing her master, VIXEN immediately unclenched her jaws and again lowered her head onto the ring of her emerald body, going back to sleep. I though, took a closer look at the liquid:

Forest Wyvern Poison (alchemy ingredient)

To look at it, I had a cloudy yellow viscous liquid that smelled acridly of hydrochloric acid. It had very irritating properties, even corroding the skin. It was gross all on its own, but mixed with another poison that instantly lowers Charisma, I'd have exactly what I wanted! The recipe for this poison, which was given the name Poison of Detestability, was something I had discovered long ago, but I never thought it would ever be of use to me, as reducing an enemy's Charisma in battle was one of the most useless actions imaginable. However, though I'd never have guessed it, the recipe was now coming in handy.

I went down into the captain's bunk and, clearing unneeded vials and reagents off the table, started producing some Poison of Detestability. Done! Minus twelve Charisma points — pretty weak, but I didn't yet have the ability to make a stronger poison. So now, all that remained was mixing it with the wyvern poison...

The action you're trying to perform is impossible
Your character lacks the specialization to prepare complex elixirs with multiple active properties

God damn it! I needed a special perk to my Alchemy skill. I looked at my stats. My Alchemy skill was at level 19, and its progress bar was half full. Just the right time to get up to potion cooking!

I restored my reserves of healing elixir and strength restoration potion, then cobbled together some Intelligence and mana elixirs for Valeria. I even made a burn medicine for the disfigured boatswain Staur Strong. The time then came to start on the coils of ruddy brown seaweed taking up half my bag. There had to be some use for them. So, let's see what they could make.

> *Experience received: 16 Exp.*
> *You have created a Minor Elixir of Underwater Breathing (may spend 38 seconds underwater without need for air)*
> *New recipe added to Journal*

Would you look at that! What perfect timing! Ever since I'd made the decision, I had been thinking over whether Angelica or Leon would get suspicious about the last dinghy from *White Shark* disappearing, or whether they'd connect its disappearance with the missing captain. But now, voila! I wouldn't need a dinghy — Taisha, Irek, Yunna and Gnum Spiteful could all jump overboard with me and Valerianna, and we'd reach the shore by walking on the sea floor. Valerianna Quickfoot could make an air bubble, like she'd done before with her magic. The wolves of the Gray Pack could swim in. They were great swimmers! An excellent option. I just had to prepare enough underwater breathing potions!

Alchemy Skill increased to level 20!
You may now choose your first

specialization in this skill

Finally! And although there were a great many perks to the Alchemy skill, including concentrating and strengthening the effect of potions, less use of ingredients, and lots of other stuff — I chose the ability to prepare complex multi-component elixirs with multiple active properties. Now it was time! I took the forest wyvern poison already on the alchemy table and the Poison of Detestability, and poured both mixtures into a container filled with the ground up petals of tropical flowers.

The pale-yellow mixture gave a gurgle, bubbled, and released a violet pink steam. I continued mixing the strange concoction with a long wooden spoon, watching it transform. It gradually cooled, quickly thickening and acquiring the consistency of a cream or lotion, as well as a glamorous pink shade. And then...

Experience received: 1600 Exp.

Alchemy Skill increased to level 21!

Congratulations!!! You are the first player to create this potion! It has the following effects:
— 60 Charisma, — 60 Intelligence , skin irritation (effect of level-20 Itching spell)
The effects will appear five minutes after

application
    Effect duration: 20 minutes
    New recipe added to Journal
    As the discoverer of this potion, you have the right to give it a name
    Would you like to use the suggested name: "Gift to the First Lady in Waiting," or would you like to give it a name?

    Mission received: Recognition of the Alchemists' Guild (1/10)
    Mission class: normal, personal
    Description: Visit any branch of the Alchemists' Guild and share the new recipe with your colleagues
    Reward: 80 Exp., Alchemy skill +1
    Optional condition: try the potion you just created out on yourself or any other player, record the results and share it with your colleagues
    Reward: variable

I'll admit, I was slightly taken aback by the abundance of text, but I read the messages and smiled. "Gift to the First Lady in Waiting?" Considering the properties of the synthesized cream, such a gift could only come from an envious and guileful second lady in waiting. Alright, I'd leave the name. The effect lasted twenty minutes. Not much, but it should be enough. The fact that the effects weren't instantaneous and only took hold after five minutes was the perfect finishing touch. What was more, the smell of the "gift" was nice — something like a complex mixture of peaches, vanilla, almonds and something indistinct.

Now, how would I get Angelica Wayward to take it? It seemed obvious — add it to her perfume collection. But on the shelves, there were thirty different containers, and the Dryad Dancer wasn't likely to be using all of them. Add a drop to each? In that case, the effect wouldn't be sufficient. What was more, the system wouldn't let me rifle through another player's things unpunished. If I did that, it would give me a criminal marker and penalize my ability to exit *Boundless Realm.* Even if I neglected all the negative effects and manipulated the dancer's things regardless, the biggest shame would be that the ownership of the items would be changed, so Angelica would be warned that she was trying to use someone else's perfume collection. She'd be sure to realize someone had messed with her stuff. What could I do? Maybe I should purposefully place a conspicuous container belonging to someone else among Angelica's cosmetics. She'd be sure to pay attention to any object belonging to another woman.

"Taisha," I said quietly, calling my NPC girlfriend over. The green-skinned girl gave an abrupt shudder, opening her eyes. "I saw that you were gathering objects left over from the undying on the deck of the trireme. Among them were empty vials of used elixirs, and some were even full. Can you show me your loot?"

Successful check for Taisha's reaction
Experience received: 40 Exp.

The goblin girl untied her bag and poured out ten various vials onto the bed. Elixirs of Agility and Eagle's Sight, empty vials of something used. But then I saw the one I was looking for — a carved red glass container with a wreath-like pattern. Based on the label, it had once contained an Elixir of Resist Fire. Taisha gave it to me unquestioningly, watching with interest as I filled the vessel.

Then, on the shelf among the other different cosmetics, there appeared a bright red one that immediately caught the eye with its unusual shape and intriguing label: "Gift to the First Lady in Waiting." The cork wasn't fully in, and the cream didn't fill the container — that was so it would look used. For Angelica Wayward, the jar would be shown as someone else's property. The dryad would surely notice the object, but would she stoop to testing the contents of the brightly colored vessel on herself? Hard to say. Although, her infamous feminine curiosity just might make her. What could I say? The only person to blame for possible side effects would be her.

Alright, done deal. The time had come to give instructions to the crew and leave *White Shark.*

* * *

Charisma check failed!

"Thirty coins from each and every passenger! Also, no critters allowed in the train!" the dwarven guard declared in an indisputable tone, looking over our soaked-through outfits with clear suspicion. All my attempts to negotiate or argue led to nothing.

I had already decided that there must have been a programmed-in script forbidding the price for tickets from being lowered, and started counting out two hundred forty coins for the squat stubborn man (myself, Valerianna, Taisha, Yunna, Irek, Darius, Darina, and Gnum Spiteful), but the dwarf mechanic stopped me and asked everyone to leave so he could talk privately with his countryman. They spoke for five minutes, after which Gnum Spiteful called me over and explained the new conditions:

"One hundred coins and we'll be given two carts with seats, plus grub for breakfast and lunch. The carts have windows, but they ask us not to open them. The ceilings are very low. It would never fit people or orcs. But goblins, a mavka and human children are no problem. For the wolves, they'll attach an enclosed freight car, usually used for purified silver ore, but no one will feed them. The most they can do is give them water. And now the most important part — at seven thirty this evening, the train will arrive at the Dar-Tu Switch-Room station. It's something like a suburb of our subterranean capital, Dotur-Khawe — 'Miner's Dream' in human language. And there, right before the station, even before the platform begins, we'll have to jump out of the car and quietly run before the station guards see us. All the documents on board will say these cars are empty so, if we're found, it could lead to trouble."

I was more than fine with that, especially given the fact that we wouldn't have formal tickets drawn up. Travelling like that with the blinds closed, we would be impossible to track. I counted out one hundred of the seven-sided game coins for the dwarf guardsman, and the wee bearded man instantly mellowed out, promising to bring us breakfast as soon as the train got underway.

"Amra, I'm going to bed!" the wood nymph told me as soon as she took her seat.

My eyelids were also sagging heavily, but I was waiting for us to leave. First, the dwarves attached a strange-looking long and low fired-up steam engine to the wagon train, then three more platforms of compressed peat to keep the fire going in the furnaces. After that was over, I rushed to close the doors so I wouldn't choke on the acrid wisps of black smoke pouring out of the low rectangular smokestack. Our train started moving and picking up speed centimeter by centimeter. I already knew that there would be no stops midway, and that all the subterranean villages we'd see on our path would be passed by the speeding train without reducing speed. It was impossible to see anything in the dark, identical tunnels, so I followed my sister's example, leaving *Boundless Realm.*

As soon as I crawled out of the virtual reality capsule and pulled on my clothes with my arms shaking in weariness, I got a call on my cell phone, which was lying on the table. The name Kira was shown on the screen.

"Timothy, we need to have a very serious conversation. Why did you hide the fact that you're taking care of your disabled sister?!"

Kira's voice was full of dissatisfied, cold detachment. I'd heard these words and emotions in the voice of girlfriends many times before, and I understood perfectly how the conversation would end. My legless disabled sister was guaranteed to scare any girlfriend away. Most of my relationships immediately fell apart when my pretty young things found out about Val's existence. And now it was Kira's turn... I sighed heavily and pursed my lips in vexation until they crackled. Without waiting to hear the heavy, irreversible words of my girlfriend, I first hurried to lay out my priorities:

"Kira, let me tell you everything myself, so you won't have to worry, feel awkward or look for justifications. To me, Valeria is the nearest and dearest person on the planet, and I would not leave my sister for anything! No one could ever make me refuse my beloved sister. Not mere pretty girls, and not even you! So, don't say anything. I already know everything you want to say to me. Sure, I'm a lousy creep, a fraudster and an asshole. You wish we'd never met, and so on. I won't argue. That's all well and good. Don't worry about the apartment — we don't have many things. We can be out of it today..."

"Oh, shut up!" Kira interrupted me, her voice raised to a shout. "You're such an idiot, Timothy! Have I ever given you reason to believe I'm such a nasty, self-involved egotist? Then why do you think so poorly of me?! Yes, after talking with Valeria, I got very angry at you, but for a different reason! Your little sister has a rare talent and is very independent for her age. She has figured out some specifically female problems all on her own by looking them up on the internet. But all the same, when talking with Valeria, I was horrified to discover some frightening gaps in her knowledge of elementary every-day topics. Your sister doesn't use cosmetics and doesn't even know why girls need scrubs and masks. For the last two years, her hair has gotten so bad it might as well belong to an old lady. Based on what I can see, she hasn't even visited an elementary stylist."

"What do you mean?!" I objected. "A lady who lived on the same floor as us had a lot of experience — she worked forty years in a salon until she was forced into retirement. Now, she earns money cutting neighbors' hair at a very reasonable price. It might be simple, but my sister and I simply didn't have the money to visit a better place."

"Timothy, your sister's hair was just abhorrent! Perhaps these cuts may have been in fashion half a century ago, but girls now wear completely different styles. Also, Valeria doesn't have normal woman's underwear, or any party dresses. All her clothes are old children's things she long since grew out of. And that's to say nothing of the fact that your sister doesn't even have her own razor or a single bra! And her breasts are growing... but this is for us girls. Valeria shared her problems with me as a secret, saying you didn't need to know. I believe you were trying to help your sister as best you could, but it clearly wasn't enough. She badly needed an older girlfriend to give her tips and advice, and who at least had some understanding of modern fashion."

I was not prepared for that reaction from Kira, or these topics, so I arrived to a state of utter shame. Yes, I truly had no idea of my sister's difficulties, or the questions eating her away inside, because Val didn't share her problems with me. Squeezing out justifications and gratefulness, I wanted to hang up, but Kira was in no mood to end the conversation:

"Basically, Timothy, it's like this: as soon as your sister wakes up, I'm going to take her on a big shopping outing. I'll work for her as a consultant and will help her choose stylish new outfits. Otherwise, I'm afraid Valeria will pick out old kid's stuff, like what she's used to. I'll bring you a detailed receipt — you can pay me back when you have the chance, no rush. Get to creating your next video clip now, and upload it as fast as you can."

"Why now?" I didn't understand. "I'll make it and upload by evening, like usual."

"No, Timothy, you'll do it now. This evening, no one will even be interested. The problem is the first information on the sea battle has already leaked onto the *Boundless Realm* forum, and there's a ton of activity and people watching the topic. What's more, knowing our corporate overlords, I can confidently say that they won't miss the chance to show such an impressive moment of gameplay, and that in the next few minutes, a glistening video report on the first battle between the pursuers and the owner of the wyvern amulet will be put up. So, you need to be sure to upload your video report first — that will

~ Stay on the Wing ~

significantly raise your visibility as a player and your value to the corporation."

Senior Tester

UNDERSTANDING the importance of the work, I did my very best. Thankfully, I had more than enough quality footage. The forty-minute video about my career as a pirate came out stuffed to the brim with action and battles.

The duel on the beach with the ghastly orc captain and rougarou shapeshifter. The night capture of the "trader's" galley in the bay. The liberation of the slaves chained to their oars and the short ritual of accepting the former captives as pirates, finishing with them all being branded on the right shoulder with red-hot iron, giving them all a skull and anchor symbol. Buying provisions and weapons. Leaving the bay of the Island of the Wanton Widow in the nasty gale. The shaman getting raving drunk, opening a bottle of rum with shaking hands and blessing the sailors. The raging sea, blasting waves of water onto the deck, the sharp cliffs and the wisps of saltwater. Installing the catapult, preparing the bombs. The sacrifice ritual, the rough sea battle and the capture of the flaming trireme. The bound kneeling undying, the horribly burnt executioner with chipped poleax and bloodied chopping block. My emerald-hued beauty the wyvern with the bronze amulet around her neck and the extreme scene depicting the elven bowwoman's execution. The happy Taisha wearing the captain's tricorn on her head, erotically pumping her thighs and posing for me on the backdrop of the rigging to great effect, the rope ladders, sails and catapults. Ghastly grinning pirate cutthroats and gold coins pouring like a river into the captain's chest.

I spent two and a half hours making it, but without any exaggeration, I can say it was the most successful video I'd ever made. Either the material really was that high quality and interesting, or it was just evidence of my increased experience in creating and narrating video clips, but I simply outdid myself. It was as atmospheric as could be, pulled you in and attracted the eye. The pirate life was revealed in all its colors — sea, storm, ships, drink, fighting, gold and happy beauties.

Already about to leave my work cabin, I checked my mailbox. Mainly, it was just more useless spam piling up. But two messages from

TOP clans caught my eye. The first was from a player named Andrzej Envoy [MERCS] a human gladiator of a simply unbelievable level: two hundred ten.

"Amra, our clan has just received a firm contract to help you. It's already paid, so no worries. Just present this letter at any branch of the bank of gremlins or dwarves, and the employees will give you a magical summoning scroll. Activate the scroll in case of misfortune, and at any time of day, a coordinated team of twenty warriors over level 160 will instantly come to your aid.

P.S. The reputation of our clan is worth much more than your winged beast, so don't worry about losing your wyvern — we won't be stabbing you in the back.

P.P.S. In the terms of the contract, it was written explicitly that we were not to reveal the name of our client. So, I ask you not to request this information from my soldiers — they'll never tell you. The penalty for breaking the secret is just too serious.

P.P.P.S. Making use of the occasion, I invite you to join our clan. We don't suffer fools. Our biggest value is keeping one's word. In one week, we could level your goblin and all your pets to over 100. Give it some thought and tell my guys. We'll send out a division right away to escort you to a safe place.

Andrzej Envoy, clan treasurer [MERCS]"

~ Stay on the Wing ~

I'd heard of this clan of mercenaries before — they weren't very numerous, and had just one castle. They positioned themselves as a community of disciplined professional high-level warriors, earning their keep with the blade. The services of the "mercs" were very, very expensive, but it was a surefire way of scaring off presumptuous neighbors or changing the course of a bad war.

Who that I know could ever afford a division of twenty mercenaries over level 160? The most obvious option was Kira. But the contract with the *MERCS* had been signed about an hour ago, and I knew the red-headed beauty hadn't been playing. Also, Kira had spent the whole previous night and morning in the apartment with my sister without the ability to enter *Boundless Realm*. What was more, Kira played a very specific character, which made her cautious to the point of paranoia, so she'd never advertise the fact that the queen of the harpies was somehow tied to the far-off little goblin.

Who else? Max Sochnier wouldn't have had the money. Leon all the more so. Truth be told, Veronica must have had plenty of cash. I thought that option over seriously. Perhaps this was all part of the Dryad Dancer's guileful plan to eliminate my big-eared Amra. But as for the reputation of the *MERCS* clan, their treasurer hadn't been lying. It was flawless. It could be no other way in their complicated line of work: the smallest black mark on the clan's reputation and it would lose all clients forever. So, the option of Veronica didn't make sense either. Then who was helping me? I got lost in guesses.

The second message was from a person I'd heard from before, a member of the strongest clan in the game, *Legion of Steel*:

"It brings me joy to see that you heard our warning, and that you managed to slip out of the trap on the Island of the Wanton Widow. I was also glad to see that you accepted our offer and said the watchword. We're preparing a shelter for you, and it's going to be sturdy enough to withstand an attack for seven days, even if all the clans of Boundless Realm *take part. For now, keep fleeing. I hope this letter also provides you with valuable information.*

Know that nearly all the TOP clans are now sending military divisions to the ports of the Brotherhood of the Coast *after you. They'll be everywhere. But above all else, in New Tortuga — the nearest harbor where you could repair your ships. I hope you have enough sense not to show your face there.*

Also, take this into account. One of your closest companions is leaking information about the movements of your character. There's simply no other explanation for the surprising familiarity of the Firstborn *and* Warlords *clans about the precise location of your ship at the end of the night. It is no mere coincidence. These clans were never among the TOP, and never demonstrated an ability to track a situation as it develops with such accuracy.*

So, the espionage and bribery is evident. Our analysts are 85% sure that the spy in your circle is a character by the name of Valerianna Quickfoot. There are many reasons for that guess, but first and foremost is that she's abnormally strong for a level-37 Beastmaster. A person who's only been playing for ten days should simply physically not have enough mana to do a double mirror image, but Valerianna Quickfoot has demonstrated that trick on a number of occasions. The most obvious explanation is that she has some rare equipment, or even a set, which she should never have had either the ability or finances to obtain. This is apparently from either an extreme donation, or money received for espionage. Check her.

Alexander the Great3st. Human. Level-230 Priest of the Sun [LEGION]"

I had complete faith in my sister, and didn't believe for a second that she might have been a traitor — no amount of money could have made my sister betray me, just as I could never her. Despite all their experience, the *Legion of Steel*'s analysts just had to be wrong. First of all, they didn't consider the fact that Valerianna Quickfoot was my sister. Second, Valeria had lived half of her conscious life in computer games, which had come to almost fully replace her bleak reality. My paralyzed sister didn't just play a video game, she became a fully-fledged resident of a digital world. Analyzing all the subtle factors of the game mechanics, thinking carefully through development strategies and creating surprisingly strong characters was always her strong suit. I'd have to show the message to my sister — Val was sure to be flattered by such a high evaluation of her abilities from the leading players of *Boundless Realm.*

After turning off the game message client, I just turned off the monitor and started off home. I emerged from my work cabin into the common corridor and stopped, amazed at the huge crowd of people. I had grown accustomed to emptiness and quiet on the tester floor. But now, gathered along the railings of this and the opposite long elevated walkways, there were no less than a few hundred people. I never even suspected I had this many work colleagues. But what were they all doing standing around in the corridor, and not at work? Maybe something had happened? Like, a patch roll-out or a game server reset? I got out my cellphone and activated the screen to see the time. It was eight fifty-nine in the morning. Just then, the numbers on the screen flipped over to precisely nine AM.

And at that exact moment, a little melody or timer signal started playing from many of their phones. The testers started walking toward to their work cabins, and a minute later, it was as empty as usual. Only a few people remained, hurriedly drinking their coffee and preparing for the work day. For some reason, a fit of laughter came over me. I could hardly believe all these people played on a strict schedule — enter *Boundless Realm* at nine, go out for lunch from noon to one, then finish out the work day and head home?

Could one really fully immerse in a virtual world, or even more enjoy a game with a countdown timer ticking in their head the whole time? "Another two hours and seven minutes of suffering in this damn virtual reality capsule, then I can go to lunch and chat with my colleagues." Although... As an old joke has it, millions of lemmings can't be wrong. Probably, from the perspective of most testers, my work schedule was the one that seemed strange — I came into the office at a random time, played mostly at night, and had never taken a weekend. What was more, I spent twelve or more hours in the capsule every day. Perhaps it was me behaving strangely, and everyone else was acting normal?

Immersed in such thoughts, I walked past the break area when I was suddenly called out to by familiar voices. I turned and saw both of my friends — Max Sochnier and Leon sitting at a table. The former teacher was drinking coffee from the machine unhurriedly, and the former construction worker was wolfing down a full breakfast. Although, full might be overstating it — the only things on the tray before Leon were a plate of cheap synthetic quick-cooking vermicelli and a dish containing a powdered omelet that hadn't been fully mixed with hot water. Leon was lazily stirring the barely edible mass with a plastic fork and drinking some off-brand crappy soda right from a two-liter bottle.

To be honest, I was surprised — even in our most moneyless and dark times, Val and I had never stooped to such obviously unhealthy sources of nourishment. And my colleague should have had money — it wasn't even a few days ago that Leon had invited all of us to a restaurant to celebrate his passing the trial period and the quite respectable salary he was offered of fifteen hundred credits a month. Veronica was also supposed to give him back the three thousand. Maybe she hadn't yet? I was too ashamed to get into interrogating Leon on his financial condition, all the more so given that Max Sochnier was rushing to share his news.

Max had spent nearly the whole previous night in *Boundless Realm*. The two-day storm at the Island of the Wanton Widow gradually quieted down, and the Naiad Trader had prepared for the unwanted but inevitable visit of undying to his trade galley *Tipsy Gannet*. There were already over thirty ships gathered near the island, and it wasn't hard to figure out that the wyvern hunters would be enraged when they realized that they had waited so long near the rocky island for nothing. Nevertheless, before the sun was even up, all thirty of the ships keeping the bay under siege lifted anchor and left to the northwest! The Naiad Trader couldn't believe his good fortune, but immediately awoke his crew and took advantage of the chance to leave the island, leading *Tipsy Gannet* further on its trade route.

"But I wasn't just sitting around the last few days with my flippers crossed, as you might have thought," Max Sochnier smiled, clearly satisfied with himself. "Yesterday, I discovered an underwater village of naiads and nereids near the island. If only you could have seen how many quests my character got! My eyes were splitting from the abundance of options! I reached level thirty in one day. I met lots of undersea girls, raising my Lothario skill to fifteen. I even took things to a romantic level with a nereid fish girl named Olilissa — she might even lay eggs today!"

"Wait up, she's of a different race than you," I said, catching onto that factor in my friend's tale. "You're a naiad, and she's a nereid..."

"Oh yeah? You try explaining that to a girl twice as long as you, and ten times stronger. She swims twice as fast as me. If a girl like that's got it in her head that she likes you, it's best not to argue. She even suggested that we attack the ships of the undying together from underwater, but I refused — the two of us wouldn't have managed, and my girlfriend would have just died for nothing. But Olilissa did give me a really cool pet — a two-meter level-11 swordfish! I named it Claymore. I'm gonna grow her into a ten-meter-long lightning fast killer. She'll make excellent protection for the trade galley. No pirate ship will dare come near! Also, the underwater residents placed some orders — all I had to do was remember to write it down in a scroll. Some need mirrors. Others want pearls of an unusual color that don't exist at the Island of the Wanton Widow. Some want forged iron and boards. The fish want hemp and strong horsehair nets. Olilissa wants coral beads... I feel like if I really can get all that and bring it to them within six days, I'll level up at least five times from all the completed quests. And most of the quests there are chains, so there will certainly be new orders. And, just imagine! That was all just in one village! Think how many there must be along the whole coastline! All in all, Timothy, I'm just starting to understand how to play a Naiad Trader."

My friend's emotional speech was interrupted by an account-balance-change beep. Max Sochnier dug through his pockets to see the message. I also got out my vibrating phone. A deposit of two hundred credits. More corporate employees outed as rats. And another three hundred credits for "exposing a bug."

"Woah! A hundred-credit deposit!" said the Frenchman, lighting up. "Yesterday, I found a bug in the game with converting the price of a good from credits into pearls. I immediately told tech support. They already fixed the error, and I got paid a bonus."

"I was also sent money for finding a bug with controlling the wyvern," I said, not particularly wanting to get into the full amount or reason.

"You're lucky..." said Leon, decisively pushing away the tray of his unfinished breakfast. "There's no work for me on the pirate bireme, so I've just been withering away at level twenty-seven. And I've got another four days of hardship to wait for my salary..."

Max immediately offered our friend a fifty-credit loan and Leon, slightly fighting back for appearances, agreed. I also offered the former construction worker some money, but he refused, saying that he already had enough. So then, what was this about? Either Veronica hadn't returned the loan, or he'd wasted a significant sum of money. Then my phone rang. The number wasn't shown.

"Timothy?" I only needed one word to recognize the voice of Inessa Tyle, vice president of the *Boundless Realm* Corporation. "I'm watching your video from this morning right now, and I cannot hold back the tears of joy. Timothy, this is exactly what I wanted out of you! Romance, pirates, sea, battles, steel, blood and rich booty! All in the spirit of Robert Louis Stevenson or Jules Verne. And you fulfilled my order so quickly and perfectly. It hasn't even been a day. Thank you. I have also already fulfilled my promise — the documents on your promotion to senior tester have already been sent to HR. You can drop by your department to sign the order as soon as we're off the phone. It's nice to do business with such a prompt, ambitious young man, Timothy! I hope we see each other again."

I lowered my hand with the phone still pressed in it and my lips stretched out into a stupid ear-to-ear smile.

"That was a call from HR," I said to my friends as they watched me carefully, touching up my version of the conversation. "They say the leadership is happy with my work, so they made me a senior tester with the salary to go with it! I just need to go to the department now to sign the papers!"

Both Max and Leon congratulated me, and I didn't sense a bit of envy or falsehood in their congratulations. Both were sincerely happy for me.

"Tell Veronica to hurry up in there," the former construction worker added. "She's already been talking to Mark Tobius about something for a half hour, and she still hasn't returned."

"By the way, about Veronica..." I said, taking advantage of the opportunity to discuss the slippery topic. "Explain to me why your girlfriend needed to buy the wyvern hunter amulet?"

Leon just shrugged his shoulders, not knowing the answer.

"You understand yourself that I am trying my best to run *away* from the hunters, constantly changing position and obscuring my location. But now, I've got a participant in the great hunt right on my ship! Naturally, that has me on edge!"

The former construction worker predictably stood to the defense of his new flame:

"Timothy, there's nothing for you to worry about here. I already told you that she doesn't have any weapons or combat skills. She calls herself a 'social character,' which means she gains experience by talking. What's more..." here Leon fell silent, as if considering whether to say the next part or not. "Angelica Wayward doesn't want to be in our group. Sure, I offered a few times, but she refused. She just constantly tells me that she's playing her own game and the role of second fiddle to a big-eared goblin is not for her. Veronica also said that she needs to start streaming again in order not to lose her current audience. From all that, I made the conclusion that the dryad will be leaving *White Shark* soon, so no need to worry about her. And also... I'll probably follow her ashore. No offense, Timothy, but I feel I should be helping her. I'm quite smitten, after all."

I spent some time in silence, thinking over the former construction worker's admission. What could I say? I wasn't planning on compelling him to play with me against his own will. After a heavy sigh, I said:

"Alright, I won't get in your way. Let Veronica cast her streams, earn money, and even wear the wyvern amulet. But you have to understand me as well — the presence of wyvern hunters on my ship is totally unacceptable. So, Angelica Wayward must go ashore in the nearest port. You can stay or follow your girlfriend, it's up to you. By the way, there's another medallion in the captain's chambers sitting on a table — I got it as a trophy after last night's battle. You can have it. *Boundless Realm* is dangerous, and reducing experience loss in case of death is a useful bonus."

Leon nodded, not raising his eye to me and asked when we'd reach the next port.

"Today at about six PM, both of my ships will arrive to New Tortuga for repair."

"Both? You got another ship?" Max Sochnier cut into the conversation.

"Yes, last night, a trireme of wyvern hunters caught up to *White Shark*. It was a very intense battle. Twenty pirates were killed, and another eighty were wounded. Half of my pets had to respawn. But still, we won! I captured the trireme, but the ships are damaged. They need repair. By the way, Leon, while you're on my ship, you could take a look and see what needs fixing?"

The former construction worker nodded, still not raising his eyes and feeling guilty. I bid farewell to my friends and headed to the elevators — I had to drop by the director of special projects' office and sign the papers on my promotion.

The tiny Jane looked very strange in the huge leather armchair, made for the dimensions of her immense former boss. Nevertheless, the girl was sitting at the director's table and let me know from her first words that the situation had changed dramatically, and that she was no longer the department head's secretary, but the acting director of special projects:

"Hello, Timothy. Pour yourself some coffee. It wouldn't be proper for me to serve my underlings."

Underlings? As far as I knew, Jane was only occupying the post of director, which was freed up for a day or two, until a new department head could be appointed. Yesterday, the vice president of the corporation Inessa Tyle had spoken fairly dismissively of the pretty director's assistant, saying she wore too much makeup or something like that. She couldn't even remember Jane's name. Had the situation really changed that abruptly overnight? Were they really planning on making Jane the new department head? Nevertheless, I still hadn't made up my mind to give her the hazelnut chocolate I'd bought and headed in silence to the coffee machine.

"I see you aren't very surprised at the changes," the girl noted.

"Well last night, Andrei Soloviev, the head of in-game security, told me that Mark Tobius had asked to be transferred back to his previous position in the development department. He said that, for the next two days, all complicated issues would have to be solved through you, then we'd see from there."

"That's exactly right! But to me, being honest, it was a surprise. I walked into work, turned on my computer, and found a letter in my email from HR saying I'd been appointed acting department head. Then it said that they were making a decision on who would be the next director, and how I performed in this position could move me up that list. I was given access and passwords to the director's terminal. And now, I'm sitting here getting intimate with the situation on all department employees. I'll admit, I don't understand a damn thing yet... By the way, what was it you came for, Timothy?"

I informed my new boss about the call "from HR," in which I was told to come and sign the papers on my promotion.

"I didn't get anything about that..." Jane said, flipping through messages on her screen a few times with a confused look. "Unless..." the girl stood up from the director's chair with clear displeasure and walked back to her former desk. "Ah, here it is! The email came in six minutes ago. Woah! A salary of two thousand credits... Congratulations, Timothy! I'll print it off in duplicate right away."

The printer hummed into action, spitting out sheets of paper. Wiser after my past experience, I read closely into the text. This time, everything was right, without any unforeseen obstacles. It was just an addendum to my work contract describing my new position: "Senior Game Plotline Tester," and an additional monthly salary on top of the previously existing forms of payment. I signed both copies and set them on the director's table.

"Timothy, come over here," Jane called me over. "A new advertising clip came in from marketing for me to sign off on. It's directly relevant to you."

The girl scooted over on the huge armchair, offering me a seat next to her and increasing the volume of the speakers. I carefully sat next to my new boss and stared at the screen.

There was a huge trireme of predatory appearance plowing through the waves, racing after two ships barely visible on the horizon. The great hunt continues! Amra discovered! After that, there were scenes of my big-eared goblin on the backdrop of the black pirate flag, pointing at the trireme and giving a speech before a group of fearsome orc sailors. The shaman, the sacrifice. *White Shark* making a tack under combat conditions. The ships racing at one another at full speed. The huge ballista bolt nearly scratching my cheek and slamming through the mast. Orc pirates falling all around me, the royal seamen slain by well-aimed arrows. The stone golem, cast by the earth mage right on the deck of my ship. The catapult shot. Fire and death. The ships coming up sideways on one another, grappling hooks flying, oars breaking. The dwarf greeting the paladin with his heavy two-handed sledgehammer as the man tried to jump over the water. A few sailors fallen into the sea. *White Shark* darting away from the burning trireme. The stabbing rampage and the fight for a spot in the dinghy. The downcast tied-up players. The executioner with his poleax and bloodied block. My wonderful emerald wyvern. The scream of the elf girl being eaten alive. The first battle of the great hunt was now behind Amra!

A slightly different order of events, not quite lining up with reality. And not a word about letting the players go — from the scenes in the clip, the viewers were sure to come to the conclusion that the bloodthirsty pirate captain had knocked all the captives off using the very harshest methods. But all in all, it looked very interesting, and the quality was high. The people who made the clip were clearly true professionals. A head and shoulders above the quick-and-dirty hack jobs I was producing.

"You're really on fire, Timothy!" I heard unhidden admiration in the voice of the girl sitting next to me. "Now, it's clear why they made you senior tester. Shall we approve the advertising clip?"

I had no objections. Jane sent her approval. I then tried to stand from the armchair, but the girl held me by the shoulder.

"Where are you hurrying off to, Timothy? We haven't had the chance to talk in ages! Don't worry, I'm not gonna interrogate you," she laughed, having noticed my nervous exertion. "This is just business. You do remember our understandings, right? I have some information that might interest you."

"How much?" I asked, fitfully imagining my bank account balance — Jane's past services had come at quite the cost, now with her promotion, they could run me a truly astronomical sum.

Instead of an answer, my boss just laughed and very slowly led her well-manicured nail down my neck from chin to shirt collar. It was seemingly tender, but for some reason, I was now reminded of Max Sochnier and his seven-meter-long nereid.

"You're so timid and tense today, Timothy," Jane said, taking her hand from my neck in clear disappointment. She reached for the computer mouse and opened an email. "It's free to start. Read it yourself."

It was a letter from the external security service addressed to Mark Tobius, and had been received late last evening. It said that the identities of several people had been established, who were actively talking on the phone with an employee of the special projects department playing a character by the name of Angelica Wayward. They were former classmates of hers who played *Boundless Realm,* who were now in the clans *Firstborn* and *Warlords*. The frequency of the calls grew sharply in the last few hours. No criminality had been detected in their calls; however, they had managed to connect those people with the crew of the players on the trireme *Princess Amelia*, which had left the port of Piren after *White Shark*, the location of both Angelica Wayward herself and Amra, the target of the global event.

So, there it was! Veronica had given me up to her friends with the goal of taking my valuable mount! I tore my gaze from the screen and met with Jane's face, smiling and very satisfied with herself.

"I knew you'd be interested in that email," the girl laughed, moving it from the inbox to the trash bin. "Veronica couldn't hold back her emotions either, when she saw the email. Although she assured me it was all just a coincidence and that she'd been talking with her former classmates on completely neutral topics, having nothing at all to do with *Boundless Realm*,"

"Would it be legal for her to interfere in the corporation's global event like that?" I inquired.

"Mark Tobius didn't think so. Security didn't interfere either. In the end, the sea battle took place and turned out great. Everyone's a winner. You and I, of course, not having read emails not addressed to us, have no notion of that, though. Isn't that right, Timothy?"

I nodded, giving a tortured smile. If my immediate superior was giving such transparent hints, then I must not have seen that email with my own eyes. Although, Veronica was a low-down bitch, of course!

"And now, with the introductory part over, let's talk about some other information..." Jane smiled cunningly. "Are you interested?"

"If it doesn't break corporate rules, yes," I answered carefully and repeated my initial question on how much this might run me. The girl shook her head:

"No, I'm not interested in money right now, Timothy. I am not experiencing a particular need for it. With time, I'm hoping to be made director, which would solve all my financial issues."

I couldn't believe my ears. Jane, who had been complaining to me just two or three days earlier about a personal financial crisis, was now claiming that she didn't need money? Hmm...

"Did you take Veronica for a lot by promising to erase the compromising email?" I suggested, and the smile on Jane's face was extinguished.

"Hey, I never told you about that! And if Veronica let it slip, it's none of your concern, Timothy." The acting department head stood sharply from her armchair, pulled down her hiked-up dress and started walking through the office. "All I really wanted was to invite you to my housewarming party. Not now, of course — I've still gotta get the apartment cleaned up and put all the new furniture in it. It'll be in a few days. I'll tell you when. I'm planning to invite all the members of our department, but you most of all, Timothy. After all, you're the one who found me a decent place to live."

Jane managed to embarrass me. In this case, I considered her selfish for no good reason at all. The new acting director had completely natural and understandable motives — getting to know her employees better, and bringing the team closer together with a shared activity. I promised I would attend her party.

"Alright then," Jane replied, growing calm. "And now, listen. Veronica really did come to me half an hour ago. She was wondering about two issues, both directly concerning you. First, what is the chance for the wyvern-controlling amulet to drop. Second: would the amulet drop if it wasn't the Dryad Dancer herself making the strike, but an NPC under her control."

"What thankless garbage!" tore itself from me along with a few entirely unprintable words.

"From your perspective, yes. But her Dryad Dancer is acting entirely in the bounds of the game mechanics, so the *Boundless Realm* Corporation will not be taking any action, and never could. And of course, that is true. The corporation's lawyers confirmed that there are no obstacles keeping our testers from participating in the great hunt."

Level-Up

IT HAPPENED at nine thirty. I was standing at the electrobus stop fighting back sleep and preparing to go home and get some rest when I suddenly heard a familiar beeping sound indicating a bank balance change. I got my phone out of my pocket, put the most recent message on screen... and spent a long time batting my eyelids and counting the zeros in the total, not believing my eyes.

It was a deposit for two hundred forty thousand credits. No, it must have been an error. I could not accept the reality of it.

PINCH ME!!! NO, BETTER GIVE ME A GOOD SLAP SO I WAKE UP!!! TWO HUNDRED FORTY THOUSAND CREDITS!!!

But despite that, it didn't look to be an error — the money was from the same corporate account that sent me my other transfers. In the notes section, it was written: "Your percentage for the amulets." Does this mean I'm rich now?! No, of course I had always hoped this day might come. And actually, that was exactly why I'd applied to be a tester for *Boundless Realm* in the first place. But hoping and dreaming was one thing, and seeing that money in my account was another. I could not fully believe in the reality of what had happened, to be honest!

The electrobus I wanted closed its doors right before my nose and drove off. I was standing fighting hard against the desire to scream my lungs out and release my pent-up emotions. Not a trace remained of my former sleepiness. How could I think of sleep with a world of endless possibilities revolving under my feet? Two hundred forty thousand! That was... my breath was taken, my thoughts scattered.

Where to start? An apartment? Although that wasn't so necessary now — we'd just gotten set up and Val was totally fine with our new place. A car? But for that, I'd have to first take lessons and get my license... Clothes, furniture, all the other necessities of life — that was all nothing, I could get that later.

Legs for my sister! That was exactly it!!! In the very best clinic, pay for the very best prosthetic specialists, who would implant electrodes into the paralyzed girl to reach her nerve endings and make her a pair of fully obedient biotic legs. The process was not fast, and could take a few months to heal and acclimatize, but then my sister could walk on her legs again!

I'd give Val the gift today. She'd asked for a virtual reality capsule, and that's just what she'd get. And I'd make sure it was the very best one out there! I opened a search engine on my phone and looked it up. Yes, I was interested in the very newest and most modern models. I found them. Sixty-two thousand credits, and with delivery and installation included. For that kind of money, you'd have to hope so. What's the hold up? I'll go buy her one now.

I searched again for a route to the store on public transportation. I was probably the only person in the world who took an electrobus with two transfers to buy a virtual reality capsule for sixty-two thousand credits. Oh well, though. My sister would be happy. She'd earned this!

I woke up at five in the evening. And it was all on my own with no alarm clock. It had been a long time since something like that had happened to me. My sister hadn't yet returned from her big shopping outing with Kira, so she didn't know about my surprise for her yet.

The big virtual reality capsule, shimmering

with silvery-blue lacquer, was at the wall of her bedroom. I purposely asked for it to be positioned as low as possible, so my sister could comfortably crawl into it from her wheelchair. All the cables were already attached, and the sensor suit had been tested and sized for Valeria's body. The service center workers had already checked all the settings at midday. All the equipment was completely ready to use.

It was six o'clock, and my sister had left home at eleven thirty. How long could one really spend in such shops? I'd already begun to worry slightly, and called Val. My sister answered me with an unhappy and annoyed voice:

"What do you want, Timothy? I'm doing fine. I'm in a cosmetic shop right now getting some work done. Kira's with me. I remember that I had to be in *Boundless Realm* by seven thirty. I'll be home in an hour and a half. I won't be late."

My sister hung up. I then paced pensively through the apartment. I warmed up the lunch Kira had made in the microwave, and ate with gusto. Going to work without seeing my sister first and giving her the gift was something I had no plans of doing. I had to wait. I crawled onto the *Boundless Realm* forums. The most discussed news was the new advertising clip about Amra the pirate and the night battle.

The wyvern hunters were being rewarded with all kinds of unflattering names for losing the battle with such a colossal initial advantage in level and number... I just laughed, reading the replies of some "boarding-operation specialists" who couldn't even get their thoughts onto the forum cohesively. For some reason, I was sure that these "professionals" would have done no better than that crew of screw-ups. Nevertheless, they considered themselves to have the right to give advice and teachings to others. What could I say? As the famous poet Rustaveli once said: "Every man imagines himself a strategist, watching a battle from the sidelines."

There was no information about new meetings between any players and *White Shark* or *Princess Amelia*. Nevertheless, that put me on edge. How were my ships doing? Would they manage to reach the harbor of New Tortuga in peace? And then a genius idea came to mind of how to see the situation on my bireme right now — Veronica had been planning to stream the adventures of her Dryad Dancer live today! Even if it was for money, ten credits per day didn't seem like a serious obstacle to me now.

Finding Angelica Wayward's channel was no challenge. Paying for it and turning it on all the less so. I had to confirm my age to register, as the stream was in the 18+ category. But I naturally overcame the age barrier with ease and, leaning back into the living room couch with a glass of whisky in hand, I prepared to watch the video on the big in-screen wall.

Angelica Wayward's channel had seven and a half thousand viewers. Not bad! And every one of them was paying ten credits a day for the right to watch. Seventy-five thousand per day! Two million credits a month! And by the way, the viewers could leave their comments and desires for the player, which ran across the bottom of the screen from the right, and Veronica saw them.

Veronica preferred her streams not to be "first person" but with the camera behind her back so the dryad herself was constantly in frame. By the way, my conception of what the dryad would look like was way off base. In the in-game race guide, the dryad looked like a half-plant-half-woman with a rough woody bark instead of normal skin and with little branches and outgrowths coming out of the body in random places, covered with flowers and leaves.

Veronica had significantly improved upon the standard dryad model. Her character was a long-legged woman with an exaggerated figure. She had snow white ruffled hair and ash-gray skin smattered with whimsical tattoos of malachite green stems and leaves. The dryad really wasn't wearing any clothing, and even the loincloth by default on all new characters was nowhere to be seen. But at that, the Dryad Dancer had plenty of things on: long emerald earrings, and rings with expensive gems on her fingers, a braided gold belt and gold bracelets on her wrists and ankles.

The simplistic amulet in the shape of a green wyvern on a bronze chain looked badly out of place when compared with the dryad's other accoutrements. Nevertheless, the girl decided this would be the necklace for her, and not something fancier. I suspected that many of the accessories had magical properties, as I saw bright sparkles come periodically from inside the expensive stones, and washed-out colorful halos around the bracelets.

By the way, the Dryad Dancer had leveled up to 38 today. Say what you will, but Veronica was a talented player. I recognized the surroundings right away — Veronica was in my captains' chambers cursing, airing her dirty laundry to someone.

"No, fatty, that's not how it's gonna be. You need to understand: I can't play normally or make any plans until I know the complete situation on the ship. Where's that pretty little redheaded thief? I ordered the crew to go through the whole ship. They checked every room five times, but no one's seen her since morning!"

"I already told you, the dinghy's in place, and all the sailors assure me that Taisha hasn't left the ship. It's just that she's the captain's pet, so when he exits the game, she disappears. As soon as the Goblin Herbalist enters *Boundless Realm,* Taisha will show up," came a voice that must have belonged to Shrekson Bastard.

"Oh yeah? Just yesterday, I saw that overly curious bot in the game while her master was out. His beasts disappeared, yes. The rest of the goblins also. But that thief was following me all day and spying on me. I'm telling you, she stole my wallet yesterday, not thieves in the port! Where else would she have gotten the dough to buy that jar of expensive cosmetics?!"

Angelica turned around, and the familiar shelf came into view, crammed with all kinds of vials, vessels and bottles. The Dryad Dancer walked up closer and took the intricately adorned red vial.

"Maybe it belongs to Valerianna? Or maybe Amra bought it for his NPC girlfriend?" the Ogre suggested.

"Valerianna practically never comes to the captain's chambers. I already asked the orcs that. Mmm... It smells good. Gift to the First Lady in Waiting... Pretty name. Sounds very exclusive. See, Amra buys these awesome gifts, even for NPC's! He even purposely put it next to mine to annoy me. When will you give me something like this?"

"What about the emerald necklace I bought you?"

"Ha! That three-thousand-coin trinket? No, no. I'll never wear that abomination. The wyvern medallion is better — let Amra fear me! But you still haven't answered the question I asked you ten minutes ago: are you ready to follow me through fire and water? Time for thinking is up. I want an answer."

Angelica Wayward sharply turned and I finally saw the Ogre Fortifier. Absolutely naked, he was lying on the bed staring thoughtfully at the ceiling. A wave of enthusiasm swept over the messages running across the bottom of the screen — many were suggesting the dryad make love with the titan again. But Angelica ignored the viewers' wishes and threw herself at the Ogre Fortifier with more complaints:

"Why are you staying cooped up? It's time to finally choose what's worth more to you: playing with me and reaching new heights, or vegetating in minor roles with the big-eared pipsqueak?"

Pipsqueak? My indignation caused me to even spill the whisky from my glass. She just had to bring height into it! The Dryad Dancer was just a couple centimeters taller than my Goblin Herbalist in the first place, and was herself a total midget compared to the ogre!

The ogre, meanwhile, answered that he had made his choice long ago both in real life and in the game. So, he was prepared to follow his girlfriend through fire and water. He extended his huge paws, trying to pull the naked girl to him, but the dancer skillfully slipped out of his awkward embrace:

"Then that's great. Get dressed and come up on deck. We'll see the port soon. We have to act!"

As soon as the door closed behind Shrekson, the Dryad Dancer dashed to the perfume shelf, took a generous scoop of the thick pink cream with her clawed palm and spread it on her neck, temples and armpits. Over the girl's head, there appeared a red criminal marker — the computer took this action as theft. Angelica pushed the nearly empty container away, placing it behind the other jars with the words:

"And no one can prove a thing! That vile toad is about to learn what it really means to have something taken away!"

I gulped down the rest of my whisky and, the glass set on the table, clapped my hands together a few times. Angelica had just put my thoughts into words. I'd never have put it better myself!

Stealing the property made the viewers glad. Their elated comments were just piling in. I first didn't understand the reason for such stormy glee, but quickly realized from the messages running past that Angelica Wayward had earlier declared that she strictly followed three principles that were stated clearly in the description of her channel. One: she would never kill anyone. Two: she would never steal anything. And three: she was in fact playing a dancer, and not a wayward nympho who'd gone off the rails. So, though there would occasionally be sex scenes, the viewers should not count on watching the Dryad Dancer throw herself at anything alive.

But now that her first moral precept had fallen, there was a storm of acrid and joyful comments marking the occasion. I was also glad, but for a different reason. After setting my phone's countdown timer for five minutes, I sat back in the couch and waited for the continuation of the show.

The dryad's appearance on deck was met with a storm of glee from the pirates. The fearsome orcs bowed their heads low before her, some just fell down in a full bow or laid right down on the deck, so the Dryad Dancer could walk over their backs. Angelica Wayward accepted the admiration of the crowd with favor, sending air kisses in all directions and smiling to everyone.

"Lights on the horizon, madam," the lookout boy directed the dryad's attention. "New Tortuga."

The dryad extended a hand demandingly and Johnny humbly handed her the spyglass. The girl twisted the lens and spent a long time looking at the far-off port.

"There's so many ships there..." she stated thoughtfully, after which she turned to the Ogre Fortifier. "No more pussyfooting around. We'll be in port soon. The time has come for us to take the reins. Amra said something about six PM, but it's already five thirty. He should appear in *Boundless Realm* at any minute. I'll manage the herbalist myself, but you're gonna have to neutralize the mavka. As soon as Valerianna Quickfoot enters the game, just walk up to her and snap her neck while she's loading up and not expecting you to attack. Can you do that?"

"It just seems so despicable..." Shrekson said in hesitation. "It looks too much like treachery. How will I look my friends in the eye after this?"

"Now you've found something to worry about! Leaving your family for a young lover, and abandoning three young daughters seems much more treacherous to me. Nevertheless, you did that cynically and with full awareness. In comparison with that, getting hold of a valuable prize in a virtual game, and thus distancing yourself from some self-assured gapers is nothing."

I looked at the timer. The poison hadn't yet taken affect, but nevertheless, Angelica Wayward had stomped the pride and ego of her companion so deep into the mud that I was left marveling. But Leon kept quiet, frowning gloomily and squeezing his huge fists. Would the giant really just swallow such offensive words from his girlfriend? But still, I didn't manage to figure that out — the timer gave a beep and it was as if Angelica Wayward was replaced with someone different. Her face twisted with rage, poking the Ogre with her clawed finger. The Dryad Dancer said quietly:

"You've disappointed me again, Leon. You

promised to follow me through fire and water, but you can't even carry out my first order without falling into a stupor. You might have realized long ago that I am not okay with such unconfident grunting — not yes, not no. I need my partner to agree with me absolutely and without speaking, obeying all my orders. I wish we'd never met. I should have found a more decisive companion or just done it all on my own. We're done. I don't need you anymore. Kill him!"

Ten pirate sabers immediately came down on the Ogre Fortifier, and the titan collapsed, bathing the boards of the deck in his blood.

Experience received: 270 Exp.

Achievement unlocked: Player killer (1)

The dryad just laughed uncontrollably, spinning away in a wild emotional dance, getting the half-mad crowd even more worked up by the fresh blood. The viewers of the video clip were running amok together with the wild orcs, noticing the fall of the second moral precept. Based on all that, the poison must have taken effect — the dancer tried to scream something to the gathered crowd, but constantly broke down into stupid giggling, sometimes even breaking into an animalistic whine. At that, the dryad couldn't stop scratching herself frantically, like a flea-bitten dog, and having no shame of it. But there, Angelica stopped sharply and, calling the pirates to silence with a gesture, got up on a barrel and cried out:

"I is you new girl-captain! Is all to forget about much dummy Amra! Is for me that orc should be obey! And hear now, orc crowd. My very first is ord..."

Charisma check failed

Damage taken: 188 (210 Punch — 22 armor)

10 second Deaf effect

The powerful punch to the ear of the Dryad Dancer made her fly away and fall on her back. The life bar immediately jumped down by two thirds, reaching the orange zone. The image became blurry. She couldn't focus her vision for a long time. And when the head spinning had passed, in the center of the screen, appeared First Mate Ziabash Hardy, rubbing his wounded right fist. Shaman Ghuu, standing next to him, pointed at the deafened dryad with his staff and shouted:

"Capture the mutineer and tie her up! As if it wasn't enough that her treachery caused the fall of many of our brothers in our last battle with the undying, now she wants to do the rest of us in!"

The green and blue markers of the NPC pirates on the mini-map instantly changed color to yellow and even red. A great many powerful hands instantly grabbed the lying girl and placed her into a vertical position with a rough jerk. The dryad's arms were forced behind her back and tied up very professionally. The shaman walked around her in a circle unhurriedly, looking over the troublemaker, who still had yet to come to her senses and stated loudly:

"This is exactly what Captain Amra warned us about. He's wise and had already figured out that this wayward woman might want to dominate you all with her evil charms. This morning, the captain predicted that the dryad would try to take over the ship. Now, on an order from Captain Amra, throw this witch overboard!"

"But she's so pretty..." one of the orc sailors said falteringly, looking over the naked dryad with a pensive gaze and loudly blowing his stuffed-up nose.

The shaman walked around the tied-up captive once again, being especially careful to look at her blood-soaked neck. After that, he looked at the wild pirate crew crowding up on the deck in anticipation of his decision, after which he waved his hand:

"I don't see any diseases, even though the dryad is itching like a mangy piglet. But alright, you devils, I'm convinced... But after you're done, she goes overboard!"

The elated whooping of the pirates made my

ears ring. Based on the delighted replies constantly running along the bottom of the screen, the viewers of the video channel were simply in ecstasy. There was a constant flood of monetary rewards coming in for Veronica, and some of them that jumped by were quite significant — up to several thousand credits. Her viewers must have decided that Angelica had been intending for this to happen all along.

The content from there was very much in the 18+ category. I spent a few minutes watching, then decisively turned the screen off — I'm not much of a fan of adult films. After that, I took out my cell phone and called Leon. No, I wasn't planning to admit that I had been watching him and his flame. But it did seem to me that my friend might need some moral support. And I wasn't wrong — from his first words, I could tell by Leon's tone of voice that the former construction worker was simply dead with suffering.

He spent some time rambling, occasionally mumbling out utterly unconnected phrases on feminine cunning and thanklessness. Slightly calmed down and his spirits gathered, my friend said:

"Timothy, I have to warn you about Veronica. She's planning to capture *White Shark* and attack you as soon as you load up *Boundless Realm*. And she just sent me to respawn for trying to stand in her way."

Trying to stand in her way? Is that how she's calling it? I just saw him standing in tacit approval of all her actions. But I didn't say those words aloud. Quite the opposite, in fact. I reassured Leon:

"Don't worry — she won't be able to do it. I gave the pirate crew an order not to impede Angelica and for them all to pretend together that they were falling for the Dryad Dancer's charms. Say what you will, but there is very little entertainment on the ship. In her, the pirates have a pretty dancing girl, singing and making eyes. And they don't even need to buy tickets for the striptease. So, I didn't want to interfere with Veronica's playing — no matter how you look at it, she's a work colleague. She needs to earn experience too. But if the Dryad Dancer forgets her role as a guest, and does try to declare herself captain, the jokes end right then and there. The crew will restrain her and throw her overboard. That was my order."

Leon spent a long time thinking, then said with obvious tooth grinding:

"I mean, I trusted her... And she ruined my life... The bitch... Are you sure the pirates will drown her right away? It's just that Angelica and I have the same respawn point — a big apple orchard next to the port of Piren... Oh how I'd like to meet her there and have a heart-to-heart talk!"

"She might not get drowned right away... After all, the pirates also wanted to 'have a heart-to-heart talk' with the dancer. But in any case, before *White Shark* reaches the port of New Tortuga, she will be sent to respawn."

"So, I don't have long to wait. The port was already visible with a spyglass. I listened to the sailors talking. They said in an hour and a half or so, we'd be in the harbor. Alright. I'll wait that time at the respawn stone. You can't even imagine how badly I want to talk with Veronica now, Timothy, when the masks are off, and she's exposed her true self. If we can't come to an agreement in peace, I'll acquaint that piece of trash with my sharp poleax. She just killed me, so she'll be a criminal for eight hours. That means she won't be going anywhere! I'll send her to respawn over and over until I've gotten all my money back to the very last coin."

I had absolutely no cause to feel sympathy for the cunning Dryad Dancer, but nevertheless, I was shaken by how quickly Leon's character shifted. The former construction worker was always associated in my mind with the prototypical hard-working good guy — perhaps a bit of a simpleton, but an honest and reliable companion to the end. But now he was embittered and prepared to kill his girlfriend time and time again just to get back the coins he'd loaned her. That was precisely the opposite of my image. Acting like this, Leon didn't arouse any sympathy either.

"Leon, I cannot believe I'm saying this, but I beg you not to kill the dryad! She might have had some reason for behaving the way she did. If need be, I can pay back the rest of what you loaned her. I have money now, and I am prepared to part with it just so I don't have to see you spoil your nature. You were always the most just and honest of our group. Everyone loved you for your essential virtue. It would be for the best, if you could remain that way."

I managed to embarrass Leon. The former construction worker spent a long time in thought, then promised me that he wouldn't attack Angelica Wayward at the respawn point as long as she didn't display aggression first. Leon categorically refused the money I offered him, saying that he wanted to handle all his problems on his own, both in *Boundless Realm* and in real life. But still, he thanked me for my willingness to help.

The trill of the doorbell made me end the conversation with Leon quickly and run to open up. Kira, giving me a kiss on the cheek as she walked, rolled the wheelchair into the apartment. The pile of bags and boxes stacked up on it was so huge that I didn't even see my sister right away. But when the purchases were placed on the floor,

I saw an obviously embarrassed Val before me with a new outfit and haircut.

I couldn't even recognize her. This was the first time I realized that my little sister, who I was accustomed to thinking of as a child, had finally grown up and turned into a beautiful lady. Fashionable haircut, smooth skin on her face, false eyelashes, bright shining lipstick. A stylish blue dress with a deep neckline, a necklace with beads made of sparkling little blue stones, sapphire earrings in her ears and rings on her fingers. Valeria was also wearing a plush plaid on her knees, covering her lack of legs.

"Well, how do you like it?" my sister asked timidly.

While I was admiring my sister's new look and stylish purchases, Kira tried to slink away unnoticed. I caught her in the doorway.

"I got a bit carried away, and wasn't thinking about the numbers," my girlfriend said in embarrassment, crumpling some papers in her hands. "But don't worry. As I already said, you can pay me back later. Or just consider this my gift to your sister."

I outstretched my hand demandingly and, unclenching the beautiful redhead's fingers one at a time, took the stack of rumpled receipts from Kira. I straightened out and read the receipts, adding them up in my head. Six and a half thousand credits... no problem in our new circumstances. I picked up the phone and, after looking through my old transactions for Kira's account, transferred six and a half thousand to it. My red-headed girlfriend's brows shot up in surprise. Before they managed to come back down, I invited both of the girls to come see the gift I'd gotten my dear sister.

* * *

Of course, I was hoping my sister would like the gift. But reality surpassed all my boldest expectations. The shrieking and screams of joy made my ears ring. Even without legs, the girl managed to jump up in her seat and shout out that I was the very greatest brother in the world! As if in far-off careless childhood, Val extended her hands upward, demanding that I lift her up. And she embraced me vigorously by the neck, sobbing in joy and smearing her makeup. Kira even walked aside and furtively dried some tears.

When the initial rapturous oohing and aahing had passed, Valeria dove head first into the thick manual describing the virtual reality capsule's settings. A sharpened pencil appeared in my sister's hand, and she started taking notes in the margins. Some of the parameters and instructions she even transferred into a notepad where she'd long kept her secret diary.

Kira pulled me into the kitchen and quickly

cut up some sandwiches. While the kettle was warming up, her voice lowered to a whisper, the beautiful red-head said:

"You really came through with that gift! By the way, I wanted to talk to you about Valeria. While your sister was undergoing the cosmetic procedures, I got in touch with one of the best prosthetics clinics and found out everything. It will take about three weeks to do all the implanting for the anchors on the bones, electrodes on the nerve endings and servos for her artificial muscles. For that entire time, she'd have to be under constant observation in a clinic, as the process is complicated and specialists would have to make sure she didn't start rejecting the prosthetics..."

"I can hear you!" came Val's voice from the bedroom. "And I repeat again: I don't want it!"

Kira must not have known that my sister had very keen hearing, and went abruptly silent. After that, with a sad chuckle, she added in a normal voice:

"That was exactly how Valeria reacted earlier when I told her about biotic legs. She didn't even want to listen when she heard about the three weeks in a hospital bed. She even threatened to purposely impede the healing process and rip out the implanted elements if she's brought to the clinic by force. I probably shouldn't have raised that topic with her — I should have just let you talk to your sister. Treatment costs a lot and takes some time, but it will need to be done one day."

A silence descended after Kira's words, making the cell phone ring that broke it sound jarring. The number was unfamiliar, but that had stopped surprising me — who hadn't called me in the last few days...?

"Timothy? When are you going to enter the game?" came the voice I was least expecting to hear, that of Veronica.

"I don't know yet. I've got some business in the real world. I need to handle it first. I might not be there until tomorrow morning. What's happened?" Did she really think I'd reveal my plans to her after all her crafty scheming?

"But you have to come play *Boundless Realm* today! You've only played six and a half hours, and the rules of the 'great hunt' say that the wyvern master has to spend at least eight hours a day in game! There's a timer on the forum showing how long you've been playing each day. That's how I know."

Oh really... As it turned out, the players were carefully watching to make sure my character followed the rules of the event. Although, with such a valuable prize and such a large number of participants, I guess I could have expected it.

"Oh yeah? Well, then I'll be in later. Near nightfall. But you still haven't explained why you need me."

"Well, you see..." the girl slightly faltered before answering. "I've found myself in a bad position, tied up by your pirates. I'd like you to enter *Boundless Realm* and order your crew to let me go. It doesn't have to be you. Your sister would work, too."

What?! Veronica knew that Valerianna Quickfoot was my sister? The only way that was possible was if Leon had blabbed. That was probably also how she got my number, when they were close. I tried not to get surprised at how informed Veronica was, but I tried to squeeze more information out. Naturally, I didn't admit that I was watching the broadcast.

"Strange. The pirate crew got a clear and unambiguous order from me not to interfere with the undying on my ship and even to indulge them however necessary. The only exception was if any of you tried to declare yourself captain and seize power on *White Shark*. In that case, I ordered the orcs to throw the mutineer overboard. That's all. I haven't given any other orders relating to you, or Leon. What might the uncomfortable situation be?"

"It has to do with the lotion you snuck onto my shelf. You can't tell me that the jar of First Lady in Waiting's Gift just showed up just by chance! I immediately noticed it wasn't mine and tried some out cautiously. After that is when the problems started — I lost control of my character and the

Dryad Dancer did some strange things. She killed the Ogre Fortifier and taunted the pirate crew..."

Wow! Veronica had the gall to implicate me in the fact that she stole something that wasn't hers! And my hearing was also cut by the phrase "my shelf" — it seemed the dryad already considered herself master of the captain's cabin. And, by the way, she had an interesting interpretation of events, especially in light of the fact that I had seen it all with my own eyes... Well, what was to be done? If she didn't want to be honest with me, she certainly couldn't expect the truth in return!

"That was a trap to catch a thief. For the last few days, someone's been regularly lifting valuable items from my captain's chambers, even though it's been locked. But I haven't been able to figure out who. There are a hundred and fifty sailors on *White Shark*, and any of them might have the lock picking skill. Even if I forced each of them to show me their inventory, that wouldn't do a thing –the compromising items were probably stashed away. It would be stupid to carry such things around, so I put a special lotion in that jar, which was bright and flashy, but the lotion would cause an unbearable itch. If any crew member started scratching, I would know they were the thief!"

"Strange trap. It was stupid to think that a wild orc would start using woman's cosmetics. But still, you're right — there definitely is a thief on your ship. Yesterday, they took my wallet with a very significant amount of money. Over thirty thousand coins and expensive stones. And the first in the list of suspects is your companion, Taisha. She's a thief by profession and was constantly messing about next to me. Also, it would be very easy for her to take your things — you let that bot into the captain's quarters yourself!"

"That's exactly why the trap was made specifically to catch a curious girl, not a moping coarse orc, who doesn't even know what cosmetics are."

The story came together. Veronica even believed it. But I thought also that I'd have to get on Taisha about the theft of thirty thousand from the Dryad Dancer, and commend her for her luck if she really had done it.

"In the end, the pirates grabbed my Dryad Dancer and really were about to throw me into the ocean, though not right away... Loss of experience and an hour for respawn is unpleasant, but not fatal. But it looks like I ruined everything. When I got control back over my character, I started convincing the pirates not to kill me. It worked, but at a hefty price... Instead of simply drowning me, they placed the dryad in a barrel to sell along with the other slaves 'in accordance with the captain's order.' And now, I need you to load up *Boundless Realm* right away and intervene. Because right now, these dolts are about to sell me to the captain of the drekar *Drake of the Morning Star*, which will be leaving to the Eastern Continent in a few hours! Of all the slavers in New Tortuga, he's the cruelest! Twelve days underway! In a barrel, with my hands and legs tied! And at that, from what I overheard, they're planning to feed and water my dryad only once every two days, just enough so I won't die. And they have no plans to untie me!"

I couldn't hold back the emotions and laughed uncontrollably. It was some time before I was settled. I was not expecting this to turn out so horrendously for her. Finally, I finished laughing and explained the reason for my joy:

"You see, Veronica... I really did order my first mate to sell everything unneeded on the ship as soon as they arrived to New Tortuga. Everything they definitely wouldn't want for the rest of the journey. And when you convinced the orc pirates not to throw your dryad overboard, the NPC had a difficult choice on how to treat you. His programmed algorithms must have bizarrely classified the Dryad Dancer as 'something that won't be needed for the rest of the journey,' with all the consequences that come with that."

Dotur-Khawe

KIRA TOOK ME to work. This time, the beautiful red-head was not behind the wheel of her exclusive Black Crystal, but of a totally normal electric car of a popular brand. There must have been tens if not hundreds of thousands of them in the metropolis. We even had to wait in a traffic jam for a bit. During our trip, Kira's phone rang a few times, but every time, she refused the call. She clearly didn't want to talk to anyone else in my presence.

When we were near the entry to the building, the red-headed lady raised the question of biotic prostheses for my sister again. Kira had no understanding of the reason for the girl's categorical stubbornness. I was much more familiar with Val's nature and understood that, for my sister, the very thought of having to stay in a strange place surrounded by totally unfamiliar people caused a sense of panic and alienation. Nevertheless, I promised her I'd speak with Valeria and gradually begin to impress upon her the necessity and importance of the medical procedures. Meanwhile, I'd already set aside money for the purpose, one hundred nine thousand credits, in a special deposit account.

When I entered the corporation, the automated system scanned us and the gates moved aside. Although there was no real need for it, a muscular security guard ran out of his booth and greeted my companion with a respectful bow.

"The guards must know and respect you," I said, turning Kira's attention to the man's unusual behavior. "When I went to get your lost ring, too, no one asked me for any signatures or documents. They all knew you."

"Come on..." Kira smiled happily. "Timothy, I've been working for the corporation practically since their first day. I've successfully taken part in a lot of projects and mass events. I've earned more than one ten-million-credit prize. Some of the money was immediately invested in stocks of the *Boundless Realm* corporation, so I've got skin in the game, and want our company to do well. It's not written in my personal record what job I have exactly, but the guard sitting in front of the monitor sees my red access level and understands that the person in front of him must be from leadership."

After parking the car in the underground lot, the beautiful redhead let me out and bid me farewell. Kira had to go up to the highest floors of the skyscraper for some business. I though, had to go down to the tester floor.

"I say we should go out tomorrow morning after work for breakfast," Kira said, smiling as she kissed me goodbye.

In an excellent mood, at eight o'clock, I entered my game cabin and turned on the screen. So, what's the news? There was relatively little mail, but one message lit me up. It was a level two hundred sixteen dwarven warrior I already knew by the name of Headshots_For_All from the *Keepers* clan:

"Amra, we took the Goons' *castle! They clearly weren't expecting our attack. There were almost no guards. To be honest, there wasn't very much loot — their leader, Mariam Standing_Right_Behind_You [GOONS] threw almost all the clan's resources into organizing the hunt for you. Practically the whole clan has left their normal place and dashed off on the chase. You must have gotten them really mad! Exactly what we wanted! As we agreed, ten percent of the loot is yours. Present this letter at any branch of the bank of dwarves, and you'll be given twenty-eight thousand coins."*

Alright! Very pleasant news! I closed the

message, grabbed my phone and called my sister, saying I'd arrived at work. After that, I closed the lid of the virtual reality capsule and started the procedure of loading *Boundless Realm*. Half a minute later, my big-eared Goblin Herbalist opened his eyes, still in the very same dwarven train car.

"Finally! I was starting to worry — in twenty minutes, we'll reach the Dotur-Khawe station, and you undying just wouldn't show up!" Gnum Spiteful groaned.

Taisha also complained her fill, saying that I was gone for too long and she had grown very bored and felt uncomfortable. But I didn't manage to answer her — Valerianna Quickfoot appeared in the seat next to mine.

"That's what I'm talking about!" The mavka's eyes were wide open in elation. She rushed to share her new impressions. "Now, I understand the difference between playing normally and full immersion in a virtual reality capsule! Tim, I can clearly discern the smells of cinder and smoke! I can sense that the seat below me is soft and made of leather. There's a draft coming from that crack! This is just all unbelievably awesome!!!"

The dwarf, as predicted, let the idle chatter of the undying pass by his ears unnoticed. But Taisha, sitting opposite, was looking at me with alarm and making a "screw loose" gesture, pointing at the wood nymph with her other hand.

I reassured the NPC thief with a smile, saying that my sister had entered *Boundless Realm* by a slightly different means this time, so that was why she was acting strange. Taisha didn't understand anything of my explanation, but still stopped being afraid for Valerianna Quickfoot.

"Enough chatter! Do you feel it? The speed has already started to gradually fall. The stokers have stopped throwing turf into the furnace. That means we'll be at the station in ten minutes," said the Dwarf Mechanic, who was even more impatient than usual today. "After all, I still don't even know what you want in the city of dwarves, or where to bring you. Dotur-Khawe is a huge city. It would take you more than a week to explore all its levels and corridors."

I answered this question almost instantly:

"Gnum, I'm not planning to stay in Dotur-Khawe long. There are three locations in your city that interest me: The Bank of Thorin the Ninth, the Alchemists' Guild, and any store where I might come by good equipment."

"How good?" the small persnickety man immediately clarified.

"The very best!" Taisha answered for me, and Valerianna Quickfoot repeated these words.

I nodded in agreement. I had money now, but the equipment I'd once bought for my Goblin Herbalist at level fifteen or twenty had grown much too old a good while ago. Actually, we all needed new things.

"And also," I clarified. "I want the place with the least undying. Better if there were no undying at all."

"In that case..." the Dwarf Mechanic stood decisively from his seat and cracked open the blinds on the window, trying to see something in the dark corridor. "We'll have to get off a bit earlier, before the railroad point. There's an old track there that leads to old mined-out copper pits and the old part of town. They have a branch of the Subterranean Bank of Thorin the Ninth there, and an Alchemists' Guild building, as well as a whole block of good craftsmen. Undying are known to enter the old part of town, but very infrequently. All in all, it's just what you asked for... Although, it looks like we've already gone past it... Ah, no. Now I'm recognizing familiar places. Two minutes from now, we'll have to jump out. Get ready. But for now, I'll go and warn your companions and open the door for the wolves."

"Jump!" the dwarf's cry caught me off guard, as I supposed we still had another minute to go.

My big-eared goblin took a decisive step toward the wide-open door and jumped into the darkness. The second I spent in flight put my heart in my throat. I landed hard on my feet, making

Amra tumble and roll headfirst down the stone floor, nearly slamming into a massive stone column.

Successful Agility check
Experience received: 200 Exp.

Dodge Skill increased to level 22!

Acrobatics skill increased to level 16!

Taisha landed gracefully next to me, taking a little run and not even falling. But then Valerianna Quickfoot flew with a frightened shriek down a side corridor. I grew afraid for my sister, but a few seconds later, her enraptured voice reached me:

"Holy shit! That was awesome! It was like jumping off the swing when I was a kid!"

Irek, Yunna, Darius and Darina as well as the animals all jumped out of the train without incident. The most surprising thing was that the fat and heavy dwarf mechanic jumped almost best of all, staying confidently on his feet.

"That way!" our guide called out in an even tone, pointing down a weakly lit tunnel with rails on the floor. It was as if jumping off a train was business as usual for him, so he didn't see anything worthy of discussion.

We tramped down the ties for ten minutes,

passing by the occasional lit lamp on the walls. In that time, a few paid messages landed in my mailbox — nothing but nonsense. Pure spam. But these messages meant that the pursuers, after Amra entered the game, had not discovered him in the port of New Tortuga and were trying to determine his new coordinates. Then, after yet another bend in the tunnel, we suddenly saw a bright light.

"We're almost there. Ah, old town... My old stomping grounds... It's been so long... I thought I'd never ever return..." nostalgia and pity could be heard in Gnum Spiteful's voice.

"So, why'd you leave?" I asked just because, without any secret motive.

*Successful check for Gnum Spiteful's opinion
Experience received: 200 Exp.*

Level thirty-six!

What? Just a level-up? But where were the usual bumps to poison or cold resistance?! I opened my character guide. Clearly, the resistances simply wouldn't go higher than eighty percent, and full invulnerability to two types of damage was impossible to achieve by raising level alone. But what a shame... After placing my free stat points as usual — one in Agility and two in Charisma — I closed the computer information and got ready to listen to the dwarf's story about why he'd left his home.

But our guide was behaving strangely — looking up into the distance, where a big group of dwarves was coming our direction with picks. Gnum Spiteful burst from place unexpectedly and ran out in front, crying out joyfully:

"Daddy!!!"

One of the bearded dwarves dropped his tool and ran in our direction, his hands parted and crying:

"My daughter!!!"

"Daughter?" I asked out loud in surprise, trying to see even one feminine feature in the singed-bearded face of our companion.

"Yes, that's a lady dwarf. Just a girl, in fact. And by the standards of her subterranean folk, she's actually quite pretty," Taisha assured me. "Many lady dwarves have beards, so there's nothing surprising here. While you were gone, her and I spent the whole day chatting in the train, and she told me about her life. Our friend's real name is Vanessa. And her original nickname was 'Hamfist' or 'Shithand.'"

Valerianna was just snickering away. I couldn't hold back a smile either. Darius, who had no sense of tact whatsoever, was cackling away loudly. Taisha looked unhappily at all of us and said:

"She bungled some work that her whole

family had spent the week prior making in the forge. It was because of the insulting nickname that Vanessa left her family, and went somewhere where no one would know her. First, she went to the humans, where she was given the new name Gnum Spiteful due to her rotten nature and habit of rushing into a fight after the fifth glass of beer. After that, she was captured by the orc pirates. What happened from there is obvious..."

We walked up to the embracing pair of dwarves, and Vanessa pointed me to her father:

"Captain Amra freed me from the pirates and took me on in his crew."

The black-bearded dwarf took a decisive step toward me and embraced me tightly with his big strong calloused mitts, causing my bones to crackle.

Successful Constitution check
Experience received: 20 Exp.

Damage taken: 76 (122 Physical damage —
36 Armor)
Hit points: 233 of 309

Damn! I managed to take a strained breath after the extremely warm reception. My whole body ached. Every muscle was announcing its existence with pain. If that was what the system called a successful check, I was afraid to even imagine what would have happened with a failed check. Broken ribs, punctured lungs, death and respawning on the Island of the Wanton Widow? I shuddered just to think of it!

"Your captain's pretty flimsy!" the dwarf guffawed in good nature. His comrades laughed as well. "But in any case, thank you for rescuing my daughter! I invite you all into my home! We're having a big celebration today!"

The dwarves all whooped in joy, hard hats and even mining equipment flew upward. Gnum Spiteful or, probably I should be calling her Vanessa now, took advantage of the occasion and whispered into my ear:

"Don't think about refusing, Amra. That would seriously offend them. And I ask you not to talk to my relatives about the composition of the crew of *White Shark* — pirates are not thought well of here. Orcs either."

* * *

"...then, the proud and extraordinary daughter of the glorious subterranean folk shouted out that her shot on the enemy trireme was sure to hit! Otherwise, she'd make a mop with her red beard and wash the deck of *White Shark* with it."

"Oh! Ooh! That's what I'm talking about! A really serious oath!" the energized howl of hundreds of dwarven voices drowned out my words.

I took advantage of the pause and suggested everyone refill their mugs and glasses to the top, because the next part was the most interesting. My suggestion was met with shouts of approval, and the underground humanoids hurried to the drink barrels. Val furtively elbowed me in the side and suggested I not repeat the mistake I'd made on the Island of the Wanton Widow.

"Don't worry about that, Val. I've got the situation totally under control. My resists have grown much higher since then, and I've passed every check for resistance to alcohol so far. Plus, it's such a wonderful chance — all the key NPC's of the old town are gathered here in one place! I'm simply telling them the story of my adventures, and that's gotten me through two levels of the Socialization quest! I'll finish the third part of it really soon, too!"

After graciously accepting a big foamy mug of *King of the Depths* from the hand of the master of the house, I continued my tale. In passing, I noted that Vanessa's mother had sent one of the young relatives out to the market for more malty beverage, as the reserves of beer and moonshine in the house were coming to an end.

"So then, Vanessa managed to prove that her words were not just idle talk! She spent a long time carefully aiming the catapult, and when the enemy ship, it seemed, was just about to hit us with their battering ram, she fired!!!"

I went abruptly silent and took a big gulp from my mug, enjoying the excellent brew with purposeful composure.

Successful check for Poison Resistance
Experience received: 80 Exp.

The crowd was silent, patiently awaiting the rest of the story. Hundreds of eyes were fixed on my big-eared goblin. I was constantly getting messages about successful checks for the reaction of dwarf smiths, dwarf mechanics, dwarf traders and members of other professions. The markers of the hundreds of NPC's around me on the mini map had already long since changed from yellow to green, and there were more blue ones every minute. Experience was gushing in like a river — I'd leveled up twice in an hour and a half just talking with dwarves about my adventures on the high seas!

"And what happened after that?" rang out an impatient voice from somewhere in the back rows. "Did Vanessa hit the pirates?"

"She did! And did she ever! A fiery hell rained down on our enemies! An all-devouring flame rolled over the deck. The pirate ship lit up like a candle!"

The dwarves gasped in delight all at once, as if they had just lit fire to a pirate ship themselves.

Mission completed: Socialization Dotur-Khawe Old Town 3/3
Experience received: 8000 Exp.

Finishing the quest meant that the key NPC's' average opinion of me was now over +75. Leading my eyes over the message, I continued the story:

"You'll never believe it! Trying to get free of the flames, the burning pirates jumped to *White Shark* one after the other. There were a lot of them! But the most dangerous was their captain. He wailed horribly in rage, got a running start, made a powerful push off and jumped to our ship! It was a level one hundred eighty undying human paladin bound in a suit of black armor covered in spikes!"

Everyone gasped in fear. I then thought belatedly that I should have claimed the pirate captain had a different profession. After all, paladins were, by definition, lawful and good warriors. Such a person would be entirely out of place among pirates. Before any of the guests managed to notice that contradiction, I rushed to continue my story:

"It already seemed that the ghastly opponent would cut us into a fine mince with his terrifying two-handed sword. But Vanessa saved the day again! She bravely ran out in front and met the flying enemy with a two-handed hammer! The ringing when the hammer struck the black armor was so loud that fish in the sea got stunned and floated belly-up to the surface. The pirate captain flew back in his heavy armor and immediately fell to the sea floor as crab food! For that feat, the brave Vanessa got the right to be first to take loot from the captured ship!"

The end of the story drowned the crowd in elated screams. They all congratulated the brave lady once again and made toasts in her honor. I didn't go without attention, either. Unknown dwarves walked up to me, squeezed my hand and thanked me for saving their fellow dwarf.

Attention!!!
You have reached the maximum opinion with the residents of Dotur-Khawe Old Town
Hidden mission completed: Socialization 4/3 (Dwarves)

Experience received: 7200 Exp.
Charisma increased by 2 points
Automatic +5 to the opinion of all Dwarves
Status received: Honored Guest of Dotur-Khawe
Foreman Skill increased to level 24!

Level thirty-nine!

I'd leveled up three times in just an hour and a half! That's what I'm talking about! But now, the time had come to gradually wrap things up — it was already nine in the evening, and the branches of the Subterranean Bank and Alchemists' Guild, as far as I'd managed to tell, closed at nine in Dotur-Khawe.

But as soon as I even hinted about leaving, the master of the house, barely able to stay on his feet, gestured for me to wait and, a minute later, was dragging behind him a dwarf who was drunk as a skunk, saying this was the very alchemist I needed to talk to. The dwarf, having drunk to excess and tripping over his tongue, promised me that his alchemy shop would stay open all night for me, so there was no reason to rush to leave the celebration.

With great doubt, I looked at the alchemist, who just could not stay on his feet. It was a massive effort for him to even sit, but still I told him about the new poison I'd created, Gift to the First Lady in Waiting, and its effect. My story made the alchemist laugh. He even fell onto the floor guffawing, where he immediately fell asleep. Fortunately, the quest managed to finish nonetheless:

Mission completed: Recognition of the Alchemists' Guild (1/10)
Experience received: 80 Exp.

~ Stay on the Wing ~

Alchemy Skill increased to level 22

Considering the state the quest giver was in, I had no cause to hope I might quickly continue this mission chain. But where was the reward for completing the optional condition, even if it was variable?! After all, I honestly did test the effect of the elixir on the Dryad Dancer and described the effect! Then, I noticed a thickened vial of bluish transparent liquid roll out of the unbuttoned belt bag of the dwarven alchemist sleeping at my feet.

Insufficient Intelligence to identify object
Requisite Intelligence: 90

The game system gave me no warnings about the object belonging to someone else, though. So, with a clean conscience, I picked up the vial, considering it likely my reward. The mavka read the information with ease — it was an Ice Bomb, which made a hail of ice chunks and caused a deep freeze effect. A useful item. I put it in my bag.

Then the master of the house reappeared. This time, he came to present me his honored neighbor, head of the local branch of the Subterranean Bank of Thorin the Ninth. The silver-haired dwarf banker was wearing a luxurious crimson velvet suit and, in contrast to all the other dwarves, was completely sober. As, it should be noted, were his two vigilant armor-suited bodyguards, who had yet to take their hands off the handles of their sheathed blades. I extended the dwarf banker two letters that looked like parchment scrolls. He took out an old-fashioned pince-nez and read the contents.

"Everything is in order, Captain Amra. The summoning scroll and your gold will be brought to this location post haste. Is there any chance that a client as important as yourself would be interested in any other services of our bank? Converting notes into hard gold? Perhaps you'd let us keep your savings. Or maybe you'd like to invest in goods or stocks of subterranean companies?"

I didn't manage to answer — a young beardless dwarf, who'd been sent out for wine, ran into the yard panting. He threw a quick gaze over the crowd of guests, saw me, ran up and, blurted out:

"There are many undying near the old market! They look like big-time gangsters. All are armed. They're behaving rudely, utterly boorish. They're asking the locals if anyone's seen a goblin by the name of Amra. They asked me too, and I sent them to the District of Smithies in the opposite direction. But, I'm afraid I might not have managed to trick them for long."

Ugh, I guess I never should have showed my face in the big city! And I really shouldn't have stayed in one place this long. It seemed searching with magical messengers had shown the pursuers to Dotur-Khawe, and one of them had found a portal scroll to the dwarven capital. I had to get out right away.

"We can protect our valuable guest!" Vanessa's father shouted menacingly, and the drunken crowd took up that cry.

But I shook my head in doubt. A group of high-level undying would sweep away any number of local NPC craftsmen without even noting particular resistance. Although... In any large city in *Boundless Realm*, there had to be areas where players could feel safe, under the protection of NPC guards. I asked Vanessa if there were such areas in Dotur-Khawe.

"Of course. In the Central District, the District of Guilds, and in the New District, the streets are patrolled by the subterranean guard of our king. In fact, my brother serves in the king's guard. They're all very capable soldiers, who can take down even the undying!" the bearded girl assured me.

> **ATTENTION!**
> **The forbidden spell Astral Explosion has just been cast in the city of Dotur-Khawe!**
> **The criminal has been apprehended and transferred to municipal prison**

For the next 12 hours, portals, summoning magic and teleportation scrolls will be impossible to use in all areas of the city

An unexpected twist — our enemies had pushed the limit, cutting the dwarven city off from the rest of *Boundless Realm*. Now, you couldn't jump here, nor leave the city via portal. Most likely, our pursuers were now sure that Amra was hidden somewhere in Dotur-Khawe, and they'd decided to kill two birds with one stone — not let their victim flee from the hunt, and not allow other competing clans near their valuable prey. I could read obvious panic in the wood nymph's eyes.

"They're blocking the ability to leave the city by magical means! There are probably undying watching over every way out of Dotur-Khawe now, too. Amra, you need to exit *Boundless Realm* right away!!!"

"No, Val. That's not up for discussion! First, I haven't completed my eight daily hours. Second, the pursuers will just find the place where I exited from and, there, they'll just wait for Amra to appear in *Boundless Realm* again. What we need to do is leave Dotur-Khawe. The city of dwarves is lousy with underground passages. They can't possibly cover them all! There are probably some unused abandoned corridors that go to the surface somewhere."

~ Stay on the Wing ~

Just then, one of the banker's bodyguards walked up to me — he handed me a scroll, and a heavy bag of coins. After hearing my words about abandoned corridors, the armor-bound dwarf burst out in inspiration:

"I know one such passage! The boarded-up shaft next to the old fountain. It leads to long-ago mined-out copper pits on the surface. Humans used to have a prison there, where the inmates mined copper veins on the edge of the Great Desert."

"But it's dangerous!" Vanessa shouted out in fear. "I've heard of that place. The catacombs there are full of arachnids, spinners, scorpions and all kinds of many-armed ghastly beasts. That passage was boarded up ages ago, and for good reason. Six miners were eaten, from what I've heard..."

"It's nothing, we'll make it through!" I announced decisively. "The most important thing for us is to get far enough away from Dotur-Khawe, so I can summon a division of strong soldiers."

* * *

Our crew ran to the old fountain. For speed's sake, Darius and Darina were told to turn into wargs. I even used Darius as a mount. Valerianna Quickfoot rode her Pirate. Taisha rode Blanca. And Irek and Yunna rode Lobo and White Fang respectively. Vanessa was opposed to riding a wolf for a long time, and did her best running on foot. Only when it became clear she'd be left behind with her parents did the girl resolve to hop up on Akella's back. He was the strongest of my pack, and none of the others could have possibly supported the weight of the thick-set Dwarf Mechanic.

We managed to pass the District of Merchants unnoticed — there was a huge room lit brightly with tall powerful columns. It was so impressive, I just couldn't bring myself to call it a cave. Our division was already getting near the old fountain when Valerianna shouted suddenly in fear and demanded we stop at once. My sister said that she saw lots of undying markers on the minimap, and that they were gold, meaning they were participating in the great wyvern hunt.

"Let's turn back!" I ordered, but my sister said in a drooping voice that there was no point now, because we'd already been spotted.

"Then, screw that. Let's ride forward! We should be obnoxiously calm and even rude. This is a big city and a protected area, where we are under the protection of NPC guards. Any undying who tries to attack us will quickly be killed by the guard of the subterranean king. Vanessa, that massive construction over there is the barracks, right?"

The Dwarf Mechanic confirmed that it really was the guard's barracks. What was more, among the soldiers responsible for maintaining order on the square, Vanessa had seen her brother, and pointed me to him.

Level-200 Dwarf Elite Warrior

He was a severe bearded soldier bound in gilded plate armor and holding a large rectangular shield with an ax in his strong hands. To me, all the dwarves of the king's guard looked identical, as if they had been made by carbon copy, but I trusted Vanessa's words that she recognized her brother. I could only whistle in surprise after seeing the strength of the local guard — they were all level two hundred! And the officers were all the way up at two hundred fifty! And most interestingly to me, they were all shown on the minimap as green triangle markers, or friendly NPC's!

"We ride to the guards. The undying are to be ignored. Do not engage them in conversation. And I warn you in advance — don't give into their jabs and provocations! You are not to attack first under any circumstances — that's exactly what our opponents want. And now, let's ride!"

I counted fifteen undying. They all surpassed me by more than fifty levels. The enemies were heading in our direction unhurriedly, renewing defense spells on themselves and calling their pets back to them. It was barely possible to make out the player name or clan tag but, when I did, I strained to hold back a groan. *Goons!* Worst-case scenario — I'd never manage to agree to peace with these guys. What was more, the threat of being punished for killing a character in a safe zone would not stop them.

Before the group of enemies on a huge shaggy snow-white dog was riding a pretty elf girl with skin the color of ivory and bluish-black hair that came down to her very heels. As soon as she gave the sign, all the other *Goons* stopped behind her.

Mariam   *Standing_Right_Behind_You*
[GOONS]
Level-198 Moon Elf Assassin

Well, well! The leader of the clan in the flesh! Her outfit was really incredible — overflowing with different colored flickers, her armor was made of the pelt of an emerald dragon. All her items without exception were from a single set. It seemed she had the full Kingslayer collection. Even the throwing knives. And what a pretty mount she had!

Fimbulthul Élivágar Guardian
Level-57 Mythical Hound (unique creature)

A private message came in from Valerianna Quickfoot:

~ Stay on the Wing ~

"Look at that dog! What a beaut! See if your artifact of Fenrir can lure that handsome boy over to our side."

I opened the Gray Pack control settings. Six of the seven available slots were filled with my wolves and wargs, one was still empty. I selected that field to see the possible options:

Fimbulthul, Level-57 Mythical Hound (inactive)

Pirate, Level-31 Seasoned Wolf (inactive)

From what I could remember, only after the victorious battle with Belle Sweetypie had I received the option to take her pets. So, I formulated my mission clearly in my head: I had to outlive Mariam Standing_Right_Behind_You in the upcoming battle by some means. But I didn't really know how. She was way too tough for me. But in any case, I didn't minimize the Gray Pack control window.

"You've put me through a lot of trouble, little goblin," the moon elf chuckled when the distance between us was just seven meters. "But now, it seems, the hunt is finished! You have no chance of escape, and the generous offering I brought to the temple of the gods of *Boundless Realm* raised the drop chance in the upcoming battle to 97%, so you're sure to lose the amulet. This has come at great cost to me. Actually, the whole hunt ran me quite a bit. I put all the clan's coffers and all my reputation on the line just for this encounter. And I never bet wrong!"

"Is pretty, this white doggy of you," I blurted, utterly out of turn.

"Amra, speak normally. You can do it. I've seen it!" flared the leader of the *Goons.* But, despite the bad timing, she didn't lose the chance to brag about her animal. "The mythical hound? Yes, he is my pride and joy. A week ago, I got the coordinates of an underwater location with a unique quest from a noob who wanted to join the clan. His name was Trong Diver, a naiad by race. I think you may have even met him. I saw him in one of your videos. The boy was entirely out of control, and a drug user at that. I kicked him out of the clan on day two — he was a complete imbecile who played *Boundless Realm* high as hell, having no idea whatsoever of where he was, or who. Even the *Goons* don't need people like that. But I passed that quest, and without any help from my support. There were certain difficulties in working under the ice of a frozen river, but none of that matters now. The important thing is that I got this beauty!"

"He really is an excellent beast," I agreed, now in normal language, not warping my words. "And now, I have no idea why you need another mount. After all, you already have one unique one!"

"What do you mean why? Because I can take

it. That's reason enough."

"Oh yeah? But the amulet that controls the wyvern will go only to the person who makes the final blow," I laughed as jeeringly as possible, pointing with my hand at the many guardsmen of the subterranean King. "It seems you'll have quite the challenge ahead of you!"

"Do you seriously not think I considered that? Amra, I played for a year in the *Suicidals* clan. They specialize in murders in cities for the sake of a valuable drop. And you can believe me that the game mechanics for getting the criminal status in locations under guard are something I've studied in the greatest detail, so I won't slip up!"

The elf girl called all her soldiers closer with a gesture. It seemed the conversation with Mariam was coming to an end, and they were preparing to kill me. But then the wood nymph standing next to me said some incomprehensible phrase. I didn't catch even one word. But Vanessa, it seemed, understood perfectly. The Dwarf Mechanic squealed as if she was being stabbed, and started shouting hysterically, pointing her finger at the approaching *Goons*. She was screaming in her dwarven language, and I didn't understand a word until she said a sentence in the common tongue: "Help, I'm being attacked!"

From all ends of the square, NPC guardsmen ran in our direction, getting out their weapons as they ran. It looked impressive, of course, but I still didn't understand Valerianna's point — calling the guard was, after all, too little. We had to force the guardsmen to act somehow. But there was a problem with that — the NPC guard wasn't going to intervene simply on the basis of an unfounded accusation, especially such an obviously false one. They'd have to see a real crime.

At one time, in *Kingdoms of Sword and Magic,* my sister and I had also occupied ourselves with helping rich losers part with their money using PvP in defended zones, so we knew this stuff well. Not every gamer's nerves can hold out when a wild barbarian runs at them hollering and waving a huge gnarled club over his head. Some inexperienced players would yield to such a provocation and try to strike the "attacker" first, automatically becoming criminals, who could then be killed unpunished with the help of the city's NPC guards. Now, the city guard was playing the role of aggressively attacking barbarian, but it wasn't likely that the highly-experienced Mariam Standing_Right_Behind_You would submit to such provocation.

And she didn't. However, not all the *Goons* in her division were so cold-blooded. Right away, two or three soldiers shot at the approaching dwarves with their crossbows, while a fire mage cast a ball of flame, hitting not only the guards, but also killing one of the peaceful citydwellers. He should not have done that... Now, the NPC guard could distinctly classify the *Goons* as criminals and enemies of the city, and not just those who'd directly attacked the city guard, but all those standing in the group.

"What have you done? Idiots..." Mariam groaned and, with a decisive shake of her head, commanded in a sharply changed powerful tone: "All pets hold back the guards! Tanks in a line, hold back the nearest dwarves for at least ten seconds! Healers, get to work! Everyone else, cover me!"

Realizing at the very beginning of Mariam's phrase that I should not keep standing here, I turned around and spurred Darius on, trying to add more distance and make some time while the high-level NPC guardsmen rounded up or destroyed the enemies. But I didn't manage... The warg below me gave a short squeal and collapsed. The icon for Darius in my pet list went gray and disappeared. My big-eared Amra rolled headlong over the stones of the square.

Successful Agility check
Experience received: 80 Exp.

Acrobatics skill increased to level 17!

I don't know if it was from the mayhem of the critical moment, or if Taisha started lagging again, but the world turned into a series of slides that flowed one into the next. As if in a slow cinema, I saw my Amra trying to get to his feet and turn toward the enemies unimaginably slowly. I noticed a throwing knife flying at me, leaving a purple trail behind it in the air. But it was already too late for me to turn away from the flying death...

But what followed forced me to think for a long time afterward. In the path of the flying knife, I unexpectedly saw the Dwarf Mechanic. I still don't know if Vanessa did it on purpose, or just fell clumsily off Akella, who was jumping away in fear, but the curved, razor-sharp knife plunged into the dwarven woman's left side all the way up to the hilt.

She thudded heavily on the stones a meter from me. The eyes of the NPC were looking thoughtlessly past me at something, then glazed over. Vanessa's life was in the red, and was falling fast — she was just gushing blood. More blood was pumping from the fearsome wound with every heartbeat.

At that moment, I really didn't think that the person before me was an NPC — a soulless piece of programming code that a living player had no business caring for. No! Before me was a brave dying lady, who had sacrificed herself to save my life. And I couldn't abandon her, saving myself by fleeing and taking the valuable amulet away. A moment later, I had a bottle of Middling Elixir of Life in my hands. But how could I get it down

Vanessa's throat? She was lying unconscious, and her jaws were clenched tight so she was in no way planning on taking the healing potion.

I had to act quickly and coarsely — I yanked the bloodied knife from the dwarf's side (it was from the Kingslayer set) and then I applied the knife like a crowbar and unclenched Vanessa's teeth. It seems I accidentally broke a couple of the woman's teeth, but that was unimportant. The NPC's life bar jumped slightly upward, but immediately rolled back down.

Here, I noticed a heavy clatter and turned. Twenty of the dwarven guardsmen with their big body-length shields were standing in two lines, blocking me and the wounded Vanessa from the *Goons*. The first group of ten was in close formation, with their short spears protruding through special gaps in their shields. The rest of the dwarves took a step forward and had their shields raised at an incline, creating a second row of defense. The word "hird" instantly sprang to mind — this was the precise name of the military formation the dwarves were using against their higher-level enemies. The dwarves took a decisive step forward. I returned to the wounded girl.

I had to close the wound with a bandage or some gauze but, first, I'd have to get to her! Removing chain mail from a heavy body lying on the ground was a long and difficult task. But not in *Boundless Realm*. I had no idea how it was technically possible, but I looted the unfeeling, but still living body, throwing the equipment Vanessa had been wearing on the stones. A cloak, chainmail, a warming undershirt... I immediately ripped the undershirt into strips.

Successful Strength check
Experience received: 200 Exp.

One more Middling Elixir of Life, because Vanessa Hamfist's hitpoints were nearly at zero. And another, the last of the middling ones. I had four Minor Elixirs of Life, but they were far too weak. So, no time to think about that now. What I had to do was place the gauze and bandage.

Successful Agility check
Experience received: 200 Exp.

With the corner of my eye, I noticed the grayed-out words "*Fimbulthul. Level-57 Mythical Hound*" had suddenly lit-up white. Just for one second, but I managed to activate it! The beast's icon flashed among my pets and immediately dimmed out. Someone must have done in the white hound right after its master. What could I say, I'd see in one hour who he'd respawn next to — me or Mariam Standing_Right_Behind_You.

Alright, bandage ready. The speed of the health loss was reduced, but didn't stop, so I had to pour another elixir down her throat. There were three left. Two. One. And that was all... I didn't have any other way of supporting the life of the Dwarf Mechanic, and the life bar of the NPC was still going down.

Just one method remained — bite Vanessa and make her a vampire with regeneration ability. But I would have to do that in full view of hundreds of NPC dwarves and several players. The question: "Is the life of an NPC worth such sacrifices?" did not exist for me at that moment. Vanessa saved my life, and I owed her a debt of gratitude for that. Yes, it was hard to understand from an outside perspective, but at that moment, I was ready to reveal my essence as a vampire.

Fortunately, such a sacrifice was not necessary — the life bar of the Dwarf Mechanic shot up, reaching the orange, then yellow zones. Healing magic? From where?! I turned. Behind me, there was a high-level player, and they were wearing a wyvern hunter medallion around their neck. It was a harrier-gray old dwarf with a knee-length beard:

Torino Granite_Muncher
Dwarf
Level-108 Healer

"You should get her dressed quickly, Amra. For local women, being naked in public is a great shame. They'd sooner die that be subject to that. And I should know. I've been living among the dwarves for two years and have studied their ways."

Trying not to be surprised, I quickly replaced the equipment I'd removed from the Dwarf Mechanic. Other than the undershirt — that was bandages now.

"Mhm, much better. She'll live, but it's a serious wound. She has a torn lung and a broken spine. The debuff is very serious — her lower body will be paralyzed for two days, then she'll limp for the rest of her life."

After following my gaze, which was boring into the hunter amulet, the healer gave a good-hearted laugh:

"Pay that no mind. I only bought the amulet because the advertisement got to me. But after I looked into your ordeals — constantly in fear, running away and hiding... I decided that I didn't want to participate. It just wasn't for me! No thanks! Plus, I'm too old for that life. Let my grandchildren run around *Boundless Realm* in search of adventure. I've got my clinic here in Dotur-Khawe, a calm existence, constant patients, good neighbors..."

Valerianna Quickfoot, now level-40, rode up to us on her level-32 Seasoned Wolf. She was looking at the Dwarf Healer with obvious suspicion, but still didn't say anything about him.

Instead of that, she pointed to the distant Taisha, who was digging through the possessions of dead *Goons*:

"The drop is just a dream. I've never seen anything like it. The enemies lost almost all their equipment. I'm walking on the edge of over-encumbrance, and I took only valuable items. I even found one unique. And if you get the chance, you should shake down 'your girly' — she was the first to get the idea of looting Mariam Standing_Right_Behind_You. I suspect we might see an NPC thief running around *Boundless Realm* wearing a full Kingslayer set in the near future."

"We will not," I answered, looking at the bloodied throwing knife, the properties of which I could not discern due to my low Intelligence. But still, I saw the level limit. "The items from this set are limited to level 180+, so Taisha won't get the chance to try on the emerald-dragon-hide armor for a long time. But, all in all, it was quite the unexpected outcome. I bet the leader of the *Goons* is not happy that she brought the drop chance up to 97% before the battle. By the way... Right at this fountain, there's a respawn point!" I turned to the healer. "I'd pay a thousand coins for a video of Mariam Standing_Right_Behind_You being reborn in nothing but a diaper!"

The old Dwarf Healer laughed good-heartedly, stroking his beard:

"That is possible. But it doesn't seem very

likely the cautious moon-elf lady chose our fountain as a respawn point. In any case, the *Goons* will be very mad when they come back. You should get as far away from this place as you can. Bolt like your lives depend on it!"

"That's exactly what we're going to do," I assured the elderly player. "As soon as we bring our wounded companion to her parents to be cared for, we'll immediately race full bore out of this subterranean city. After all, I bet that wasn't the only division of *Goons* in Dotur-Khawe!"

The Hunt Comes to a Close

WE HAD ALREADY been galloping down the mined-out shaft for an hour and a half, ignoring any forks or boarded-up tunnels. The only source of light was a magical bluish-white torch summoned by my sister that accompanied her everywhere. I didn't even try to call up night vision, because there was plenty of light as it was. The floor was slippery in places, covered with a thickly overgrown mold, but in large part, that was the only difficulty.

A few times, we encountered abandoned conduits — heaps of empty slag, old smelt furnaces, empty store-houses and rusty narrow-gauge rails that went off somewhere into the darkness. We didn't find anything useful there — the fastidious dwarves had taken everything of any value out of the tunnel before closing it up. But I still didn't understand the residents of this subterranean city, who had boarded up this entirely adequate and, based on what I could see, safe corridor. But suddenly, our path ahead was blocked by a huge spiderweb...

"Dumbo, let me remind you that I've been afraid of spiders since I was a kid." said the mavka, raising her voice after a long silence.

"I also cannot bear spiders, even the littlest ones!" Yunna echoed. "But this one's web is as thick as a finger. The spiders around here must be big as wargs, if not bigger."

I hurried up to the obstacle. The spiderweb was very old, dried out and covered with flecks of dust. Nevertheless, I was unable to break the web with my hands. Cut it down with a knife? Or burn the web?

The mavka also jumped off Pirate and walked up closer. After looking over the walls, the wood nymph pointed to a lattice of deep scratches next to the old spiderweb:

"I have a bad understanding of arachnid language, but my Polyglot skill will allow us to decode some of the symbols at least. Scratched into the wall, it says: 'border' and 'forbidden.' And also, there's what looks to be the dwarven rune for 'death.' I think these many-armed creatures made this as a sort of boundary, the crossing of which is punishable by death. And also, for the record, I see a vague motion somewhere in the distance on the minimap. There are monster markers popping up and disappearing. For me, they have red skulls."

Red skulls? The beasts were more than twenty levels higher than my sister? Bad news...

"Maybe we should go back to the last fork? Then we can try to get around the obstacle down a side passage." Taisha suggested. But I shook my head "no."

"That won't get us anywhere. If we go farther than this spiderweb, we'll be attacked. Also, the dwarves of Dotur-Khawe were quite insistent that we not leave the main corridor leading to the surface, because lots of tunnels are in critical condition, and getting lost in this gigantic underground labyrinth would be easy-peasy. It seems the time has come for me to use my rainy-day trump-card..."

I took out the ribbon-bound summoning scroll and, decisively breaking the wax seal, unfurled the parchment. A moment later, five steps from me on the stone floor, there appeared a big glowing blue circle six meters in diameter. A plethora of bright, indecipherable runes were flowing along its inner edge. And, a few seconds later, a big group of fighters appeared inside the circle — mages with spells already activated in their raised hands, soldiers hiding behind shields wearing heavy armor, bowmen with the bow already pulled, a ton of zombies and spirits floating in the air. The experienced crew was prepared to enter battle at any second, and now started looking around in search of an enemy, somewhat bewildered.

I took a step forward, attracting the attention of the mercenaries.

"Mercs, your mission is to surgically clear this corridor here all the way to the surface, after which the contract will be considered completed. The enemies are spiders and other subterranean beasts of levels 60 to 90. It shouldn't be any issue for you."

"Please clarify the mission," said a level-170 necromancer who stepped forward in a torn shroud, wooden sandals bound with twine and a mask in the shape of a three-eyed skull. Disregarding the strong magical aura coming from the tear in his garment, one might think the player was trying to save money on equipment. "You don't want us to 'steam-train' so you can level quick? Just walk down the corridor cutting down everything in our path?"

"That's exactly right," I confirmed. "There's a hunt after us, so our biggest concern is speed."

"In that case..." said the necromancer, clearly in charge of the group, as he looked at the web and corridor, "first and fourth group of five, advance! Get to the exit! The third group is to remain with the client and take down anything the strike group misses. The second group will go in the opposite direction to meet the pursuers. Hold them at bay, even if it costs you your life!"

~ Stay on the Wing ~

There were no arguments or objections. The mercs split into groups in silence, ready to carry out the mission.

"Wait!" I said, stopping the soldiers, who were already getting into action. "I've got an idea for the second group. There's no reason for them to die. Here in the old underground corridor, there are places where the tunnel is practically held up by matchsticks — the girders are old and bending, and little stones pour down from above at the slightest disturbance. I suggest you collapse the tunnel, blocking it off entirely." With these words, I took out the ice bomb and extended it to one of the mercenaries from the second group of five.

The half-orc assassin looked over my gift carefully, tossed it up and caught the charge in midair with his wide palm, giving a bark of approval:

"Now you're talking! This will blow so hard, it'll take the dwarves more than a century to clear. If that isn't enough, I've got another four grenades in my bag, even if they aren't as powerful."

"Then let's not waste time!" the necromancer said, making a decision. Then, pointing at the momentarily flickering spiderweb, he walked after the assault group, leading the stinking zombies and hovering spirits after them.

We were told to wait fifteen or twenty minutes, after which point we could walk forward down the cleared passage. As soon as I gave the command to rest, the wolves and wargs laid down on the stones, having lost all interest in what was going on. Valerianna Quickfoot also asked to exit *Boundless Realm* for a few minutes. The group of five guards that remained with us stepped aside in order to, and I'm quoting their commander here: "Not embarrass the client with our presence." The mercs didn't embarrass me at all, but I didn't want to impose with my company. One of the mercs placed a torch in a crack in the wall so I didn't have to sit in darkness, then went off after his comrades.

For some time, I sat with my goblin and looked at the smoking torch, dripping burning resin. But suddenly, Taisha broke the prolonged silence:

"Amra, please give me that throwing dagger you took near the fountain!"

Well, well! What a request! The magical throwing knife was already worth quite a lot on its own, and was also part of a very expensive and rare set called Kingslayer, which significantly raised its value.

"What do you want it for, Taisha? After all, you don't have the skills or level to use it."

My green-skinned companion shrugged her shoulders and smiled craftily:

"It's hard to explain, Amra. It's just that I feel with my skin that this object should belong to me. I have an unbearable desire to possess it, but I cannot express that in words. I do not want to steal the knife from you, or buy it, which is why I'm just asking."

Hrmph, an explanation that was simply in the best traditions of female logic: "I don't know why, but I want it, so you need to give me that expensive thing." What could I say? I'd had girlfriends like that in real life before. Unlike them, Taisha was at least useful. So, I took out the curved and fairly heavy throwing knife and simply gave it to my companion.

Mission completed: A Gift for Taisha
Reward selection in process

I remembered this quest perfectly. It had been sitting in my queue for quite a long time unfinished. Back at the goblin wedding, my NPC bride had demanded I gift her an object meant for her and no one else. I'll admit, over the last few days, I'd been busting my brains trying to think something up that could really be for no one but Taisha. I didn't know why, but the throwing dagger of the leader of the *Goons* had met this criteria. Strange, of course, but the mission had finished, and that's what mattered. But I still didn't know what it meant by "reward selection in process."

And meanwhile, Taisha, not at all ashamed by the presence of Irek and Yunna, started getting undressed. The dark, form-fitting thief's clothes, which had served as the source of a great many nasty jokes, flew onto the stones. In an instant, Taisha was wearing just a thin loincloth and, a moment later, she was standing in a full suit of luxurious sparkling armor made of the skin of an emerald dragon!

"Wow!" was all I could say. "Excuse me?!"

Taisha laughed happily, very satisfied at my surprised and enraptured reaction.

"The secret here is simple: the full set has a special bonus: 'No level limit.' So, it was important for me to have all ten objects from the set. I took nine off that moon elf, and the other was a gift from you... And for that, I'll give you something no worse than that. I'm sure you're gonna like it!"

The NPC thief unclenched her fist, showing me a massive silver ring lying on her hand with a milky-white oval stone in the setting.

Ring of Ice Stream
+20 Resistance to Cold, +25 Strength, +25 Agility,

Summon Mythical Hound (no more than 1 time per day)

Unique object from the set Twelve Élivágar Guardians

But this was... Such a valuable object... And perfect for my goblin! It was practically made for him! I couldn't find the words to express the emotions overflowing from me, so I simply took a step toward Taisha, who looked amazing in her new armor, and gave her a kiss.

Reward received

As soon as I'd taken and put on the Ring of Ice Stream, a new portion of messages appeared before my eyes:

Mission completed: Get higher Agility than Taisha
Experience received: 48000 Exp.
+20 to any check of Taisha's opinion

Level forty!
Attention!
You have reached level 40
You may now improve your character's survival by choosing a modification

Wow, a real red-letter day! I opened my character's stat window: The ring had given me complete immunity to cold! Beautiful! And what about the Gray Pack settings? There it was, Fimbulthul the level-57 mythical hound had become my pet! I still couldn't summon him for seventeen hours — clearly the time since his previous owner had summoned him had not passed yet, but still.

"Looks like I guessed right with the gift!" laughed the NPC thief, picking up her old rags and placing them in her inventory. After noticing my gaze, Taisha commented on her actions: "I can still wear this around the house. After all, I can't very well roast fish or mop the floor in my sweet new emerald armor. And also, why hide it, it was pleasant to catch your admiring gaze on my body, undressing it."

At that moment, somewhere in the distance behind us, I heard a muted plunk, and a few seconds later, a burst of air stirred past my wide ears. They'd caved it in, cutting us off from our pursuers. Alright then, one problem down. Now I had to wait for my sister to return, and we could get going.

My sister entered the game looking overstimulated. Her eyes were burning as if she was rushing to share a new portion of fresh news.

"News of the hour! On the *Boundless Realm* forum, they're writing that Mariam Standing_Right_Behind_You has disbanded the *GOONS*! In parting, she said her fill of rotten things about the intellectual capacity of her former clan-mates, who somehow managed to fail all her most important orders of the last days. They'd frittered away the clan castle together with all its stores.

~ Stay on the Wing ~

They'd wrecked a ship on the cliffs out of their own idiocy together with a hundred of the strongest soldiers. After that, they sunk another ship in battle with the *Keepers* — a drekar they'd purchased with a loan from the bank of gremlins. And, at the pinnacle of their stupidity, they'd aggroed the NPC guard against themselves and let Amra and his flying mount go. I also read that Mariam Standing_Right_Behind_You has already applied to join the *Mercs* clan."

"That's true," confirmed the half-orc mercenary who emerged from the darkness. "In the clan chat, they're writing that our leader invited Mariam himself, as she now had nothing to do. But her application will only be approved after the contract with you is up — we don't want a conflict of interest. By the way, the assault group says the corridor has been fully cleared, and they're now checking the side corridors and area around the exit. There's less than a kilometer between here and the surface. Hurry!"

I jumped onto Akella and commanded my crew to move out. My sister summoned the magical torch again, so I could make out the picture of the bloody struggle revealing itself a hundred meters in front of us in great detail. There were shells of big insects chopped into sauerkraut... Body fragments lying here and there... Jointed feet... Decapitated heads with many-faceted eyes and fearsome mandibles...

Chitin sheets... Wings... Bits of web... It was all smeared with a greenish orange sludge that covered the whole floor and was splattered on the walls.

Despite the nausea creeping up my throat, I decisively jumped off the wolf:

"Friends, wait one minute. I have to collect alchemical reagents — when will I ever get such a rare chance again? Blood samples and body fragments from these subterranean creatures are quite rare."

It quickly became clear that there were four totally different species in the ghastly mess of chopped up body parts: subterranean spiders, gigantic dragonflies, arachnids and scorpions. I gathered blood samples from all those creatures and, after letting my companions get a good head start, lagged slightly behind the group and drank down the four vials of smelly viscous blood:

Achievement unlocked: Taste tester (37/1000)
Achievement unlocked: Taste tester (38/1000)

Achievement unlocked: Taste tester (39/1000)

Achievement unlocked: Taste tester (40/1000)

~ Stay on the Wing ~

Regeneration improved to 5 HP/Minute

Five hitpoints per minute wasn't so very much, but it was still nice! I caught up to my companions, who were stopped in the next room. The necromancer, leader of the group of mercenaries, met me there and reported back that the contract was completed:

"Amra, the path has been cleared. We overcame all the NPC monsters. We met one living player. In fact, in this very room, but he ran nimbly up the vertical walls and jumped into that shaft. I sent my soldiers out after him, but they returned with nothing. The arachnid was far too fast."

"An arachnid player?" I asked in surprise.

"Yeah, we were surprised, too," the necromancer confirmed. "We've already checked the knowledge base. It was only recently made possible to play this race. But, it seems, it has not gained significant popularity. After all, I'd never heard of people living on the edge like this before. Perhaps this was a game tester, a company employee. I've heard that the corporation tests out new and unusual paths and races before advertising them to normal players. In any case, the runaway arachnid doesn't present a threat. That upward corridor there goes to the surface. We checked the surroundings meticulously — no dangerous beasts, and no living players. So, I consider the contract to have been completed."

I squeezed hands with the mercenary, thanking him for the help. The group of mercs wished me luck and headed back to meet up with the group of five behind us, so they could all return together in one portal to their castle. We then headed for the surface.

There was an enchantingly beautiful starry night ensconcing the rocky desert. The innumerable bright stars and huge moon made so much light that it seemed like day. Myriads of crickets, having crawled up out of their burrows, were cutting through the air with their chirping. My big-eared goblin took a deep breath of the chilly air and said blissfully:

"Woah! It's really nice here! And the weather is perfect for night travel! We have the whole night ahead of us! We should try to get as far from Dotur-Khawe as possible. There are still a whole seven hours until the sun rises, so we can easily make it two hundred kilometers on wolfback. What do you say, Val?"

Instead of an answer, my sister just shrugged her shoulders unconfidently and smiled a tortured smile. I noticed that she was wrapped up tight in a light cape, even though the night was warm. Maybe Valeria was getting sick?

"Hey, what's that thing over there behind those ruins to the east?" asked Yunna, pointing at some dark wreckage, barely distinct from the distant cliffs.

"Maybe those are the abandoned copper mines Vanessa told us about!" I suggested. "We should be going that way, anyhow. I planned to run east through the Great Desert, so let's ride up closer to the ruins now and see with our own eyes."

A few minutes later, we were already standing next to a brick fence and stone arch adorned with metal letters that had darkened with time: "Pr_ka Copper Pit." It was missing one letter, so I couldn't read the last word. Praka? Prika? Pruka? I didn't know. All that was clear was that it was a proper noun, as it was written with a capital letter. Probably someone's name.

From the stone arch, we caught a glimpse of the deep wide pit with small rectangular buildings at the bottom — just bare walls with no roof. The depth was substantial. At least a hundred meters. There was a forking path leading to the bottom, in places entirely covered with sand. Having stared into the abandoned pit long enough, I wanted to get on our way to the east, but the wood nymph stopped me:

"Based on the mini-map, there's a spring down there. This seems like a great time to fill up on water, if we're planning to cross the Great Desert."

My sister's voice was hoarse and quiet like she was sick, which just further confirmed my suspicion that Valeria was unwell. I had no desire to go down there, but the wood nymph was right the slippery sand path. It was a miracle the descent didn't break my neck. I led the wolf to the stream, which emptied into a small round pond. Scaring away the many level-1 Rats taking water near the pond, I gathered fresh water in a canteen from the spring, and drank a swallow.

Endurance points restored

Well, well. This spring contained special water! Even a small gulp of it fully cured my fatigue. This was the first time I'd encountered such a wonder. After filling my vessels with the magical water, I took a look around.

The mavka had already drunk her fill and was headed for the ruins of what looked to be a barracks. I followed after her. Based on the remains of a smelting furnace, broken bellows and abandoned old tools, this had once been a smithy. Under our feet, there were bunches of old copper wire. Over a stone step, leading across the smoke-stained brick walls, there was a snaking gnarled message carved, in places totally rubbed out: "_oss_did_time_her_." Although the first letter in the first word bore a great resemblance to the letter "P," I could clearly tell the intended word was "boss." After all, from what I'd heard of the dwarves' tales, there had once been a prison here. And what could I say? This was a pretty sweet spot for a boss, in the warmth near the furnace, and with a good view.

But just then, my sister suddenly stumbled and fell face down. I was next to her instantly, helping her up, and holding her there, as the mavka's knees were shaking. My sister was completely weak. She was shivering all over. After returning to me and focusing her gaze with difficulty, Val said:

"I'm sorry if I'm not doing good enough, Timothy. But it should be working. I thought it all through carefully..."

The mavka's eyes closed. What was she talking about? What was supposed to be "working" or "not working?" I shook my sister with all my might and Valerianna Quickfoot peeked open an eye with difficulty. I demanded that she explain herself. The mavka gave a tortured smile and said in a barely audible voice:

"In the virtual reality capsule settings, I turned off... shutdown in case of emergency health issues. I took a strong sleeping medicine... A whole pack..."

"Why did you do that?!" I shouted out in fear.

Valerianna focused her gaze on me with difficulty and smiled. Then she slowly raised her arm and led the tips of her fingers tenderly over the cheek of my goblin.

"Timothy, I want to live fully, not just exist as a legless cripple... Don't worry, Tim. I've read all the existing literature about digitizing consciousness in a virtual reality capsule... Many famous authors have described successful cases when a person became part of a game forever... And I want that for myself... I decided a long time ago and was preparing for this moment... I was waiting for the chance to get into a virtual reality capsule, if only for a few hours... And I followed all the instructions to a 'T...' It should work..."

Valerianna's eyes closed. Her arms fell limply downward. I held the hand of my sister's dying body and didn't know what I should do. It would be pointless to give Valerianna Quickfoot healing elixirs — after all, she was dying in real life, and her bad feelings were just being shown through the character. But there was some feedback here, and the virtual reality capsule was transmitting some effects to the body, but clearly not enough to save a poisoned body. What should I do? Exit immediately? But what about the thirty-second delay before opening the virtual reality capsule, specially formulated to allow the player's consciousness time to reorient? A whole thirty seconds! My sister might die in that time!!!

So, I did something else — I activated the in-game menu and opened the window for paid calls directly from *Boundless Realm*. Yes, it was expensive, but for me now, the price had no meaning. My sister's life was incommensurately more important. After calling the emergency services number, I told them about Val's overdose, then gave her age and our address. The operator confirmed that she had received the information and asked me to give a phone number for them to call back. I dictated my number and reminded her again that the issue was very urgent.

"The ambulance team is already on the way," the operator assured me, and the call ended.

"What's happening, Amra? Why isn't Valerianna Quickfoot getting up?" There was no time to indulge Taisha's curiosity now, so I just waved her off — I had no patience for her at this moment.

The main thing was that help was on the way! But I was still in a state of alarm — what if the ambulance didn't make it?! I made use of another paid call, this one to Kira. If her Black Crystal was here in the underground parking lot, that would be the fastest way of getting to the apartment. But my red-headed acquaintance didn't pick up — she must have already been in *Boundless Realm.*

Then I used another paid game function and called a magical messenger. After dictating my message to the winged pink demon that appeared, I sent him to the ruler of the Land of Gloom, the queen of the harpies Kirra'ellita, Huntress of the Night.

But Taisha just wouldn't buzz off and continued the interrogations about what was happening. I answered just to get her out of my hair:

"Taisha, my sister took poison in the realm of the undying so she could stay here in *Boundless Realm* forever."

It was surprising, but the NPC understood everything and even came to certain conclusions:

"Valerianna Quickfoot decided to live here in *Boundless Realm* and never leave? Did she want to become like me? What's so bad about that? There she's a cripple, here she's a beauty. Any girl would want to do the same in her position!"

"Fool! Stay out of matters you don't comprehend!" I burst out with rage at my NPC girlfriend. "If you want to be useful, don't just stand there like a stone. Give the mavka artificial resuscitation. In the world of the undying, that might help. But right now, I've gotta go to my sister."

Successful check for Taisha's reaction
Experience received: 200 Exp.

"Amra, when should I expect your return?" Taisha asked, taking a seat next to the wood nymph's lifeless body.

"I don't know, Taisha. I'll try to be back soon, but it isn't up to me now. I can say one thing for certain — if my sister does not survive, I'll never return to *Boundless Realm*. So, pray for my sister to pull through."

* * *

Over the half-deserted night streets, the taxi driver raced to our residential neighborhood, having received a generous bonus for increasing his speed. I ran across the vestibule and called the elevator. The elevator rose unbearably slowly to the 333rd floor. I was just all wound up in terror. But then the elevator doors opened, and I threw myself down the hallway to my apartment. Hooray! The door was smashed in — the ambulance beat me here!

"Where is she? Where is the girl who took sleeping medicine?" I blurted out in the doorway to an unfamiliar man in a police uniform.

"She was taken away a few minutes ago by the medics," a mustached policeman with sergeant patches told me, demanding that I present my papers.

The sergeant scanned my identification card with a special device. Then he suddenly got on edge, placing his hand on his holster and demanding I immediately explain what I was doing at night in an apartment that didn't belong to me, and asking where the owner was.

"I am the owner!" said Kira, looking disheveled. She ran into the room at the perfect moment! "Everything's fine, sergeant. This is my common-law husband, Timothy. His younger sister also lives with us in the apartment."

The beautiful red-head placed her hand under the scanner beam readily, and the vigilant policeman read the data from the identification chip implanted under the girl's skin.

"Kirena Tyle... Yep, everything looks right," the policeman said, immediately growing calm and buttoning his belt holster shut. "The ambulance team was forced to break in the door to get into the apartment. So go through the rooms and check to see if all of your things are in place — I need to write up my report."

Kira tried to object, saying that there was no need for her to check all that, because she'd crossed paths with the ambulance brigade in the vestibule. The medics, wearing hospital whites, hurriedly pushing a stretcher to their vehicle with the lifeless girl and an oxygen mask. She didn't see any of her possessions. But the policeman was a pedant and insisted all rules be followed — if protocol said she should look over the apartment and sign a report, then that was what had to be done.

As soon as Kira was off looking over the rooms, the sergeant said quietly to me:

"I heard that your sister's heart stopped. The ambulance brigade called a special quadrocopter by radio with resuscitation equipment... So..."

My heart was just pounding wildly as I

listened to the horrible news. My eyes glazed over. Val, how could you do such a thing?! How will I live without you?! But meanwhile, the policeman continued:

"There have been a lot of such cases before. As soon as the virtual reality capsule came on the market, an epidemic of suicides began. There were even groups in social networks where inveterate gamers would discuss how to kill one's self in order to later be reborn in the game. They even thought up a term for it: digitization. There were always rumors swirling about someone meeting a player in the game after their death. Nonsense, of course. Not a single instance was confirmed. The police tried to track down these groups of suicidal maniacs and stop them, arrest activists, but it only got worse — these fanatics thought the government was trying to hide the truth from the people. But after that, all the noise about virtual reality capsules and 'digitization' fizzled out. There haven't been any cases like this in my area for two years. It's actually strange that your sister decided to try so late..."

The sergeant went silent, because Kira came up to us and said that all her things were in place. The policeman extended a tablet, and the apartment owner placed her palm on it, authenticating the report.

"You should call a locksmith to get a new lock put in," the mustached policeman said, already in the doorway, to which Kira answered that her husband could take care of it.

The policeman left. I, though, took a seat in an armchair, entirely overcome with sorrow. So, I didn't hear Kira's words right away, she had to repeat herself two times:

"Why are you sitting there? Let's fly off to hospital number four. That's where they brought Valeria. We can get the latest updates."

My first hope, a very timid one, flickered up in my soul. Maybe this wasn't the end? Val wasn't dead? It would seem I asked that question out loud, because my redheaded girlfriend started frowning:

"Timothy, what are you talking about?! I talked with the doctors at the elevator, and even had a brief chat with them. Yes, it's a severe case. They even told me that your sister's heart stopped for a minute and a half. But the ambulance came in time, and the medics pumped her stomach right away. Valeria has already expelled the pills, so the poison has left her body and your sister should be on the mend soon. Timothy, are you crying?! Calm down, everything's fine now!"

I turned away, embarrassed to show my feelings.

"Sorry, I couldn't hold back. I'll get myself in order, wash up, and we can go."

Once in the Black Crystal, racing across the night sky, I started a conversation:

"So, does this mean your full name is Kirena Tyle? You wouldn't happen to be related to the vice president of the *Boundless Realm* corporation Inessa Tyle, would you?"

My companion clearly didn't like the topic. Kira cringed in dissatisfaction.

"I was hoping greatly that you wouldn't notice that... Although, I suppose you would have found out sooner or later anyway, so maybe this is for the best. Yes, Inessa Tyle is my grandmother. But that doesn't mean I had any privileges in comparison with the other testers! I achieved everything in *Boundless Realm* on my own. My influential relative never once came to my aid!"

By the end of her speech, Kira was nearly screaming. I became firmly convinced that the close relationship of my girlfriend with the vice president of the corporation had served as a reason for conflict with colleagues on a few occasions in the past. Or perhaps, they had caused suspicions she wasn't playing fair. I apologized to the girl for the tactless question. The beautiful redhead calmed down and said:

"Timothy, you shouldn't be apologizing, I should. I feel very guilty. I'm actually the one who bought the sleeping medicine for Valeria. They'd never sell such a dangerous medicine to an underage person. It's just that your sister told me a secret, saying that in the last few months, her breasts have been growing a lot. And her left faster than the right. And that the process was very painful, so much that she couldn't even touch them. And your sister said she was unable to lie down, either on her stomach or side. And I couldn't imagine that Valeria would use the sleeping pills for other purposes..."

It was my shortest, and at the same time saddest video. I honestly admitted to the viewers of my clips that the wood nymph Valerianna Quickfoot, who had accompanied my big-eared goblin in *Boundless Realm* from day one, had been none other than my very own little sister. And that something bad had happened to my sister in real life, so she was now unconscious in intensive care, attached to an artificial breathing device. I told them I simply was physically unable to have fun in a virtual game, because my thoughts were now occupied only with my sister's wellbeing.

So, I honestly told them the coordinates of my Goblin Herbalist. I offered anyone who wanted the Royal Forest Wyvern to come to that place and wait for me there. Sooner or later, I'd enter *Boundless Realm* and even allow myself to be killed unanswered, because I had volunteered to take part in this massive hunt as the runaway victim.

I made the video the day after the incident

near midday, when it finally became clear that Val's treatment might take time, and that the doctors couldn't give a one-hundred-percent guarantee of a successful outcome. The girl's heart had stopped two times in the night, and only the swift intervention of the brigade on duty each time had saved my sister. Valeria was still unconscious as before, hooked up to the medical device.

As soon as the video was published online, all my friends got in touch with me. Max Sochnier was very worried for Valeria and expressed a readiness to help with money for her treatment. But I assured my friend that I wasn't having any financial problems. And in fact, I did have money. What was more, I'd received yet another huge transfer from the *Boundless Realm* corporation — this time, it was for a whole three hundred forty thousand credits as "my percentage for amulet sales." But today, the mountains of cash brought me no joy...

Leon called as well. He also expressed words of support and wished my sister a speedy recovery. The former construction worker told me he had returned to his family, where he was accepted very warmly both by his wife and three daughters. His crisis of family relations had ended smoothly. What was more, my friend gave me some transparent hints that he and his wife were already thinking about a fourth child.

My new boss, as could be predicted, also

called. Jane wished my sister a speedy recovery and inquired about when I'd be back at work. Unfortunately, I couldn't tell her a precise date, because I didn't know myself. Jane was clearly upset, but still said that she understood me, was in no rush and would try to smooth the issue over with the stalled event on her own. Perhaps, she'd organize a pause in the great hunt, or think up something else.

I also got one call that I wasn't expecting at all, from Veronica, although it was surprisingly warm. The girl was sincerely worried for my sister and wished me patience and strength. She also offered to forget all our past disagreements and to make peace. Veronica also said that her Dryad Dancer managed to take advantage of an opportunity when the drekar captain wanted to look at his take, and escaped from her imprisonment in the barrel. And now, she was the fully-fledged master of the drekar *Drake of the Morning Star*, and her three hundred crew members were willing to go through fire and water for her.

I dozed off sitting on a little sofa in the hospital hallway embracing Kira, who had crashed from fatigue. But suddenly, I was awoken by an employee of the medical facility, who told me the ailing girl had regained consciousness. A doctor had already looked her over, talked with her and allowed her to be transferred to the general-care ward. What was more, relatives were now allowed to speak with her without any limitations. Kira and I instantly shot up and, throwing on our white hospital gowns and rubberized slippers, hurried after the nurse.

Val was lying on a hospital bed with black circles around her sunken eyes. There were plastic tubes protruding from my sister's nostrils, leading to a strange metallic apparatus. There was a glucose drip in the girl's left arm. As soon as I appeared, my sister lit up and started speaking completely distinctly, although in a very quiet voice:

"Forgive me, Tim... I was wrong. I'm such a fool! I understand how badly I scared you."

I walked up to my beloved sister, took a seat next to her on a chair and held her cold, child-like hand in mine. I mostly stayed silent. Valeria wouldn't quiet down for a second though, trying to say her fill and share her fears:

"Next time I get this notion, Timothy, remind me that digitization doesn't exist! I've tested it on myself... There was no 'splitting of the mind,' as some authors describe. There was no digitization. In fact, I lost control of my character... If only you knew how scared I was when I realized my error... I tried to immediately exit the game, but I was too weak. And you forgive me too, Kira! I changed my decision, and now I want to get biotic legs. Plus, seeing how I'm already in the hospital, I want to start the procedures right away to implant all the electrodes and other wires."

Kira and I exchanged glances, surprised at the sharp change in Valeria's bearing. My redheaded girlfriend answered that she was very glad at the girl's desire to get legs, but in any case, that decision would have to be made by the doctor. And only after Valeria got her strength back.

When we were already out in the corridor, after speaking with the attendant physician, Kira stopped me and said:

"Timothy, I say we should split the cost of Valeria's recovery and biotic legs down the middle. And don't even try to argue — I won't accept any other way! To me, Valeria is not just some mere stranger, and I sincerely want to help. But now, excuse me, I've got to leave on urgent business."

I'd completely forgotten about this arrangement. And, I'll admit, I didn't even immediately realize what Jane wanted from me. I supposed my new boss might try to chew me out for not coming into work for the third day in a row now. But Jane was calling about something else:

"Timothy, what are you talking about? Remember! My housewarming party... All of my direct employees are invited... And you promised to come to the party!"

"Yes, that's true. It must have slipped my mind. When should I show up?"

"Today at six PM! A gift won't be necessary, just make sure not to be late!"

Jane hung up, leaving me in a pensive state. At six PM? That was fine, I still had a boatload of time. But as for "a gift won't be necessary..." If I'd heard those words from any old person, they'd have meant: "a housewarming party is simply a pretext to get everyone together. We're expecting a wild time, all the workers will get to know each other, there'll be a bit of alcohol and dancing." But in Jane's mouth, those very same words had a slightly different meaning: "I won't kick you out without a gift, of course, but I will definitely start thinking of you as cheap." Well, I guess this meant I'd get her a gift for the housewarming party.

The clock was showing one thirty PM. I was in my apartment waiting for the movers, who were coming to haul the virtual reality capsule to the clinic for my sister. Her doctor was surprisingly lenient and allowed Val to spend four hours each day in the virtual reality capsule. What was more, the doctor even approved of her spending time that way, saying it stimulated the muscles and nerve endings in her damaged legs, so it should have a positive effect later on the process of her growing accustomed to the biotic legs.

Installing and connecting the virtual reality capsule went off without a hitch, but Valeria unexpectedly refused to enter *Boundless Realm* without me. So, my sister and I had agreed to enter at nine tonight, when night was falling over the Great Desert, and my big-eared goblin would no longer be threatened by imminent death from the rays of the sun. I tried not to think about the other problems — hunger, thirst for both water and blood, how there would probably be a ton of people near the place I'd appear, and that my first game session after a three-day break would almost certainly be vanishingly short.

It was hard to believe, but over the whole time since Val's suicide attempt, I had not once played nor even opened the forums of *Boundless Realm*, so I had absolutely no idea what was going on in the game now. I even astonished myself — as soon as I even thought about the game, I started feeling a sense of revulsion. Clearly, I was sick and tired of *Boundless Realm* after so many days of playing actively without a single break. So, I spent my time talking to my sister and doing a bunch of interesting things in real life.

For example, I fixed the door and changed out a leaky faucet in the apartment. I fully replaced my wardrobe, having bought up high-quality and stylish items. I signed up for driving classes, and had even attended two of them. And for the first time in a long time, I made it to the gym — I worked actively on pullups and parallel bars, then played soccer with the guys and got back to pullups.

The exercise was surprisingly easy. I set, and immediately broke personal records for pushups, pullups, cartwheels, and other workouts. The active, adventuresome life of my Goblin Herbalist in *Boundless Realm* must have been having a very positive effect on my health. My biceps were bigger and noticeably stronger. On my stomach, you could distinctly make out abs. My excess fat had totally disappeared. It was unusual and fun to sense the interested and evaluating gazes of completely unknown girls on my body. Seeing a young strong man in stylish athletic clothes clearly drew their gazes. It was pleasant, devil take me!

At five minutes to six, I was standing outside Jane's door with a big box tied shut with a bright ribbon in my hands. I wasn't sure that my gift would be to her liking. But still, I hoped that my boss would appreciate the living flower. Created in a lab by geneticists, it was capable of recognizing its owner from among hundreds of other people. It would then modulate the color of its petals, as well as the character and intensity of its aroma to suit the owner's mood. From behind the door, I could hear loud music and voices. I pressed the doorbell, but discovered that the door was unlocked, and entered.

I immediately stopped sharply, finding myself nearly face to face with a group of unfamiliar people covered head to toe in gang tattoos. I jumped back, but the exit was already blocked by two guys of a similar, obviously criminal appearance.

"Come in, Timothy, I've been expecting you!" came Jane's voice from the neighboring room, and soon, my boss appeared in my field of view in a shockingly short dress with a compact audio player in her hands. She pressed the pause button, then the music and happy voices I'd heard from behind the door disappeared.

I didn't manage to come to my senses from all the events before the gift was taken from me, along with my mobile phone and all the coins from my pockets. They then slammed a fist into my stomach a few times and tossed me in a deep chair. Another minute later, my arms were tied tight to the armrests of the chair, and my legs were tied to its legs.

A hulking skinhead with a Nazi swastika tattooed on his neck punched me hard in the cheekbone, which made my head fly back and nearly tear clean off.

"That's for my sister, bucko. She's the one you hit in the clinic! And that's just the beginning!" the gangster hissed, sputtering with rage. Hatred was flickering in his eyes.

~ Stay on the Wing ~

He gave me another box to the ear, then tried to kick me in the groin, but his friend pulled me away from the off-the-rails psycho just in time.

"Don't overdo it. I need him conscious," Jane said in an even tone, calmly observing the goons. "Timothy, do you understand why they're here?"

I nodded slowly, at that watching somewhat distantly as the blood from my broken nose trickled onto my new white shirt.

"What, don't you like it?" Jane asked with warm-hearted mockery. "Now just imagine how much I liked it when these thugs broke into the apartment at night, demanding I pay them back five thousand credits right away, or they'd break my arms and legs!"

"But we quickly realized our mistake..." came one of the cutthroats, carefully listening to our conversation and playing with a butterfly knife as he did so.

"They realized it but, all the same, those unpleasant minutes were enough for me to realize I never want to be treated like that again. They almost raped me. I'm still covering up the bruises on my face with concealer. And to my mind, the person responsible for that was you, Timothy! You blatantly set me up by giving this address to the social center and setting the Grave Worms gangsters on me! Then you fled to another apartment, without even warning me about the danger!"

Well, shit... So that's how this whole story got started — Val had taken the papers with the survey, but the lady from the center must have already managed to enter some of the data into her computer and passed that information along to the gangsters. Bad news... Having lived a few years in the criminal outskirts of the megalopolis, I had all too good an understanding of the harsh character of this gang, and knew what Jane had to go through that night.

"Timothy, they practically left me paralyzed! And I had to pay for the 'false alarm,' even though I had nothing to do with all your problems. To my eye, it seems that you are at fault in all my sorrows. So, listen to me very carefully, because your life will depend how you react. Timothy, you transfer all the money you got from the corporation over the last two days to my account. Trying to wheedle or deny is useless here — all the payment orders came from accounting through my computer, so I know the exact total of all your payments: six hundred twenty thousand credits. And that is more than enough for me to share with my new friends," said Jane , nodding at the gangsters in the room. "As soon as you pay, we'll untie you and set you free as a bird, alive and well. The broken nose doesn't count. That's minor. As you see, it's all simple."

"Mhm, that's what I thought. There'll be a search for you," I chuckled with broken lips.

"Timothy, with three hundred thousand credits, I could just disappear in the megalopolis, making myself a new appearance and documents. It wouldn't even be hard. Or I could just leave this city once and for all and travel for the rest of my life to the best resorts on the planet."

"I see. And what if I don't agree?" I asked, though I understood the answer wouldn't be to my liking.

"There's no 'if' about it, punk!" said a gray-haired gangster with an evil gap-toothed grin. "Your choice now is this: either you pay voluntarily, or my guys will make you pay. I've got a group of specialists here with me, so sooner or later, you'll give up the money just to make the torture stop!"

"But if you will not work with us, no one can guarantee your safety," Jane added, admiring her well-cared-for nails. "You see, Timothy, these guys and I have a certain understanding. I found you for them, and will get my share somehow. But if you don't agree voluntarily, my share will be quite small. Then, I won't have enough to pay a cosmetic surgeon, or get new documents. So, you must understand, I simply cannot leave you alive, because you'll give me up right away."

"You won't be able to leave in that case either — the corporation will be searching for me, and it won't take them long to look your direction!"

Jane laughed, took a seat opposite me in the

chair, crossed her legs and took out a cigarette.

"No one will be searching for you, Timothy. As your direct boss, I'll simply fire you for missing work. By the way, I have the complete authority to do that. And the event with the hunt can then continue just fine without your participation — someone who owns a silver dragonfly agreed to take your place and serve as the new victim of the great hunt. For the last two days, our advertising clips have been showing not your green wyvern, but a tireless, handsome dragonfly, and none of the players even came out against the change. By the way, for my handling of the crisis after you bowed out of the event, the board of directors officially appointed me the new director of special projects. You might even congratulate me on the promotion, Timothy! So then, I'll repeat once again. No one will be looking for you, and in two or three days, everyone will just forget you ever existed..."

Jane spoke coherently and convincingly. She really did manage to force me to feel all the weight and danger of the situation. What could I say? Maybe I should just agree to part with the money — at the end of the day, life is too precious. But I was then stopped by the lack of any guarantee that I would be set free after that. In fact, from what I knew of the ways of the Grave Worms, they would stop at nothing to rid themselves of a witness as dangerous as me. They wouldn't let Jane go either, especially with all that cash in the girl's account. They'd clear her account out, then keep withdrawing until they hit the overdraft limit, leaving her far in the red. It was too bad that Jane didn't understand that herself...

Time passed, I stayed stubborn, and the gangsters got angry until they lost their patience.

But then, a very bright spark blinded me and a horrible scraping sound cut into my ears. I nearly lost consciousness, having completely lost my sense of orientation. But when my vision and hearing came back, I saw that the situation in the apartment had changed radically. All the bandits were lying snout-down in the floor with their hands cuffed behind their backs. Jane found herself in the same position. There were armed soldiers moving about the room in futuristic-looking armored suits and helmets with opaque face guards. The armored chestpieces all of them were wearing shone out with the emblem of the *Boundless Realm* corporation. There was also a logo in white, winding its way over the black air tanks on their backs: "Security Service."

One of the fearsome assault soldiers approached me. An electric knife appeared in his hands. With a couple quick, nearly indistinguishable motions, the ropes binding me fell to the floor. The soldier put his weapon away and lifted the mask of his helmet, showing his face. Well, I'll be! I knew this man very well. It was the head of Kira's bodyguard team. Talk about the last person I expected to see here! This meant the guards of my redheaded girlfriend were also employed by the *Boundless Realm* corporation!

"I see they touched up your face a bit, Timothy," the guard smiled happily. "We got here just in time. Can you stand?"

I shrugged my shoulders tentatively and tried to stand. I was leaning slightly to the right, but all in all, I needed no support. I could stand normally. The Security Service guard extended me a bag of my things: telephone, keyring, and ID card.

"Go to the stairs. There, you'll be met and brought to a safe location. You don't need to see what's gonna happen here," said Kira's bodyguard, turning away from me, letting me know that the conversation was over.

I took one last look around the apartment that nearly became the site of my death. All the glass was broken, and the door had been broken away together with the jamb. On the floor, there was a fallen butterfly knife. It looked like the old gangster's head was busted in — there was a dark black spot of blood spreading out on the back of his gray-haired head. Jane was lying with her hands tied behind her back moving her lips without a sound — she was seemingly praying to herself. My boss didn't react at all when I left.

Near the elevators and stairs, I met Kira.

Instead of the fashionable dresses I was used to seeing my girlfriend wear, she was now wearing a dark leather suit, on top of which she had a light armor plate. Every time I tried to start a conversation, Kira just grumbled:

"Not here. We can talk in the car."

This time, we were riding in a big armored limousine with darkened windows. Kira told the driver the address, then took a seat next to me.

"How did you find out that I was in danger?" I finally asked.

"From a clue your sister gave me. Today, I visited Valeria in the clinic, and she said that you were supposed to be at a housewarming party for the new director of your department at six, and that she'd invited all of her underlings. To be honest, I was surprised. Six PM is high work time for testers, so who would ever schedule a party then?! Not long after, your sister got a call from a tester by the name of Leon. He wanted to find out how she was doing, and get some clarifications on his character's skills. I asked Valeria to ask him about the party and found out that Leon had no idea about it."

Kira took a heavy sigh, then gave a bitter chuckle and continued:

"After that, I called in to work and asked all my colleagues if the special projects testers were all at work. As it turned out, the whole department was there, and had no idea there might have been a company event in half an hour. But the head of the department had, in fact, left work early..."

Kira came up closer to me. The girl's lips were quivering, and tears were welling up in her eyes. I embraced the beautiful redhead, who looked so soft and funny when upset and kissed her tear-soaked cheeks and nose a few times. But still Kira wouldn't calm down. Bawling uncontrollably and swallowing her words with salty tears, she tried to say her fill quickly:

"Just look at it from my perspective: I heard about a young girl leaving early from work and inviting my man to her place at the same time. I expected to see a completely predictable scene. I was just shaking in rage. So, I used my position at work to send the security service out to check up on what was going on at your little 'work party.' They planted listening bugs and video cameras on the windows, and set up an observation point in an empty apartment in the opposite building. From there, they had a good view, and I was getting ready to look with a heavy heart. But nothing was happening the way I expected..."

I'll admit, during the drive, I was occupied by Kira's story and was not watching the road. So, I was surprised when the driver stopped the car next to my building. Kira and I embraced as we walked through the vestibule and, once in the elevator, she said:

"I know I wasn't behaving properly, being

suspicious and having you followed. I don't want you to hold that against me. So Timothy, I promise to fulfill any wish you can dream up!"

"What do you mean 'any?'" I smiled, turning Kira's face toward mine and looking the girl right in the eyes.

"Just that, 'any,'" KIra confirmed, blushing with unexpected intensity.

I waited out a short pause, observing with interest as the girl's cheeks filled up with crimson. I truly do not know what wish she had in mind, but my wish couldn't have been simpler:

"Promise you'll never spy on me again!"

"Ok, I promise..." Kira confirmed, after which she added with reproach: "I'll admit, Timothy, I was expecting a wish of a totally different nature... More personal. Adult. Intimate even..."

It became clear that I had slightly disappointed my girlfriend by not catching her mood in time. But I tried to rectify matters immediately:

"Do we really need to wish out loud to be together?"

I opened the door, took one key off the ring and immediately put it in Kira's hand. After that, I invited my girlfriend in with a gesture. Kira closed the door behind her and said, unzipping her leather suit, getting out of it in the entryway:

"Timothy, you promised your sister you'd be

in *Boundless Realm* at exactly nine. We've got an hour and a half. Let's not waste even a minute! This time is precious!"

Epilogue

HUNGER. THIRST. No, I'd even say: THIRST!!! The whole world was painted in red tones. My big-eared goblin was unable to think about anything other than the immediate need to drink fresh hot blood. Amra absolutely would not obey my orders and was rushing off into the darkness, where his nostrils sensed the presences of a living creature. MEAT!!! I saw a little jerboa or rat, didn't make a difference. After grabbing the quivering creature, my goblin vampire sunk his fangs into the flesh of his victim. Just what I needed!!!

Sating the Thirst: 3/30

The world started to revert to a customary gray night-time shade. My control over my character returned. A step from myself, I saw

Taisha, terrified and holding a live rat in her outstretched hands, but prepared to leap back at a moment's notice.

"Everything is fine, Taisha, I've come back to my senses! Thank you!"

Nevertheless, I took the second rat from the goblin girl's hands and drank all its blood, increasing my Sating the Thirst bar by three more points.

"If you want, there is more living food here," said Taisha, pointing at a whole pile of half-strangled little creatures near the entrance to the tent. "VIXEN has been collecting them for you. She doesn't trust me — she hisses and spits poison if I get near the heap. In fact, it's time to throw out the ones at the bottom of the pile. They're starting to stink pretty bad..."

"Where'd you get the tent?" I asked, looking interestedly at the sewn pelts stretched over the wooden frame.

"I ordered the orcs to build it in the place where you left *Boundless Realm*. After all, I didn't know what time of day you'd return, and in the day, it's pretty sunny here..."

"A reasonable precaution. Thank you for the care," I praised my NPC companion. "Wait up... What orcs?"

"Our orcs from *White Shark*, silly. Who else?" Taisha walked up to the tent door and raised the flap, pointing me to the orc camp around the pond.

"When you showed me how to send messages, I immediately sent a messenger to Ziabash Hardy. I described the situation to him, and showed him the place on the map. Yesterday evening, they arrived — three hundred soldiers, Shaman Ghuu, and the little boy Johnny with them. And that tent over there is for the dwarves that came this morning. Gnum Spiteful is still limping, but she's on crutches. And she brought ten soldiers from the royal guard with her. I didn't call them here, they found out about you on their own. From what I understood, it's a contingent of Vanessa's relatives, sent to accompany the limping girl and make sure the Dwarf Mechanic met her captain without incident."

Dang... I stood, my mouth hanging open in surprise. I was trying not to even think about the fact that NPC's were not supposed to be able to use magical messengers. I was surprised by something else entirely — my crew had come this whole way to help out their captain! That must have meant I wasn't such a bad leader. After all, they'd come for me.

And then, as if I didn't have enough other impressions from my return to *Boundless Realm*, into the tent came a huge terrifying shaggy creature of a camouflage gray-and-black coloration. I only didn't squeal in fear because, at that very moment, I looked at the mini-map and noticed that the monster marker was blue — ally.

Fimbulthul Élivágar Guardian
Level-57 Mythical Hound (unique creature)

The strange color of the mythical hound's fur was explained by the Gray Pack settings, in which I had chosen a camouflage pattern for all members of the Gray Pack. The coloration clearly didn't agree with Fimbulthul, though. The mythical hound looked much cooler with snow white fur. But as for the beast's appetite, everything was just fine — without the slightest degree of hesitation, the overgrown dog went straight for the pile of dead animals and started wolfing them all down, both the dying and obviously decaying ones.

Valerianna Quickfoot then appeared in the tent. Tears were streaming down the wood nymph's face. I was first afraid for my sister's wellbeing, but she just waved off my concern and answered that she had a different reason.

"I've been sorting through my inbox, and I'm just blubbering away, unable to stop. Such a huge plethora of players in *Boundless Realm*, I'm now finding out, care about me! So many words of warmth! They're all wishing that I get well soon, expressing a willingness to help, inviting me to clans... Four have even proposed," the mavka giggled, displaying her sharp teeth. But then, she shuddered in fear, having just then turned to see the source of the satisfied munching sounds, the Mythical Hound.

I was glad for my sister. A good amount of messages had also fallen on me, but I hadn't yet gotten around to sorting through them. But then I realized something: where were all the enemies?! I asked that question aloud.

"Wyvern hunters did come, and quite a few of them, but only on the first day," Taisha told me. "The *Legion of Steel* stopped them up top at the start of the path. Some were killed, others scared off, but none of the enemies were allowed to get down here. After that, they all went somewhere else and, the next day, the *Legion of Steel* also left."

What does all that mean? Where'd they all go? Why didn't any of the pursuers stay here to wait for me? I probably would have kept busting my brains over this problem for a long time, but then, down from the night sky directly to my tent flew the glowing winged figure of the Keeper. With a barely visible gesture, he moved Taisha and Valerianna aside, after which he covered us both with a canopy of silence.

"You entered the game, finally. And I see that you're surprised," the angelic figure chuckled.

"Indeed I am," I said, not trying to deny it. "I entered the game expecting a slaughter. I thought I would see hordes of players here, thirsting to kill me, but for some reason no one wants my head. Strange."

The glowing opaque figure laughed happily and lowered down to the earth, his wings folded up compact behind his back.

"You must not have read the news on the *Boundless Realm* forum. After your video about the tragedy with your sister and your readiness to sacrifice yourself to fulfill your promise to the participants of the great hunt, the corporation was flooded with a wave of messages from the players. Of course, the opinions expressed were varied, but the overwhelming majority were in your support. The players demanded justice — after all, no one had caught your goblin. You had skillfully avoided all your many pursuers, so it wouldn't have been fair to take your mount away. The board of directors had a talk and officially announced that you had successfully passed and would be made an official tester for the *Boundless Realm* Corporation. Your Royal Forest Wyvern can be kept but still, selling it will be categorically forbidden, because you still didn't hold out to the end of the hunt."

Not believing my ears, I asked the Keeper to repeat his last sentence and the glowing angel confirmed with a smile that VIXEN had again become a normal mount, and would no longer drop if I died.

So, what did this all mean? I got to keep my pretty, and no one would ever be able to take her from me? That was the best outcome I could have hoped for! I mean, I wasn't planning to sell VIXEN even before but, now, I didn't even have to justify that fact.

"Such a compromise decision was completely acceptable to the players, and the fuss immediately quieted down. What's more, they found a very timely replacement with the Silver Dragonfly..."

Here, the Keeper went gloomy and told me that he knew what had happened between Jane and I. After that, he totally dumbfounded me.

"By the way, this is my last shift as Keeper. Starting tomorrow, I'm being promoted — I'll be taking the vacated seat of the director of special projects."

I didn't grasp what the Keeper had said right away, but it soon reached me that I was now talking with my future boss. It must have been reflected somehow on my face, though, because the Keeper laughed:

"There are whispers in the corporation that the position is cursed. After all, it's seen three directors in just two weeks. But I'm not superstitious. All the same, I decided I should personally get to know you given that, in some way or another, you served as the reason for the last three directors of special projects getting fired. Timothy, I expect to see you in my office tomorrow to discuss your future plans. It seems to me, given that the corporation has already announced your official hiring as corporate tester, we should play that up — I should assign you some bone-rattling mission, now that you've earned the famous flying mount. Something that lots of other players have broken their necks trying to do. For example, you could map out Dragon Ridge, track down the Master of the Swamps, or find a path to the Land of Gloom... Alright, we can talk later. But now, go meet your flying snake!"

Then, I heard the flapping of wide wings in the night sky, and near the entrance to the tent, VIXEN landed. I could hardly recognize my beauty, she'd grown so much! She was now level twenty-eight! Almost seven meters long!

By the time she was on the ground, the Keeper was nowhere to be found — the opaque figure dissolved without a trace into thin air, taking his magic canopy with him. Taking an incredulous look at Fimbulthul, who had already managed to eat up all the food stores, and was now looking around for something else to eat, the wyvern set her new prey before me.

Level-14 Steppe Chamois

What a present! I embraced my huntress, then pulled the half-strangled body into the tent in a business-like manner and closed the flap so no one would be disgusted by the unpleasant spectacle.

~ Stay on the Wing ~

Racial ability improved: Taste for Blood (Gives +1% to all damage dealt for each unique creature killed with Vampire Bite. Current bonus: 24%)

Great! As soon as I opened the tent flap again, the Mythical Hound popped inside and ate the rest of the chamois. I guess he was a bit of a glutton!

To my surprise, the wyvern hadn't flown away while I was gone, and was waiting patiently for me lying belly-down on the stones with her short legs drawn up. Was she offering to let me climb up on her back?

Seeing that I was hesitating for some reason, the Royal Forest Wyvern unfurled a wing and lowered it to the earth, offering me an even more convenient way up. I had no doubts remaining — VIXEN was allowing me to sit on her back. What could I say? My beauty, I've been waiting for this moment for so long!

As soon as my Goblin Herbalist had sat down, VIXEN gave her wide leathery wings a flap, immediately gaining a significant altitude. My big-eared little goblin was clutching fearfully onto outgrowths on the scales of the flying snake. As soon as my initial instinctive fear passed, I shouted out in elation. Finally! I can fly!

All of *Boundless Realm* was spread out at my feet now. Dragon Ridge? The Domain of Swamps? Land of Gloom? No problem — I'll fly there and see it all first-hand! All the far-off dark recesses were now within my grasp. Millions of unknown locations lured me with their mysteries and treasures. My funny little big-eared goblin smiled a happy smile from ear to ear. Now, the real games could begin!

End of Book Two

About the Author

Michael Atamanov was born in 1975 in Grozny, Chechnia. He excelled at school, winning numerous national science and writing competitions. Having graduated with honors, he entered Moscow University to study material engineering. Soon, however, he had no home to return to: their house was destroyed during the first Chechen campaign. Michael's family fled the war, taking shelter with some relatives in Stavropol Territory in the South of Russia.

Having graduated from the University, Michael was forced to accept whatever work was available. He moonlighted in chemical labs, loaded trucks, translated technical articles, worked as a software installer and scene shifter for local artists and events. At the same time he never stopped writing, even when squatting in some seedy Moscow hostels. Writing became an urgent need for Michael. He submitted articles to science publications, penned news fillers for a variety of web sites and completed a plethora of technical and copywriting gigs.

Then one day unexpectedly for himself he started writing fairy tales and science fiction novels. For several years, his audience consisted of only one person: Michael's elder son. Then, at the end of 2014 he decided to upload one of his manuscripts to a free online writers resource. Readers liked it and demanded a sequel. Michael uploaded another book, and yet another, his audience growing as did his list. It was his readers who helped Michael hone his writing style. He finally had the breakthrough he deserved when the Moscow-based EKSMO - the biggest publishing house in Europe - offered him a contract for his first and consequent books.

Want to be the first to know about our latest LitRPG, sci fi and fantasy titles from your favorite authors?

Subscribe to our NEW RELEASES newsletter:
http://eepurl.com/b7niIL

Thank you for reading *Stay on the Wing!*

If you like what you've read, check out other LitRPG novels published by Magic Dome Books:

The Dark Herbalist LitRPG series
by Michael Atamanov:
Video Game Plotline Tester
A Trap for the Potentate

Reality Benders LitRPG series
by Michael Atamanov:
Countdown
External Threat

Perimeter Defense LitRPG series by Michael
Atamanov:
Sector Eight
Beyond Death
New Contract
A Game with No Rules

An NPC's Path LitRPG series by Pavel Kornev:
The Dead Rogue

Level Up series by Dan Sugralinov:
Re-Start

The Way of the Shaman LitRPG series
by Vasily Mahanenko:
Survival Quest
The Kartoss Gambit
The Secret of the Dark Forest
The Phantom Castle
The Karmadont Chess Set
Shaman's Revenge
Clans War

**The Expansion (The History of the Galaxy) series
by A. Livadny:**
Blind Punch
The Shadow of Earth

The Sublime Electricity series by Pavel Kornev
The Illustrious
The Heartless
The Fallen
The Dormant

You're in Game!
(LitRPG Stories from Bestselling Authors)

You're in Game-2!
(More LitRPG stories set in your favorite worlds)

**The Game Master series by A. Bobl and A.
Levitsky:**
The Lag

Moskau by G. Zotov
(a dystopian thriller)

More books and series are coming out soon!

In order to have new books of the series translated faster, we need your help and support! Please consider leaving a review or spread the word by recommending *Stay on the Wing* to your friends and posting the link on social media. The more people buy the book, the sooner we'll be able to make new translations available.

Thank you!

Till next time!

00293

Made in the USA
Columbia, SC
07 July 2019